THE PEOPLE

They were farmboys, slum kids and children of the aristocracy when they embarked on their profession. But by the time they emerged from Med School, each saw himself first and foremost as a physician, single-mindedly committed to healing the sick.

These were the men and women Dr. Nick Gorlin chose to staff his model clinic, for he would have only the finest. But in looking only to their excellence, he failed to recognize their very human frailties. And in a neighborhood where the cunning prey on weakness—however subtle—the clinic would become a prime target for the lost and the lawless. . . .

THE NOVEL

Seething with the drama of love and vengeance, faith and despair . . . a passionate, explosive saga of hope, violence, and death in the corridors—and on the doorstep—of

THE GORLIN CLINIC

Other Avon Books by
Barbara Harrison

The Pagans	09597	$1.25
City Hospital	11374	$1.75

THE GORLIN CLINIC

Barbara Harrison

AVON
PUBLISHERS OF BARD, CAMELOT, DISCUS, EQUINOX AND FLARE BOOKS

THE GORLIN CLINIC is an original publication of Avon Books. This work has never before appeared in any form. All characters in this book are fictional, and any resemblance to persons living or dead is purely coincidental.

AVON BOOKS
A division of
The Hearst Corporation
959 Eighth Avenue
New York, New York 10019

Published by arrangement with the author

ISBN: 0-380-00446-1

First Avon Printing, December, 1975

AVON TRADEMARK REG. U.S. PAT. OFF. AND IN OTHER COUNTRIES, MARCA REGISTRADA, HECHO EN CHICAGO, U.S.A.

Printed in the U.S.A.

For Philip Schneider,
through the years.

PART ONE

1

Then and there they would begin. In winter, in long shadows of gray cold, they would go now and be doctors . . .

THE SKY was ashen with January. A pale, angry snow muffled the city. But in one small, reconverted tenement building on the Lower East Side there was none of the quiet of winter; there was only triumph, young and sure and bouyant. It was a party, Nick Gorlin's party, and they were celebrating the coming true of an old dream, the coming true of The Gorlin Clinic. They gathered there, all the shiny, brand-new doctors, to applaud Nick, for Nick was their friend and their teacher and their strength and, most of all, one of their own. They wouldn't be hushed on this night; they would have their hurrahs.

The party was scattered through the five floors of the new Clinic, but the largest concentration of guests was settled into the big, square, main-floor reception area. Thirty or forty young men, beer cans in hand, grinned and back-slapped and tossed their laughter into the air, telling story after story of their medical school days, their days as interns and residents, recalling old professors and old hospital rounds, cranky nurses and first patients with such hilarity that new laughter spilled from them before their anecdotes were half finished. For these men residency was only just over, their memories bright about them and they shared not only their City Hospital and Bellevue backgrounds, but the particular, graceful confidence born of the rigors of exacting training—the brutal, gut-wrenching experiences—at those exacting institutions. They were like men who won the battle that won the war—a little surprised, and a little relieved. There was a tiny sprinkling of women in the room, but their presence was incidental, the gathering might have been a fraternity party, so heavy was the air of masculine camaraderie. It was their party and their group, self-sealed and self-contained, and that was the way they wanted it; they shared the experience of being men and being doctors, and for them at that moment it was enough. They were in their early thirties, though they seemed, in their ease, much younger. In jeans and corduroy slacks, in turtlenecks and sweatshirts, in sneakers and old boots many times resoled, they looked like careless boys. They were tousled, their faces smooth and clear, and their eyes were crinkled and damp with laughter, for everything on that Saturday night was very funny indeed.

In the center of the group stood Nick Gorlin—tall and wide-shouldered, his hair a black shock tumbling onto his forehead. He was a large, trim man, handsome in a vigorous, irregular way. His eyes were black fire, thickly, blackly lashed, and his smile was very white. At thirty-four, there was a solidity to him, a rough-cut virility, and there was an intensity. His friends said he had some tall, special flame, that he dominated the circumstances of his life. He had grown up on these same slum streets and had had defiance when he needed it and pride always. But above all, Nick Gorlin cared. He cared about his work, about the *people* his work served, and if his temper was the size of a mountain, his compassion was a mountain times two.

Now, Nick listened to yet another funny story. It was a City Hospital story and a large fondness spread across his face as he remembered the days of it.

The young man, a resident when Nick had been Chief Resident, took a deep breath to control his laughter and then turned back to the group. "So Nick here just closed his books, draped the skeleton, and said, 'Gentlemen, if that's your attitude, there won't be any more classes.' And he walked out. Damned if the next day there aren't sixty students looking stupid and lined up outside Nick's office with a *written* apology."

That story reminded another doctor of another time and he launched happily into his recollection as Nick drained the last of the beer from the can, the harsh overhead Clinic light sending quivers of brightness onto his flushed face. He turned, his eyes searching, then raised his arm and waved his hand in the air that was already heavy with disinfectant.

"Sam . . . Sam, over here," he called. He left the group and squeezed past clusters of guests until he reached the open space toward the back of the room. "Sam, I've been looking for you."

"My optimistic friend. Do you think anybody can find anybody in this mob?" the man said as he shook Nick's hand. He was Sam Matthews, the balding, harried, Chief of Staff at City Hospital, a man who'd watched Nick go from student to intern to resident to Chief Resident; he'd been among the first to recognize Nick's brilliance. He remembered Nick then—the fierce desire, the demand for excellence—and he looked at Nick now and could see no difference. He smiled broadly. "What are the chances of getting a drink at this fancy establishment?"

"I happen to know the owner. Come with me." Nick led Sam a few steps away to a long lab table that had been set against a wall. The metal table was laden with food at one end and liquor at the other, mounds of paper plates and cups in the middle.

Sam poured some Scotch into a cup and took a quick sip. "That's better. You want some?"

"I'll stay with this," Nick said and reached down into a borrowed metal trashcan filled with ice and beer. He plucked a can free and ripped the tab away. "Let's find some quiet. Back there," he said and guided Sam away from the deep circle of men to a narrow stairway in the middle of the building. They sat themselves on the bottom step and for a moment just listened to the party sounds drifting around them—the chatter, the bellows of laughter, a lone doctor singing along with the Beatles.

The two men sat where they were and said nothing for there was so much to say. So many thoughts, so many emotions. They went back so far and had been so close.

In the strict sense, Nick and Sam hadn't been friends; they hadn't sought each other out when their work was done, they hadn't exchanged confidences or searched each other's souls or sat into the night talking of the mysterious future; the difference in their ages, in their outlooks, had prevented that. After all his years at City, Sam Matthews was an amiably cynical man, but Nick was still young, still tilting at windmills; their two personalities had clashed often. Arguments, deep, black, furious affairs, had been frequent, Nick's voice crashing cymbal-like as he fought his battle, Sam sitting silent in his chair, shaking his head back and forth, holding his ground. In the early years of Nick's time at City, Sam had won all the skirmishes and was prepared to go on winning until he discovered that quietly, and behind his back, Nick was winning the wars. A deep respect was born on that day, and while the arguments went on, the two men never again argued against one another personally, only against points of view. They understood each other and it was an understanding that would grow. For what they had shared and shared still was the bond of their work.

Nick sipped his beer and put the can on the floor. He leaned back against the stairs and looked at Sam, so proper in dark suit and vest and tie among the sea of dungarees. "You look like you're going to a budget meeting," Nick said with a smile.

Sam shook his head. "In my day when you went to a party or to a meeting, you put on your good suit. No more. There was a surgical committee meeting the other day and Cole came in in worn-out pants like you're wearing and a shirt my wife would use to dust the piano. And the younger doctors? Take a good look," Sam laughed, waving his hand at the party, "at our young doctors. In my day it was the patients who looked like hell, now it's the doctors. All hair and old clothes," he said and then turned to Nick. "But it's not my day anymore, it's yours. That's why I came tonight, I wanted to say that."

"Sam, I—"

"Don't worry, I'm not going to make a speech. You never listened to my speeches anyway," he smiled. "I'm only going to say that I'm proud of you. That everyone at City is proud of you. Tessa gave me the tour, it's a fine setup, fine."

"It's still hard to believe. When I remember the shoestring I was prepared to work on. Leasing equipment, using volunteer doctors . . . and then the grants began coming in. From all over, Sam, they just kept coming. Tessa kept saying, 'Well of course you'll get support, of course you will,' but I never believed it. Then one day we were notified of the first grant. Twenty thousand dollars, I'll never forget it. And then the others followed."

"So. The Clinic is rich."

"You know better than that. But at least we were able to *buy* the equipment we needed. And," Nick laughed, "instead of my standing on a ladder with tools and ten thumbs, we had the building professionally renovated. Most important of all, I have a full-time staff. They're not getting top dollar the way medicine is today, but they're getting a decent salary."

"I heard. Is the staff all filled in?"

"Five full-time doctors, including me. Two part-time consultants. Five nurses. And I've got a bunch of volunteer residents from City and Bellevue who'll help. We're going to be open twenty-four hours a day."

Sam Matthews shifted his body on the stairway and took a pipe from his pocket. He lit it slowly and puffed on it for a long moment. "You've never heard of doing things halfway, have you? Well," he shook his head, "you know what you're taking on anyway, this is your neighborhood."

"I was born two blocks away, it's mine as much as it's anyone's."

"Nick," Sam said quietly, "you've worked your rear end off ever since you were a kid. How many jobs did you have to get yourself through your training? Never mind, I don't want to know . . . you're a brilliant doctor, you had offers from every medical center in the country. Yet here you are, back where you started. Do you know what you're giving up?"

"Yes, I know. But what do you think all that work was for, was *always* for? It was to get back here. To take care of people who can't take care of themselves. Sam . . . when I was a kid I saw neighbors, friends—my own father—die because no one was willing to take care of them. They had two choices: the clinic at City or the clinic at Bellevue. *Daytime* clinics, clinics where you had to wait forever, clinics that took the last shred of . . . dignity. I know poverty, I know what it does. It's not just that there isn't enough to eat, that you can't buy a pair of shoes for your kid . . . it's that it kills the spirit. The gray ghost, I used to call it, because it was always there, haunting every moment of your life until one day you looked around and saw that you had no life. That hasn't changed down here . . . the colors have changed, there's a lot more black and brown, there's less white, but no matter the color of the people, they see that gray ghost too."

A small, half-smile played around Sam's mouth. "I gave you common sense and you always handed me nobility."

"Medicine used to be a noble profession."

"Young people make me tired." Sam sighed. "Nobility, indeed. Three quarters of the young men and women who pass through City now are interested in one thing. It's not a ghost and it's not gray. It's green, the color of cash money. Nobility!"

"That's theirs to decide, Sam. I've decided differently. All of us here have. I always thought it was pure stupidity to go into medicine for money. If money is the thing then go into business—in business you don't have to spend twelve years learning and training. You can make all the money you want and you can steal. Why the hell go into medicine for money? You go into medicine because you give a damn about people, and any other reason is going to make a very bad doctor. It's like going into law hoping to become a judge so you can be a crooked judge."

Sam laughed. "You'll never change, Nick. You'll be a hundred years old and still arguing the plight of the people. And the joke will be on you because eventually you'll find out that the *people* don't give one goddamn about *you*. They'll resent you, in fact. You'll be feeding them and they'll be biting your hand."

Nick ran his hand through his shaggy, thick black hair and looked closely at Sam. "I'm not a fool, I never was. I'm expecting a lot of resentment down here. At first the people in the neighborhood will think they're being condescended to and they'll be belligerent, I know that. I also know that I've got an extra problem: a lot of the people around here are people I know . . . used to know. I grew up with half this neighborhood.

Kids I used to play stickball with, some of them are still here. They're struggling now like their parents did. We've got the older sisters of guys I knew, the younger brothers. The best hitter on the old team—a three sewer guy, steady—he's still here. Runs numbers now. He's been in and out of jail I don't know how many times for a variety of things. He—our *leadoff* man, for God's sake—now carries a gun and he's always half loaded and he doesn't mind knocking women around," Nick said. "If you don't think he's going to see red when he sees me around here . . . ," his voice trailed off. "Same age, we went to the same school . . . his mother worked in the same factory in Russia as my father. Christ, we go back. And now he's . . . doing what he's doing, and I'm doing this. Of course he'll resent it—I would—and that's the story of a lot of people down here. They won't mind the other doctors so much, but they'll hate me."

"So for the privilege of their hate, you—"

"Sam," Nick smiled, "you're not fooling me. Why have you stayed at City so long? City's a poor, starving, municipal hospital with poor patients. It's twice the work and half the money and no bouquets for you. But you stayed."

Sam's shoulders rose and fell with a small sigh and he looked at Nick. "You were right about one thing. There was a time when being a doctor meant something. It's forty years since my medical school days . . . yes, it meant something then. Now, people make rude jokes about doctors and the doctors deserve it. Half the medical community is a disgrace . . . They wouldn't stop to tend a dying man in the street because maybe they'd get sued, or horror of horrors, maybe they wouldn't get paid." He paused, looking out at the young men standing by the makeshift bar. "There's a lot of talent in this room, Nick, but yours is extraordinary. I don't like to think it will go to waste."

"This isn't a waste. If I can prove this Clinic is successful then there'll be other Gorlin Clinics in other neighborhoods like this one. We'll keep on with them until there is finally a system of free neighborhood health centers in our cities."

"I see. Today East Fifth Street, tomorrow maybe the South Bronx."

Nick laughed and reached for the beer, taking a long, deep sip. "You know what I mean, Sam. You know very well. You know our whole group at City. . . . We may be the last of our kind for some time. Look how it's come out. Ted Michaelson's already in Oklahoma setting up a small clinic." Nick smiled. "Tendin' Indians, as he puts it. David Cord's already decided on public health. Dan Phillips is staying on at City. Porter's going to L.A. to work at the Free Clinic. And three of the guys from City's GYN are working at the free birth control clinic in Harlem. That's not a bad ratio."

"And you've got Brian Morgan with you here."

"I have. That's nine of us. Nine out of our original intern group of thirty-five."

"Young people make me tired."

"I decided against drug maintenance, though; that should please you. We're not doing methadone."

"That pleases me very much. Even though I'm sure your reasons for not doing it are different from mine."

"They are. I want us to be doctors, not cops. There are a great many drug clinics but very few medical clinics because nobody understands that it's not enough to get a man straight. You've got to get him healthy too. Say a user has a few dollars in his pocket and a boil on his nose. What's he going to do, get the boil treated or get a fix?"

"Nick, just don't expect humanity in return. You won't get it. How well I know. We struggle along, literally working day and night, and we manage to pull a difficult case through. Afterwards we say, 'We'd like to see you in the clinic to keep an eye on you.' What does the patient say? Now keep in mind this patient has had some of the finest doctors in the world—City doctors, staying with him round the clock. This patient is paying nothing for the equipment and the drugs and *couldn't* pay for the care he got. We saved his life. And what does he say when it's all over? Fuck you, that's what he says. After thirty years of fuck-yous, a man is not the same man he was. Except you." Sam laughed. "You'll be the same. They'll say fuck you, Gorlin, and you'll say, 'Yeah, but come in tomorrow for your X rays.' "

Nick frowned. "Then why do you stay on?"

"At City? Oh, I suppose I was a lot like you at one time, I suppose I'm schizophrenic. . . . I'd prefer to believe and so I do while all along the other part of my head knows my cocker spaniel has more humanity than most people I know. Of course, every once in a while there's a surprise and maybe that's why I go on. Tessa . . . She was a surprise. We . . . you saved her life, and when it was over she didn't flounce out and forget it. She came to care about City, about what we try to do. A surprise like that keeps you going for another five years." Sam smiled at Nick. "She's looking more beautiful than I remember. She's so proud and happy."

"We have a good marriage, Sam," Nick said softly. "We've both found . . . a measure of peace. When God smiles He grins: I have the Clinic and I have Tessa."

"It was so obvious from the very beginning, you and Tessa. But how you fought." Sam laughed. "At last I caught you in a mistake. I waited years for you to make one."

"Yes, I was wrong. But it's very hard to come to terms with the kind of money she has. I never had any and I won't ever have any. My salary from here, that's it. Psychologically, I had to work it out for myself."

Sam was about to speak when a roar went up from the crowd, ten steps away. He and Nick looked up and then laughed, for one of the doctors was doing an imitation of the dean of City's medical school.

"Mike's got poor Steven down to the last hair," Sam said.

"You should have been around earlier, when he did you."

"They always do me." Sam smiled. He looked at his watch and then turned back to Nick. "Is Grady Malory definite?"

"Yes, he is. He'll be running the Clinic with me."

"I'm glad. He had a fine reputation at Bellevue, fine."

"I got to him as soon as I was sure Ted was going back to Oklahoma. You know, he reminds me of Ted in some ways. He's got the same kind of easy-going manner, the same charm . . . but the same intensity when he works. And the same vulnerability."

"Vulnerability? I hope not, not here."

"I don't mean physically. He . . . he looks like he could be hurt. Easily hurt. Inside."

"But you'll take care of him in no time. Straighten him right out. Nick, you're a perennial broad shoulder."

"You know you approve of me, Sam. Admit it."

"Yes, but I worry about you too. It's not an idealistic world anymore, if it ever was. In this world now you need every advantage you can take . . . you need thick skin, not to mention locks on the windows and guards at the doors."

"Not here. Not at my Clinic. That's the point, Sam."

Sam stared at Nick for a moment, saying nothing, and then looked again at his watch. He stood. "Time to be getting my weary body home. Estelle waits up for me," he said and then laughed. "That's the kind of marriage I wish you and Tessa . . . married twenty-nine years and she waits up for me. . . . Well," Sam said and stuck out his hand, "my congratulations again."

"Thanks, Sam. Your coming tonight meant a lot to us."

"Say goodnight to Tessa for me. I'll see you Thursday. Are you teaching the five o'clock or the three o'clock?"

"The first years are five o'clock."

"You've got the first years? Good luck to you . . . hard heads, every single one of them." Sam smiled and started away from the stairway. "Don't see me out, stay and enjoy yourself. You'll never have another night like this one." Sam smiled again. He looked around him. "And watch yourself. Not all your backing is from well-wishers. Some of it came from doctors who would like to see you fall on your face . . . or hang yourself. They're giving you just enough rope."

"That won't happen, Sam."

"No, I don't think so." He smiled at Nick. "You'll beat them at their own game, the bastards." He laughed then and it was a young, mischievous laugh; suddenly Nick had an intimation of the man Sam Matthews had been thirty years ago. Just as suddenly, he was struck by a feeling of loneliness and he didn't want Sam to leave. He called out, but Sam was already lost in the crowd of people and noise.

Nick turned away, and after a brief hesitation headed toward the back of the narrow building. He walked to their new, red-doored elevator—the elevator that stood where, not too long ago, garbage had rotted and mice and rats had made their shelter. He pressed the button and the door slid open.

Nick rode to the fifth floor, his mind absorbed in the past; he thought about the long, long years of his training, the days of joy and of pain, the blue-black nights that would not end. Those years flashed through his mind and he felt the dull ache of something lost.

The elevator door opened with a sharp click and Nick looked up. He stepped into the corridor and slowly walked past several closed doors. The fifth floor was the only non-medical floor in the building, containing the laboratory, the supply room, a tiny medical-library room and a large room that was the staff office.

Nick walked to that room and then stopped at the door, staring inside.

Tessa Gorlin was there, and her beauty, familiar as it was to Nick, made him stand very still. She sat at his desk, reading, and in the thin light of only a small lamp her beauty took on fragile, tender poignancy. Her golden hair was piled in a simple, graceful puff atop her head, tendrils curling over her ears to rest on tiny earclips of pearl. She wore something long and dark-blue and soft, the fabric ruffled at her pale throat. Her hands were very still, her dark lashes casting long shadows as she moved her head to the next page.

"Tessa?" Nick said softly, entering the room.

She smiled at him, the deep navy-blue of her eyes sweeping up to his gaze. "Don't tell me it's over already."

"No, it's going on and on. I'm expecting another shift from City in about an hour," he said and sat in the chair opposite her. They were four floors above the party and there was an enormously peaceful quiet in the room, the only sound that of the fierce winter wind rattling at the window. Nick glanced toward the sound and for a long while stared at the snow falling past the window in irregular patterns, the bits of whiteness catching and swirling in the wind.

Tessa regarded him closely, smiling slightly. "Happy?" she asked.

Nick looked back at her and his pitch-black eyes were very gentle. "I'm happy."

"And sad too."

Nick looked away and then back to his wife. Slowly, very slowly, a grin spread across his face. "You know me too well. Do I look sad?"

"A little lost."

"I don't know what happened. Sam started to leave and suddenly I felt . . . all alone. I started thinking about the old times . . . the early days at City."

"I think you finally realized that come Monday morning you've got yourself a clinic. And that the old times are over."

"Why should that make me sad? That's exactly what I wanted."

Tessa sat back in her chair, her big eyes fast on Nick. "The beginning of something is always the end of something else, that's hard. Remember that McMurtry book? *All My Friends Are Going To Be Strangers*?"

Nick leaned forward. He smiled. "Tessa, my friends aren't going to be strangers."

"No, but it's that feeling. Something ends and it's that feeling, something begins and it's that feeling. The day we were married . . . my happiest day, and yet I was sad."

"That's a hell of a thing to say."

"Not at all," she laughed. "It's not easy to let go of what you've been for a long time . . . good or bad. There's a kind of melancholia. Any kind of good-bye is a little blue. That's what you're feeling . . . just a little, blue, good-bye."

Nick left his chair and sat himself on the edge of the desk. He reached down and took Tessa's hand. "Did you get over your sadness?"

"Very quickly."

"Tessa . . . you're not . . . sorry about all this?"

"I'm delighted about all this. About us, about you, about your Clinic. You don't have to ask, you know the answer."

"Sam began talking about—"

"I know. He did to me too. Nick, he just wants you to use every bit of your talent, of what you have to offer. And I think he'd like to see you have an easy life for a while. He said, 'Tessa, he's a fine boy, fine, but he's never had a chance for a life. His life has always been medicine, it's always been work.' I think that's all Sam meant. He knows you could make a fortune somewhere else and have some leisure. That's practical Sam

565-5080 Ma[illegible]
Insurance

~~Dorchester Motor Lodge~~
~~(603) 747-0961~~

Cell 2 Morning report No.?

[illegible]

DEPARTURE - February 18 - ALLEGHENY #782

Leaves Pittsburgh - 4:30 pm
Arrives in Scranton - 6:04 pm

RETURN - February 20 - ALLEGHENY #981

Leaves Scranton - 5:55 pm
Arrives in Pittsburgh 7:30 pm

Accommodations have been made for LG, and Larcom at Nicholes Village (717)587-1135 (2 single rooms) talking. His other side knows that this is where your happiness is."

"And you?" he asked softly.

"I couldn't love a man who didn't care. I couldn't love a man without compassion. And," she smiled, "I couldn't love a man who was unhappy all the time. You in a three-hundred-dollar suit at some big medical center, that would be awful for you. And for me: I'd be Tessa Cabot all over again, pouring tea and going to clever dinners. I'd hate it. Nick, look around you, look at the Clinic, at the good it will do. There are no apologies to make to anyone, least of all me."

"Will you marry me?" he smiled.

"Sorry, my husband wouldn't like that."

"Worst luck."

"Terrible," she laughed and stood up. "Haven't you got a party going on somewhere around here."

"I believe I do."

"Then you're being rude. Go back and enjoy yourself like the rest of the children."

"Children? Some of the most promising doctors in the city are downstairs."

"I'm glad their patients can't see them now. Has Grady come in yet?"

"I haven't seen him, he's probably still at Bellevue. He was very upset about that patient."

"Don't forget to remind him about dinner tomorrow night."

"I won't," Nick said, his face growing serious. "Grady Malory . . . I hope we get along, because now that I've got the Clinic it's time for me to step back."

"Step back? How?"

"The whole story of this Clinic is going to be Grady . . . Grady and the other doctors. It's like my story is over and now it's Grady's chance. And the others'."

Tessa put her arms around Nick and they kissed; for a long time they just held each other. After a while Nick held her away from him, staring into her eyes.

"There should be something very special to say to you on this night."

"Just that you're happy. That's all I want to hear, I know the rest."

Nick smiled and kissed her lightly on the forehead. "I am. All's right with my world."

Tessa walked the few steps to the door with Nick. She stroked his hand lightly and then let it go. "Have a good time."

"Won't you come down for a while?"

"Not a chance." She smiled. "Tonight's for old boys getting together."

"Do you want anything? Can I bring something up?"

"Nick, just go and *have a good time*," she laughed. "Go on, get out of here."

"Okay, okay," he said and walked into the corridor. He stopped this time at each of the doors, reading the brightly stenciled signs with a fresh excitement. The sadness was gone now and all he felt was an anticipation, a certain soaring spirit that made him lightheaded. He stepped briskly into the elevator and rode downstairs whistling to himself. When he got out at the main floor he hurried back into the crowd of men. He waved as a new group of doctors burst through the door, their shifts over, their faces burnished with cold as they made their noisy way into the party. Their voices were loud and laughter was all about them.

Outside the clinic, the snow drove frenziedly around on the deserted street, pushed by a stiff wind. A lone man made his way down the stormy street, his shoulders hunched against the cold, his cinnamon hair waving in the wind. Grady Malory, Dr. Grady Malory, come to join the party.

PART TWO

2

He was a moody man, he was a merry boy . . . one no more than the other . . .

"WHEN A BOY IS BORN in Texas he gets a football and an American flag," Grady Malory was fond of saying, "but all I ever wanted was a doctor kit." And it was true enough. Growing up in rural, oil-rich, ranch-rich East Texas, Grady Malory had spent his young years dreaming another kind of life for himself. He'd wanted no part of commerce, of Texas business or his father's life; he'd wanted something special, something his own. He'd been a lonely child, wandering the wide land of his home by himself, stopping now and again in fields of Indian paintbrush and wild bluebonnets, but always moving on again restlessly. He was looking for something—something he couldn't call by name—and only vaguely did he understand that what he looked for was identity, an identity of his own. It was in his fourteenth year, on a bright yellow summer day, that Grady came upon his way. After that he did not waver.

There had been an accident, not a particularly bad one but before the child could protest he was in his father's car, Lucas Malory at the wheel, and on the way to the hospital. The child said nothing throughout the twenty-mile ride; he was only remotely disturbed, for remote was the way he felt about most things. But when they reached the hospital Grady's plans for his life began.

He'd never seen such whiteness. The hospital walls and the shades on the windows were white; the men and women wore white; even the equipment, in the reflection of bright light, had a whiteness to it. When a young doctor came forward, Grady felt comfort; more than that he felt the first stirring of desire to be a man who would comfort. It was the first time he experienced serenity and he would know that serenity again only when he was in places of medicine among people of medicine.

If Grady the romantic thought doctors heroes, Grady the realist thought to learn about doctors at close range, and so he began to divide his time between school and the hospital, working as aide and orderly, watching every move the doctors made. It didn't bother him when he learned that doctors were only men after all, that some were noble and some were not; it didn't bother him to learn that the color of blood was not burgandy and that there was little grandeur in ailing bodies. He was a young boy resolved and the once-indifferent student found the seriousness that lay at his core and worked harder than he ever had. He *needed* to be a doctor, to be a *fine* doctor, better than the rest, for in that was his only definition of himself. He studied and he learned. He grew to a manhood still bright in the imperatives of his youth. Now, sixteen years out of Texas, sixteen years in New York, there was still the passion, still the fire that burned too brightly, and now it was no longer the musing of a boy but the deliberation of a man who would have to prove himself a thousand times at The Gorlin Clinic.

Grady Malory at thirty-three still possessed a wry

combination of shrewdness and innocence; a wide, frank stare; a quick, defensive smile; a prairie-lean body. Standing just under six feet, he had a kind of good looks at once boisterous and delicate. There was a sensitivity in his face, and in his eyes a quiet compassion.

Grady was a man of moods; he knew great high spirits most of the time, but when his mood shifted there was no deeper darkness. He was enigmatic and wary, and above all he had an old Irish instinct for nuance, sensing things long before they happened. He knew the rain before the sky turned gray, he felt the wind while leaves were yet still; he knew when a woman would cry.

He had the ease of a man brought up with money. It wasn't moncy as Texas money went, but it was solid, fourth-generation comfort. His great-grandfather had made his way across an ocean to New York and then across the young country in the pursuit of money; the fourth generation—Grady, his brothers Garth and Logan—took money for granted, treating it lightly, honoring it not at all. And of all of them Grady cared the least. Grady had passed up the favors of the Ivy League for N.Y.U. med, and since arriving in the city he'd lived a casual, unspectacular New York life, blending in with the city. He'd long ago become accustomed to the narrow spaces of the city. He felt uncomfortable in suits and seldom wore them, wearing instead tan jeans and one of twenty or so turtleneck sweaters hanging in his closet. During his hours at the Clinic he added a white jacket, and on occasion he'd been talked into wearing dark slacks and a blazer jacket. He owned one tie, a broad, blue-patterned affair, and two shirts, one blue and one blue-striped, and no jewelry save for a wristwatch and the St. Christopher medal on a gold chain around his neck. He owned sixteen pairs of jeans, each of them slightly worn at the back pocket and a little faded. Boy and man in the same body, they said he was a bit of a character, a character who could charm the sun from the sky or bring the clouds, according to his mood. They said too that for all the childlike man he sometimes was, he was as intense about his work as any they'd ever seen. And Nick Gorlin agreed.

Grady's large, powerful hands were jammed into the pockets of his jeans, his curly head still damp from the shower and his eyes focused downward in thought as he approached the clinic. Spring was on the city, the Clinic was five months old, and in those months he'd formed a pattern—each day riding down as far as Fourteenth Street and walking the rest of the way, using the time for his thoughts, collecting himself for the day. It was not yet seven o'clock of a billowly June morning; soft spring clouds were just beginning to unfurl in the sky, and Grady was a preoccupied, lone figure on the streets. The morning was cool and the long, square shadows of the early sun were crisp, their angles arching before him, though he didn't notice. His clear blue eyes were absorbed and some small sadness flickered across his face.

Grady turned into Fifth Street and looked around, as he always did, at the squalor of the neighborhood. The streets were narrow and had a uniform, gloomy brown to them. The five- and six-story tenement buildings were a dull brown, their old limestone stoops and façades aged into sameness, their only real color the graffiti that was everywhere. The metal fire escapes that hung from the front of every tenement had rusted into a kind of brown and the garbage that wasn't spilled onto the streets was stacked in torn, greasy, brown bags. Grady knew that as much as spring was around the city it wasn't here; here were only weary, decrepit tenements, some with missing windowpanes, some with cracked windows, one missing an entire door. He knew that inside the narrow, dim hallways there would be winos and junkies sleeping off their drugs, there would be mice and rats in the old walls, and roaches on the floors, there would be grime and worse on the tile stairways.

Ruin was everywhere in the neighborhood, and despair. Quickly he walked toward the Clinic door.

The Gorlin Clinic was another piece of brown. Stained by dirt and sweat and a thousand tired months, battered by weather, old with age, the reconverted tenement looked like all the other buildings around it—as if it had never seen the sun. The Clinic was as sad-looking as the structures that flanked it, yet for the five months of its existence the Clinic had been the one slim hope in that raped, grimly poor neighborhood. The residents of the neighborhood—blacks, Puerto Ricans, later-generation Poles and Italians and Jews—were realists who harbored few illusions; one generation of slum was breeding another generation, partly from indifference, partly because there was no choice. There was too much to fight, too many battles raging in hearts and heads and spirits, in needles and wine bottles and guns and knives. Suicide was routine, the murder rate the second highest in the city. Children of twelve were treated for venereal disease and any eight-year-old could point you to a pusher. Policemen walked in twos in that neighborhood . . . when they walked at all.

Into all of that had come The Gorlin Clinic—come to mixed and sometimes vehement reactions. To some, Nick Gorlin and his doctors were "messing around where they didn't belong," but to many, the same doctors were a very real salvation. The one certain thing in that neighborhood of anger was that everyone had an opinion and all Nick and Grady and the other doctors could do was go about their work and hope in time to be accepted; they listened to those who wanted to be heard, they talked to those who wanted to talk, they were largely silent with those who chose silence, they tried never to interfere. If they made judgments, the judgments were private and among themselves and never—not by hint or innuendo or reference—displayed before their patients. They were trying, doing the best they could with what they had.

What they had was a deep, narrow building that still bore some resemblance to the building it had been. The building had little width, and though the old railroad apartments had been ripped out, the basic structure remained the same. Instead of railroad apartments there were railroad examination rooms, six to each of the first four floors. The walls had been painted a stark white, though they were already graying in the dirt of the neighborhood and small cracks had begun to appear. The building had been rewired, and very bright light spilled down from the ceiling, but occasionally, when a subway car rumbled by underneath, the ceilings would tremble. A narrow tiled stairway bisected the building, and for convenience and the old and the emergencies, a small elevator ran at the back of the first floor. Each of the four, cork-tiled, medical floors had a nurse's station, which was no more than a large, formica-topped desk and two yellow file cabinets. Each station had a call-director board and a single telephone connecting to the paging system that ran to all floors. The first-floor desk was also the reception and referral area and was staffed by two nurses, usually one female and one male, the latter a huge man from the psychiatric division of City Hospital who had handled all manner of violence during his career. Off the reception area was the small emergency room, furnished with a refrigerator, an examination table with pull-up, criblike sides and restraints, and oxygen and transfusion equipment. The Clinic had its own pharmacy and pharmacist and a telephone line direct to City Hospital.

Operating on rotating schedules twenty-four hours a day, the Clinic had five full-time and two part-time physicians, a surgical consultant, five nurses and a dozen newly trained aides from among the neighborhood people. The staff worked together in a harmony based in part on the fondness they'd acquired for each other and in part on the fondness they shared for the idea they served; if they had disagreements they were no more serious and no more frequent than those of any group of people working under pressure in close quarters.

Grady was frowning now, absorbed, as he closed the Clinic door behind him. He entered the building slowly and then slouched along until he reached the stairway, taking the stairs two at a time to the fifth floor. At the top of the stairs he saw a doctor at the end of his night shift coming from the lab. Grady waved vaguely, going by him to the staff office. Nick Gorlin was already in the office, already at his desk, his head bent over a manila folder. He glanced up, smiled briefly at Grady and returned to his files.

Grady shook his head and smiled for the first time that day. "What the hell, Nick. Whatever damn time I get here the chief's already at his desk."

"I just came in a few minutes ago," he said and sat back. "Work's piling up."

"Don't look at me. I've been pulling a full wagon."

"I'm not looking at you, you know better than that," Nick said easily, though he looked appraisingly at Grady. In the five months of side-by-side work he'd become familiar with Grady Malory's moods. But that was not to say he liked them. Nick saw the rapid dips from easy nature into quiet brooding, sometimes brief anger, and he'd learned by now to detect them early, in a certain angle of Grady's shoulder, an abstract look in his eyes. The moods disturbed Nick, for he'd never gotten over the habit of worrying about his doctors; it was a habit that had begun the day he became a senior resident looking after interns, and it was a habit he felt most strongly in Grady's presence. Nick wanted to protect more than Grady's work; he wanted to protect Grady himself, for he'd grown fond of him. Now his black eyes measured Grady as he watched him walk the few steps to the large coffeemaker on the windowsill.

Grady poured the hot brown liquid into a white mug and took a long sip. "My mouth's been waiting for this all morning." He smiled and went to his desk. He set the cup on top of a cork coaster and fell into his deep leather chair.

"This is your late morning," he said to Nick. "You should be home."

"There's too much to do. A dozen lab reports, a dozen applications from new doctors, requisitions, eight new patients . . . I've divided it up, the yellow stack on your desk is for you."

Grady looked at the pile of papers and folders and nodded. He turned to Nick and then smiled. "It wouldn't be that you're really here early to check Brian's files?"

Nick shrugged. "You're right, I am. I'm going to keep an eye on him until I'm satisfied."

"Satisfied about what?"

"That's just it, I don't know. He was at City for three years and now he's here and I still don't know him any better than I did the first day I met him. He worries me, he just doesn't seem . . . happy, he never did. I don't think I've seen him smile twice in all this time. What if he doesn't like his work here? What if we made a mistake with the guy?"

"It's not the Clinic or his work. I think it's just the way he is. His nature."

"Maybe."

"He does everything we ask. He gets along with the patients, he works extra shifts, he's never late. And in five months of checking, you've never found even one mistake in his cases. What more do you want?"

Nick smiled. "You're a little anxious to keep Brian here, aren't you?"

"Damn right. I've still got splinters in my seat from interviewing doctors. I don't want to go through that again unless there's a good reason. You know how many doctors I talked to?" Grady asked and leaned back, stretching his legs on his desk. "Lots. That's how many. Damn right, I'm anxious. Besides, he's the best around in his field right now who wants to work here."

"He bothers me."

"You don't have to take him to the prom, Nick, you just have to work with the man." Grady grinned.

Nick laughed and looked back to the folder on his desk, the smile still broad on his face. He appreciated the odd flair Grady had about him, the certain fond absurdity, as if he'd examined the world closely and found it a little foolish. "Okay, let's both follow Brian for a while. Maybe there's some way we can bring him out of his shell. Maybe he needs some friends here. I like a man to be serious about his work, but he takes it too far."

"Okay, mother hen. If he's got a bone of friendship, I'll find it," Grady said, and sipped his coffee. Nick returned to his work and Grady stared at nothing in particular, listening to the morning silence. The Clinic was not yet awake; there was little activity at this time of day. An hour from now there would be noise and the rush of doctors and nurses. The page would start and keep on until it was dark; patients would come and go, asking questions, being afraid and surly and loud in five different languages. Children would cry in the hallways and things would drop to the floor and telephones would buzz and ring and file drawers slam shut. Traffic in the street outside the Clinic would whistle and clank and cough its noise into the building, but not for a while yet. Not now, for there was peace. Grady turned his head and watched the sun creep into the room through the yellow curtains, watching as it caught the top leaf of their avocado plant, watching it tease the leaf and then slink away. He took his blue eyes from the plant and looked absently at the room. It was not large but it was adequate, a white-walled square that was filled with all the paraphernalia they needed. There were twin filing cabinets, and next to them a wall chart with movable pins to follow the location of each Clinic doctor. A wide bookcase, its upper reaches made accessible by a small stepstool, was stacked with medical reference books. There were single armchairs at both Nick's and Grady's desks, and behind them a long work table and several chairs for the other doctors. There was a small, new sink, and above it a paper towel dispenser and a plastic soap dish. A table held a pile of medical journals, a Spanish-English dictionary, and a transistor radio. Grady's eyes returned to their desks and he smiled, for the difference between the two pieces of furniture was so great; Nick's desk was the scratched and battered piece of wood from his intern days, its surface crowded with folders and notes and odd pieces of paper; his own was sleek and polished and neat, his papers in orderly stacks, each held in place by a small glass paperweight.

"Nick, do you have a busy schedule today?" he asked.

"No more than usual, why?"

"I'd like to get over to Bellevue and take a look at Mrs. Vaqua . . . if you can take my patients for an hour or so. I'll be back in time for the polio vaccine tonight."

"Sure. What time?"

"About five. It's quiet about that time. I've got two scheduled, but I think I'm getting transfers from Hank. Mr. Jackson and some new woman."

Nick nodded. "Yes, all right, I'll take them, but be sure you're back by seven. I'm expecting half the neighborhood. Same story all the time, everybody waits until the last day to get their kids immunized and then there's a scramble."

"I'll be back. I only want to take a look and see how she's doing. She was so damn pale the last time I was there. Nothing's showing in the blood, but something's funny," he said as Nick flipped his folder shut and opened another.

"Are they doing blood every day?" he asked.

"Hah. I asked them to, but you know how hysterical they get when an outside guy walks in. Christ, they act as if I was looking to get their jobs from them. Residents spook so damn easily."

"You were a resident once." Nick smiled.

"I may have shied a couple of times but I never spooked. I was too full of myself."

"Or it," Nick said, hiding his smile with his hand.

"Well, well," Grady said through a wide grin, "the man's wearing his funny hat today. Sure I was full of it. *It* is what keeps you believing you're a little better than the next man. Ever know a good doctor who wasn't full of it?"

Grady gave his head a small toss and swung his legs off the desk, taking his cup to the coffeemaker and refilling it. "Want some?"

"No, thanks, I've still got some."

Grady took his cup back to his desk and sprawled in his chair. "I think my stomach's just going to fall out one of these days. You know now much of this I'm drinking every day?" he said, holding his cup high in the air.

"You're supposed to know better."

"Why? Because I have my M.D.? People think just because a man's a doctor he's a sensible man. Not true. Not true at all, and you have me to prove it by," Grady said. Suddenly the tone in his voice had become ironic, a little sad, and Nick looked sharply at him. He regarded Grady quietly, seeing not a mood exactly, but some small, near thing without a name dimming his eyes. It was a tiny, uncertain unhappiness and, perhaps, thought Nick, even Grady didn't know what it was.

"By the way, why are you here so early?" Nick asked.

Grady shrugged his trim shoulders, waved his big hand in the air. "No special reason." Then he smiled. "You're not the only person who can get here before daylight. An old country boy like me is used to getting up early."

"Since when?"

"There's nothing to it. The alarm clock rings and the thing to do is get up and look smart."

Nick ran his hand through his hair and then spoke. "You're still not sleeping well, are you?"

"I'm all right, Nick. I decided to get up and do some work on the report. It's almost done. Another couple of nights is all I need."

"Grady," Nick said with concern, "there's time on the report, I'd rather you get some sleep. We'll get it finished, I'll help you."

"No. You finished your part of it and I want to do mine. It's bad enough as it is, you here all hours night and day. Plus teaching at City. Plus meeting with people who want to set up their own clinics. You almost never get home. I'm surprised Tessa hasn't started yelling. It's not fair."

"She understands," Nick said quietly.

"I know she does, but that's not the point. The least I can do is my share, if we're going to present the report at that A.M.A. convention, we might as well make it good. We need every bit of ammunition we've got. We're not going to convince anybody about neighborhood clinics with pretty talk. They want cold facts. There are a lot of facts in the five months of our operation, and I want to be ready to lay them on."

Nick nodded his agreement. "It'll be a start. But that's all. We have years of reports ahead before we make any serious impression. Men who read the stock market report before they read the medical journals aren't going to care much about what we have to say."

"I know it. Sad," Grady said. His brows grew together in a slight frown. "Tessa really does understand, doesn't she? She's happy."

"Yes . . . why?"

"Oh, I don't know. It's nice is all. That she's happy. Knowing it, that's nice," he said quietly and looked off.

Nick took a small breath. He wanted to reach Grady in some way, to find out what was wrong, but he knew

Grady well enough to know that he couldn't be pushed, he couldn't be badgered; he could only be left alone until he was ready to be joined.

Grady took up the first of the folders on his desk. "Nick, you know who's coming in this morning, don't you?"

"Carlinos. Mother and son," Nick answered, and there was a new, automatic stiffness in his voice.

"Well?"

"Well, what?"

"Please don't stall me. I've talked myself blue . . . asking you to let Frankie Carlino work here during summer vacation. You promised me an answer and I'd like it now."

"I was hoping you'd forget about it."

"I haven't. I still think we could train him as an aide, just as we're doing with the other kids."

"Frankie Carlino working *here*," Nick muttered. "All the warning bells are going off in my head."

"I wish you wouldn't keep taking that attitude about him. If he's working here he'll be off the streets. And the environment may just do him some good."

"I don't think so," Nick said shortly. "I think *he'll* influence this environment, and not for good."

Grady's eyes stared stubbornly at Nick, but he held his voice and slowly thumbed through Frankie's file. After a while he turned again to Nick, his lips pursed. "Why does it have to be that open and shut?"

Nick hesitated, his expression troubled, and then looked at Grady. "I think it probaby is, that's why."

"*Probably*? Probably isn't good enough. Not when we're talking about helping a kid."

"Every bit of my instinct tells me it's too late to help Frankie."

"Fifteen years old, Nick. That's a long way from too late."

Nick frowned and exhaled a great breath. "Where you come from fifteen is a kid. Down here fifteen is a grown man," Nick said intently. "Frankie's a bad one—" When Grady tried to speak Nick held up his hand. "I don't mean because he's been in trouble . . . most of the kids we're taking into the Clinic have. I'm talking about what Frankie *is,* what's inside him. I grew up here, Grady, and believe it or don't, but I can spot the bad ones a mile away. Look at that gang of his. You know what they do, don't you? They ride around on buses and subways terrorizing people . . . they take their money, their trinkets, but they *terrorize* them first. They come back down here and scare the old men and women almost to death, waving their blades, cursing them, daring them to make a move . . . shoving them around. For the few dollars they get? No. Oh no, for the *fun* of scaring defenseless people, for the fun of the torture. Fridays, when the welfare checks come in, the Social Security checks, there isn't a man or woman who'll go out in the streets if that gang's around. Schwartz gives them ten bucks a week just so they won't go into his store and threaten people. So does Goodman and so do Vargas and Mateos. Those kids are big and they're strong and they've got knives and chains and they're sadistic," Nick said, shaking his head. "Frankie may be the worst of them. I'm not sure, I can't prove it, but there's a look he gets in his eyes sometimes that tells me I'm right. I see the insolence and I can imagine the cruelty."

"There's nothing I can say to that, it's all true."

"Then? Then why do you harangue me about him?"

"Maybe he deserves to be written off, maybe he does. But what if what he needs is a chance? What if he needs a chance and we can give it to him but don't?" Grady paused. "You've got what you want now, you've got your Clinic . . . maybe that means you can sit back and dodge the hard problems."

Nick's eyes grew dangerously quiet. "I didn't hear that . . . I'll let that pass. This once," he said in a very low voice.

"Don't let it pass, I want you to think about it. When you came to me, when you first told me about the Clinic . . . you said we had a chance to be more than just doctors . . . that we had a chance to make a difference in people's lives . . . that if we kept only one bad kid from destruction we'd be doing more than most doctors do in their lifetimes. Okay, where is all of that when it comes to Frankie?"

Nick rose suddenly. He crossed over to the window and stared out, his hands in tight fists as he tried to control his anger. His face, when he turned to Grady, was very pale. "All of that is right here and you know damn well it is. It's in everything we do . . . the couple of jobs we've been able to find for a couple of people who were desperate for them, the family we got to enroll their boy in drug rehab, the mother we talked into keeping her girl in school . . . the landlords we've forced into making repairs," Nick said, his voice beginning to rise. "The sessions Brian sets up on his own to tell kids about V.D. and birth control . . . the outings Hank Mitchell arranges for the children, the club programs you push them into . . . the lawyer you talked into volunteering two nights a month. It's in everything we do . . . taking care of people, their bodies, yes, but looking further . . . looking to see what needs to be done with their *lives*. You accuse me of turning my back, of *dodging*?" Nick shouted. "You dare accuse me of that?"

"Nick, I—"

"You're sorry? You didn't mean to say what you said?"

"I didn't. You know I didn't."

Nick turned away and leaned his hands on the windowsill. He stood that way for a while and then straightened up, passing his hands over his face. "All right, I know you didn't," he said, his voice calmer. "Frankie Carlino's been an issue around here since our very first week. Why? Why him? There are a lot of other kids in this neighborhood who need help."

"Maybe because that's what everyone's always said . . . help the others. It's too late for Frankie. The fact is we don't know that because nobody's ever tried."

"And you include me in that."

Grady shrugged. "Look, if he turns out to be trouble we don't have to keep him on. If he's trouble, we'll boot him out the door, but in the meanwhile . . . I don't want to start an argument all over again, but what kind of trouble do you think he's going to make here?"

"I don't know, dammit. It's not something I *know* at all, it's something I feel." Nick looked at Grady. "Brian couldn't handle him at all, that's why I switched him to you. I regret it now, I think he's got you conned. What did you see in Frankie that the rest of us missed? What is it about him?"

Grady looked away, but not before Nick saw the sudden melancholy in his eyes. Grady spoke then, in a soft, distant voice. "I saw a boy barely more than a child . . . defiance that's really bravado for the fear . . . a fifteen-year-old with no place . . . loneliness." Grady shook his head slightly, as if bringing himself back from a dream.

The furrows deepened between Nick's brows; he'd heard the words, the tone of them, and he was suddenly sure Grady was talking about himself, himself at a different time.

Grady caught his look and spoke rapidly. "And I saw the challenge. I'd be less the doctor I have to be if I avoided that challenge. I can't be any doctor, Nick," he said urgently. "I have to be good, I have to be the best. *Have to be,*" he finished, his glance firm and clear.

"That's a romantic perception of—"

"This whole Clinic is a romantic perception," Grady cut in quickly. "Young doctors giving up big fees to go to a slum and serve the poor. What makes *my* romantic perceptions worse than yours?"

Nick smiled slightly and returned to his desk. "Okay, but we're getting off the point. The point is Frankie. I'll agree," he said slowly, "that Frankie got a particularly bad deal from the start. I've known his mother since I was a boy and she was never any good. I used to play ball with her brother and she was always around bitching at us. She was a bitch then and she's a bitch now . . . she nagged at her husband until he couldn't take it and became a drunk. She kept on nagging and he walked in front of a car. Then she started in on her two children and she's been on their necks ever since. Poor Marie. She's the kid I really feel sorry for, she's such a sweet, gentle girl. But Frankie? He's been mean since the day they buried his father."

"Is that surprising? After what you just said?"

"No, not at all, I'm not saying he doesn't have cause, I'm asking if there's anything we can do about it. I think it's a long shot."

Grady's head shot up. "Worth taking?"

Nick was silent for a long moment, staring at Grady. Grady shifted once or twice in his chair, almost feeling the deep black of Nick's eyes on him.

"I think the odds are enormous. . . . But if you feel that strongly, if you are that sure . . . yes, worth taking."

Grady smiled, nodding his head at Nick. "You were going to say yes all along, weren't you? But you just had to give me a hard time first," he laughed.

"I decided this weekend that I'd try once more to talk you out of it. I also decided that if you still felt that strongly I'd let you have your chance . . . because it's always been my rule to go with my doctor's instincts if those instincts were strong and if there was any possibility they might be right. Some damn good doctors matured on that rule. You'll get your shot."

"Uncle Nick patting the kid on the head." Grady smiled again.

"Uncle Nick knows what he's doing," he said and returned the smile. "Uncle Nick isn't the newcomer to this Clinic you think he is. . . . Grady, I've wanted this

Clinic for so long, I've been running this Clinic for so long in my head that I feel like I've been here for years. I'm prepared for tough decisions and I'm prepared for grief with some of them. You're not. You have to learn."

"There's a theory that you run the Clinic—"

"There are a lot of theories about how I run this Clinic. A lot in interpretations. *My* theory is that it's run first for the benefit of the patients and then for the benefit of the doctors. Same theory I had at City. Well, you're not going to do Frankie any harm and you may . . . *may* do him some good. That's my first responsibility. My second is to my doctors, to you. I started out with some good students at City and they became *fine* doctors, finely honed. I start out here with some fine doctors and they will become finer. A year or so here and you'll all be better than you knew you were. Brian has to learn involvement; Hank, how to relax. You . . . I'm not sure about you, but I suspect you have to learn to lose and not feel diminished."

Grady smiled thinly and turned away. He remembered another time he'd heard words like that, a time when he was fifteen years old himself, lonely and afraid and having no place. He remembered a gift, a gift from his father—a palomino that wouldn't be broken. Time after time he'd mounted and been thrown, until Lucas Malory had come forward and dragged him away. Grady remembered his shame and his rage at the failure. And he remembered his father. "A man's got to learn how to lose," he'd said. And, "You won't be worth a damn to anyone till you can lose and pick yourself up and go on to the next." But Grady knew he couldn't lose, for losing was failure and with failure came that strange feeling.

Grady shook himself out of his memory and sat very straight in his chair. His eyes were cool on Nick. "My father was always saying a man had to learn how to lose, but I never saw him lose a damn thing in his life.

Not a fight, not a woman, not a card game, not a business deal, not a bet. In our town people used to say God created Lucas Malory to beat Him at chess."

Nick's mouth opened to speak and then snapped shut. He recalled what Ted Michaelson had once said; "Only thing wrong with Grady is he's never lost a close one. I think he'd take it personal."

Nick sat back in his chair. "What gives you the idea Frankie's going to take the job? We've been arguing theory, now let's talk specifics."

"The truth is this wasn't exactly my idea. I was trying to find some way to reach him when he mentioned it. . . . I gave it a lot of thought before I brought it to you."

"*Frankie* mentioned the Clinic?"

"He didn't come right out with it. Not exactly. But it was what he was hinting around at, I'm sure of that. One of the boys he goes to school with is starting here in a few weeks. . . . Frankie said how that was making him a big man around the neighborhood. The other kids calling him doctor, things like that. He said very pointedly that you'd never let *him* work here. He said he always gets the shaft from everybody."

"Did he mention he always *gives* the shaft to everybody?"

"Come on, Nick, you see what I mean now. I'm sure this is the right way to go."

"Tell him we'll take him on if he wants. But tell him it's conditional. He's on day-to-day trial here and *I'm* the trial judge. One second of trouble and he's out, sad stories or no. There's only one reason he wants to work here, you know."

"What's that?"

"He won't have to go looking for people to torment, he'll have a captive audience right here."

Grady smiled. "Can we keep an open mind?"

"You keep an open mind. I'm going to watch every move he makes."

Grady grinned and the old warmth came back into his eyes with the light of his smile. His face relaxed and the tension seemed to leave his features. "That was—" he said and then stopped as the door opened and their huge male nurse, Jim Trankos, lumbered into the room. He was enormous, taller even than Nick and almost twice as broad across. In white pants and jacket he looked like an aging wrestler wearing someone else's clothes. The last thing he looked was medical; the first thing was mean. He had short, thin, brown hair and leathery features, indistinct, with thick eyebrows and small eyes bordered by squint lines. He had a nice, easy smile.

"Morning," he said amiably. The two men smiled up at the building of a man, his muscles bulging and bumping under his white coat. "Here's the mail," he said, tossing a large, cord-tied bundle on Nick's desk.

"Anything going on downstairs?" Nick asked.

"Nothing. Jean just came in, she's straightening up. See you," he said and turned his body around and out the door. Nick was used to Jim's girth, for they'd worked together at City; he turned to the mail, but Grady still stared at the doorway.

"Jim's wife is about five feet four." Nick smiled, looking over the mail. "It's funny."

"I wonder how funny she thinks it is," Grady mumbled. "Anything?" He gestured to the heap of mail.

"Something," Nick said slowly, reading the paper in his hand. "Something you are going to like." He smiled and handed the page to Grady.

"I knew it, I knew it. Man, I knew it. Somebody should kick some ass at City for scaring that woman the way they did. I knew they were wrong."

"You called it. I guess everything I've heard about you is true . . . you're pretty good."

"*Pretty* good?" Grady smiled. "Where's the control sheet?" he asked, and Nick passed another paper across his desk. "Good . . . good. That's the way I'd like to start every week," Grady said and then fell quiet. He put the paper into a file on his desk and leaned over the Carlino folder. There was silence in the room for a few minutes, and then the door burst open and another Clinic doctor hurried into the office.

"Morning, Nick . . . hi, Grady," Hank Mitchell said as he went quickly across the room. He dipped his head into the closet and searched around until he came to the plastic bag marked MITCHELL; he ripped one of the freshly laundered white jackets from its hanger and put it on over his blue work shirt. He stopped to pour a cup of coffee and then rushed to the door, holding the cup high to keep it from spilling. "Nick, I wish you'd talk to the cleaning crew. They did something to the fourth floor . . . the floor's too damn slippery."

"Especially on Monday, when your footing's not so good," Grady laughed.

"Funny . . . funny man," Hank Mitchell called and disappeared down the stairs.

"The dervish." Grady smiled.

"The playboy," Nick said, though he was amused.

Grady made a notation in the Carlino file and closed it, moving it to one side of the desk. He didn't expect the Carlinos until eight, and so he relaxed, reaching over to Nick's desk for the newspaper. He scanned the front page and then put it down, sighing.

"What's the matter?" Nick asked.

"Nothing."

"Why the big sigh?"

"Who knows? Some mornings I'd swear I have my head screwed on backwards. Not that there aren't people who'd tell you that's the way I was born." He smiled.

Nick stared at Grady. "Is something wrong?"

"Nothing. I suppose I'm a little edgy. Maybe it's Courtney. . . . She's been so damn . . . restless lately, it's catching."

Nick was silent. Courtney Ames. He wondered if she and Grady would ever get it all straightened out. He scowled when he saw Grady light a cigarette.

"Back to those?"

"Well, Nick, I'm sitting here with one in my hand, so, I'd say I was. You know how I am. I go in spurts, off one week, on the next. I'm edgy, that's all. Courtney's going to make me white haired and old and I know it." He grinned. "At least," Grady said lightly, "when I smoke I don't drink coffee. I don't know which is going to kill me first."

"Take a guess," Nick said and then ducked as Grady threw the newspaper at him.

"You've been around me too much, Nick, you know that? You're getting what you call your smart mouth." He laughed.

Nick picked up the paper from the floor and put it on his desk. He drained the last of the coffee from his cup and leaned back, rubbing his eyes. He yawned and looked at his watch and then reached to a coatrack at his side, pulling his white jacket free. He slipped it on over his yellow shirt and tugged at his broad, flowered tie, straightening the knot.

"Almost time for today," he said.

"That it is," Grady said and stood up. He went to the closet and took a jacket from the package marked MALORY. He slid into it and then slipped his stethoscope around his neck, checking his pocket for notebook and pen, taking up the small, clip-on flashlight and flicking it on and off. Satisfied and prepared, he took a puff on his cigarette and stubbed it out, walking then to the sink to wash his hands. The water splashed loudly in the bowl and he soaped his hands twice, rinsing them carefully, drying them slowly.

"We should be hearing about John Woods today," he said, turning to Nick.

"I'm not anxious . . . I don't think it's going to be good."

"Are you coming?" Grady asked.

Nick glanced briefly at the wall chart and moved the pin bearing his own name to a different location. He stared at it for a moment and then turned and went to the door where Grady waited.

"Don't tell me, let me guess." Grady smiled. "You're going to work on Brian's floor for a while."

"For a while," Nick said. They left the office and headed to the stairway.

"Dr. Malory . . . Dr. Malory. First floor. First floor," the page sounded, and Grady buttoned his jacket. The two doctors went quickly down the stairs.

3

Monday, a new week beginning. They would hardly notice how busy they were . . .

GRADY LEFT NICK at the second floor and continued down the stairs to the first floor. He went directly to the nurse's station near the front door and Jean hung up the paging phone. She smiled. "Good morning," she said and handed him a long list attached to a clipboard.

"Morning. Nice weekend?" he asked, putting a checkmark next to his name.

"Not bad."

"They here?"

"Only Frankie," she said and took the clipboard from him. She shrugged her shoulders, her head tilting back. Jean's eyes were bright but resigned as they always were, as if nothing would ever surprise her again. Her hair was short and black and gleaming, a neat polished cap about her small face. "Frankie muttered something about his mother coming in later, on her way to work."

"Damn. I wanted to see them together. That was the whole point."

Jean shrugged again. "Do you want his file? Or hers?"

"No. No, not today," he said in a preoccupied voice. "Which—"

"Room three," Jean said and then looked away as the door opened and a patient came into the Clinic. Grady walked a few steps to the examination room and quietly opened the door. Frankie Carlino sat in one of the two chairs in the narrow room, his face vacant, bored. He didn't turn his head when Grady entered. Grady regarded him without expression as he took his seat.

Frankie looked older than fifteen, several years older. He had a somewhat sensual appearance, neither attractive nor unattractive, and there was a hint of swagger about him. His skin was sallow, with small, oily patches around his thin, sharp nose. His black hair was long and badly cut, though it was clean and shiny, for he was vain about his looks and especially his hair. He had a soft, full mouth, insolent at the corners, and his brows were thick and rose to odd points above the center of his dark eyes. His chin was firm and strong and his cheeks full, though he was a slim boy. Already tall, he was still growing; his jeans were a little short on him.

Grady looked at the boy's face and saw the defiance in his eyes. "I was hoping to see you and your mother together."

"Ma was just gettin' up when I was leavin'. She's comin' on her way to work. She says it better be good 'cause she ain't got no time to waste," Frankie said. He had a deep, dull voice, flat without intonation and curiously thick, as if something were stuck in his throat. He wore a denim jacket over a blue body shirt, the first four buttons open. Frankie took a package of cigarettes from his pocket and threw it on the desk. "Want one?"

"No, thanks."

"Okay," Frankie said and grabbed the package. He shook a cigarette out and lit it, making a great show of inhaling. "So what do you want?" he asked finally, one eye narrowed against the smoke.

"To talk. I wanted to talk to you and your mother about the summer. About summer vacation."

"You want to send me to camp, Malory?" he sneered.

"Do you want to go to camp?"

"Sure, man. Arts and crafts and basketweavin'. Man, can you see it?" he laughed rudely.

"No," Grady said easily. "I think you need the streets."

"Streets need me. This neighborhood ain't nothin' without me. I'm it, man."

"Agreed, but have you thought about what you'll do this summer?"

"You kiddin' me, Malory? What do I always do? Me and the guys . . . we hang around, we got things to do."

"Such as?"

"Such as none of your business, big shot. Who are you, my old man all of a sudden? Even my old man never asked me such as—" Frankie snapped and his eyes turned angry, though it was a chilly anger. It was ice and Grady understood what Nick meant about the look in his eyes.

"Sorry. What I meant was, what's the percentage in just hanging around? You have the cops to hassle you, and—"

"The percentage is, on a good day the guys and me we pick up fifty, sixty bucks. And the cops don't do no hasslin' of Frankie Carlino. They come around, make it look good, but no pig lays his pig hand on me. Me and the guys, we take care of ourselfs and we take care of each other," he said, opening his jacket wider. He drew it back elaborately and Grady saw a length of chain rolled up in an inside pocket.

"All that's going to do is land you in jail one day."

"Malory, I'm a *juv-e-nile*. You know what that means? That means it's a sweet life."

"All right, let's stop playing around. I want to offer you a job here at the Clinic for the summer. And I want to know how you feel about it."

"You jivin' me, man?"

Grady shook his head and sat back in his chair.

Frankie stared at Grady, his soft lips pursed, and then a small, sardonic smile edged across his face. "You're askin' me to work here this summer? I got you right?"

"You got me right."

"Don't you never talk to your pal Gorlin? Ain't you heard yet I'm poison?"

"I've already talked to Nick. There's no problem with Nick."

Frankie dragged on his cigarette. "What's the joke, Malory?"

"No joke. The offer's real and I want to know how you feel about it."

"How come you think I want in? I got my action on the street. Plenty."

Grady sighed. "Frankie, when we talked about Bobby the other day I had the idea you were interested."

"Yeah? How's that?"

Grady leaned back and shook his head. "Why all the fencing? Either you're interested or you're not. It's true we'd like to get you off the streets, even if it is just for the summer . . . and we'd like to give you a shot at straightening yourself out. But we're not going to twist your arm. *I'm* not going to plead a case. I'm only going to tell you that you're welcome here if you want to be welcome. That we'll give you something better to do with your time than scaring little old ladies in the street. Anybody who's big and young can do that, Frankie, but not everyone is asked to work here. The point is I want to help you."

"Why?"

"Does it matter why?"

"Yeah."

"Let's just say I think you can do something with your life. You're a smart boy, smarter than most of the other kids around here, but you're not doing anything about it. You're going to look around one day and see that you're a gang leader with no gang to lead. The time to think about that is now. Later is too late."

Frankie said nothing. His eyes grew a shade darker and they narrowed by the tiniest fraction as a quietness came over him. It was as if he were coiled, about to leap, and Grady couldn't even guess what thoughts traveled through the boy's mind.

"Yeah," Frankie said softly, almost to himself. "Where would I work around here?"

"All around. The aides work all the floors."

Frankie looked down at the floor, his unblinking eyes deep in thought.

"We pay three-fifty an hour," Grady said.

Frankie looked up, a twist of a smile on his face. "I make three-fifty in three minutes, standin' on the corner," he said simply and then looked away again.

Grady drummed his fingers on the desk impatiently. After a while Frankie looked at Grady and his look had cleared; he seemed to have settled something in his mind.

"When is this supposed to start?" he asked.

"When the school term's over."

"And Gorlin won't give me no hassle?"

"No."

Frankie smiled, though it was a thin, cold smile. "So I come to work here and all of a sudden life is cool, huh? All of a sudden I got no more problems?"

"You come to work here and maybe you'll get a different outlook. That's all I'm hoping for. It won't hurt you to be around decent people, Frankie. I want to give you an alternative to the streets."

"Maybe you got yourself a deal. I'll think about it,"

he said and stubbed his cigarette out. "Why'd you want Ma?"

"I have to talk to her about this. You're only fifteen, I have to—"

"My old lady ain't got nothin' to do with nothin'," Frankie said quickly. "Frankie decides what Frankie does, nobody else," he said and stood up. "You ain't learned much about this neighborhood, Malory. Nobody goes to nobody's old lady to say can I. *I'll* decide."

"All right, you decide. But I have to mention it to her anyway," Grady said quietly. He stood and looked at the boy. He was pleased and yet he felt no pleasure. Indeed, an indefinable disquiet affected him. Grady shook himself to rid the feeling. He'd wanted Frankie to join the Clinic and now he was certain he would, yet he felt no happiness. He smiled to himself at his own foolishness; it was the anticlimax, he was sure that was all.

"I'll be calling you, Malory," Frankie said at the door. "I'll let you know," he said and walked into the corridor.

"Fine. That's fine," Grady said and followed the boy out of the door. They walked together in silence toward the Clinic entrance.

When they reached the desk Jean called out, stopping Grady where he stood. "Mr. Benke's in five. Chest pains," she said and handed a file to Grady. He took it and turned back in the direction from which he'd come. He didn't see the terrible look of hate on Frankie's face as he left the Clinic.

Egon Benke sat atop the paper-covered examination table in room five. His shirt and shoes were already off when Grady walked in.

"Well, good morning, Mr. Benke," Grady said, then grinned, for the man was wreathed in his familiar, almost toothless smile. It was nice, Grady thought, to see a smile in those rooms, for they were bleak and depressing and there was no help for it. The rooms were necessarily small, cube-shaped, and the walls were graying badly. Each examination room held one examination table, a desk, two chairs, a scale, and a locked cabinet in which doctors kept their prescription pads and blood pressure meters. Each room had a lab schedule printed in English and Spanish and a series of posters that warned against drugs. The room in which Mr. Benke sat had a window, its shade rolled up halfway to allow the sun; the brown cork floor was a part of the same floor that ran throughout the Clinic. A slim screen was placed against one wall and a pile of paper gowns rested on a small shelf near the table.

Grady walked to Mr. Benke and picked up his wrist, checking the rhythm of his pulse against a watch. "What seems to be wrong today, Mr. Benke?" he asked.

"Pain. Bad pain. Here," he said and thumped his heavy chest.

"Let's have a look," Grady said and put his stethoscope to the right and then the left side of the chest. "Lie back, please," he said. While Mr. Benke arranged his large body on the table, Grady went to the cabinet and removed the pressure cuff. He wrapped it around his arm, inflating it and letting the needle fall back, inflating again and once more letting it fall back. "Sit up, please," he said and repeated the procedure. Satisfied, he nodded and again put his stethoscope to the man's chest. "Well," he said, standing away, "I don't hear one thing that shouldn't be there." He smiled. "When'd the pain begin? After dinner?"

"Was a terrible pain. Like fire."

"Was it around dinnertime, Mr. Benke? Maybe after dinner?"

"Yes. I eat good and then the pain. Like fire."

"I think you just have another case of indigestion," Grady said and turned away. He returned the equipment to the cabinet and locked the door, depositing the key in his pocket. He looked back at the man. "Do you still have the pills I gave you the last time?"

"Yes, I got."

"Did you take them?"

"No, I didn't know. Maybe the heart. My heart is old. I am sixty-seven next week."

"Mr. Benke, your heart's going to live longer than my heart," Grady laughed.

"You only boy," Mr. Benke said. He looked disappointed and Grady smiled indulgently.

"Okay, let's make sure," he said. He handed Mr. Benke his shoes and smiled again. "Put those on, we'll go get a cardiogram. C'mon, bring your shirt."

"With the machine?" the old man asked hopefully.

"With the machine," Grady said and picked up the file, opening the door for him and leading him out. "Just go into the front room there and we'll get the machine going."

"Doctor," Mr. Benke said as they walked through the corridor, "maybe, is my heart?"

"Maybe," Grady said, for he knew how much the man enjoyed the attention. "But if it is I think you've got a good chance to beat it. All that . . . kielbasa you eat . . . makes you strong." He smiled and made a fist. "Go ahead, go in, the nurse'll be right there," he said and turned to the desk. "Jean, set him up for an EKG."

"Again?"

"He gets a kick out of it. Hell, it's cheaper than going to the movies and safer than taking a walk. It's something to do."

"Okay." She nodded and took the man's file from Grady.

"Mrs. Carlino's waiting in two."

"On my way." He took a few steps and called over his shoulder, "Let me see the EKG tracings before you let him go." Jean nodded again and left the desk. Grady took another step and then whirled around as the Clinic door crashed behind him. He sighed, seeing it was only Jim Trankos, obscuring the door as he walked inside.

"Woman on Hester Street busted her leg. Hank's waiting with her until the ambulance comes," he said in explanation, and Grady shook his head up and down.

"One of ours?"

"Nope. Never saw her before. Her kid called and Hank and I went over to see what was up," Jim said.

Grady smiled, watching the big man deftly slide his weight behind the desk to dive for the ringing telephone. "I'm in two," Grady said and walked on to the second room on the left. He paused only briefly at the door and then pushed it open. "Mrs. Carlino, how are you?" he asked, seating himself behind the desk.

"I didn't come here for chitchat, I got work waiting."

"I'm sorry," he said. He stared at her—a woman in her late thirties who looked much older. Bad diet, he thought absentlv, for her complexion was dry and dull and too wrinkled for her age and her thick hair was lifeless. She was plump, though her waist was narrow and her hips were slim for all the round bulb of the stomach. She wore green eyeshadow and bright red lipstick, but even with all the color her face was tired. Grady felt a quick sympathy for her. "Frankie was in this morning," he said quietly.

"So?"

"We talked about his—"

"I'm not interested. I come for my prescription, that's all I'm interested in. You wanted to see him, I told him. He came, that's okay. He didn't, that's okay too. I just want my prescription," she said and lifted a large black plastic handbag to the top of the desk. Grady pushed himself away from the desk and went to the cabinet. He drew out a prescription pad and roughly tore off a page. He returned the pad to the cabinet and slammed the door, locking it.

"I'm going to give you your full prescription this

time, but I want you to start cutting down," he said, scribbling on the paper.

"I need 'em."

"You're beginning to rely on them. Once in a while is one thing, but every night's too much."

"You don't want to give me the pills, all I got to do is go on the street. I can get anything I want on the street. You're supposed to be so smart, you should know that."

Grady handed her the prescription and leaned forward to her. "Let's talk about Frankie."

"I got nothing to say."

"Then I'll talk. Mrs. Carlino, all we're trying to do is help the boy. Why do you fight us? He's your son, not ours."

"I don't need no reminder."

"Please . . . at least listen to me."

"Look, here's a message from me. The kid's on his own. Last time we was at the court I begged the judge to send him away. The judge says no, the kid's entitled to another chance . . . he shouldn't be mixed in with reform school until he gets another chance to straighten out. So okay, I'm doing my part. I give him a roof over his head, a bed. I cook food for him and I give him clean clothes. I do that, but it's all I'm going to do. I don't care no more about Frankie. He's no good. He's bad for my Marie and he don't do me no good either."

Grady leaned back, trying to control his feelings. It was always like this, he thought; he began by feeling sorry for her and then had to keep himself from railing at her hardness. "You must care something for the boy," he said evenly.

"No. I already said it plain. Sooner he gets out of my house the better. Like I say, he's no good for my Marie."

"Your Marie, your Marie. What about your Frankie?"

"I had him but he's not mine. No . . . he's another

Gus Carlino, that bastard I married. Before I was married, I looked around good, picked my guy careful. I picked Gus Carlino because he had ambition. He was going to be a cop and we was going to get out of this stinking neighborhood. A house in Queens, Gus said. So Gus goes and turns out to be a no-good bum. You know what the neighborhood said when he got run over by that car? They said, 'Thank God' . . . yeah, 'thank God.' And Frankie . . . he's just another Gus. Like from the same cloth. He's got his old man in him. Frankie loved only one person in his whole life and it had to be that bastard Gus . . . because the two was just the same. They was alike, that's why. If Gus'd lived, you could see it. Two of a kind."

"Mrs. Carlino—" Grady began.

"No . . . I'm going to say it once and then I ain't going to say no more. You sonsabitches ain't going to tell me no more what to do. Nick Gorlin," she said disgustedly, "I used to wipe Nick Gorlin's nose and now he comes around like a big man. And he brings his pals . . . more big men who they don't know what it means to live down here. I had one dream, Malory, only one. To get out of this neighborhood . . . somewhere where I can sleep with the lights off and not worry the rats is coming out of the holes . . . somewhere where there's no bums doing their business in the hallways. Somewhere where I got heat in the winter. Well, I didn't make it with Gus and Frankie's gone bad, but I got a chance with my Marie. I brought her up good. Every penny I make goes into her."

"An investment?" Grady asked softly.

"Yeah, you could say. I fix it so she has nice clothes and she's learning how to talk good at the charm school. She got a good Catholic education and this summer she's taking a shorthand class to improve her skills. Then she'll start work. Respectable. She'll work at a nice office, meet a nice man. Anyways a man with some money and a future."

"And he'll marry her. Then it'll be the three of you, that it?"

"Yeah, he'll marry her. She ain't giving nothing away. I catch her fooling around I'll break her head, she knows it. She'll get married, all right, and when she moves to her house I'm moving right with her. She owes it to me."

"And Frankie?"

"There's no room for Frankie in my plans. Her boyfriend won't even know she got a brother."

Grady stood up and walked away from the desk. He wanted to pace, to walk off his anger and frustration, but there wasn't room and he returned to his chair. "It's all worked out for the two of you. Or doesn't Marie know about your planning?"

"She'll know when it's time for her to know. Right now she's learning shorthand."

Grady shook his head, his eyes were chilly. "You're his mother."

"Don't make it sound so holy, being a mother. Anyways, I'm what I got to be, and I got to be my number one . . . anyone who can't help me, I don't need them. So you sit there and you think what a rotten woman Anna Carlino is. Well, I know what it is to live in a garbage can all my life. I *know*, Mr. Fancy Doctor. What do you know? You think because you put on a white jacket and work down here that makes you understand? Where do you live? Not around here, you don't. And neither does Mr. Fancy Doctor Gorlin, not anymore . . . big men, the both of you. You ain't even got your names in the phone book. I know 'cause I looked the both of you up. Sure, when the two of you go home, when all of you go home, you go to nice places. I go home and I go to a garbage can. I—"

"Mrs. Carlino, I wasn't making judgments, I'm not here for that. I wanted to talk about Frankie, that's all. I was wrong to try," he said. He felt suddenly awkward before this woman. He saw the stiff, sprayed beehive of her hair, the small beads of perspiration on her upper lip, the hard, sly eyes under the green shadow; he saw driving hate and selfishness, yet he pitied her as much as he abhorred her, for he knew that each moment of her life had passed in a relentless, unquiet desperation. "I'll talk directly to Frankie from now on," he said finally. "Unless it's absolutely necessary to involve you," he added, standing up. He glanced at his watch. "The pharmacy should be open now."

"Don't sound like you're doing me such a big favor, Malory. It ain't such a favor. What's here to get, I'll get, I got it coming. I learned that much from Gus at least."

Grady wiped at his eyes tiredly. "Let Gus rest," he said and then was sorry. Her face colored violently as she jumped from her chair. "Don't push me, Malory, I'm warning you nice. I don't need no smart cracks from you. I seen your girl . . . and I seen Gorlin's wife. He don't know it, but I seen her the same day I seen your girlfriend. Both of them, so delicate, so pale," she said angrily, "such fine ladies. You push me and I don't mind getting the word to the nigger boys about all that fine white stuff."

Grady was around the desk in an instant, standing over her in his own rage. His eyes were hard, blue steel, his cheeks stained red; when he spoke his voice was very low but its tone was fierce. "Listen carefully, Mrs. Carlino. I don't ever want to hear you mention those girls again. From now on those girls don't exist. Do you understand that?" he demanded. She took a few steps back from him toward the door. She tried to reach the doorknob but he was there quickly, blocking the way. "One thing more, so you don't forget what I said. Anytime I want to I can sit down and have a long talk with your Marie, your precious Marie. She may not be interested in your plans after we've talked. Think about that, think about it very hard before you even *think* about mentioning those girls again."

Anna Carlino emitted a high moan that turned into a scream. Her eyes were bright with apprehension, and before he could raise his arm, she lifted her handbag and hit him full in the face, hitting at him again and again, cursing him loudly until someone started pulling her away. It was Jim Trankos, silent, calm, locking her arms behind her.

Nick Gorlin rushed in the next second, looking first at her and then at Grady, seeing the cut on his face. "Stop it," he said sharply. His black eyes were fiery as he spoke again. "I could hear—"

"Nick, you tell your pal . . . you tell him—" Mrs. Carlino began, but half-crying, half-senseless with anger. She stopped trying to speak and instead struggled against Jim. "Let go of me," she cried, but Jim stood firmly until Nick shook his head. Then he released her and she ran from the room.

Nick looked quietly at him. "It's okay," he said. Jim left the room, closing the door softly behind him. Nick waited a moment before speaking. He took a breath and sat on a corner of the desk, facing Grady calmly though his eyes were stormy. "You okay?" he asked.

Grady took a handkerchief from his pocket and held it to his cheek. "Mean as a jackal, that one is."

"Did you touch her?" Nick asked stiffly. He crossed his arms over his chest, his hands in tight fists.

"I never hit a woman in my life. Not that I didn't think about it, just now," Grady said and grinned suddenly. He shook his head, one cinammon curl slipping down on his forehead. "You were the man said fight fire with fire."

"What happened?"

"She got tired of threatening you and me. Started up on the girls. I gave her back and she turned colors and socked me right in the face."

"The girls?" Nick asked, and a quick wariness flashed across his features. "You mean Tessa and—?"

"Just talk," Grady shrugged, "but I wanted her to know I didn't like it and wouldn't sit still for it."

Nick frowned. "A fight with a patient. If a thing like this had happened at City I'd have had the doctor's head, you know that, don't you?"

"This isn't City, this isn't Bellevue. That's over with," Grady said. He leaned back against the examination table and looked off. "We all had our best dreaming when we were residents. There was nothing that couldn't be handled by being kinder than the next fellow . . . I remember, I haven't forgotten. But what we *didn't* know then. Christ, when I *think* what we didn't know. Then we were working at places where patients came and went. We weren't living with them, like here. Here we're all in it together and we're living in a small town. Someone sneezes on Fifth Street and there's going to be someone on Houston saying God bless you. Sometimes it takes a kick in the ass. You keep telling me to learn the neighborhood." He looked at Nick. "Well, I'm learning that they must know they can't just walk all over us."

"There's too much of it going on. Hank took a punch in the mouth from a guy he was treating last week. If Brian hadn't stepped in Hank would have punched the guy flat out."

"I heard. It's going to take a while, Nick," Grady said and looked at the bloodstained handkerchief he was holding. "But meanwhile we have to show we're not ready to lay down and take it. We show them we're scared, just once, and we might as well pack up and get," he said. He crumpled the handkerchief into a ball and stuck it back in his pocket.

"Them and us. That's what's wrong, the attitude of them and us . . . two separate camps."

Grady glanced away and then back to Nick. "Mrs. Carlino said just about the same thing. Angry that we don't have our apartments down here too. Really angry."

"I can understand that. You will too eventually."

"I felt very defensive about it. And then when she mentioned our not being listed in the phone book, I—"

"How does she know?" Nick asked quickly.

"She looked us up."

"That proves it's necessary. Who else might be looking up our home addresses? I can't expose Tessa to that. I can't expose any of my doctors to that."

Grady was silent for a moment and then looked closely at Nick. "It's all very strange . . . we have to exist on two levels down here. To care about the people and to fear them at the same time."

"It's not fear, it's knowing the possibilities."

Grady smiled. "You're playing with words. However you put it, there's a division. It's like being willing to go anywhere but not being willing to turn your back. It's like Mrs. Carlino drives me up a wall but I feel sorry for her too. There are two attitudes in everything we do, it seems."

"What I'm counting on is that time will blur the divisions. When the neighborhood knows we're sincere . . ." Nick said and left the thought dangling. "You talked to Frankie?"

"I think he's in. He's going to keep me waiting for a day or so, but he's going to take it."

"It was really that easy?"

"That easy. I told you, it was pretty much his idea in the first place. No screaming, no pleading, I just said we wanted him."

"I'll be pleased to be wrong about him, you know that."

The page sounded suddenly and both men looked up. "Dr. Gorlin, telephone, Dr. Gorlin, telephone." It was Jim's voice calling, and they left the examination room, walking rapidly down the corridor. Nick turned to take his call and Jean handed several long, slim strips of paper to Grady. He ran them quickly through his fingers, nodding as he read the wavy lines.

"It's what I thought. Nothing. Send Mr. Benke home." He smiled. Jean left the desk for the E.R. and Grady turned away. He leaned his body against the desk, waiting for Nick.

Nick hung up the phone and looked at Grady. "John Woods." He shook his head. "It's inoperable, they're releasing him this morning."

"Damn. I'm sorry about that. How long?"

"Four months. Maybe."

Grady looked down at the floor, his eyes very still. "Does he know?"

"He said he'd rather hear the news from us. He's coming directly here," Nick said and expelled a great breath. "It's always the nice ones."

"Jesus!" they heard Jim say, and they both looked at him, following his eyes to the doorway.

"Hurry," Nick said, and all three moved quickly to the Clinic entrance. A woman sagged in the doorway. They knew her only because they recognized the small child hanging onto her legs. They would not have known her from her face, for she'd been beaten, her skin bloodied and torn. The right side of her face seemed to be separating from the left, blood was everywhere, and her right eye was already closed and swollen. The woman was mute with her pain, her arms hanging loose at her sides; the child was still in her nightclothes, crying and confused, as if she'd been pulled very suddenly from her bed.

Jean untangled the child from the woman and took her to the desk. Jim gently lifted the woman in his arms and carried her to the table in the E.R. He settled her body on the table top and then left, leaving the doctors to their work. Grady soaped his hands several times and went to the cabinet. He removed swabs and disinfectant and cotton padding and took them to a tray by the table. He leaned over and cleaned the woman's face, murmuring softly to her all the while. Nick bent over her, his stethoscope at her heart, his face closed in concentration. Grady continued to wipe the blood away while Nick pointed a small flashlight into the pupils of her eyes.

"Hold her," he said to Grady and then gently pried open her right eye, searching into it with his light. He sighed and nodded his head. "Lucky," he said quietly. "There's no damage. Missed by a quarter inch," he added and went to the refrigerator. He took a syringe and filled it with clear liquid, carrying it back to the silent woman. He swabbed her arm and injected her; she was so numbed by her pain she barely noticed the needle going into her. Jean returned to the room and stood at Grady's side.

"Finish this," he said, motioning to the woman's half-cleaned face. He stepped away and drew Nick aside.

"It looks worse than it is, but her forehead's going to need some stitching."

"I know. Let me get her pressure," Nick said, wrapping the sleeve around her thin arm. He leaned over it, inflating several times before he was satisfied.

"She's okay . . . just stunned. Give her a few minutes before you start sewing."

"Finished," Jean called to them.

"Librium ten," Nick ordered, and Jean raised the crib sides on the table and went to the cabinet.

Grady looked at the injured woman and then at Nick. "What are we going to do about this? I hate to keep sending her home; next month she'll be back just as bad."

"She loves him," he said quietly.

"That's fine, but he's going to kill her one day. He gets drunker and drunker each week and he's hitting harder."

"I've talked to her, Grady. She won't press charges and Sergeant Mendez won't pick him up again unless she'll agree to. The last time he picked him up, she denied the whole thing." Nick looked away. "The problem is she *expects* to get knocked around, she accepts it as part of the deal." Nick paused, his eyes soft. "You see, he doesn't mean it, he doesn't mean to hurt her, but it's something he can't help. His frustration builds and builds until he has to hit out."

"And we're supposed to let it go on this way?" Grady asked in exasperation. Grady saw sudden weariness in Nick's eyes.

"No," Nick sighed. "Tonight I'll go and have a talk with Tony. Another talk. I'll tell him that this time he missed her eye by a quarter inch . . . that she might have lost it. I'll tell him all of that. And do you know what he'll do? He'll cry. He'll pour me a glass of beer. He'll tell me how it was in his country. He'll tell me he wishes he never came here . . . how he can't earn enough money to feed his family . . . how he takes it and takes it and takes it until finally he starts drinking and he gets angry and he hits her. He'll tell me how the other day he flushed the toilet and a rat flushed into the bowl. How a junkie jumped his kid for the twenty cents lunch money he had. He'll tell me about the neighborhood, Grady. And his hate." Nick lowered his head and kicked absently at the floor. "Only he doesn't have to tell me. I know. For five years Tony Nadez has been kicked around, *mauled* by this neighborhood, and he kicks back the only way he knows. It's not right, but that's the way it is. He finishes off a couple of six packs or a pint of rum and he dreams of a sunny place and the palm trees and a place where people are occasionally nice to each other. Then he looks around him and sees the way it is . . . roaches marching up the walls, four kids jammed into one bedroom no bigger than a closet. The broken plaster, the exposed wires, the holes in the floorboards where the mice live. He sees the apartment freeze in winter and roast in summer and he sees that his wife looks like an old woman from all the worry and the work. He gets mad," Nick said quietly. "He gets very mad."

Nick passed his hand over his face. Grady looked away, for he didn't know what to say. He watched as Nick returned to the woman. "Rosa . . . you'll be fine," he said kindly. "You rest for a few minutes and in a little while Dr. Malory will . . . patch up your cuts . . . you know? Patch up?" he said and gestured with his hands. She nodded at him and tried to smile. He saw her look at Grady and he saw her eyes darken with fear. She looked questioningly back at Nick and he took her thin hand.

"We won't call Mendez. I promise," he soothed her. She looked again in Grady's direction, and Nick held her hand tighter. "Dr. Malory won't call Mendez either. Rosa? Tonight I'll come to your house and talk to Tony. We'll talk about things, like we always do. Okay? Is that okay?" He smiled gently at her until she relaxed and the wariness left her eyes. "Good, Rosa. Just rest a while and we'll fix you up. Connie is fine. She's with Jim . . . you know, big Jim?" Nick smiled again and held his hand high in the air. He left her then and went to Grady.

"While it's handy, do something about that cut."

"It's all right."

"Do it."

"Yes, Mama, I'll do it," Grady said, but he didn't smile. His eyes were downcast and very quiet, for watching Nick with Rosa Nadez he'd suddenly felt like an outsider.

Nick patted him lightly on the shoulder. "Feeling a little left out?" he smiled.

"You understand all this," Grady said, staring at the woman on the table. "Sometimes I think I never will."

"You will, Grady. You'll be sorry, but you will," Nick said and left the room.

Grady looked after him, smiling slightly as he remembered one of the City doctors saying, "Nick reminds me of what Yogi Berra said about someone: he learns you his experience."

"Grady, I think she's ready now," Jean said.

"Set up the tray." He nodded and bent to Rosa Nadez. Gently he touched the swollen skin around her eye. "We're going to take care of those cuts now, all right?" he asked, pushing her brown hair back from her brow. "Will you help me "

The woman moved her lips slightly and her eyes softened. "I help."

4

Morning grew louder as it reached toward afternoon. Patients asked and demanded and pouted and joked and glared and smiled. Doctors obliged and tended, frowned and laughed. There was one doctor whose expression never changed, who smiled only seldom . . .

"LIE BACK, PLEASE," Brian Morgan said as his fingers deliberately, carefully examined the patient on the table. He took his time and proceeded slowly, for Brian Morgan was a cautious man, given not at all to suddenness or fancy. He moved logically from A to B to C, unhampered by haste, unmoved by audacity.

He had a good face, a fine, trim mouth, and his hair was shaggy and brown, the color of winter chestnuts. He had beautiful eyes, gray as smoke and large and rimmed with odd golden lashes. A lively intelligence was in those eyes. And his was a quick, agile mind, though his thoughts, for the most part, were his alone to know, so closely did he hold himself.

He stepped away from the examination table and slid a broad white screen into place. "You can get dressed now," he said and went to the sink. He washed his hands and dried them carefully, leaving the office then for the nurse's station.

"Where is—" he began, but then he saw what he wanted and he went to it, taking a single blood set from the dozen or so arranged on the lab cart. He looked around only briefly.

The second floor was crowded; young black faces peered out beneath Afros, young white faces with uneven, home-clipped hair stared at each other suspiciously. Some of the children played noisily on the floor, pushing wooden blocks and toy trucks around with great concentration while their mothers watched them. Poverty that was not noticeable in the children was clear in the women, in the pitifully cheap, ill-fitting clothing they wore. The younger women, the mothers tried hard to look modish but what, at a distance, looked fashionable was, close up, a melange of plastic shoes and flimsy seams, of marked-down fabrics and glass beads; the older women, the grandmothers, didn't try at all—they wore shapeless housedresses.

Brian stepped nimbly around the children and returned to his office. He turned at the door and looked back, nodding impassively at Nick as he led a child into the adjoining room. He waited until he heard the door close and then rejoined his patient. He tied an elastic around her arm and patiently slapped at the skin until a vein was raised. He drove the needle in and watched as the blood flowed into the syringe. "We've got the infection cleared up now. Starting next week you'll be seeing Dr. Sturgis."

"Aw, Doc, what for? How come?"

Brian pulled back on the needle and applied a small cotton pad, bending her arm back to hold it tightly. He snapped off the elastic and put it and the blood into a wire rack. The young woman slipped off the table and sat down in the chair by his desk, watching as he wrote in her file in his neat, large hand. After a moment he put down his pen and looked at her.

"Dr. Sturgis is an obstetrician."

"What's the difference, you're a doctor."

"I'm not an obstetrician," he said quietly. "You *do* want this baby? You are sure?"

"Yeah, I'm sure. I know I could get rid of it if I want, but I want to keep it. Maybe Petey and me'll get married, maybe we won't, but I want the kid. I'll take care of it."

Brian nodded and closed the folder. "You shouldn't have any trouble with your pregnancy. A second pregnancy—"

"I didn't have no other kid," she said quickly.

"No, but you had another pregnancy. Abortion or no, this counts as a second pregnancy."

Mary Ganter looked at him and then looked away. Absently, she put her hand on her stomach, though in her second month there was little to feel. "Petey don't know about the first time."

"Are you going to tell him?"

"I don't know. Maybe if we get married, I will. I don't know. He don't have to know, does he?"

"That's up to you."

"Would you, if you was me?"

"Mary, you're very young. So is Petey. You both have many, many years. I wouldn't want to see those years spoiled by old secrets that really don't matter anyway. Everybody makes mistakes, you're not alone in that."

"I make more than anybody. I got some kind of jinx, Doc."

"That's wrong to think. You're human and you're young, that's all. You have to start thinking about the future now. Forget what's already done," he said quietly and stood up. "And if you have any questions about anything . . . come and ask Dr. Sturgis, or ask me. Don't try and get your information . . . any information . . . on the street. It's usually wrong and probably dangerous. You have to think about the baby now."

"Yeah, okay." She nodded and stood too. Brian looked at her for a moment, his eyes unblinking, and then he bent to her file and removed a printed folder. He handed it to her.

"This is about a residential home. A place where you can go and live until the baby is born. Read it. If you're interested we'll talk about it."

"A home?" she asked, and her eyes were wary.

"Just a place where girls live until their babies are born. They're not institutions, it has nothing to do with police or the law or anything like that. Just a place where you can get good, solid care. I thought you might be interested. Read it and see what you think."

She looked suspiciously at the booklet and then stuffed it into her bag. "I'll read it, but I don't want to talk about it with that other doc. Even . . . even if I got to see him instead of you, can I still talk to you? About . . . things. If I want to."

"Of course." He nodded. "I'll be right here," he said and went to the door. He opened it and followed her out, watching as she went to the nurse's desk to make her next appointment. He watched while she shook her head and then nodded and walked away to the stairs. Fourteen years old, the acne fresh on her face. Brian turned and looked at the line of patients. He went to the woman nearest him, a woman struggling to hold a tossing five-year-old on her lap.

"Hello," he said and took her file from her hand. He looked at the name at the top and then looked at the child.

"Aretha? Good morning, miss. Let's take a ride inside," he said and carried the child into the office. He sat her atop the table and turned to her mother. "What seems to be bothering her?"

"Another damn sort throat. That's the fourth one she has this year, since the winter. And her glands is all swoll too. I swear, ever' time I turn around she's hanging on to her throat."

Brian looked carefully at the notations in the child's file and nodded. "Come fall, we'll have to think about removing her tonsils."

"No . . . no!" the child pouted.

Brian leaned closer to her. "You get all the ice cream you can eat."

"Don't want no ice cream."

Brian unclipped his flashlight and tilted the child's head back. "Open wide. Make an O," he said softly.

"No no no no no," the child said stubbornly, shaking her little head back and forth.

"No," Brian said. He leaned against the edge of the table, his arms crossed, his back to the child. "I bet you don't know how to do anything but say no."

"Do too."

"Can you say . . ." he looked around, "window?"

"Window."

"That was too easy. I bet you can't say . . . Ohio."

"I can! *Ohio,*" the child said, punching at his back.

Brian turned around. "Louder."

"Ohio."

"I can't hear you," he persisted.

"*Ohio,*" the child screamed, and in an instant Brian's flashlight was looking into her throat.

"Louder, louder . . . I still can't hear you," he repeated over and over again until he had a full view. None of them noticed the man standing at the doorway, watching. It was Nick, taking in the scene with great amusement, his face draped in a grin. He watched a while longer, waiting, waiting for Brian to break into a smile. But Brian did not smile; he went about his work without expression, and Nick turned away.

A nurse called to him. "John Woods is on his way up." She turned in her swivel chair and reached to a stack of files. She handed the folder to him without comment, although she saw the sudden dark look on his face.

"Bad?" she asked finally.

"Bad," Nick said curtly. He slammed the folder against his leg as he walked down the corridor.

5

A break in the chaos, a break in the noise. Remember well the years before this year, the times before this time. The moments. Remember quietly . . .

BY TWO O'CLOCK the surge of patients had slowed and Grady wandered down the main-floor corridor to the nurse's desk. He glanced at the patient schedule and then said a brief word to Jim before walking on to the inside basement door. By day, the basement was a lunchroom for the staff; during evening hours, it was a recreation room for the neighborhood youngsters. It was not much of a lunchroom, but it sufficed for the doctors and nurses and aides who used it. It was a large, deep, basement, furnished with old but comfortable things. There was a secondhand pool table, a small stereo, a worn, round coffee table littered with sports magazines, and a saggy blue couch. There was a soft drink machine and a machine that dispensed coffee and soup. A candy machine leaned against one tan wall and, across from it stood a cigarette machine. In one corner was a brassy new pinball machine, the gift of a visiting doctor from Chicago; in another corner, a rectangular metal table. There was a large refrigerator in the room and half a dozen chairs.

Grady walked into the room and went to the metal table. He filled a plastic plate with salad and cold cuts, balancing the plate with one hand while he poured coffee into a plastic cup. He carried the food to the couch and sat down, nibbling at his lunch. His eyes were hazy and far away in the empty, still room, his body hunched forward over the coffee table. Idly he thumbed through one of the sports magazines, paying small attention, occasionally pausing to look at a picture. He jumped when he felt a hand on his shoulder. He looked up and saw Nick standing there, a sandwich in his hand.

"You're a million miles away," Nick said and took a seat next to Grady. He took a bite of the sandwich and chewed it rapidly, hungrily. "Well," he said when he was finished, "I saw John Woods. I told him."

"How'd he take it?"

"About the way I expected. He said not to do any crying for him . . . that he's still got some time and he intends to use every minute. Quote," Nick said quietly.

"Quite a man. Nothing but niceness to him. I tell you, if I'd led a life like John's, a good life, a decent life, and someone came along and handed me cancer . . . man, I'd be screaming. Count on it. But not John."

"No, not John," Nick said slowly. He turned then and looked over at Grady. "Where were you when you were a million miles away?"

"No place special. Here and there," Grady said, then looked up as the basement door opened. Brian entered the room.

Grady waved. "Join the party," he called. Brian glanced in their direction and walked over to them. He said nothing, studying them closely, taking in the bandage on Grady's cheek, the subdued look on Nick's face.

"Rough morning?" he asked, looking from one to the other.

"Par," Nick said.

"Hey, Brian? Guess who's going to be working here this summer?" Grady asked.

"Who?"

"Frankie Carlino."

"Oh."

"Is that all you have to say?" Grady smiled.

"He's not my favorite kid. I don't think he's anybody's favorite kid."

"Do you mind that he'll be here?"

"No, not at all. He probably needs all the help he can get," Brian said quietly, then turned to leave.

"Why don't you get a plate and eat with us?" Grady asked.

"Thanks, but I brought this," Brian said and pulled a worn paperback copy of Updike stories from his pocket. He left them without another word and went to the lunch table, sitting down with his back to them.

Nick shrugged. "See that? See what I mean?"

"Let it alone, Nick. Don't force it." Grady smiled. "Not everyone can be as charming as I am."

"Or as modest."

"Or as modest," Grady said and then fell silent, his eyes traveling restlessly around the room.

Nick leaned back against the couch and stretched his arms above his head. "How's Courtney? Besides restless?"

"Courtney's Courtney. I never did know how to describe how she was. . . . I told you, she's in a kind of funny mood."

"You told me."

"That's all there is to tell, I guess."

"Okay."

Grady took a cigarette from his pocket and lit it. He inhaled and then sat back, watching the smoke tailing away. "I was thinking last night about the first time I saw her," he said softly, as if to himself. Nick looked at him but said nothing. Grady turned his head very slightly and slowly continued, "Coming to New York for the first time, seventeen years old and scared. Lonely. You couldn't have a horse or even a decent-sized dog. I didn't have a friend. And all those tall buildings . . . it was something. The Empire State Building knocked me out flat," he said and paused.

"That first time with Courtney . . . we met in the garbage room, did you know that? My aunt . . . she sent me to the incinerator room one night. I'm in my robe and feeling really dumb walking in the hall half-naked, holding *garbage* in my hands." He stopped to smile briefly. "I got to that incinerator room and there's this girl standing there with *her* garbage. I nearly jumped out of my skin. I dropped the garbage, I remember that." Nick smiled. "What got me . . . if that had happened down home, it would have been all different. The girl would have gotten all giggly and run away blushing. She'd hide the curlers with her hand and pull her robe to and make a great thing of it. But that girl . . . Courtney, just stood there and smiled. Then she leaned down and helped me pick up my garbage, for Christ's sake. She was about sixteen then,"—Grady shook his head—"but poise? She could pour tea for the Queen of England. And pretty. Very, very pretty." Grady took a long, lazy breath and stretched his legs out in front of him. "At home, the nearest town to the ranch was Norther. I went to school in Norther . . . went with the prettiest girl in Norther too. Debbie Ann. Next to Courtney, Debbie Ann was a mess. She was nothing." Grady pushed the curls from his forehead and went on: "So this girl . . . Courtney, puts out her hand and introduces herself and smiles a smile like I'd never seen before. Or since, for that matter. She points out her parents' apartment and says we should come by for a drink one day. I was overwhelmed, really was. At the time it seemed to me like something from a movie . . . country boy meets Grace Kelly."

Grady stopped speaking, but Nick perceived the vulnerability that was so plain in his eyes. He saw again how perishable Grady was and he sighed, for he knew it was tied in with Courtney Ames and he wasn't at all sure how to take her. There were times when he thought he liked her very much and other times when he couldn't decide; she was strong, Nick thought, she might go to the edge but she'd never break, and he didn't know who else he could say that about—not Tessa, not himself, certainly not Grady.

"For the first time," Grady said, "it really sunk in where I was. No more Norther, not for me. My head was saying so long, Debbie Ann." He took a final puff of his cigarette and flipped it into an ashtray. "Small-town face, small-town voice, small-town mind. Here was a girl named Courtney and she was going to be my friend, my person. The wonder of it all . . . yeah, that's how I felt about it," Grady said quietly.

Nick waited until he was sure that Grady didn't intend to say any more, then looked at his watch. There was time yet and he was glad of it. "What's really on your mind, Grady?"

"Hell, I never will forget that first time," Grady said as if he hadn't heard Nick's question. "I was never so . . . struck in my life. I thought she was better than the Empire State Building. I guess I still do," he finished quietly.

Nick regarded Grady thoughtfully, his lips pursed, trying to decide what words should be said.

Grady felt Nick's stare and he turned. "Why're you looking like that?"

"Is there trouble with Courtney?" Nick asked.

"That's a stupid thing to suggest."

"Not so stupid. It's worth sorting out."

"Nothing to sort. I've been trying to figure out Courtney and me for a long time . . . you don't have any answers I don't have."

"I have one."

"Oh, sure. The whole damned world is out getting divorced and you preach marriage. What kind of sense does that make?"

"What the whole world is doing has nothing to do with you. Besides, the whole world is *not* getting divorced. I'm not, for example."

"That's different," Grady said quickly.

"Why? Why is it different?" Nick paused, staring intently at Grady, and then spoke again. "Grady, I don't like to see my doctors all screwed up. Or misfunctioning because their personal lives are messy."

"I'm functioning just fine, thank you very much," Grady said amiably.

"These mood swings of yours are not just fine. Maybe they'd be tolerable if you were a simple businessman, but you're not a simple businessman. Medical pressures build up fast and they build up before you're even aware of them. They're hard enough to handle if your life's in order, if your life's not in order they can be too much to take. Years in medical school, years of internship and residency, one point is made over and over again and no one really pays any attention to it. I don't know why, because it's the most important point that's made in all those years."

"What is?" Grady asked impatiently.

"That doctors are ordinary men but they can't *be* ordinary men."

"I don't know what the hell you're talking about."

"You know, but you're doing what you always do when a subject bothers you, you're ignoring it. Grady, I mean that doctors above all have to be stable. If they don't have stability they have to learn it."

Grady looked quickly at Nick. "Are you calling me unstable " he laughed.

"I don't know what I'm calling you. I only know I've

been watching your moods get a little more unfathomable. And I think it's because there's uncertainty at home."

"I tell you about meeting Courtney in a garbage room one night and I get the Gorlin special lecture. I'm not some wet-behind-the-ears intern, Nick," Grady said softly. "You're not talking to a kid. I paid my dues. I'm here. You're not at City anymore . . . you can't make everyone over in your image anymore."

"Is that what you think I want?"

"I think you want what's best. But your view of what's best isn't everyone's. My personal life is none of your business."

"Every doctor is this Clinic is my business. And that includes his personal life because what affects a doctor's personal life affects his work. I'm not trying to interfere, I'm trying to help—that's my responsibility as much as any patient is my responsibility."

"Why?" Grady asked, the humor gone from his voice. "Who made *you* responsible for everybody? There are some of us perfectly willing to be responsible for ourselves."

"It's not that easy. This place has a lot in common with City, and one of the things is that here, as there, we're going to find ourselves in very tight corners. Sooner or later we'll be in a chips-down situation, it's bound to happen. And what I want to know for sure is how we're going to handle it. It won't be a time for moods. I worry about Brian, and in another way about you, because in neither case can I guage how fragile you two may be."

"We'll hold our own."

"I'm not so sure. That's why I worry."

A hint of a smile came onto Grady's face. "You'd feel better about my chances if I married Courtney, is that it? You'd feel better about Brian if he smiled?"

"Don't do that, you know what I mean. I'm not telling you to marry Courtney, I'm not telling you to marry anyone. I'm certainly not telling you that marriage is the answer to anything. I *am* telling you to take a good look at yourself. Face whatever it is you're always brooding about. Something's troubling you."

"Nothing."

"Grady, either you can't pull yourself out of bed or you don't sleep at all. One moment you're roaring with laughter and the next you're in a black funk. I know you're using a tranquilizer, it's in the pharmacy records. The nights you're not working you're always . . . *always* rosy with bourbon. Sometimes I look at you and you're far, far away from the reality of the moment . . . deeply preoccupied. If a patient came to you with that background you'd tell him to take a good look at his life, wouldn't you? You'd tell him there was reason for concern?"

Grady laughed, his eyes bright and almost mischievious. "I wouldn't hire him to work at this Clinic."

Nick smiled. "I haven't seen any trouble in your work. But don't think it's only Brian's files I'm keeping an eye on."

"Oh swell."

"You wouldn't have it any other way," Nick said and stood up. "I have to get back."

"So do I," Grady said, checking his watch. Nick picked up their few dishes and carried them to a plastic hamper. He took a quick, appraising look at the food supply and then turned to Grady.

"Did Courtney tell you she's going to work with Tessa? Raising funds?"

"Yes, she did. They have a meeting today, I think. She's excited about it."

"So's Tessa. With the two of them handling the money end, we won't have to worry at all."

"I hope not," Grady said as the two men walked up the stairs to return to their work.

6

She was a shimmer of soft colors. There was quiet about her and sometimes unease . . .

COURTNEY AMES, in white floppy slacks and blue, soft shirt, stood by the neat, polished sideboard in the apartment she shared with Grady Malory. It was not yet three o'clock; there was time before Tessa arrived, and so she slowly poured a measure of deep red wine into a crystal goblet. She walked across the room to the couch and sat down, catching her reflection in the glass of the framed print on the opposite wall. She was a pretty woman, a sleek, cool lemonade blonde. She was the kind of woman you thought of when you thought of the best of New York; there was grace and style and gloss and a youth that seemed as if it would go on forever. Her fine, pale hair was swept back from her face, falling to her shoulders. Her skin was very, very white, her eyes a subtle blue, and in her thirty-first year she was all shadows and secrets and moods like fine gray-blue smoke. There was something—too much—of innocence about her for her age and there was, too, a certain solemnness, a solemnness of knowing; there were times when she seemed very tired, times in a brief, sudden look in her eyes or in the stillness of her hands when it seemed she knew what there was to know very well and was wearied by it and sometimes uneasy. But through all of her was quiet. She moved in whispers and often tentatively.

Courtney was a writer; she worked at home, writing short stories in the apartment that had been hers and Grady's for five years. It was a spacious, sunny floorthrough in a small, noble old brownstone on Sixty-eighth Street, and their living had Grady's style stamped vividly on it. It was Grady who'd had years of paint and plaster stripped away to find the original brick and then splashed it with gallons of whitewash, Grady who dressed the apartment until it looked a little like the southwest and a little like New England, the two places he loved. The floors, old, dark wood, were burnished to a high shine and all about were shiny glass things and old pewter and bright, glowing copper. Spanish moss hung in clay pots above the brick fireplace and the furniture was a series of tans and beiges and golds—large comfortable pieces with throws the colors of Mexican shawls. There were curly bentwood rockers and plump footstools covered in needlepoint, huge framed prints and unframed oils, hundreds of books.

The sun shone through the two large bay windows, and Courtney watched as a long ribbon of yellow light wrapped itself around a bowl of daisies. She saw a bud beginning to emerge from its green shell and she smiled at it, for Grady had a way with flowers. She leaned toward the bud, touched it lightly with her finger, and then picked up her glass, swirling the wine thoughtfully before she sipped it. She let the warmth trickle slowly into her, letting it relax her, letting it dull the edge of the nervousness she felt now day and night. Courtney didn't know when it had begun but she knew she could not rid herself of it; it was tiny, like a faint stirring of some uneasiness, and it made her restless. Her own work took little of her time, three or four hours a day, and that was no longer enough; she needed to be occupied by more than her own words and her own characters, she needed a supplement, something outside herself and, in a way, outside Grady. The Clinic project had seemed ideal. It was worthwhile, and that pleased her, for she felt the need of being useful; it involved working alongside Tessa, and that pleased her too because she hoped that Tessa's serenity, her peace, would visit her own life. She needed that now, as buffer to her confusion.

Courtney looked up quickly as the doorbell pulled her from her thoughts. She crossed the deep room and opened the door to a Tessa golden and elegant in a bright yellow coat.

"Come in," Courtney said and stepped back as Tessa passed. "What's all this?" she asked, taking a sheaf of folders and notebooks from Tessa.

"Your new reading material. You'll have to get yourself familiar with all of this, but don't worry, the key word is capitalization. Whenever a paragraph starts with 'capitalization,' read it." Tessa removed her coat and draped it on a chair and then sat down on the couch.

Courtney glanced at the folders and then laid them aside. "Would you like some wine, or a drink?" she asked.

"Wine sounds nice, thanks."

"Red or white?"

"Whatever." Tessa made herself more comfortable on the couch.

Courtney went to the sideboard and refilled her own glass while she poured a fresh glass for Tessa.

"To something," she said, raising her glass.

"Something," Tessa nodded and sipped the wine slowly, looking quietly around her. "It always looks so *nice* in here, I don't know how you manage it."

"It's Grady who manages around here. I'm an absolute pig and he's neat as a pin. We're not very well matched, I think sometimes." Tessa looked quickly at Courtney and Courtney smiled. "I mean that sometimes it's frustrating to live with a man who does everything better than you do. He's a better cook, a better shopper. He's even a better cleaner, when he puts his mind to it."

"Nick's not a bad cook, but he's not keen on cleaning."

"Neither is Grady, I don't think," Courtney said and then paused. "But he does it anyway. God forbid he might ask *me* to do something extra around here. . . . He insists on doing it all himself."

"Maybe he doesn't want to take advantage."

Courtney looked at the dark red liquid in her glass and a small, sad smile came to her mouth. "Advantage? Living with a man for five years . . . knowing that same man for fifteen years . . . I don't think it would be taking advantage to let me . . . to let me feel like I wasn't a guest around here," she said softly. "People being people with each other, nobody catering, that isn't taking advantage."

A slight frown crossed Tessa's forehead, and then disappeared as she looked speculatively at Courtney. "Does he cater to you, is that what you mean?"

"He does," Courtney said and looked around. "In all these years I've never felt like I lived here, like it was my apartment too." Courtney turned to Tessa. "Sometimes I feel we're two paper cutouts."

"I've never seen two people who are less like cutouts with each other than you and Grady," Tessa said slowly. "Whenever you're together you manage to be touching hands . . . or Grady is playing with your hair or you're leaning close to him. There's such fondness between you two."

"Yes, there's that." Courtney smiled. "But this is

silly, how did we get started on this? You're here to talk about the Clinic and here I am . . . wandering."

"There's plenty of time. Wander, if you want." Tessa leaned forward a bit, smiling gently at Courtney. "What's bothering you?" she asked.

"It's the strangest thing, I don't know. It's Grady, in a way, but in *what* way I'd be hard put to say."

"Nick told me Grady's been moodier than usual."

"That's my fault. I get into one of my things and then Grady gets into one of his things."

"Have you talked."

"We talk all the time. We just don't talk about the things closest to us. . . . It's probably just as well, I haven't any idea what I'd say. Something is wrong, I think we both feel that . . . and it's not some sudden thing. It's more that something's been building in bits and pieces for a long, long time, until it's almost complete. Words are hard," she said, waving her glass around, "and even if I had the words I doubt I'd use them. Grady gets so uneasy whenever I discuss anything really personal. It's as if he feels more comfortable not knowing too much," she said. "Do you know . . . once something was bothering me, I don't remember what now . . . something was upsetting me and I finally wrote him a *letter* about it? I did. Wrote it and stamped it and mailed it. To *our* apartment. Then I went to a movie so he could read it alone. When I got home he didn't even mention it. It was something like three weeks before he even brought the subject up. And another two or so before we talked about it."

"Grady's very reticent, I know that."

"Reticent? Is that what you call it? Deaf and blind is what I'd say: if I close my eyes it'll go away. Only when he's feeling the bourbon do we really talk, and then it's not talking so much as it is going around in circles. Charming circles, but circles." She stopped. "I guess what's wrong with me is that I feel rootless . . . I don't belong anywhere. This situation . . . I don't make much sense either, I guess," she said, seeing the smile creep onto Tessa's face.

"No, no, it's not that," Tessa laughed. "I was thinking how everybody's running around crazy to *become* rootless. Break those ties that bind, get rid of the obligations, you know?"

Courtney's pale blue eyes were suddenly amused. "I believe, madame, you have reference to the lib gang? Ah yes, ah yes . . . well, that's fine if you need it, but I've always been liberated. Going way back. My parents always gave me a wide berth; my schools treated me like a responsible, intelligent human being. The first job I had I beat out a man for and thought nothing about it. I dated whom I wanted and there was never any role-playing," she said and drank some of the wine. "My parents had the great wisdom . . . and kindness to understand that a life is what you want from it, not what other people say it *should* be. I wanted to write and I quit work and started writing. I wanted to take off for a weekend, I took off for wherever I wanted, no obligations, no guilts chasing *this* person. I wanted to move in with Grady and I moved in . . . no restrictions, never any demands. You couldn't get any freer than I am, everything's always been on my own terms." Courtney spoke very softly. "I think that's the problem . . . all that freedom. I've had it too long. Tessa, I think I've come to a point where I would like demands made on me. Responsibilities for more than myself. I'd even like it if someone took me for granted once in a while. Once, if just once, Grady walked in and said, 'Where the hell's dinner? . . . Where's the stuff from the cleaners? . . . I'm tired, let's go to bed.' But no, with Grady everything's 'would you like to . . . would you please . . . would you mind if . . .' " Courtney's voice suddenly became troubled, quiet with thought. "You can get goddamned tired of unlimited freedom, you know. And you can get scared by it."

Tessa sipped from her glass and put the glass down,

her eyes intent on Courtney's face all the while. She reached absently for a cigarette and lit it slowly, still staring at Courtney. She saw the spots of color rise on the high cheekbones and then fade away. She saw the uncertainty in the pale eyes and the unhappy set of the mouth.

Tessa sat straighter and tried to inject more cheer in her own expression, in her voice. "Grady will grow up one day. Men eventually do, even men like Grady."

"Men like Grady?"

"The ones who can't stand failure. It's odd, you'll see them take some real chances once in a while, almost tempting failure, but in their personal lives . . . when it's close to home, they don't dare. They simply don't dare."

"What would he be risking? What would he be daring?"

"Grady could make a demand on you . . . he could bare himself enough to show you he wants something from you . . . even if it's a tiny thing. But what then if you didn't come through? If you told him no, forget it? He'd feel like a fool . . . and knowing Grady, he'd feel like a failure in dealing with the woman he loves."

Courtney looked at Tessa. "How do you know those things about Grady?"

"I don't really, I'm guessing. Too, there are a few things Nick's said and a few I've noticed. You see, Nick's compulsive about doing everything right because he insists on everything being done right. With Grady, it seems more that he insists nothing be done wrong."

"Do you think he's measuring himself in those terms? Not willing to be wrong?"

"Could be. It happens sometimes . . . the shadow of a strong father, all that."

"Grady's brothers are nothing like him and they had the same father."

"Grady's the middle boy. That's not always easy."

Courtney smiled. "I didn't mean for this to get so analytical. But I would like to know exactly what went wrong . . . why it's going wrong, if that's where it's going."

Tessa finished her wine and looked levelly at Courtney. "It's always easier from the outside. From the outside, a person can hear what the words mean, can see what the eyes say."

"Then tell me. Tell me what's nagging at me." Courtney leaned forward in her chair.

Tessa was quiet for a long time, the lashes of her downcast eyes painting long, wispy streaks on her pale cheeks. She seemed to be considering, but when she looked again at Courtney she seemed to have made up her mind. "It isn't for me to tell. For one thing, my impressions may be way off line, and for another, it wouldn't mean a thing until you sorted it all out for yourself. We all have needs, Courtney, I'll say that much. And they change with time. We can go along for years and years and everything's fine until one day it just isn't fine anymore. Just like that, it isn't fine."

"I don't know what you mean."

"No, I see you don't," Tessa said quietly. She felt the shadow of worry come over her, a suspicion, an intuition that Courtney and Grady were somehow nearing trouble, somehow nearing pain. She wanted to warn Courtney, to offer cover, but realized she could not; whatever it was would have to come to them as it willed. It would try them, test them, and Tessa felt sadness, for she didn't think they—they in their awful innocence, their blithe carelessness—would be equal to it. So deep in her thoughts was she that when the telephone rang she jumped.

"It's only the phone." Courtney frowned as she reached for it.

"Hello? Hi, Grady," Courtney said, her face suddenly bright and shiny with her smile.

Tessa smiled too, for she had seen that look before: on Grady whenever he looked at Courtney, and on

Courtney whenever Grady was around. They shared the same pleasure in each other; in both of them it was an almost childlike glee. Indeed their happy moments sparkled, Tessa thought; their unhappy moments must give them terrible pain, must be like a fall from sunshine into darkness.

" . . . Okay, I will," Courtney laughed into the phone and then replaced the receiver. She stared at it for a moment and then glanced at Tessa. "Messages from Garcias—Malory and Gorlin. Let's see . . . Nick and Grady will both be late. After polio vaccine tonight, Nick's going to call on some patient's husband and Grady's going to stay at the Clinic and do charts until Nick gets back. They'll try and call later, but if not we should just go ahead and have dinner. And they apologize." She smiled.

"*They* apologize?" Tessa laughed, a light, high ripple echoing through the tall room. "You mean Grady apologizes. Nick is quite accustomed to working twenty-hour days without apology," Tessa said fondly.

"You should see your face, Tessa. What's it like to be that happy?"

"It's about the way you looked when you were on the phone with Grady . . . very, very nice." She looked away. "I'd about given up, until I met Nick. Everybody always assumed I was having the time of my life. . . . All the Cabot money, all the Cabot everything. But this, this is real, we've got a beautiful marriage. He's all mine. Terrible thing to say these days, isn't it? He's mine? But it's true. I never thought I was particularly selfish but, Lord, how selfish I am about him," she said and then grew quiet. "Courtney, he's mine in the way Grady is yours, in the way you belong to each other. I hope you'll both remember that." She shook her head. "Speeches, lectures. You're allowed to tell me to shut up."

"I like to listen to you. You're a whole happy ending of your own . . . the kind I used to write."

"But you don't write them anymore. I just finished the suicide story."

"It's not my fault. It's what people want, and nobody wants a happy ending unless the story takes place in the nineteen-fifties. My last three stories ended with a death, a divorce, and a suicide. Tells you something about the way of the world these days, doesn't it?"

"I'd rather not think about it."

Courtney looked at the slim gold watch on her wrist and stood up. "I'd better see what we have for food. You'll stay?"

"Love to. Nick can pick me up here. Can I help?"

Courtney looked off in the direction of the kitchen and then sat back in her chair. "Come to think of it, there's a big pot of chili, if you don't mind leftovers."

"Chili Malory? I could eat that every day."

"Grady practically does." Courtney smiled. She rose and went to the table by the door, taking the folders back to the coffee table and spreading them out before her. "I suppose we should get to this stuff. We'll have plenty of time for talking later."

Tessa leaned toward the mass of papers and fingered the top folder. "You'll have to read all of it, but this one's the most important. This one your should almost memorize. And soon. I've made an appointment for you, I hope you don't mind."

"No, the sooner the better. Who's it with?"

"Joint Charities of America. They have an extra hundred thousand to give away this year in grant form, or so my spies tell me. One Peter Joshua makes the decisions and signs the checks. He's your appointment."

"Starting me at the top. When do I see him?"

"In two weeks. He's based in Washington, but he'll be in the city for ten days or so to see applicants. It's a big chance. That hundred thousand would put the Clinic in the clear through next summer, but it won't come easily. So . . . these folders, all the possible questions and answers are in them. Also about a dozen different ways to slant our application. You'll probably need every one of them. I hear he's a bit whimsical, our Mr. Joshua."

Courtney's eyes swept over the folders and then to Tessa. She smiled. "I can't wait to tell Grady about all of this. He didn't think I'd go through with it."

"Why not?"

"He said it would be dull."

"It will be." Tessa smiled.

"Not as dull as Irene and Justin. I am sick to death of Irene and Justin."

"Who?"

"The story I'm writing now," Courtney laughed. "Irene and Justin are the most tiresome people I've ever come across. Besides, I need something entirely different to do before my nerves collapse in a heap. No matter what Grady thinks," she added.

Tessa looked quickly at Courtney. "Grady doesn't mind your doing this?" she asked.

"I don't know. He wouldn't say if he did." Courtney went to the sideboard and refilled her glass. She turned back to Tessa. "We love and we love and we love," she said quietly, "but somehow we don't get close. I suppose what I mean is we don't get . . . personal. Grady's policy of noninterference. No criticisms, no compliments." She smiled. "Except once he told me I walk through doorways like Joan Fontaine. I guess that was a compliment."

"Courtney, it can't be as bad as all that, or your face wouldn't shine so when you're together."

"Oh, I love him madly when he's around. When he's on the telephone to me. When I look out the window and see him coming. It's just when he's not around, or on the telephone, or in sight that I begin to wonder what's wrong, what's missing." Courtney raised her glass to her mouth.

7

The June evening grew later, nearly ten. A night of gray lace and gentle with spring . . .

"WHAT ARE YOU DOING HERE?" Brian Morgan asked as he walked into the office. "I've got the night duty this evening."

"I know," Grady said, glancing up from his desk. "I'm just catching up on the chart work until Nick gets back."

"Want some coffee?"

"Thanks. Anything downstairs?"

"Quiet. Nothing at all so far."

"Then you can sit awhile, talk. I'm about finished anyway."

"Okay," Brian said. He put a cup of coffee on Grady's desk and took his own to Nick's, seating himself in Nick's chair. There was a peaceful stillness in the office. Brian sipped his coffee slowly, while Grady watched him, his lips pursed.

"You happy here?" Grady asked suddenly.

Brian looked up in surprise. "Happy? Yes . . . I

haven't thought about it in that way, but yes, I'd say I was. Why in the world do you ask?"

"You've got Nick worried."

"I? Worried about what?"

"Well, he's thinking maybe you don't like it here. He notices things like you never smile, or anyway not much, never showing much emotion," Grady said, watching Brian closely.

Brian stared at Grady for a moment, "All my life people have been asking me if I was happy," he said evenly. "My mother used to chase me around the house asking if I was happy, if something was wrong. 'Brian, is school getting you down? . . . Are you hungry? Do you feel well?' The truth was I was fine. School wasn't getting me down, I hadn't had a fight with Stanley next door. I wasn't hungry, I felt well."

"Yes? Then?"

"Then what?"

"What was it?"

Brian opened his gray eyes a little wider and almost smiled at Grady. "Why, it was nothing at all. It was just the way I was. Am. I never found it strange. Do you?"

Grady shrugged and picked up a pencil, fiddling with it while he considered his answer. Finally he shrugged again and grinned. "I'm embarrassed for asking. I always figured a man had a right to be any way he wants to be. I can't say I paid any special attention to you, your ways, until Nick mentioned it."

"Nick hasn't made the transition yet."

"What transition?"

"From City to here. He's tried to recreate City here, and in a way he has, but he can't recreate the doctors. The way it was. It was very close." Brian looked off. "We worked ridiculous shifts, we hardly ever had any free time and many of the doctors lived at the hospital as well, so that we hardly ever left the hospital at all. It was like a small community and Nick was mayor and police chief and fire marshal and town clerk and spiritual advisor, all in one. He was the finest City's ever seen, almost singlehandedly kept everything in line, kept the seams from splitting. And he did it his way, which was to keep a tight control over his doctors, over the students. He knew their thoughts before they knew them. There was a harmony of line, a smoothness. Except for me. I always made him uncomfortable. I still do, I see," Brian said quietly. "That surprises me, because I'd have thought that by now Nick would understand that what existed at City won't exist again. Certainly not here. I'll make him uncomfortable until the time he realizes that, I'm afraid," Brian finished and picked up his cup.

Grady smiled. "That's the most words I ever heard you speak. You've given Nick a lot of thought, obviously."

"Some. Before I joined the Clinic. I didn't come here because I wanted to do the work of the people, particularly. I'm not nearly so inspired by the people as Nick is, but I am every bit as devoted to being the best doctor I can be . . . as Nick is. He'll make me that and I know it. He opens my mind farther than I thought it could be opened . . . just sitting and reviewing cases he does that. And thanks to him, I am already developing a pure instinct—the ability to sense things, to anticipate them. That's why Nick will always have young doctors anxious to work at his Clinics . . . and I'm sure there will be more than this one. Some will be missionaries, of course, doctors who believe as strongly as he does in the tragedy of the poor. But many more will want simply to work with him, because working with him develops *them*. Nick has yet to learn that this is a very practical world—that his doctors have different goals, we're not all as he would have us. But it'll be a sad day for him. I feel sorry for anyone discovering it's a very practical world."

"Okay, that explains Nick."

"And me? I'm what I seem, Grady. No more, no less. I never really had any friends, I suppose."

"Never wanted them?"

"Never thought about it. I never had your charm and I never had Nick's . . . intensity. I never had the humor that Hank Mitchell has, nor the exuberance of Pete Sturgis. It never bothered me, particularly; it was fact, the way it was. Is. I'd like it if Nick accepted me as a pal, but until he does there really isn't anything I can do about it. But I am happy here. I'm using all of myself, thanks to Nick, though he can't see it that way. Yet."

"Nick will never stop clucking over his chicks, I don't think."

"I hope he doesn't, but he will learn to accept their differences. Maybe at first because of you. After all, you don't exactly toe the party line on life-styles. At City he would have given you an ultimatum. So he's already learning to give a little."

"If you call that giving. Maybe it is giving, now that you mention it, giving lectures." Grady laughed. "Day in, day out, I get the straighten-out-your-life special."

"That's no secret," Brian said, and a brief irony glimmered in his eyes. "Nick's voice carries."

"Hell." Grady smiled. "I don't think I'm moodier than anyone else. It's my artistic temperament, my old Irish blood. Nick's never satisfied. He's worried because I'm moody and worried because you're not."

The phone rang then and Brian pressed a button and lifted the receiver. "Yes . . . yes, I'll tell him . . . absolutely quiet," he said and hung up. "Nick's downstairs."

Grady stood up and peeled off his jacket, throwing it into a large laundry bag at the back of the room. He took his keys from his pocket and put them in a desk drawer and then turned to Brian. "I'll be on my way. You need anything before we leave?"

"No, thanks. I'll hold the fort."

"See you tomorrow," Grady said at the door. "Hey, Brian? You didn't mind my—"

"Not at all," Brian said quickly. "I'd like to be closer with you and Nick both, but I'm afraid you'll have to take me the way I am," he added evenly.

"Deal." Grady smiled and left the office. He hesitated by the elevator and then took the stairway, going rapidly down the four flights. At the bottom of the stairs he went to the door and then stopped, taking a look around the Clinic's ground floor. He didn't like it the way it was at that hour—sheathed in a half-darkness, the nurses and aides long gone, the page switched off. From the basement he could hear the sounds of music playing and kids laughing and shooting pool. He heard the long, hollow roll of a cue ball and then a crash of wood. The sound jolted him from his thoughts. He looked at his watch and quickly walked out into the cool, gray night. Nick was standing a few steps from the Clinic talking with a neighborhood man, and Grady joined them.

"Good evening, Mr. Stimik, Nick."

"Hi, Doc. We's just talking about the weather. Nice for June, ain't it? Bet it'll be a hot summer. This nice in June always means a hot summer."

"I wouldn't be surprised," Grady said. "How's the leg? Been giving you any more trouble?"

"No, Doc. You guys fixed it good."

"Grady, you ready to go?" Nick asked.

"Sure," he said and waved to the man as they left. "Don't you drink all that tonight." Grady smiled, pointing to the brown bag that contained, he knew, a pint of rye. "Save some for tomorrow," he called as they crossed the street.

"Of course he won't," Grady said to Nick as they reached the corner.

"No," Nick said, and then both men were quiet. They walked the next block at a moderate pace, both of them strongly aware of the neighborhood around them.

There were a lot of people out in the pleasant evening—very young children clustered around a stoop taking turns with an old rubber ball, older boys and girls, teenagers, dressed in beads and platforms and bright colors, the old people, reminders of another time, looking timidly from windows, not daring the streets. Music poured from some buildings, quick Latin rhythms fighting hard rock, and somewhere a television set blasted a ball game. There was a seeming normalcy about the neighborhood, but neither Grady nor Nick was deceived. They knew this time of night in these streets, knew that it was the beginning of the hard, tough, often violent hours. Nick and Grady walked slowly through the poorly lighted streets, but they watched carefully, staring into shadows they didn't trust.

They reached another corner and Grady looked over at Nick. "I had a nice talk with Brian."

"Good."

"He's a little odd, maybe, but he's okay. I think we'll have him over to dinner, Courtney and I."

"What did you talk about?"

"Different things. About you, the Clinic," Grady said and looked again at Nick. "Something on your mind?"

"My talk with Tony. It was what I expected. . . . He didn't mean to hurt Rosa, didn't mean to do any damage."

"What did he mean to do?"

"It started Saturday," Nick said quietly. "He was on his way home from work. He'd worked an extra shift to get some money to pay for the little girl's First Communion dress."

"And?"

"Don't be so impatient, Grady. Don't be so impatient with him. You have to try and see it the way he sees it, the way he felt it. He was on his way home and he was walking through St. Marks Place. Passing all those boutiques . . . you know, where they charge a hundred dollars for a cotton blouse? Well, he saw all the people . . . well-dressed people, people not from the neighborhood, coming out of those shops, arms loaded with all that expensive stuff. He said he didn't pay much attention then, but as soon as he got home he started getting mad. More of the kitchen ceiling fell down. It fell into the soup, so they had to have rice again and it was the last of the rice until the new food stamps. The bathroom plumbing was broken and the landlord said to pay for a plumber if they were in such a hurry to get it fixed. The six-year-old had a bad toothache and Tony had no money for a dentist. And then Rosa told him that the man from the television store said if they didn't make their payment in three days they would lose the set." Nick paused as they turned into another street. "Tony got to drinking. And he got to thinking about how it was for them, for his family, and about all the . . . fancy people, he calls them. The fancy people who were at the boutiques buying all those expensive things and laughing about it. He said he felt ashamed that his family had to live like animals while all the fancy people were spending so much money and laughing."

Grady shook his head. "And one thing led to another."

"Exactly. By Sunday night he was in a rage and he took his rage out on Rosa. The funny thing is he loves her, really does. I see the way he looks at her, talks about her. If he *didn't* love her he wouldn't get so angry, he wouldn't feel so useless. All he wants is to do for his family. To be the man, he calls it. Meanwhile the poor guy can't even make the payment on his television set."

"But he works."

"He works, but what does he earn? He's illiterate, he has no skills, and he's a Puerto Rican. Every day he goes to that dank little factory in Queens and twists wires in lightbulbs. He begs for overtime . . . but still, what does he earn? He'd be better off on welfare, but he won't do it. He's fighting to hold on to what small pride he has left, but he's losing that battle too. The day he signed up for food stamps nearly killed him. Now he just dies a little more each new day."

"What are we going to do about it? Rosa—"

"He will wind up killing Rosa one day. Not meaning to, but killing her. He'll be sent away and the kids will be shuttled into homes. Close the books on Tony and Rosa," Nick said in a low, flat voice. "That's this neighborhood, Grady. What I said about Tony and Rosa could be a hundred people down here, a thousand. Meanwhile we root around for temporary solutions. Like what to do about his television set."

"Nick, I can take care of that, it isn't much."

"No," Nick said firmly. "That's where we have to begin to define ourselves. If it's Tony's television, then why shouldn't it be a winter coat for Mrs. Soma, who walks around in a sweater in twenty-degree weather. Why shouldn't it be the rent for Roosevelt Johnson? A few decent meals for the Rodrigos? It breaks my heart but we can't start doing that. What we give to one we have to be prepared to give to each. Otherwise we'll be dividing our own house."

"All right, but I have an interest in keeping Rosa safe for awhile. Her eye won't take another beating."

"That's why I'm making a small exception. But we're not giving anything to Tony. He's going to work it off. I'm going to take care of the television and he's going to paint the basement storeroom. And he knows this is an exception, that we won't always be able to do something like this because it's unfair to the others."

"That's nice of you, Nick."

"It's like treating a broken leg with a Band-Aid, dammit, but it's all I can think of to do. It's not enough, but it's all I can think of."

They reached Nick's car and got inside, driving slowly and very quietly uptown.

"Good night, good night." Courtney smiled at the door. "Thanks for the wine, Nick. Tessa, I'll see you tomorrow."

"Thank's for dinner," Nick said.

"You have to thank Grady for that," Courtney smiled at him. "Right?" she asked Grady.

"That's right. An old family recipe."

"Are you sure you have to leave?" Courtney asked. "It's still early."

"Yes, really," Tessa said. "Since these two insist on starting work at the crack of dawn."

"You married a doctor," Nick smiled at his wife.

"And I'm not complaining," Tessa said and turned out of the apartment.

Grady waited until Nick and Tessa were out of sight and then he closed the door. "Nice evening."

"Yes . . . nice day too," Courtney said and flopped down on the couch. "How was yours?"

Grady joined her on the couch, draping his arm around her shoulders, stretching his legs on the coffee table. "Half and half. I was able to tell a lady she didn't have leukemia. I was able to get one of the neighborhood kids working with us for the summer. The bad part is no matter what we do I know we should be doing more."

"Is that why you and Nick were so glum when you walked in?"

"Poor Nick, he feels it more than I do. I forget it after a while but he carries it around with him."

Courtney sighed and relaxed back against Grady, burying her head under his chin. "Did I tell you there's a letter from your father?"

Grady glanced over his shoulder at the desk and saw the small stack of waiting mail. "It'll keep till morning. Another offer to set me up in practice down home, I'll bet."

"He only wants to help, Grady."

"I know it. And I appreciate it," he said quietly. "I

just want him to understand I can make it on my own . . . and in the big, big city. Christ, I'm thirty-three years old, time and then some to achieve something myself."

"You have. Bellevue, the Clinic, you did that on your own."

"I haven't done anything yet. I'm still learning when it comes to the Clinic. And I can't say I've really had any kind of big challenge to face yet. That's what he always said, my father, it takes a tall challenge to make a tall man."

Courtney laughed and moved closer to Grady. "The wit and wisdom of the great Southwest," she murmured.

Grady grinned broadly at her. "Something wrong with it?"

"It's outrageous." She smiled.

"Well, everybody can't go around talking like Irene and Justin, thank the Lord. Did you finish them yet?"

"Almost. Boy doesn't get girl, girl doesn't get boy."

"They're both very lucky, I wouldn't want either one of them. I have read nicer people in my time."

Courtney laughed again and took Grady's hand, holding it in her own. "Here's the deal. I won't make remarks about the great Southwest if you don't make remarks about my writing?"

"That's the deal, huh?"

"That's it, take it or leave it."

"Okay, I guess I'm stuck with it." He smiled and leaned closer to her. He kissed the tip of her nose lightly and then rested his chin on her head. "I like your nose. Did I ever tell you I like your nose?"

"No. Anything else?"

"See? See how that is? Give a female an inch . . . ," he said softly and held her more tightly to him. "Can we go to bed now? Let's go to bed."

"Poor thing. Poor tired Grady. Are you dying for sleep?"

"Well . . ." he said slowly and stood, pulling her upward from the couch, "sleep's nice too." He smiled and slid his arm around her waist as they walked to the bedroom.

Tessa sat brushing her hair at a small table in the blue and white and yellow Gorlin apartment on Irving Place. The deep, thick gold shimmered over her bare shoulders to the top of her lace-bordered nightgown.

Nick lay in bed watching her. "Did you have a good day with Courtney?"

"Fine. It's going to work beautifully, I think. She *needs* this project."

"Needs?"

"To take her mind off . . . to take her mind off whatever it's on."

"And what's that?"

"She's in a kind of limbo. At least that's the way she's feeling these days. It's upsetting her."

"She seemed okay tonight. She seemed great tonight. Both of them were in great form."

"Oh yes, they're good together. Perfect together. But I can understand . . . ," Tessa said and looked from the mirror to Nick, "I can understand that when they're not together the uneasiness sets in. She's alone, she has a lot of time on her hands and she begins thinking about the fact that something's missing."

Nick watched the twisting smoke from Tessa's cigarette in the ashtray. "Missing with Grady or with her?"

"I mean with *them*. She doesn't understand it herself yet, and I hope she doesn't for a long time. What she's feeling is the absence of Grady saying, 'Look, this is it for us. You, me, together, sharing each other's lives.' "

"They've been doing just that for a very long time."

"In that nice, easy arrangement called living together, yes. They've been sharing the same apartment, the same bed, but they haven't been sharing each other. She wants something more now. *I* know that, I only hope she doesn't figure it out before Grady's ready to cope."

Nick swung his legs over the side of the bed and sat up straight. "Courtney Ames is damned independent, she'll do as she pleases."

"That's unfair, darling. Strong-willed, yes, and stubborn, but she's not the immutable force you think she is. That independence you talk about is coming back to haunt her now because she needs more than that. She needs something she's never had—an anchor. She and Grady have lived together for five years, yet their relationship lacks . . . commitment. She's growing faster than he is, I think; she's willing to take a chance on a commitment. Grady isn't."

"He adores her, you know he does."

"The question is why the doubt? Why five years later is there still an escape hatch in their relationship? He's going to lose her to that doubt, mark my words. Because she *is* stubborn, she *is* worried, and whether she knows it or not, she wants affirmation. From him. What's acceptable in one's twenties is often rethought, reevaluated, in one's thirties."

"What does she want?"

"More than she's got. She wants Grady to get close to her."

Nick shook his head. "We talked about that today, sort of. He's so hard to figure out. He's not happy either, though he won't admit it. I can almost see it coming. . . . His personal life is going to get more and more complicated, and Grady—"

"Will not know how to handle it," Tessa cut in softly.

"That's right."

"They're both such children, in their ways," Tessa said and left the dressing table. She sat next to Nick and absently took his hand. "It makes me so angry sometimes. The two of them, stubborn, spoiled children who will have their way . . . except they aren't having it at all. They're careless about things, Nick. Blithe spirits when the sun is shining."

"I'm glad we don't have those problems, Tessa. I'm so glad about us," he said quietly. She kissed him and he held her very close. Tessa reached out and dimmed the light.

Twenty blocks from the Gorlin's apartment, seventy blocks from Courtney and Grady, Frankie Carlino and two other members of the Savage Snakes gang sat on the roof of an old brown tenement building. It had been a high, hysterical evening, for they'd drunk almost two half-gallons of sweet wine, smoked a handful of grass and made their plans. More exactly, Frankie Carlino had made his plans theirs. His white teeth flashing, his soft, full mouth moving rapidly in talk, and in coarse, rude laughter, he'd kept their attention for hours—the boys sometimes clapping their hands in approval, sometimes slapping his palm in elation. One of the boys had fallen asleep now against the hard stone of the roof, but the other one, Charley, a broad, black boy no older than Frankie, stared proudly at him, and Frankie relished the attention with an almost sensual pleasure.

He tossed his head back and tipped the cheap glass jug to his mouth, swallowing the last drops of wine. He flipped the bottle away, rolling it across the roof, unconcerned about those who were sleeping below, knowing they wouldn't call the police. Frankie leaned back, satisfied with himself.

"Man, that's what we call our phase one," he sneered, the insolence thick in his voice. "Yeah, man, phase one. He's *givin'* me my ticket in. You ever seen a dumber dude than big shot Malory? Man, we got ourselves a party." He laughed and Charley laughed with him. "Phase one, man, just stick around for my next bulletin," he said, and his face was ugly, shot through with venom. "I'll show the bastards who Frankie Carlino is. I'll show them all."

"Man," Charley Jefferson said, his eyes glinting in the half-light of the moon, "you the baddest dude they is."

8

It was Friday, a city relaxed, though for the doctors it was not yet the end of the week . . .

THE CLINIC was crowded, choking with patients, and for most of the afternoon the page had been one monotonous wail, demanding, insisting, until the doctors were numb with the sound of their own names. Jean was running the page from the ground floor and by six o'clock, when at last the pace quieted, she leaned her arms tiredly on the desk and looked at Jim Trankos, sorting charts beside her.

"Dr. Sturgis's wife picked a fine day to get sick. We'll be here all night handling his patients."

"You won't be here all night," Jim said lightly. "It's past six, you should have been out of here an hour ago."

"With all this going on?" she said. Her hand flew in a wide arc at the patients waiting in a line of chairs.

"You know Nick's rule, no women here after dark."

She looked toward the door. "It's not dark yet. It's getting to be summer, staying light later."

"Did you ever see Nick mad? I mean really mad?"

"I've heard about it."

"Believe me, hearing is better than seeing. If I were you I'd leave before Nick gets back from City."

Jean glanced at her watch and then shook her head. "He's got another hour with his class. He's not through teaching until seven."

"Have it your own way. Just remember I warned you."

"Okay, I'll—" she began and then stopped as the door banged open. "What in the . . . ," she said and left the desk. "Clovis . . . what is that in your hand?" she asked, peering down at the child, at the small, feathered creature he held.

"A bird," he said and fastened his dark, stubborn eyes on her. He was nine years old, a small, coffee-colored boy with a serious face and a somber, quiet nature. He looked at people suspiciously and Jean saw the suspicion rising now.

"Clovis," she said softly, "You can't bring a . . . a bird in here."

"I already brings him."

"Take him right outside again, there are sick people here."

"He sick too," the boy said without moving. "His wing is broke."

Jean leaned closer to him and took a better look at the little bird; his tiny eyes didn't blink. She saw that he'd been cruelly sprayed with a metalic paint, the paint matting his yellow feathers. She shook her head and looked at the child. "Clovis, where did you get him?"

"In the alley by Third Street."

"You really can't bring him in here. He's probably full of germs."

"They has germs too. They has bigger germs than him," Clovis said, gesturing at the waiting patients.

Jean looked questioningly at Jim. He stood up but remained where he was, waiting watchfully. The child saw the massive man rise but wasn't swayed or intimidated. Clovis looked down protectively at the bird and Jean was surprised to see an unusual kindness sweep his features. She knew about this child; this child had lost his oldest brother to an overdose, another brother to Vietnam, and had stood their deaths stoically. This child had sent his mother to the Clinic with a broken rib, a rib broken by his tight-fisted punch when she'd tried to keep him home one night. This child was not emotional, or so they thought—yet this child stood there now with kindness in his eyes and a small tenderness in the way he held the skinny, dazed bird. She sighed and put her hand on the child's slight shoulder.

"Why did you bring him here?" she asked gently.

"Doctor Mogan fix him up."

"Dr. Morgan's not a vet."

"He a docker, ain't he? Docker good enough for folk, good enough for him here."

"But, Clovis, there are people waiting, *patients*. Sick people."

"I waits my turn like the rest," Clovis said, and she knew he wouldn't be persuaded. She looked at Jim again and shrugged.

"Ask Grady," Jim said.

"Ask nobody," Clovis said and walked past her to the stairway.

Jean laughed despite her annoyance and Jim bent to the call director board and pushed a button. "It's Jim. Clovis Williams is coming up with a bird. A sick bird," he said and then was silent. He listened for a moment and then hung up, smiling at Jean.

"That guy is something. All he said was, okay, he'll do the bird after he finishes with the rash and the twisted ankle." Jim laughed and looked toward the second floor. Jim and Jean both turned when Grady came out of an examination room and into the corridor.

"Who's next?" he called.

Jim took a chart and walked over to him. "Ellen Train," he said.

Grady nodded and walked off. "Ellen?" he said. "Come on in."

Ellen Train rose and entered the room, closing the door behind her. "How are you, Grady?" she smiled.

"That's my question."

"I feel great."

"Good, glad to hear it," he said and pulled the changing screen to the examination table. He handed her a paper gown and stepped away. "Everything off, please," he said and went to the sink. He washed and dried his hands slowly and then went to the desk, removing the paper wrapper from a syringe.

"Ellen, the nausea all gone?" he asked, glancing over her chart.

"Every once in a while I feel a little green, but it's much better."

"Good, I think we've about got it beat. . . . Ready?"

"Ready," she said, and he pushed the screen out of the way. Gently he prodded her abdomen and the area around her liver and then he snapped an elastic around her arm.

"I think you're a ghoul in your spare time." She smiled as he inserted the needle into her vein.

"I don't have any spare time," he said, watching the blood flow into the syringe. "Anyway, you know we need this. That liver problem of yours was no joke."

"After two weeks in the hospital I'm not laughing."

Grady removed the syringe and unsnapped the elastic. He took them to the desk and dropped them into a wire holder, then turned back to her. She was a pretty young woman, a nice young woman. In her early twenties, her light hair was glossy and long, in a thick braid down her back. Her face was clear and earnest and well-bred and he knew it didn't belong in this neighborhood.

"Are you still living in that hellhole of yours?" he asked with a smile.

"It is not a hellhole. It's . . . deprived, that's all."

"Ellen, when you were at City you promised you'd think about moving."

"I did think about it, but I can't move. I love it here. This is a vibrant, exciting neighborhood, despite our bad press notices."

Grady's face grew suddenly serious. "Do you know how patronizing you sound?"

"Patronizing? I don't mean to. It is exciting. Vibrant. I think it is."

"If you don't *have* to live here. If you don't have to live here, it's colorful. Ask some of the people who have no choice and see how *vibrant* they find it," Grady said and bent again to her, again pressing his fingers gently on her skin. "Did you hear me?"

"I heard you, but you know what I meant." She smiled. "I have a little of Italy and Puerto Rico and Harlem and Israel and Poland down here. And Chinatown's in walking distance. And the East Village still has a strong artists' community. I don't want to leave that. What for? A tall glass box with thin walls and ridiculous rents? Some midtown street in the middle of traffic?" She laughed. "Besides, *I've* got no choice now. Big daddy cut off the bread."

"Did he?" Grady said and eased her farther back on the table. "When did that happen?"

"Last week. Mother's hysterical but she won't cross him. He said I've botched up my life on his money long enough. It's come home to Dearborn and accept his help or stay here and forget about his help."

"That's laying it on the line."

"That's how Chrysler dealers are in Dearborn. They lay it on the line." She smiled. "But I'm staying."

"Stay, if that's what you want. But you don't have to stay down here. You could wash your feet and go uptown and use that fancy education of yours."

"And meet some solid-citizen type and get married. I'd wind up just like Mother, and that's boring," Ellen said. She wriggled her toes, dusty from her sandals, from the grimy streets, and smiled up at Grady. "I won't leave yet, maybe not ever. Drew's just getting started . . . his things are finally beginning to sell."

"Yes?" Grady said, and a picture of the young man slipped into his mind—Drew, her big, affable, California student-turned-potter. "Is that what you want? Drew?"

"We're happy, Grady. His work is getting better and my jewelry is starting to sell."

"I've done my best. Don't say I didn't try." Grady shook his head. "I won't say any more."

"We may have a showing next month."

"Send me an invitation."

"If you'll bring your checkbook."

"Just like all the rest, only interested in me for my money."

"Poor Grady," she said, and he looked at her in surprise, for suddenly she sounded like Courtney and suddenly he saw that he felt protective toward her because she reminded him of Courtney.

"That's a very strange look on your face, Doctor," she teased.

"For a minute you reminded me of someone."

"Someone terrific?"

"Yep. Terrific." He smiled. "Sit up, please," he said and listened briefly to her chest. "Okay, all done."

"No more medicine?"

"The inflammation's way down, another month or so you'll be fine. Just *please* watch your diet. And take those vitamins," he said and dragged the screen back to the table. He sat at the desk and wrote quickly in her file, his light, curly hair falling forward as he concentrated.

"This terrific person," Ellen called, "how come I've never seen her around here?"

"I don't like her to come around this neighborhood. If you have your show I'll bring her along."

"Is—"

"Never mind all that now." He grinned. "The joy of being a doctor is you get to ask personal questions but you don't have to answer any."

The metal frame of the screen made a loud, rasping sound as Ellen Train pushed it away. She walked over to the desk and looked down at Grady. "She's that special, is she?" Ellen said softly.

Grady looked away, unwilling to answer, for he knew the answer too well and *special* was not a good enough word—she was not special, she was his whole world.

"Clovis," Brian Morgan said at the entrance to the examination room. The child stood up and carefully carried the bird inside, laying him gently on the paper-covered table.

"Sorry-looking thing," Brian said. "Who'd be mean enough to pour paint on a little parakeet?" Brian asked, as if speaking to himself.

"He be a parakeet?" Clovis piped.

"Yes. They talk, you know, if you teach them. He's in a bad way." Brian turned his gray eyes on the child.

"You fix him."

"I don't know that I can."

"You can try . . . 'stead of just standing around, talking at me."

Brian crossed his arms over his chest and returned the boy's serious, quiet look. "If I get him well, what will you do with him, Clovis? He's a house bird, he wouldn't survive outside. Will you keep him?"

"My mama, she probly cook him for supper. She a bitch," Clovis said. Brian regarded the boy silently, without expression, staring deeply into his dark eyes until he realized he had to do what he could for the creature. He had to because he saw more than the hardness, the shrewdness in the child's eyes—he saw the blind innocence. Brian uncrossed his arms and picked the bird up, holding the stethoscope carefully to its chest. He heard a minute, faint heartbeat and he put the creature back on the table. "He's alive. We'll start with that," he said and leaned over his desk to write on a prescription pad. He tore the sheet off and handed it to Clovis. "Go downstairs and get these things from the pharmacy. And go down to the basement and get a piece of bread. Can you do that for me?"

"I be right back," he said to Brian and then went and stood over the yellow bird. "I be right back," he said.

Jim knocked on the door and handed a chart to Grady. "Good luck," he whispered, smiling. Grady looked curiously at Jim and then closed the door. He glanced at the new patient and then at his chart, frowning as he sat down.

"How long were you in detoxification?"

"Got through with detox last week. After two months."

"Two months?" Grady said and made a notation. "That's not bad."

"Not bad for you," the man said curtly, and Grady looked at him, a tall, thin, black man in his thirties. His face had one long scar, cheekbone to chin, and a smaller scar at the corner of his mouth. He had small, unfriendly eyes, and there were several gray hairs in his high Afro.

"Have you stayed clean?" Grady asked.

"Is it any of your damn business? This ain't no damn drug clinic. Damn, I just got used to one white man . . . now they come hand me a new one. And it got to be the one from the South. A *Southern* whitey, top of it all."

"I'm not a Southerner, no matter what you heard. I'm from Texas."

"You the one I heard about, all right. Big ranch man."

"My father's got the ranch, not me."

"Yeah? Your father also got a bunch of black men he treats like niggers?"

Grady glanced up from the file and took a long, steady look at the man. "My father doesn't discriminate," he said quietly. "He treats his white men like niggers too."

The man stared back at Grady through narrowed eyes and then a smile began that became a low, amused laugh. "Man, maybe I let you take care of me after all, Whitey. You mind if I call you Whitey?"

"Smile when you say it." Grady grinned suddenly, and this time the man laughed loudly, a full, rich chuckle that dissolved the tension.

"You got yourself a new patient, man," he said and rolled up his sleeve.

"I'm glad," Grady said. And he meant it; he felt good.

Nick walked quickly through the Clinic door and stopped short when he saw Jean standing at the desk. His jaw clenched and his skin paled a shade. He took a deep breath and then marched to the desk.

"How many waiting?" he asked Jim bruskly.

"Only the three down here," Jim said and tapped the files in front of him.

"Come with me," Nick commanded Jean. She followed mutely behind him, not daring to say anything, for the tone of his voice was furious. In the E.R. she sat quietly in a chair and stared up at him as he paced, his eyes threatening, his hands clenched white with anger. He looked at her finally. "Do you know what time it is?"

"A little past seven, but it's been busy, Nick. I've never seen it so busy."

He took a step toward her and she drew back, her eyes blinking rapidly, for Nick was an awesome picture in his rage.

"What is the rule around here?" he demanded. "What time are nurses supposed to leave?"

"Women are supposed to leave by five, I know, I know. But it's not really that dark and—"

"For Christ's sake," Nick thundered. "Do you think I send you all home because of the *dark*? I want you all out of here by five because by five it's getting ugly out there. Everything that lives in the woodwork starts coming out then," he hollered, his eyes two stark pinpoints of black. "They start *needing* then. A fix, a lay, a bottle, a fight. Jean, do you think I make Clinic rules just to have something to do? Do you think I sit and figure out ways to be arbitrary? I know this neighborhood, and goddamn it, when I say it's dangerous here after five o'clock, I *mean* it's dangerous. It's your ass I'm trying to save, not mine. The first thing I told all of you was that you were to obey safety rules and obey them absolutely. Do I have to remind you every goddamn morning? Every goddamn day?"

"It's just this once," she said quietly, turning away from him. He took her arm and swung her around to face him.

"Just this once! Some creep who's *needing* something isn't going to know it's just this once. He's going to *take* what he needs. *Grab* it, you understand that? You think I'm being dramatic, go ask Sergeant Mendez. Ask him about this neighborhood after five o'clock. A man may have some chance to defend himself. *May*. What do you weigh? A hundred and ten pounds? Around here a ten-year-old kid can deal with a hundred and ten pounds." He released her arm. "You do this once more, just once more and you're out of here."

"Okay, okay, do you have to scream?"

"Apparently I do. Apparently I have to worry about you because you won't worry about yourself. You think it's a game . . . one big happy family. The night you run across a junkie who's itching you won't think it's such a game."

She stared at him for a moment and then spoke quietly. "I'd like to think that this neighborhood is becoming my neighborhood too, that it doesn't just belong to the men here. Why should I be shut out just because I'm a woman?"

Nick shook his head. "This isn't a matter of discrimination, it's a matter of safety. A woman is fair game around here. Maybe you want to take the chance, I don't. You will do it my way or you won't do it at all. Yes or no?"

"Okay, I said okay."

"Come on now, Jim will walk you out. How do you get home?"

"Subway."

"Wonderful. A subway in this neighborhood," he said and glared at her. "You'll take a cab tonight, if there's one around here."

"But, I—"

"A cab!" he ordered and walked with her silently to the desk. "Go with Jean," he said to Jim. "See if you can find a cab somewhere. I'll take the next patient," he said and snapped up the top chart from the desk. He walked off a few steps and then looked back. "Do you need some money?" he called to her. She shook her head and Nick continued on his way.

"Sam Greenberg?" he asked the waiting patients, and an old man rose, nodding as he entered the examination room.

Grady walked into the corridor and saw that one more patient remained. He was tired, but still he felt good and he passed his hand quickly across his face as if to wipe the fatigue away. "Hello. I'll just get your file. Sorry you had to wait so long. What's your name?"

"Doc Gorlin got my file in there," the woman said. "I'm waiting on him."

Grady looked at the closed door and then went to it, knocking softly.

"What's up?" Nick asked through a crack in the doorway.

"Do you want me to take her?"

"No, I'll be finished here in a minute, I'll do it."

"I'm going upstairs then," Grady said and walked away, going to the elevator. He stepped inside and pressed 5, wearily stripping off his white jacket, crinkling it into a ball in his hands. The door opened and he walked into the fifth-floor corridor, going directly to the office. He stopped abruptly at the door when he saw Brian and Clovis bent over something small and bright on a desk top.

"What have you got there?" he asked, walking into the room.

"I hope you don't mind my doing this here," Brian said without turning around. "Come take a look."

"Yeah, cowboy, come on you take a look," Clovis said, his dark eyes cool on Grady. Grady shrugged and took a couple of steps to them, peering down. He stared and then laughed out loud, a great, deep, exclamation.

"He no bird of paradise," he laughed again.

"He a parakeet," Clovis said impatiently.

Grady looked at Brian. "A little veterinary medicine on the side?" he asked, smiling.

"Courtesy of Clovis," Brian said quietly.

Grady reached down and touched the bird gently with his finger. "He's painted up like a peacock," he said.

"I already tells you, cowboy, he a parakeet."

Grady smiled at Clovis and looked again at Brian. "What are you doing for him?"

"I managed to make a small splint and get some of the feathers unstuck. We were going to try and give him some water now," Brian said, holding up an eyedropper. "Clovis, take a cup and get some fresh water and some cotton pads from the supply room, please."

Clovis regarded Grady sternly and then reluctantly edged out of the room. "Docker Mogan, you keep you eyes on cowboy," he said and left.

Grady looked after him and he felt his good spirits

waning. "I just made a convert downstairs . . . but Clovis is another story. That kid won't like me, no matter what I do."

"The accent," Brian said mildly.

"What accent?"

"You still have a slight accent, noticeable enough around here. Clovis spent his first five years in Alabama, did you know that? He remembers. He told me once they used to call him woolhead down there."

"And what do you think they do *up here*?" Grady said, suddenly angry. "Nobody comes right out and says it up here, but they're thinking it just the same. Do you think it's better that they talk a good game and then won't let a black move into their precious Forest Hills? Somebody ought to write a book about the politics of a Southern accent," Grady said and slammed himself into a chair.

Brian stared at him quietly. "Grady, what's got into you? I know you're not a racist. A bigot. I only said that Clov—"

"I'm sorry," Grady interrupted. "It's just that I was feeling so great a minute ago. I guess he let the air out of my balloon." Grady lit a cigarette and then went to the desk and looked down at the bird. "Will he be all right?"

"I think so. But what are we going to do with him?"

"We'll keep him here. Clovis needs something to love."

"Here?" Nick Gorlin's big, deep voice entered the room. Brian and Grady turned and saw Nick, with Clovis in tow.

"Nick," Grady said, "take a look at . . . Clovis, what are you going to call him?"

"I like to call him T.K."

"Nick, take a look at T.K."

Nick crossed the room and looked from the bird to Grady to Brian. "Whose handiwork is that?" he smiled, pointing to the splint.

"Mine," Brian said. "It's not bad, considering I had to work with a tongue depressor."

Nick looked again at the bird. "We'll have to get a cage."

"You're not going to give us an argument?" Grady smiled at Nick.

"Clovis took the trouble to bring him in." Nick paused. "Brian took the trouble to fix him up . . . T.K.'ll be a Clinic project," Nick said, while wondering anew about Brian—methodical, unemotional Brian, who'd taken his time to attend a scruffy bird. "Clovis, we'll keep him here in the office. You can come up and play with him whenever you want. You'll have to take care of him, feed him, keep his cage clean. Do you understand?" Nick asked gently.

"I can do it," Clovis said eagerly. He stepped forward and looked down at the bird. "I be seeing you, T.K.," he said and then glanced sideways at Grady. "You be careful, Cowboy, you do him good till I sees him next," he instructed and then looked at Brian. The child seemed about to say something and then abruptly changed his mind and nodded at Brian instead. He took a last look at Grady and walked wordlessly out of the room, his small back straight and his shoulders squared, his job done for now. The doctors watched him leave and then looked at each other.

"He's a puzzle," Nick said.

"He makes himself clear enough when he wants to," Grady said with a smile. "He doesn't trust me with T.K.," he said and stretched. "I'm going home. Brian, are you leaving? I can drop you off."

"Ready. Unless Nick wants something."

"Nick doesn't. Except where are today's files?"

"They're all collected, same as always."

"All right, go on home. See you Sunday."

"And not before. Tomorrow's one day off I'm going to enjoy."

The two men turned and walked to the door. Grady

looked back at Nick. "Where's your help for tonight? You're not going to handle a Friday night here alone, are you?"

"I've got two City residents coming over later. Go on, before I change my mind."

"No, no, don't do that." Grady smiled. "Come on, Brian, or the mean man will keep us after school."

Nick smiled after them and then sat down. He looked around absently, his eyes falling on the bird. He stroked the yellow feathers lightly and smiled again. "Welcome to the Clinic, T.K."

9

Friday night, almost Saturday morning, and people would have some time for themselves . . .

COURTNEY rinsed the last dish in the sink and placed it in a yellow rubber rack nearby. She dried her hands and left the kitchen, walking into the living room where Grady sat watching television, his face drawn tight in concentration. Courtney shook her pale yellow head. "A boy and his color TV. It touches me to my soul." She smiled and sat down next to him on the couch.

He slipped his arm around her and grinned, his eyes still on the television set. "Are you making fun?"

"Maybe. Maybe a little. How's the game?" she asked, glancing at the screen.

"The Mets are getting their asses beat in San Francisco, that's how the damn game is."

She looked at him curiously, wondering at the sharp tone in his voice. "You're in a fine mood tonight."

"Mood. I'm getting sick of hearing that word."

"What word would you like?" she asked gently. "You haven't been your usual charming self all evening. No snappy patter, no witty sayings, no jokes."

He smiled slightly. "No magic tricks, no time steps. I'm sorry . . . half my mind's been on the Clinic. The . . . children. Remember I told you about the parakeet, that Clovis named him T.K.?" he asked. She nodded. "I didn't tell you what Brian said on the way home."

"What?"

"About Clovis. He was just a baby when his father left them. And he's never seen him since. Yet when he finds a little bird, finds something he loves, he names him after his father, T.K. Williams. What does that tell you?"

"I don't know what you mean."

"Courtney, when a kid gets a pet, any kind of pet, he names it after someone he cares about or he gives it a neutral name. Rover or something like that. Clovis gave the bird a personal name, but all he could find was the name of a man he never even saw. He has no one at all in his real life, not even someone to name a bird after. What are we going to do with those children, Courtney? What can we give them? Hell, why are people always leaving people? Why are they always walking out?" he said very quietly.

"People aren't always—"

"They are. They're always leaving. Sooner or later, everyone takes a walk."

"You're still here, I'm still here."

He looked at her then and held the look for a long moment. She saw the hurt, the sadness in his eyes, and she was suddenly afraid. "Anyway," she said slowly, "you and Nick and everybody are giving those children all you can. Look at that boy you're taking into the Clinic for the summer . . . you're giving him something he's never had before."

"And it's going to work." He grasped her shoulder harder. "I can do it and I'm going to do it," he said intently.

"All right, Grady, but do I have to give my arm in the cause?" she asked softly. He felt the pressure of his fingers then and he took his hand away, peering at the whitened flesh where it had been.

"Sorry. I guess I get carried away, times."

"I guess."

"Did I hurt you?"

"The brute doesn't know his own strength," she laughed, swinging her arm through the air. "It's all right though, I'm right-handed."

He looked again at her shoulder and smiled. "You're going to be black and blue."

"People will think I got it fair and square, in bed."

"How you talk." He grinned. "City women, my father warned me about city women."

"Your father likes me."

"For a city woman he likes you."

"He said I was so pretty I made his eyes tear." She laughed. "Why don't you ever say things like that?"

"You know you're pretty," he said quietly, then brightened. "Besides, that's what you call your sexist remark."

"You're impossible, Grady, what will I do with you?"

"Love me," he said in a low voice. "For as long as you can," he added, pulling her head to his shoulder. She slipped her arm around the curve of his back and hugged him tightly. She looked at him and smiled and he smiled back and for a moment they just sat that way, bathed, it seemed, in each other's reflection. After a while he lightened his grasp on her and leaned back. "I think I could do with some thirst quencher. Would you mind fixing a drink?"

Courtney slid out from under his arm and went to the sideboard, pouring bourbon into a glass, adding ice. She poured a glass of wine for herself and returned to the couch.

"Thanks," Grady said and took a deep sip.

Courtney reached for a sheaf of folders on the coffee table.

"Are those Tessa's?" he asked.

"The last of them. My first meeting's coming up and I'm going to know as much about the Clinic as you do."

"Good. Maybe you can finish my A.M.A. paper for me."

"What are we going to do tomorrow?" she asked, looking up from the file.

"What would you like?"

"You decide."

"Whatever you'd enjoy."

"Grady, stop it."

"We could . . . we could go riding. Go riding in Central Park if it's a nice day, would you like that?"

"A long, long ride. Yes, I'd like that. Away from everything. Away, Grady, really away."

He heard the desperation in her voice and he looked away, back to the television. "Damn, that guy throws a ball like he has all the time in the world."

"Grady?" She shook his arm. "A long, long ride? Can we?"

"Sure," he said, then looked closely at her. "Away from everything." He felt a quick ache in his spirits and took a gulp of the drink in his hand. He sensed her strange unrest.

Courtney leaned back, sighing. "It's that I feel kind of closed in lately. I'm in one place and I want to be in another. I go to another place and I want to go back to the first one. Days . . . when you're not here, when nobody's around . . . I can't seem to sit still," she said and looked at the papers in her hand. "I . . . I start working at the kitchen table and before I know it I'm sitting at the desk. Then I find I'm at the coffee table . . . then I find I'm back in the kitchen. I can't settle myself down. . . . It's like the apartment is too small for me, the city is too small, but that isn't it. I'm looking for something but I don't know what. Myself, maybe," she said and looked at him. She saw his eyes fixed firmly on the television screen, she saw the tension in the tightness of his mouth. Courtney wasn't surprised, for she knew she'd dipped too deeply into herself and made Grady acutely uncomfortable. She felt a brief flicker of annoyance and then laughed softly, running her hand through Grady's hair, splaying light, shiny curls onto his forehead.

"Okay," she said lightly, "my innermost has its clothes on again . . . it's safe to look."

"What?" he asked innocently.

But Courtney saw the relief in his eyes. "Never mind." She smiled. "I talk to myself sometimes . . . just for the hell of it."

Grady leaned over and kissed her on the forehead, then he held her face in his hands. "I'm doing the best I know how to do, Courtney," he said quietly. He held her glance another moment and then looked away, a trace of uneasiness in his eyes.

She regarded him in silence and then shook her head. She reached over and poked him in the ribs, a good shot.

He hunched over in surprise. "What in hell was that for?"

"That's for nothing," she laughed. "What are you going to do about it?"

"You know, in Texas a woman has more respect." He grinned. "A man's lord and master . . . you don't see any Texas woman shoving a man around. I should teach you some respect."

"Tomorrow. I'm too tired for respect tonight."

"We can watch the rest of this lying down. Want to?" he asked, pointing at the television.

"Good idea," she said and stood up. She went around the room turning off lights and Grady went into the bedroom. She heard the sound of the portable starting up and the rustle of linen as the spread was swept back from the bed. She heard a whoosh as Grady fell onto the bed and she smiled, as she took the glasses to the kitchen. She listened to the quiet, familiar sounds of Grady, of their nights, and a great, sudden warm happiness flowed over her. In the peaceful, homey sounds she felt her love for Grady as if it were an actual physical presence in every part of her. Her mind was on many things and on nothing as she went about rinsing the glasses, straightening the kitchen, her fingers flying as she hung up a cloth, wiped a spot of grease, closed a cabinet door, reached for the light switch. Courtney had taken a step out of the kitchen before she realized she was crying. She froze in her steps, reaching to touch the small tears streaking her face. She was frightened and she shook herself to rid the feeling. She went back into the kitchen and bent her head low over the sink, gripping its sides until the nameless fear passed, until the twisting she felt inside her ceased. Slowly she walked from the room, bitter confusion in her face, for there was no reason she knew, none she could understand, that would explain her tears. Near the bedroom door she heard the reassuring sound of Grady mumbling at the television set, and just when she thought the small spell was gone she felt new tears slip down her cheeks. She turned away from the doorway and made her way to the couch, sinking down quietly, her pale face in her hands.

"What's *wrong*?" She whispered to herself. "What is the matter?" she asked over and over again, though silence was the only response in the darkened room. Her thoughts spun and buzzed around her as she tried to piece it together. Happiness in one moment, she thought, and then . . . and then what?

"Courtney?" she heard Grady call her. "Courtney, aren't you coming in?"

She fumbled in the pocket of her long blue skirt, looking for a tissue, finding only a paper clip and the stub of a pencil. She felt a quick, hard anger at that moment, and flung the pencil across the room. She heard it hit the air conditioner with a small ping, and looked quickly toward the bedroom.

"Courtney? . . . Courtney?" Grady's voice came again. "What's keeping you?"

She looked at the doorway and forced herself to take deep, regular breaths.

"In . . . in a minute," she said bleakly. "Just . . . give . . . me another minute," she added and stood up. She felt a shiver at the back of her neck, a new, strange loneliness in the shadows of the room. She cursed out loud, though not loud enough for Grady to hear.

"Courtney?" Grady called, his face grim and his eyes very dark. Without looking at her, without seeing her face, he knew from her voice that she was upset. He wanted to go to her—to run to her and hold her and make it well. He sat up, about to crawl off the bed, and then sat back again, his face as sad as it had ever been. He couldn't go to her, couldn't offer himself; something in him held him where he was. He leaned back again, grieving for what they were losing—a little bit more every day.

10

The last day of June was hot and thick with early summer. The air was gaunt. Tempers would be short . . .

"I'M NOT INTERESTED in your sad stories," Nick snapped into the telephone. "Just get your rump over here and fix this thing," he shouted and slammed down the receiver. "Brand-new air conditioner," he said to Grady, "the first time we have to use it, and it doesn't work. Do you believe that?" he asked, black eyes furious.

"Is the guy coming over?"

"Who knows? The American repairman . . . the new American elite. They do as they damn well please to do," Nick said and left his desk, going to the small panel that ran the central cooling unit. He smacked it with his fist, hard, and Grady looked around.

"That's not going to help any."

"No kidding," Nick said and leaned against it, looking at Grady. "And while I'm at it, what are you doing here so early? You're scheduled for the late shift tonight."

"Sturgis called me at home. His wife's sick again, he couldn't get in. He just did get in about fifteen minutes ago," Grady said and then regretted his words, for he saw Nick pale with anger.

"Again?! I wonder what kind of hustle Sturgis is running around here."

"Hustle?"

"Hustle. Haven't you noticed how his wife gets sick when it's snowing, or when we're going to be jammed, or on Friday afternoons . . . or today, when it's hot as hell?"

"Now that you mention it." Grady smiled.

"Crap. You've noticed just as I did. How many times have you covered for him, all told?"

"I haven't kept count, Nick. Several, that's for sure."

"At least twice a month for each of our six months. That's what *I'd* say. Sure, he's found himself a sucker . . . good, old Grady Malory at his service."

"Well, what am I supposed to do? Leave a floor uncovered?"

"Don't worry, you don't have to do anything. I'll do it. I'll take care of Sturgis's butt this afternoon."

"I wish you'd calm down first. No use screaming, not with him. He's got to be talked into it."

"Talk? Oh, I'll talk, I'll talk a blue streak. I'll do some talking about U.C.L.A. Medical Center and see how he likes it. He's just marking time here until he can join the Center next year, you know. Well, what friend Sturgis may have forgotten is that the Center's going to take my word on him. I say no, they say no, I say maybe, they still say no. He can unpack his bathing suit if he keeps this up."

Grady nodded but said nothing; he watched Nick thoughtfully, measuring the tight anger in his voice. "What's got you so worked up?" he asked finally.

"Everything. It's sloppy around here, sloppy. I come in this morning and I see a blank bulletin board. Two weeks ago I asked Jean to put up the notices . . . the sandlot baseball games, the Boys' Club swimming and basketball, the P.A.L. ball games, all the things the kids around here could use. One week ago I reminded her. Three days ago. Today, I blew my top. Then the air conditioner . . . it must be a hundred and ten outside and they hadn't even bothered to turn the damn thing on. Okay, it's not working, but they didn't know that. Then I noticed the aides hadn't bothered to put out fresh gowns, nor to circulate today's charts. . . . There are four cracked test tubes sitting in the blood sets. You're in when you shouldn't be, Sturgis is out when he should be in. Herb tells me the pharmacy has been out of tetracycline for six days. . . . Two of the lights on the call director board aren't working. . . ." Nick shook his black head in disgust. "The small things start breaking down and it isn't long before the big things go to hell." He flipped the spigot on the coffeemaker roughly and a stream of coffee sloshed into the cup he held. He took the cup to his desk and slammed it down, spilling some of the liquid. Grady got up slowly and took a paper towel to the desk, quietly sopping up the wetness.

"Yeah, I guess all that could do it."

"*Could* do it? Did do it."

"You were a little touchy last night. When we talked on the phone?" Grady said pleasantly.

Nick looked at him quickly and then sat down behind his desk, cupping his chin in his hand. For a long time his eyes were abstracted, vague, and then he looked at Grady. "I was, you're right," he said quietly.

"Problems?"

"I don't know."

Grady went back to his paperwork without comment, knowing Nick would talk when he was ready. He turned a page and then leaned back in his chair, lighting a cigarette. He drew on it for a while and then again bent his head to his work.

"Tessa promised her father we'd spend a week at Cabot's Landing."

"Is that bad?"

"I don't know," Nick said and looked off. "I thought we'd settled the question of the Cabot money. I should say I thought I'd settled it and could live with it. I mean, we worked it out so that Tessa uses whatever she wants but *we* live together on what I earn."

"What's that got to do with spending some time at Cabot's Landing?"

"Grady, you know how I used to spend my summers? Stickball in the streets . . . open fire hydrants to get cool, public pools and Coney Island if my mother had the subway fare. Tessa . . . her summers were spent at Cabot's Landing. I've seen pictures of it. It's an estate. One big, enormous house and then about half a dozen guest houses. They're right on the water *and* they've got a pool. Private docks. They've got a boat . . . Jesus, it's more like a ship than a boat. Tennis courts. *Skeet* shooting, for God's sake," he said desultorily. "I'm going to go up there in my twenty-dollar chinos, my five-and-dime sneakers, and there'll be Jason Cabot, master of all that, in his two-hundred-dollar flannels and custom-made tennis shoes . . . looking at Tessa and knowing she could have married anybody in the world. Not some guy who used to play in open fire hydrants."

"The point is she *did* marry that guy."

"And she'll take a good look at what is hers, by right, and what she's got now and . . ."

"And what? Divorce you and go marry a prince?" Grady smiled gently. "Don't you know any better than that?"

"Of course I do," Nick said quickly.

"Then what are you so worried about?"

"I'll feel like a fool in the middle of all of that."

Grady smiled. "Do you good. Join the club. When are you going?"

"September sometime. If we go."

Grady hesitated for a moment, his face growing serious. "Tessa doesn't ask for very much."

"What do you mean?"

"That it's not worth rocking what you two have. Don't risk losing her over a stupid trip."

Nick looked at Grady in surprise. "Losing her? I'll never lose her. We'll never lose each other, we go too deep for that."

"Anybody can lose anybody!" Grady said harshly. He stood up abruptly and looked at his watch. "Time to get back downstairs. Are you coming?"

"I have a few minutes. I want to look over Marie Carlino's file in peace before she gets here."

"Okay," Grady said and turned toward the door.

"Grady?" Nick called. "What were you so angry about a minute ago?"

"Nothing, the heat—" he began, but stopped as the phone rang.

"Gorlin . . . what? . . .when? . . . yes . . . yes, I'll take care of it, I'll be down," he said and crashed the receiver back on its cradle. "That was City. Sturgis called them to cancel his consultation over there today. He said he's too *busy*," Nick said and scrambled away from his desk.

"Where are you going?" Grady asked.

"To have a long, loud word with Sturgis before I call City back and tell them to expect him. On time," he said shortly, moving rapidly to the door. The phone rang again, stopping him just short of the corridor, and with a snort he reentered the office.

Grady hurried out, taking the stairs quickly to the third floor. "Where's Sturgis?" he asked, grabbing an aide's arm. The aide pointed to one of the examination rooms and Grady hurried to it, knocking curtly. The door opened and he waved his finger at Dr. Sturgis, bringing him into the corridor.

"You wouldn't listen to me, would you, Sturgis?" Grady said heatedly.

"What are you—"

"Well, I told you it would happen and it's happened. Nick's on to you now, man, and the fur's going to fly."

Dr. Sturgis looked warily around him and then at Grady. "Did you tell—"

"I told nothing . . . though I should have, I see that now. You just better hope Nick doesn't get a notion to take a close look at your file, Sturgis. He's ready to tear your heart out as it is. . . . If he finds out there is no Mrs. Sturgis . . . that all that sick wife business was a lie . . . he'll grind you into little pieces. Man," Grady shook his head, "that's the kind of con we used to use in med school . . . a cheap, kid trick. You should have grown out of that kind of shit by now. An intern wouldn't be so fat-assed dumb."

"Grady, you know I have problems. I'm trying to—"

"Problems? You have problems?" he said angrily. "Everybody has problems. I could tell you a thing or two about problems. Do you think I live in the Garden of Eden?"

"Calm down, Grady, I—"

"You look here, man, and you listen. If you get through this in one piece you'd better do some heavy thinking about the work we're trying to do here. About cooperation. You just pull up your socks and get with it, starting now. You don't and I'll have a nice little talk with Nick. I swear I will. Fat-assed dumb, that's all it is. Fat-assed dumb. Problems! Tell me all about it," he barked and turned swiftly away and toward the stairs. At the head of the stairs a nurse bumped into him and he turned on her. "You want to watch where you're going? You just want to watch where you're going?" He stopped at the next landing and took a deep breath, wiping his damp face with a handkerchief. He tried to calm himself, to quell the storm he felt inside. It wasn't supposed to be this way, he thought, it wasn't supposed to be this way at all. It seemed more than he could stand, and however he looked at it it all came out: Courtney.

Grady took another breath and then continued to the desk, looking at it cursorily as he went to an examination room.

"Mr. Benke, you back again?" Grady asked the grinning man and then sighed, forcing himself to smile.

Nick walked into an examination room and smiled at Marie Carlino. She was seventeen years old, a dark-haired, brown-eyed girl who just missed being pretty in the same way she just missed at everything in her life. Soft-spoken, shy, in personality, in nature, she was the direct opposite of her brother Frankie, and Nick knew she was afraid of the younger child. Nick could remember Marie as a baby, soft, obliging, a baby who almost never cried. That had been his last year in the neighborhood, but in all his visits back he'd never failed to stop and visit her; it was he who'd comforted the little girl on the day of her father's funeral, he who'd taken care of her at City when she'd had a nervous collapse. So long ago, he thought, and now she was almost a woman, but she'd never lost the melancholy, the wistfulness. She was little more than a shell of a person—dominated by the mother to whom she gave unquestioning devotion, cowed by the brother who taunted her, threatened her.

"How are you feeling, Marie?" he asked gently.

She fumbled nervously with the straps of her purse. "Like always. Maybe a little stronger, since you started the injections. I . . . I'm sorry I came early but I got to . . . I have to enroll at that school later."

"That's all right. Tell me about the school."

"It's a secretarial school. My shorthand's not so good, so Mama said I got to . . . I have to go this summer and then I can get a job in the fall. Mama says I can get a good job in the fall, she says everybody's looking for a good secretary. Important people, maybe."

"Do you want to be a secretary, Marie?" he asked softly. "Or is it your mother's idea?"

"She's been telling me about secretarial work for a long time . . . since I was little. Mama says it's a way to improve myself . . . you know, through the people I meet. Uptown people, maybe."

"I always kind of thought you had your eye on Jimmy, down the street." He smiled. "I always thought you and Jimmy would get together and make your own lives."

Marie looked away from Nick, pink color rising to her cheeks. She waved her small hand in embarrassment and then looked back at him. "We been . . . we have been friends, you could say, since third grade, but Mama says Jimmy's only a waste. Not like the people I could meet . . . if I learn how to talk good and improve my manners. She got me this book, it's all about how to eat nice, like in a restaurant, you know? And how to make good conversation, stuff like that. I'm studying it."

"So, Jimmy's a waste," Nick said slowly. "He has a job, hasn't he?"

"Oh yeah . . . yes. He's a clerk uptown. He told me when he saves some money he's going to go to night school. But Mama says you can't put dreams in the bank. She says better to find a man with a good regular job. A man with a future."

"Marie, do you always have to do what your mother says to do? You're not a child, you're entitled to think for yourself. Make your own decisions."

"No, you don't understand it right. Mama always . . . well, it's like this: When Pop died Mama was all alone, the two kids to take care of and everything. And all her life she worked hard so we could have a better life than—than her . . . she. I always get confused with her and she," Marie said apologetically.

"Don't *worry* about it so much," Nick said quietly. "I hope things work out for you, Marie, I really do. But listen to one piece of advice, will you? It's no disrespect to our mother to want to do something different with your life . . . something she hasn't planned for you. It is your life, not hers."

"I wouldn't be anywhere without Mama."

"As she so often reminds you," he muttered.

"What? I mean, excuse me?"

"Never mind, Marie. C'mon, let's see how you're doing. Get undressed and we'll check your weight."

She nodded to him and stood up, walking behind the screen. He left the desk and pulled the scale away from the wall. "Did Frankie come with you?" he asked.

"Yeah . . . yes. He's waiting down in the basement. Jean says that's where you're going to teach him what to do."

"That's right. What do you think about his working here?"

There was no response and he didn't repeat the question. When she emerged from behind the screen he saw the nervous look in her eyes and he led her silently to the scales.

"Good, you gained a pound this week. The vitamins must be working. Now we'll just get some blood," he said, and she took a seat on the edge of the examination table. He took her arm and saw how frail it was, how frail she was, though despite the fragility, despite her slimness, she had a nice figure, surprisingly rounded and very soft. She would never have the voluptuous curves her mother had at the same age, but she would have a nice build and Nick was sorry only that her attractiveness was a fact that never occurred to her.

"You're looking at me funny, Nick."

"Not at all, I was just thinking that you're becoming a pretty young woman," he said, though he knew pretty wasn't the word and never would be. *Nice* was more like it, but he knew she wouldn't understand that word as he meant it.

"Go on. Mama shown . . . showed me some pictures from when she was young. She told me how all the boys was . . . were always chasing her. Jimmy's the only boy was ever interested in me. I have this pointy chin. And Mama says my eyes are too small."

"Marie," he said kindly, "what am I going to do with you? When a man tells a woman something nice, pays her a compliment, she should say thank you and then let it alone . . . not argue about it."

"Oh, you're a doctor, it's your job to be nice."

"I give up." He smiled. "Okay, let's see that arm," he said and searched out a vein. He inserted the needle and watched it fill the syringe when suddenly Marie coughed a few times and put her other hand on Nick's arm.

"What is it? Am I hurting you?"

"No . . . no, it's not that. It's about what you asked me . . . before. About Frankie. I never told this to nobod—anybody, Mama said not to . . . but I don't know . . . seeing he's going to be working for you, maybe you should know what I think."

"What's that?"

"Well, it's like I told Mama . . . I think Frankie is a little strange . . . maybe a little crazy even."

"I've thought he was strange, yes."

"But did you ever think he was . . . not right in the head?"

Nick stared at Marie. "What makes you ask something like that?"

"It's like I said, seeing he's going to work for you, maybe you should know what I think. . . . I think after Pop died he started getting . . . funny. Like the time he set the cat on fire."

"What?" Nick asked, startled.

"My cat, Mumps. Frankie came home one night with some junk from the cellar, paint stuff. He tied Mumps in the tub and the next thing I know, the cat's on fire. He died," Marie said and looked away. "Mama came home and saw what . . . she beat up Frankie with Pop's strap. She beat him up until he was bleeding and then she said never to tell what he done . . . did."

Nick hastily withdrew the needle and pushed her arm back. He felt a dull, thudding sickness somewhere in his stomach and he leaned back against the edge of the desk. "You can get dressed now, Marie," he said quietly.

"Nick? Maybe I shouldn't have said noth—anything?"

"I'm glad you did. Your brother needs a lot of help, Marie. Maybe we can give it to him, maybe we're still in time," Nick said grimly, his face closed and dark and tired.

11

The first days of July were hot and close with summertime. It was a new season, their lives would be changed . . .

"I DON'T BELIEVE IT, I just don't believe it. Not any of it," Nick said to Grady. The two men sat talking quietly, careful to keep their voices away from Clovis, who sat in a corner of the office watching T.K. hop around on the floor.

"Frankie just needed to know someone would give him a chance," Grady replied. "He's had the chance and he's responding."

"You really believe that? No, I'm sorry, I can't buy it."

"Figure it out for yourself. He's been here five full days now and what's he done? Run himself ragged, for one thing. He comes in in the morning with a big smile, does his little jobs and asks for more . . . hell, he's willing to work a lot harder than we ask him to."

"I know all that, it's the talk of the Clinic. Even Brian had a kind of stunned look on his face the day Frankie worked his floor. But it doesn't make sense."

"As long as it makes sense to Frankie, that's what's important. Anyway, I think you've watched him long enough. I'd like him assigned to the first floor now. After all, the point of this was for me to get close to him, break down some of those defenses."

"I didn't think he'd last five minutes, you know that?"

"Okay, you were wrong, don't take it out on the boy."

"Grady, I'm not taking anything out on anybody. I'm trying to be sure we haven't made a bad mistake with him."

"And just when are you going to be sure? By the time you're ready the summer will be over," Grady said loudly, and Clovis looked up from T.K.

"Cowboy, why for you likes that no-good so much?" he asked, his eyes quietly mocking.

"Don't call him a no-good," Grady said gently. "We're here to give help to people who need it . . . like what you did with the bird there. You saw he needed help and you brought him here."

"That a different thing. T.K. don't carry no chain in his pocket, no knifes."

"We're trying to change Frankie. Try and understand that—"

"Seem to me I understands okay. Black boys understands good as white boys," he said. The hostility was sharp on his small face and Grady drew in a breath.

"I didn't mean—" he began, but Nick interrupted him.

"All right, all right," Nick said impatiently. "Clovis, what we're talking about happens to be none of your business. If you start interfering in our discussions up here you won't be allowed up here. And, Grady,"—he turned to him—"you're afraid to say boo to Clovis because you know he's going to lay some black-boy remark on you. Clovis knows it too. He's a pretty good con artist for a nine-year-old." He smiled over at the boy, then turned back to Grady. "Now look, we're going downstairs and have a word with Frankie. I'll move him to the first floor tomorrow, but I want him to understand that he's on permanent probation here. I know he's been on his best behavior these first days, but I want him to know he has to keep it up. C'mon, let's go."

Grady stood and went over to Clovis. He looked at the boy and then bent down and took the bird in his hands. "T.K., T.K. Can you say your name yet? T.K., T.K.," he repeated.

"I be teaching him," Clovis said firmly, and Grady returned the bird to the floor.

"C'mon, Grady," Nick called at the door.

"Coming. 'Bye, Clovis."

"Yeah," the boy said, and Grady turned and left the office.

They took the stairs, stopping briefly at each landing to look into the waiting areas. "I'm seeing more and more new faces every day," Nick said.

"I am too. Doctor, we are beginning to make a name for ourselves." Grady smiled.

"That fact should be included in the A.M.A. paper."

"I intended something on it. Courtney brought up the point, matter of fact."

"Oh?"

"That's right. She has her first meeting this afternoon, and man, has she ever got the Clinic memorized. She knows what we've got and haven't got down to the last Band-Aid."

"The man from Joint Charities?"

"Yep. She's been fluttering about it for two days. It's like I'm not around," Grady said quietly.

Nick looked at him hard. "Grady—"

"Don't get that tone of voice, Nick. Don't start." Nick shrugged and they turned into the first floor and went to the desk.

"Get Frankie down here," Nick said to Jean. "We'll

be in there," he added and guided Grady into the E.R. Nick sat down, tapping his fingers impatiently; Grady rested against the rim of the examination table, neither man speaking until Nick looked up at Grady. "Another thing I can't figure out is why you don't seem happier about how Frankie seems to have fit in. I thought you'd be beating your chest."

"I don't know. Maybe it's because you haven't given me the chance to work directly with him. When *I'm* able to do something that makes the difference, I'll be beating my chest. Now I'm only a bystander."

"You wanted me?" Frankie asked, and both men turned. He looked like the same Frankie Carlino and yet he didn't. The insolence was missing from his soft, full mouth and in clean denims and his beige aide's jacket, there was no menace in his shuffling walk. His long hair was neatly combed, it shone, and the smile on his face was bright. In that moment he looked like any fifteen-year-old boy anxious to please his boss. Nick studied him for a moment and then managed a small smile.

"You seem to be enjoying it here, Frankie."

"I am. I ain't done nothin' wrong, neither."

"I know. That's what I'm wondering about, why haven't you done anything wrong?"

"I don't get you," Frankie said, frowning. "In the class you said all the guys had to watch themselfs, you didn't want no trouble."

"That's what I said. But, Frankie, what I've said never made any difference to you before," Nick said slowly.

"Oh . . . oh, now I get you. You wonder how come. Well, it's like this: I figured I'd see how it was to play it straight for a while. No promises," he said quickly, "but I'm goin' to try it. See, nobody never offered me no job before. The money don't mean nothin', I can make better on the street, but maybe I don't have to be no bum all my life, like my old man. You get me? See, if I could have a job here, maybe I could have a job somewhere else. Maybe someday I could move out from the neighborhood. All the time that's all Ma yaps about. Movin' out," he said and paused. "And there's another thing . . . this job makes me a big man in the neighborhood, on count of I'm the only Savage Snake you asked. You beginnin' to get what I mean? Nick, you ain't goin' to can me? 'Cause I thought I was doin' good, doin' okay."

Nick was startled to find he almost believed the boy. He ran a hand through his black hair. "I won't can you unless I have reason to. Just don't give me any reason. I'm moving you down here starting tomorrow. This floor handles a lot of old people—defenseless people—and I don't want them frightened by you. Frankie, I don't want you to take advantage of them in any way."

"Yeah, Nick, sure, I understand."

"I hear you volunteered to work in the lab as extra duty, is that right?"

"Yeah."

"Why?" Grady asked.

"I seen it the day I was deliverin' towels. It's heavy, man, all those bloods and tubes and gadgets. Can I?"

"We'll see."

"Nick, okay, you don't trust me," the boy said earnestly, "but a person could change, you know. Ma's always sayin' 'look at that Nick . . . he improved hisself, got out of the neighborhood.' I'm not going to be no doctor, but maybe someday I could be something respectable too."

For a moment Nick only stared at Frankie and then he turned away. "We'll see, Frankie. Get back to work now, we'll talk again."

Frankie left the room quietly and Grady looked at Nick.

"What do you think?"

"Who knows?" Nick said. "I hate like hell to say it, but he's convincing. Not what he says . . . not that song and dance about wanting to be something . . . but the part about trying to play it straight. The trouble is he's such a clever kid he could be conning us out of our socks and we wouldn't know it. Street-clever. I don't know. There was . . ." Nick said and paused, staring off in thought.

"What? There was what?" Grady prodded.

"I saw something like that happen down here once. There was this real mean kid, worthless. He lived across the street from Pitlik's Market, used to hang out there, annoying people. Finally old man Pitlik decided to offer him a job . . . just out of the blue. I suppose he thought as long as the boy was going to be there anyway, maybe he could get him on his side. Anyway, he took the job and the next thing everybody knew he was a different boy. No angel, but not so bad either. I don't know, maybe this is Pitlik's Market all over again."

"And we're old man Pitlik?" Grady laughed.

"Maybe, I said maybe. I still wouldn't bet the rent money on it."

"I'm anxious to start working with him."

"You'll have your chance, looks like," Nick said and glanced at the clock on the wall. "We'd better get back."

Frankie stood outside in the corridor, listening. When he heard the men leaving the room he scurried to the staircase, racing up until he was out of sight. He'd have to be careful with Nick, he thought to himself, but Grady Malory—he had Grady Malory in his pocket. Frankie chuckled and then he laughed, crouching against the wall, holding his mouth to quiet the sound; he laughed until he cried.

Courtney stepped out of a taxi onto the sidewalk in front of the Plaza Hotel. She was early but she hurried inside, anxious to be out of the midafternoon heat. It was cool inside the old, graceful hotel, and she wandered slowly through the lobby, looking at the windows in the small shops, looking at the greenery, looking at the people—laughing women in designer-styled summer dresses, erect, sure men in gold-buttoned blazers. If there were tourists anywhere around she didn't see them; she saw only New York people sitting handsomely over cocktails and business lunches and lovers' rendezvous, and she felt suddenly lighthearted. It was a splendid day in a spendid hotel among splendid people, and for the first time in many months she felt herself without the nervousness that had haunted her. She smiled at her reflection in a mirror, at the unexpected confidence she saw, and then entered the elevator. During the short ride upstairs she ran over the Clinic statistics in her mind, though her mind was less on the Clinic than on the new mood she felt, the lifting of her spirits. Courtney walked through the long, silent corridor determined to enjoy it, and more, to enjoy herself, for it seemed a very long time since she'd felt this well. She located Peter Joshua's suite and rang the bell. She was smiling broadly.

"Courtney Ames. Come in."

She looked up and was startled by the man she saw. She'd expected an attractive, assured man, but she hadn't expected *this* man. This man was elegant; very tall and reed-thin, all sharp angles and planes, his hair dark and shot through with slim silver streaks. He had a narrow, mocking smile and eyes the color of the wind.

"Thank you," she said quickly and walked into the suite. "I hope I'm not too early."

"Gives us more time together," he said easily. "Sit down. What will you drink?"

"Oh . . . nothing, I think."

"Nobody drinks nothing," he said and walked to a tray of liquors sitting on a round, gilt-trimmed coffee table. "We have everything."

"Then a little wine, thanks."

"Wine," he said.

Courtney sat in a plum-colored velvet chair and

looked toward one of the two huge windows in the room, her spirits rising even more as she contemplated the cityscape beyond the windowglass. She felt suddenly as if she belonged—belonged in this room, in this hotel, in the pattern of sun-whitened city towers she beheld. Grudgingly, she remembered the purpose of this meeting and she quickly rearranged the folders in her lap. She turned and looked again at Peter Joshua. She saw the fine cut of the soft, fawn slacks he wore, the expensive, graceful fabric, and the well-tailored striped shirt, open at the neck to reveal a bit of brown silk scarf. He wore brown Gucci loafers and a wristwatch of very thin gold. He moved easily, fluidly, and the sun in the room touched the gold on his wrist, sending bright shadows onto his angular face. She watched as he walked to her with the drinks and, inexplicably, her smile faded; she felt a small apprehension, a discomfort she couldn't explain.

"To Courtney Ames," he said and raised his glass. It was a tall glass, three quarters full, and he drank hastily. "Do you disapprove of me, Courtney Ames?" he smiled at her.

"Of course not," she said quickly.

"Then you mustn't look so serious. In this glass is twelve-year-old Scotch, and twelve-year-old Scotch is very good for a forty-two-year-old man. It works miracles. Makes him believe he's really eighty-two and about to be out of it at last. Makes him believe he's really twenty-two and just beginning. I recommend both feelings for forty-two-year-old men. I am an expert on forty-two-year-old men," he said and drank again from his glass. "I will soon be an expert on forty-three-year-old men."

Courtney stared at him, not knowing what to say. It occurred to her finally that he'd already had a great deal to drink.

"Perhaps you'd prefer another day, Mr. Joshua?"

"No, I wouldn't prefer another day. Why would I

prefer another day? Do you think I drink less on Thursday than on Wednesday? On Monday than on Friday?" He smiled, and his smile taunted her gently.

"I meant—"

"No, don't lie, Courtney Ames. You were thinking: Well, this man is drunk and I should leave. Except if I leave I may not get his hundred thousand dollars."

"Mr.—"

"Don't call me Mr. Joshua. If you do I'll have to call you Miss Ames, and there we'll be, going through life calling each other Mr. and Miss. What would the children say?" he asked seriously, then laughed, a low, ironic sound deep in his throat.

"We want your hundred thousand dollars, but I don't remember anything about children."

"Well, you see, I am looking ahead."

"To what?" She stirred in her chair.

"Don't be afraid," he said with the same taunting smile, "I will not attack you where you sit . . . or even where I sit."

"This is all very strange. Do you usually conduct—"

"No."

"I wish you'd let me finish a sentence," she said.

"Yes, go ahead."

"I . . . this is an odd way to . . . begin a meeting. Or have we met before? Have I forgotten?"

He smiled at her, measuring her with his eyes, then rose and disappeared into the bedroom. Courtney looked after him, her brows drawn together in confusion. She didn't know how to interpret him or the fact that in only a few minutes her good mood had been shattered. She jumped when she felt a hand on her shoulder.

"Recognize this?" he asked and held a slim book to her view.

"Yes, yes," she said surprised. "It's mine. I wrote it three years ago."

"*The City Stories*," he said, glancing at the cover. "And nothing since. Why?"

"It's a task . . . getting enough stories together to put out a book. Too much of a task. I write them one at a time now."

"Too much of a task," he said quietly. "Some of these were very promising stories. By now you should have done the long-awaited novel. That's what reviewers call it, isn't it? The long-awaited novel?"

"If you're Norman Mailer that's what they call it. If you're good, that's what they call it."

"I'm going to give you something to read. I don't want you to say a word. Just take it home and read it."

"Something . . . oh," she said, nodding her head. "Something you've written. You want to be a writer, that's what this is all about."

"I am a writer," he said softly. "You'll know when you read it. It's a screenplay, seventy-five percent finished, and it's good, Courtney Ames. That's something I know, it's good."

"I'm sure it is."

"Don't lie. How could you be sure? That's cocktail party conversation, Courtney Ames: 'I'm sure it is.' There's a lot of work to be done on you, I see. But we'll do it, don't worry. Today is the beginning."

"I thought today was the beginning of a hundred thousand dollars."

"Ah yes, well, that too. I don't, as it happens, give one damn who gets the money. It's my job to pull the money in and then funnel it out. That I do, and do very well. When Tessa Cabot phoned—"

"Tessa Gorlin."

He smiled. "You are as touchy as she is. Never mind, our research department is thorough, and when she phoned I got a full, fat, file on your Clinic. Included in it was the fact that Miss Courtney Ames would be my contact. Courtney Ames. And all the time *City Stories* was sitting on my desk. Interesting, I said. I wonder if it's the same Courtney Ames. I said maybe the Clinic will get our hundred thousand because Courtney Ames's niggers are probably as worthy as anybody else's niggers."

"Now look—" she began, but again he held up his long, thin hand and stopped her.

"No offense, of course. Didn't you know all fund-raisers are animals? Yes," he nodded, "we join the animal union before we're allowed to go out and collect our monies. We are not classy people, Courtney Ames. We have classy outsides, but inside we are lowlifes. Calling the noble black man a nigger, for example."

"I don't like this conversation," she said sharply. "They're doing a fine job at the Clinic. They're proud of their work and so am I. If this is what we have to go through to get your money, I think we can do without it. And I think Nick Gorlin would agree."

"I think so too," he said calmly. "As I've said, the file is very full. Noble Nick. Noble Tessa. It's a veritable royal court. But," Peter said and waved his glass at her, "it's true. I've been very bad. Even the animal union wouldn't approve such behavior. I, Peter Joshua, master fund-raiser, forty-two-year-old man, drinker of twelve-year-old Scotch, apologize. Most humbly. Will it help if I tell you I've narrowed the field down to your Clinic and just one other organization?"

"It might."

"Then consider it telled," he smiled at her.

"What's the deciding factor. Obviously you don't want to see the material I brought. You don't want to ask questions. What's going to make up your mind?"

"I want to meet the good doctors."

"Of course. You're welcome at the Clinic anytime."

Peter Joshua looked at her and laughed, a full, throaty laugh that was heavy with weariness. "*Clinic*? I don't want to go to the *Clinic*. I've seen enough *clinics* to know they don't vary, one to another. Dangerous neighborhoods, poor people, kids with runny noses and dirty socks. That doesn't appeal to my classy outside. You see, after one or two years in this nifty job I lost my social conscience somewhere. Somewhere in the vicinity of a poor, bleeding, bastard slum. Reward offered . . . but nobody turned my social conscience in. Now, with the shortage, I can't even get a new one. The shortage," he said, drinking again, "it was a blow. I was caught napping. Caught short in the shortage." He smiled. "I didn't mind the food shortage or the gasoline shortage or the power shortage or the paper shortage or the truth shortage. But the social-conscience shortage . . . lady, that's a rough one. I have to do without. Not enough coupons in my ration book. Some people would say that it's odd for someone in my particular job to go around without a—"

"You're mad," she laughed at him. "You could be Lewis Carroll."

"I could be anybody. Unfortunately, I am Peter Joshua." He leaned back and took another swallow of his drink. He stretched his long, long legs in front of him. "The point I am making is, I don't want to go to the Clinic. I want to meet the good doctors. I want to ask the good doctors some stock questions. But I don't want to go to the Clinic."

"What do you suggest?" she asked, sipping her wine.

"Dinner," he said certainly, as if he'd long since decided. "I think dinner is a fine way to get to know people, don't you?" he asked.

"In all your great cynicism you think the flaws will show, is that right?"

"In all my great cynicism I think people are more likely to be themselves at some point in a long evening than they are at a clinic. That's arbitrary of me, Courtney Ames, but there never was a shortage of arbitrary, so . . ." He spread his arms wide.

"All right, dinner. That's no problem."

"Of course it isn't." He smiled genially. "There are such real problems . . . like why you're not writing books. Like why I'm not writing books. Like what damn thing are we doing and why. Like why am I lonely," he said quietly. "Why are you?"

"I'm not lonely."

"Aren't you? Aren't you now?" He smiled thinly. "I read *City Stories*, written about three years ago. I read a couple of your recent stories only last week. Lady, behold the difference. Three years ago there was no loneliness, three years ago your men and women got along, they were close. Now . . . now you write lonely words, Courtney Ames. Alone words. Your men and women don't understand each other very well anymore. They don't talk of personal things, of close things. Separation, isolation, alienation. All the 'ations,' that's what you're writing about now."

"I'm older now," she said easily, though she turned away from his look.

"And disenchanted."

"No," she said quickly.

"Methinks all is not well."

Courtney's head snapped up and she looked at him angrily. "You're dead wrong," she said flatly. "And it's none of your business."

"Do you cry sometimes, Courtney Ames? I do. Sometimes. When it's very late, deep at night. When the twelve-year-old miracle stuff is gone . . . when the whole damn world is alone." He stared off into space. "It always gets to be the next day, though . . . somehow, through no help of mine . . . it gets to be the next day and I get up and put on my Peter Joshua clothes, my Peter Joshua face, and do my numbers. Let people do their numbers on me. I don't care. And then it's night again. Follows as the day, the night, goddamned if it doesn't. Read your stories, Courtney Ames, read them as if they were someone else's and see if you don't write lonely words," he said and looked back at her. "That's how you got in here today . . . because Tessa Cabot said Courtney Ames would handle the meeting and I knew Courtney Ames writes lonely words. Knew I would understand her, because I understand her words." He laughed. "Hell of a way to run a charity, isn't it? Well, I run it the way I want to run it. We got a citation from the President of the good old U.S. of A., and you *know* what that's worth, don't you?"

Courtney shook her head, her fine blond hair sweeping the shoulders of her white blouse.

"Not a damn thing." He smiled.

Courtney laughed and sat back in her chair. She couldn't make him out at all, yet she was intrigued; she was held by his oddness, by his irreverence.

"Has Lady Ames made up her mind yet?"

"About what?" she asked, frowning again.

"About me. Yea or nay? Do I pass? Have I spent the last ten minutes wisely? Bewitching you? Or have I been putting you off? You didn't like me at first," he said matter-of-factly.

"That's very perceptive of you."

"You bet. Perceptive Pete. That's what it says in my high school yearbook. Distinguished by his perception."

"I suppose you were the boy most likely."

Peter looked serious for a moment, his pale eyes drifting off. "I'm from the Midwest . . . where there's an unwritten rule that children between the ages of thirteen and seventeen shall have *fun*. And they define the fun for you. Cars, sports, pom-pom girls, 4H Club. This, you see, is because after the age of eighteen you're never supposed to have fun again. You're supposed to tend your farm, raise your children, pay your bills, wave your flag—"

"Tote your barge."

"You laugh, but it's a serious business. I had no part of the oomp-pa-pa. I wasn't even a member of the 4H Club, and that, my child, was tantamount to being a commie, one of your reds. People looked at me very suspiciously: Why aren't you having *fun*, Peter? This is your last chance, Peter, next year it's soy beans for you."

Courtney smiled. "I thought you were from the East. You sound it, look it."

"Born in Iowa, raised on a farm. I sat in my black room writing my young heart out while all the shit-kickers were at 4H. The scandal almost killed my father. I'm sorry to say it didn't, just almost."

"My, my."

"Yes. It was like that. One year I made the big effort to please him. One goddamned, stinking year I suffered through Animal Husbandry. I decided then that suffering wasn't my style. Not with animals anyway. Not with Iowa. Not with farms and pom-pom girls and a sonofabitch father who never gave a damn for anything in his life except his brood mares. Brood mares were his hobby, bless his withered soul."

"And all the rest is history."

"Ah, yes. Now I am the delightful Peter Joshua, toast of Georgetown. Yeah, that's what the *Washington Post* called me. And we know the *Post* don't lie."

She watched him without speaking, unable to take her eyes away from his thin, sarcastic face. Suddenly a picture of Grady, open, smiling, innocent, came to her and she felt a peculiar disloyalty. She shifted uneasily in her chair and looked back at him.

"It's worked out for you," she said, for she didn't know what else to say.

"You see before you a man of culture, of erudition. I can name the forty kings of France. And I can sit in a Plaza suite and talk about giving away a hundred thousand bucks," he said and leaned forward to her. "And I can tell you that you're not very happy with your life, too."

"Now wait—"

"But I won't, of course. I'm merely enumerating the various things I can do gracefully."

Courtney took up her glass and finished the wine.

She looked at her watch and then at Peter. "What do I tell Tessa? That you'll decide about the grant after we all have dinner?"

"That's what you tell her."

"I'll leave this material with you anyway," Courtney said and extended the folders.

"I don't want it. There's nothing you can tell me about a clinic I haven't heard before. Nothing I want to hear again. I'm tired, Courtney Ames. I'm tired," he said suddenly, vehemently. He saw the startled expression on her face and held up his hand. "I'm sorry, that wasn't meant personally."

Courtney stood up. "When do you want to meet Dr. Gorlin and Dr. Malory?"

"And Tessa . . . I'm in town for a couple of weeks, but I'd like to do it as soon as possible. Name it."

"I'll have to check with them, but can we say Sunday, tentatively?"

"We can."

"Well then, I guess that takes care of everything."

Peter rose and walked to her. "For now. I couldn't wheedle you into another glass of wine?"

"No, thanks. We have a guest coming to dinner, I have things to do."

"We?"

"Dr. Malory and I. We live together."

"Keen," he said and walked with her to the door. "You call me about Sunday."

"I will. And thank you for a . . . strange afternoon."

"You could have walked out," he said quietly. "You didn't."

"Good-bye." She held out her hand. He took it and bowed elaborately over it.

"That is another thing I can do gracefully. Good-bye, Courtney Ames," he said, and she walked from the suite and into the corridor. He watched her for a while and then soundlessly closed the door. Peter Joshua crossed the large room to the liquor tray and poured a drink. He held the glass up, looking thoughtfully at the dark liquid.

"To Courtney Ames," he said.

"Steinberg's paper on M.S.? What you want is Bradley's paper on M.S.," Grady said to Brian Morgan.

"More coffee?" Courtney asked.

"Thank you."

Courtney leaned forward and poured coffee into Brian's cup and then into Grady's. Her own cup was still full, growing cold, for she hadn't touched it. She sipped now and then from a snifter of brandy but she did so without much interest; she'd been preoccupied throughout all of that evening and had been relieved when the men had lapsed into a medical discussion.

"You're very patient," Brian said to her.

"Or something," Grady said, looking at her carefully.

Courtney saw his look and sat up straighter, smiling at Brian. "I don't know anything about medicine. I don't even watch the doctor shows on television, but I like to listen when two doctors get together. It all sounds so . . . serious."

"Courtney doesn't know anything about medicine, but she knows all about the Clinic," Grady said to Brian. "She was out fund-raising for us today and she's been in another world since." He smiled, but his tone was a little sharp.

"Any luck?" Brian asked.

"It looks promising . . . but let's not talk about that."

"Why not?" Grady asked. "Brian, I couldn't get one word out of her about her meeting. First day on the job and already she's full of secrets." Grady's smile was less than happy.

"It was very dull, really," Courtney said to Grady and then was silent, for her words didn't ring true and it bothered her.

"Brian," Grady said quickly, "did you see the Mets game last night?"

"I'm not much of a fan. Of anything. I played a little ball in school, but not very energetically."

"We're going to take you to a game one night. You don't have to be a fan, you just have to have a sense of humor."

"I'm not much on that either, I'm told," Brian said pleasantly.

"Are they giving you a hard time at the Clinic, Brian?" Courtney smiled. "Don't pay any attention to them, especially to this one." She looked at Grady. "He's got a grin for almost everything."

"It works," Brian said and looked at Grady. "I saw you with the Carlino boy today. Maybe your faith is paying off."

"We had a long talk this afternoon. I'm getting through to him, I know it. He doesn't bait me anymore, he doesn't sneer. He tells me he isn't spending so much time with that gang of his either."

"It's remarkable, if you're right."

"I've never been more sure of anything. I won't fail, Brian. I'm going to make something of him."

"I hope so, it seems so important to you."

"It is," Grady said with a quick intensity. "It's something I have to do."

Brian was surprised at the fierceness behind Grady's words. He was about to speak when the telephone rang.

"I'll get it," Grady said and went into the bedroom.

Brian turned to Courtney. "He's taking this more seriously than I thought."

"I don't know what *this* is. Grady seldom talks to me about his work," Courney said, looking toward the bedroom door, "but I know he's always looking for different ways to prove he . . . belongs. To prove his own value. I hope this isn't one of them."

"Why do you say that?"

"I don't know. Suddenly . . . suddenly I got a strange feeling. He cares too much, I saw it in his eyes. I don't want him to be hurt."

"He's very complicated, isn't he? Not the jolly fellow he always seems to be?"

"When he's happy, he's very, very happy. When he's sad . . . it's pretty terrible." Courtney looked at Brian. "You notice more than you seem to."

Brian smiled very slightly and sipped his coffee. "I haven't been much of a guest, I suppose. I'm sorry, but I'm always that way. I always seem remote and my hosts think I didn't like the chicken, or their apartment, or them, or something. I must be awfully boring," he said thoughtfully.

"That's a terrible thing to say, you're—"

"Ellen Train," Grady said, coming out of the bedroom. He had his black medical bag in hand and his motion was abrupt. "Liver's acting up, it sounds like. I'm going to take a look."

"Wasn't she in the hospital not too long ago?" Brian asked.

"Yes. Coming along well, too." Grady shook his head. "Maybe she just ate wrong . . . but I'll have to see. Brian, I apologize for running out like this," he said on his way to the door.

"Shall I come with you?"

"No, you stay and keep Courtney company."

"Yes, please, we've hardly talked at all," Courtney said. She stood up and walked over to Grady. "I hate you being in that neighborhood this late."

"I'll be fine. I'll take a cab."

"Take the car. You might not be able to get a cab back."

"Hell, the car's way down—"

"The car is one block away, Grady. Please, I don't want to sit here worrying all night."

"Worrying about me?" Grady asked, genuinely surprised. Courtney saw his look, saw that it had not occurred to him that she would worry about him, and she tossed her yellow hair.

"Grady, I want you to take—"

"Okay, okay, I have to go. I'll take the car. Brian, see you later or tomorrow," he said and opened the door. He stopped to kiss Courtney on the cheek and then was gone.

Courtney watched him down the stairs and then quietly closed the door and returned to Brian.

"I'm getting paranoid about safety. Whenever I hear about something happening down there, I think, God, that could have been Grady. Or any of you."

"It's a natural enough worry. I have it myself, sometimes. Just when I think I've got used to the area, I realize I'm not too crazy about being on those streets after dark. The night shifts are hell. I don't remember the city ever being this way."

"Drugs."

"It's more than drugs. It's . . . some kind of awful hatred. Everybody hates everybody. The drugs compound it, make it worse. They estimate a hundred and sixty thousand addicts in the city. That's more than the population of any city can absorb."

Courtney poured more brandy into Brian's glass and added some to her own. "You take a studious view of things, don't you?"

"I suppose. Rather than emotional. I'm emotionless, it seems."

"Why are you so down on yourself?"

"I'm not, I don't think. Just accurate. I'm not known for my humor, or passion . . . or even as a good dinner guest," he said easily. "I don't often get invited back a second time. This is a very expressive society, ours. Everybody's supposed to let it all hang out, as they say. That makes me odd."

"You're too harsh on yourself."

"I have two nephews, two boys. They like me and sense how I feel about them. But I don't think my brother and his wife believe I like the kids. They keep waiting for some expression on my part, and it's not in me to give. Children, for some reason, accept that. So children and I get along very well. But adults are suspicious because I can't let down. Do you know what I mean?"

"I think so."

"That's why it's so nice to be around . . . well, people like you and Grady. I watched you all through dinner. The fondness that flows between you. The warmth. I thought to myself that if I reached out I would be able to touch it."

"We have wonderful times together." Courtney smiled and self-consciously played with a strand of her hair.

"And it's all out there in the open . . . for anyone to see. That's what I'd like to have. That's what I miss. Children are like that—no walls. I relate to that very strongly. I suppose that's why I'm a pediatrician," he said quietly. He shook his head once, almost imperceptibly. "But I didn't mean to embarrass you."

"You haven't. You're not the first person to compare us to children."

"Well, it's more than that. I was telling someone about the Clinic personnel the other day, and I said there were only two bachelor doctors, besides myself. I included Grady in with the married ones because it's as if you and Grady have been married for years. Now I have embarrassed you," Brian said, as Courtney turned her head away. "I don't mean to be clumsy."

"No such thing," Courtney said easily. "What do you see when you look at us?"

"A rightness, I think. It's something one doesn't see too often, so it's very noticeable. It's very nice. I wonder if something like that will ever happen to me."

But Courtney hadn't heard his last words; she was thinking of Peter Joshua. "It's odd how different people see different things," she said thoughtfully. "Someone sees a rightness . . . someone else sees trouble in the garden."

"The garden?"

Courtney looked quickly back at Brian. "I'm sorry, I was thinking aloud. And thinking of something stupid. Tell me, have you never married?"

"No, never. Not even engaged. In high school I went steady, as was the term then, and there've been some romances since. But I never saw the colored lights."

"You may be sorry when you finally do."

"Maybe, but I want them nevertheless. I told Grady once that I thought some part of me had been left out. Perhaps it's the part that feels. I'm waiting for *the* thing, whatever it is, to come along and wake that part up."

"Maybe you should get away," Courtney said suddenly, "go to a new place."

"You mean run away?"

"No, just get new bearings. I've been thinking maybe that's what I need . . . to get new bearings. At least to take a break from everything."

Brian regarded her without expression for a moment. "Everything?"

"Well, not Grady of course," she said hastily. "The problem is his life is here, so how could we go away?"

"Even Nick is going to give vacations," Brian said quietly. "And three weeks, I think."

"I'm being foolish. There's no point in going away. You only take yourself with you, after all. But I keep visualizing a small town, if there's such a thing as a small town left in this country. Do you imagine there is?"

"I think we always idealize the direct opposite of what we have," he said slowly. "And I think I should be going. I've stayed too long."

"No, please. The lights burn late around here."

"Still, my shift begins at eight tomorrow morning," he said and stood up. "It's been a very nice evening. I thank you," he said to her. "I hope I didn't talk too much. I'm monosyllabic around Nick and everyone else . . . but when I get around you and Grady the words pour out."

"We all had a nice time, Brian. We'll do it again soon. Here you get second and third and hundredth invitations. We run a very loose establishment." She smiled.

"Thanks. You and Grady are nice people," he said quietly. "If I ever get my apartment cleaned up, I'll expect you both for pizza and beer."

"And you'll get us. Good night, Brian."

"Good night," he said.

Courtney closed the door behind him, thought about doing the dishes, but then returned to the living room. From the corner of her eye she saw the large manila envelope that had been delivered by messenger that afternoon. She walked over to the table and stared down at the package. Her had reached out and touched it and then quickly drew back. Courtney walked away from the table and toward the kitchen, but in a moment she was back, staring again at the package. With a sigh, she picked it up and undid the clasp. She drew out the manuscript, fingering it nervously, and then opened it to the first page. The note clipped to it said: "This is what we should work on. Together. In some special place where no one has been before. Peter Joshua." She carried the bound pages to the couch, stretching out full length, arranging several yellow batik pillows behind her head. She opened the manuscript to Scene I.

The small, gold antique clock on the mantel ticked the minutes away. She read for almost an hour, smiling here and there, frowning in places, sadness coming into her eyes as she approached the ironic, bitter ending. When at last she closed the binder, her eyes were like pale-blue sky, still and faraway and deep as a sky is deep. She didn't know how long she sat there after she put it down, but when she heard Grady's key in the door she sprang up and ran to him, encircling him with her arms.

"Well," he said, dropping his bag to the floor, "what's this?" He held his arms around her and said not a word until he felt her relax against him.

"Hey . . . it's okay," he said softly. "Whatever it is, it's going to be okay."

"I know." She nodded against him.

"I'm here, Courtney," he said in a whisper, "here." And he held her gently until she took a small step away from him.

"I . . . I don't know what's the matter with me. Maybe I was afraid you weren't coming back."

"Why would you think something like that?" he asked, puzzled.

"I don't know . . . do you suppose I'm getting ready for a nervous breakdown?" She smiled at him. "Do you suppose I am . . . how you say, nuts?"

He grinned despite the uneasiness he felt. "Flakey, yes, nuts, no."

"Thank you, Doctor, I needed that reassurance," she said with mock formality.

"Did you want me to run away from home?"

"Nope. Here is where you are, here is where you stay."

"Is that so? By decree of the yellow-haired girl?"

"None other?"

"Good." He smiled, though he was concerned, deeply concerned, about her mood. He looked down into her face and kissed her forehead lightly, then drew her close against him. "C'mon, let's go to bed. Now," he whispered.

She put her hand on him and then suddenly lights were turned out and clothing thrown off and they lay on the floor, tender and loud, soft and demanding, taking and giving of each other until, at the end, there was an incredible sweetness that filled them both, and pleasure that they and only they and nobody before them felt. After a while they rose, clinging to each other, and slowly, slowly, walked to the bedroom, dozing together through the night, their arms fast about each other.

12

Sunday came, a tall, pink day, quiet as a sigh. Later, perhaps a summer storm, but not now . . .

"COME IN, come in," Courtney said at the door. "You are a truly great person to come over and help me with my goddamned quiche." She paused, taking a good look at Tessa. "God, you look sensational."

Tessa's thick golden hair was piled atop her head in loose waves, her lips glossy with deep rose. She wore a soft white summer dress, its slim skirt grazing the floor, its gathered bodice haltered at her long neck. Frail, shiny gold hoops were on her ears and gold glinted on her wrist and on her fingers.

"I decided to get out the good stuff." Tessa smiled. "If we're putting on a spectacular, we might as well do it right. And you, I see, had the same idea."

Courtney looked down at her dress and nodded. "At least we match," she said, for she wore a long summer dress of black and white, a bold geometric print dramatic in the quiet day. Her lemon hair was swept back from her face and tied at the nape of her neck with a black and white ribbon; her earclips were gold and chunky, matching the bracelet on her arm, and her lips were colored a clear, cool red.

"Grady's wearing a shirt and tie." Courtney laughed.

"Nick called me from the Clinic to tell me. He couldn't stop laughing." Tessa wandered over to the couch and sat down, glancing at the fresh flowers in the bowl before her. "What happened to your quiche?"

"I don't know. I made a test one and it was awful. The rest of the stuff's ready, but that . . . I thought we'd serve it with drinks. Grady said to buy something, but, no, I had to insist on *making* something."

"It doesn't take long, don't worry about it. What else are you serving?"

"Grady made a terrific Bourguignon last night. He let me flour the meat and wash the mushrooms, wasn't that nice of him? And there's rice, salad," she said and went to the sideboard. She poured two glasses of wine and handed one to Tessa.

"Isn't it a beautiful day?" she said, sipping the wine.

"It is. Lovely. I feel lightheaded."

"I meant to ask you . . . did you and Nick settle it, about Cabot's Landing?"

"Yes. I found something out, Courtney. There's nothing wrong with having a real, knock-down, drag-out fight once in a while. I brought up Cabot's Landing again and Nick got pale and started raising his voice again . . . and the raised voice turned into screaming and I . . . I, this person, screamed right back. He was so surprised." Tessa laughed. "He just sat there and listened to me for ten minutes without saying a word. Then he brooded for a while, great black clouds around his head. *Then* he said, well, *maybe* he'd been wrong. I screamed a little more and he dropped the maybe. Anyway, we're going sometime in September. After the A.M.A. meetings here."

"Good for you."

"It really was. Good for me, I mean. I felt very good when it was all over. And Nick did too. For all these months I think we've both been scared to death that we wouldn't survive a full-fledged argument. And that we wouldn't survive the Cabot money. Now we know we'll survive arguments, and I'm pretty sure we'll survive the Cabot money."

"And there you are, walking into the sunset."

Tessa laughed. "Well, it was so silly. Thinking the money would go away if we didn't acknowledge it. Thinking Cabot's Landing would go away. Now I know as long as we speak up, as long as we don't refuse to talk about things, we've got a fair chance. That's all I ever asked Nick to give us. Acknowledging the fact of my father, of the money, is part of that chance. We're reaching a point where we can be adults with each other. It's been a nice couple of days." She smiled.

"Maybe we're all on a good streak. Grady sat up half the night writing a long letter to his father. A long, long letter."

"Oh?"

"He wrote pages and pages about some boy he's helping down at the Clinic. His ideas for the boy. He's so proud of himself. Confident, and he's seldom confident."

"I'm glad for him. I hear very good things about that boy."

"I don't hear anything, but that's par for the course. Say, what time are they leaving the Clinic?"

"Nick promised they'd be here by seven. That will give us about an hour to relax before Mr. Joshua arrives."

The smile left Courtney's face. Tessa studied her closely. "Didn't you like him? You didn't say much, you know, except that you thought we'd get the grant. And that he wanted to see us *en famille*."

"Like him?" Courtney asked slowly. "Yes, yes, I liked him quite a lot. And I didn't like him quite a lot too. He's . . . he's . . . well, you'll see for yourself, he's not exactly like anybody else," she said and looked down at the floor.

"That doesn't tell me much."

"You'll see what I mean. He's hard to describe," Courtney said impatiently and drained her glass. "Quiche time, I think."

Tessa stood up. "We'll make the mixture and refrigerate it until it's time to put it in the oven, okay?"

"I never argue with the chef," Courtney said as they walked into the kitchen. Courtney put on a large red gingham apron and handed a blue one to Tessa. She then opened the refrigerator, withdrew a bowl of eggs, and reached back into the refrigerator for cream and cheese and butter.

"Bacon?" Tessa asked.

"Right," Courtney said and added a package of bacon to the line of ingredients on the counter.

"You do the bacon while I chop the onion," Tessa said, and for the next half hour the two women chopped and beat and seasoned and poured. When finally the mixture was in the refrigerator, Tessa wiped her hands on a towel and stepped back. "We've got a masterpiece in there," she said.

"Good. Can I tell Grady I made it?"

"Of course," Tessa laughed. "Let's go back inside and sit down."

Courtney nodded and they returned to the living room. She poured more wine and put the glasses on the coffee table, settling herself in a tan chair opposite Tessa. "He's a writer," she said after a while.

"Who is?"

"Peter Joshua."

"A writer? What kind of writer? I thought he was a fund-raiser."

"Yes, of course he's a fund-raiser, but he's a writer. He . . . sent me something he wrote," Courtney said hesitantly.

"Writing's his hobby, then?"

"Oh no, no. He's too good to call it a hobby. What he wrote, it's not polished yet, not really, but it's beautiful. It's . . . if I could write that way, I think I'd never leave my typewriter."

"What does he write?" Tessa asked, and a hint of a frown passed over her delicate features.

"Screenplays. It's a screenplay. Would . . . would you like to read it?" Courtney asked, an odd note of shyness in her voice.

"Well, I . . . yes, certainly, if you'd like."

"I'd like you to see what I mean. He's really very, very good. You can't stop reading, you race along, and yet you want to go slowly because it's so lovely you don't want it to end."

"Courtney, why did he give it to you to read?"

"Oh, he'd read some of my stories and wanted to show me some of his writing."

"I see," Tessa said, though she didn't, didn't see at all. She didn't like the expression on Courtney's face, either. There was something strangely secretive that made Tessa uneasy.

"Did anything happen during the meeting that you didn't tell me about? You said so little."

"Nothing. He's not exactly like anyone else, that's all."

"Well, yes, I would like to read his screenplay. After—" They heard a noise at the door and then the scratching of a key.

"We're here," Grady said, walking into the apartment, Nick behind him.

"But it's not seven yet." Courtney jumped up. "It couldn't be."

"Five-thirty," Nick said. "Or just about." He looked at his watch. "Mr. Joshua called me at the Clinic and asked if he could come at seven instcad of eight. I got Hank Mitchell to cover and—"

"He called you at the Clinic?" Courtney asked.

"Yes. He asked for either Grady or me."

"But how did he know you were at the Clinic?" Courtney asked, sudden color rising to her face.

Nick looked at her curiously. "If it matters, he said he knew we'd be there on Sundays. He made some remark about . . . why?" Nick asked.

Courtney suddenly felt not only Nick's eyes on her but Tessa's and Grady's as well, and she smiled hastily. "No reason, just curious. I wanted to be sure I hadn't made a mistake."

"No mistake," Grady said quietly and walked to her. He kissed her on the top of her head and put his hand on her arm. "Take it easy, it's not the Aga Khan coming to dinner."

"Don't be silly," Courtney said too heartily, "I only want it to go well."

"You look overexcited to me," Grady said softly.

"I'm fine. Doctors are all alike," she laughed.

Nick looked from Courtney to Grady and then to Tessa. Tessa gave him a look to keep still, and he shrugged his shoulders. "Anything to eat around here?"

"We'll have some quiche Lorraine in a while. Be patient. Grady," she said, looking at him, "you look lovely."

"I better put the beef in the oven," he said to Courtney. "Since he's coming early."

"I'll do it," Courtney said and went quickly out of the living room. Grady stared in her direction and then looked at Tessa.

"Everything all right here?" he asked quietly.

"Yes, Courtney's a little nervous, that's all. After all, this is *her* project."

Grady looked back toward the kitchen. "She's been this way ever since she had that meeting," he said, almost to himself. "Yeah, I guess this is her project, all right." He played idly with the bottom of his tie, a broad, blue-patterned cotton that he wore against a pale-blue shirt. His slacks were pale, an off-white, and his blazer a deep navy blue with shiny buttons. Tessa saw that his curly hair had already begun to lighten with the coming of summer, and she smiled at the few freckles that had appeared on his fair skin.

"You look very sunny today, sir," she said to him. He didn't reply but continued to look toward the kitchen.

Nick shook his head and looked at his wife. "What hornet's nest did I stumble into?" he asked with concern.

"Don't be silly," she said lightly.

He looked back to Grady. "Everybody's telling everybody not to be silly," he said and looked at Tessa. "What's going on?"

"Talk to Grady, darling, cheer him up. Better yet, why don't you mix some drinks?"

Nick rose and went to the sideboard. After a minute Tessa joined him. "You look a little unhappy yourself. What's up?" she asked.

"First of all, I didn't want to leave the Clinic this early."

"And second of all?" she prodded, pushing back the black hair from his forehead.

"Mrs. Vitero asked us to have dinner at her house tonight. Grady and me. That's the first time anyone from the neighborhood invited us to their home . . . socially. I felt so good, like we were finally getting involved with the community. Then I had to say no."

"Did she understand?"

"She got embarrassed," Nick said sadly. "The opening I've been waiting for, and I had to blow it for Joshua. She won't ask again."

"Someone else will."

"Tessa, we're down there day after day, night after night. We're a regular part of the community and yet we're not. We're still outsiders, dammit."

Tessa was about to answer when Grady walked over. "Is one of those for me?" he asked Nick.

Nick handed him a glass. "I was telling Tessa about

Mrs. Vitero," he said. Grady said nothing and Nick frowned. "Grady?"

"Hmm? Oh, sorry, I didn't hear you. Tessa, would you go and see if Courtney's okay out there?"

"I'll give her a hand with the food," Tessa said. She patted Nick's arm and walked away.

Nick stared at Grady. "You're a million miles away again. What the hell's the matter?" he asked.

"Nick, don't start," Grady said shortly and turned away, taking a long, deep, drink.

They sat around the huge, old oak dinner table in the dining room, Grady next to Courtney next to Peter Joshua next to Nick next to Tessa. A pale-yellow damask cloth covered the table, which was set with plain white stoneware and fine, thin crystal goblets dark with red wine. White daisies sat in a clear glass bowl in the center of the table, near tall handcrafted oak salt and pepper mills. There was a pleasant aroma of lemon oil and wax and flowers and hot French bread and beef cooked in burgandy.

They smiled, for they were handsome people sitting before a fine dinner in a lovely apartment on a radiant night; they smiled, too, because they were nervous, everyone save Peter Joshua who enjoyed the tension in the room. He'd seen the tension take shape and grow as soon as he'd arrived and he'd been vastly amused and, therefore, charming through cocktails. That they sometimes didn't understand what he said, or the way he said it, that many looks were exchanged among them, only added to his amusement. He was relaxed, at his ease, while they smiled and laughed too frequently, trying to make easy conversation until the dinner was placed on the table. He'd admired the table and the food both to himself and to them—and he was aware that he was being very closely watched by two people, Grady Malory and Tessa Gorlin, so it was to them he directed his finest smiles.

"Yes, I do agree with that," he sad to Grady and then paused. "I wonder, though. I wonder, in fact. Because, in fact, I wonder about a few things. Do the ladies adjourn somewhere while we stay here with cigars and port, or do we all talk about the questions I have?"

"We're not offering cigars and port, so I guess we all talk together," Grady said.

"Start without me," Courtney said and stood up. "I'll start clearing the dishes."

"Leave them. I'll help you later."

"No, Grady, they'll get cakey."

"I'll help you take them in," Tessa said quickly and pushed her chair back. "Why don't you do your talking in the living room and give us a clear field in here."

"How nice." Peter smiled slowly, looking then at Grady. "You're blessed, Doctors . . . toiling in the fields of the poor by day, winning your souls from God . . . and by night beautiful women in your kitchens. And other rooms."

"Thank you, Peter," Tessa said hurriedly, before Grady or Nick had a chance to respond. She looked directly at Nick and then gave her head the tiniest nod toward the living room. He stood up.

"Grady, why don't you pour?" he said, and the men followed him to the sideboard. Tessa said nothing, piling the dishes in a neat stack while Courtney fumbled with the silverware. They carried the used plates and forks and knives into the kitchen, and still there was no word between them.

Then Courtney dropped a handful of silverware to the floor. "Damn, that's the second time tonight I've dropped something."

"I'll get it. You put the dishes in to soak."

Courtney turned the water tap on roughly and impatiently squeezed some detergent into the gathering water. She lowered the stacked dishes into the sink and wiped her hands. She turned to Tessa. "Well?"

"Well what? Peter Joshua?" Tessa said quietly. "Charming. Arrogant. A prince-of-darkness type. Consciously or unconsciously. He sensed we were uncomfortable around him and he loved it."

"It did get uncomfortable all of a sudden."

"And he's been measuring each of us."

"Measuring?" Courtney asked.

"Each of us in turn. Except you, Courtney."

"Well, he'd already met me."

"Yes. He had," Tessa said not unkindly. She looked at Courtney and sighed. "He plays with people, toys with them."

"Maybe."

"He's out to give somebody a hard time tonight . . . I don't know whom, nor why, but I think it's begun. With the beautiful-woman remark. Why? Do you know why?"

Courtney sat at the tiny, marble-topped kitchen table. "I know he's a little . . . odd. Maybe that's why. If you're right, maybe that's how he gets his fun. How should I know?"

Tessa sat in the other chair and reached into a small marble box for a cigarette. She lit it and leaned forward toward Courtney. "What do you know about him?"

"Not much. He rambled a little about his childhood. That and the writing thing, that's all."

"Umm, the writing thing. If he's as good as you say, why does he bother working for Joint Charities? There's nothing creative about working for a charity . . . and obviously he couldn't care less about charity, his or anyone's."

"I don't know, Tessa," Courtney said, looking distracted. "I suppose he makes a lot of money, doing what he's doing."

"He talks like a writer. Or as one assumes writers talk . . . except that writers usually talk like regular people. Except Bill Buckley, and he doesn't count."

"Tessa, I've told you . . . I don't know what he's all about. Why are you doing so much conjecturing?"

"Because he did so much. All through dinner. All through coffee. He was conjecturing about each of us, I could feel it. He makes me very curious, I admit."

"But do you like him?"

"I don't know, I don't think so. Does it matter?" she asked carefully.

"No, of course not."

Tessa drew on her cigarette and then smiled at Courtney. "Grady is a real person, so is Nick. When I meet a man like Peter Joshua I appreciate that even more. Don't you?"

"I don't know what you mean by real."

"I mean they leave the moonlight and shadows alone. Peter Joshua deals in moonlight and shadows. Perhaps that's why, as you say, he writes so well."

"Nothing wrong with it." Courtney smiled uncertainly. "An old American custom, moonlight."

"That doesn't put the potatoes on the table," Tessa said.

Courtney laughed. "That doesn't put what on what? Come again, madame?"

"You heard me." Tessa looked closely at Courtney. "How far can he take you on a dream?" she asked very quietly.

Courtney looked startled. Her lips fell open, as if to speak, and then she pushed herself away from the table. "Let's join them, shall we?"

Tessa stubbed out her cigarette and rose from the table, following Courtney out of the room. At the edge of the living room they saw the men talking and sipping drinks, Nick and Peter on the couch, Grady sitting on the floor.

"All your questions answered?" Courtney asked.

"I know why there are no minority and no women doctors at your Clinic," Peter said.

"Satisfied?" Tessa smiled, sitting next to Nick.

"I don't care, personally. I have what you might call a touchy board, though. Those esteemed men . . . gentlemen all, are paid to worry about what grievous sin I might commit against minorities, or women, in a moment of twelve-year-old Scotch." He looked around from face to face. "They do not care about minorities or women, but they are passionately caught up in the fight to end discrimination against fund-raisers. Among other things, that means they have to answer for everything thrown in their direction. Including minorities and women in the institutions they support."

"The Clinic wouldn't exist in the first place if we were discriminatory. Our neighborhood is minorities," Nick said shortly. "But it's hard to get minorities to serve minorities. Once a black doctor has made it, for example, he may be in no hurry to *return* to the ghetto. He may just want out."

"And who blames him?" Peter said, a small, teasing smile on his thin face. "Who casts the first stone? Not I, not I. No, I don't blame anyone for doing what's good for herself. Right, Courtney Ames?" He looked at her.

"The way you say it, it sounds selfish."

"Selfish? Everybody is, in the dark part of his soul. There are a few men like good Nick and good Grady, but even they, I think, are selfish about something. What about it, Grady?" he asked, though he kept his gaze on Courtney.

"I prefer the word caring," Grady answered, and his eyes were very clear and steady. Courtney looked at him curiously, for his tone was very soft and a little sad. She edged closer to him, but she couldn't catch his eye.

Tessa spoke quietly. "We're getting far off the subject of the Clinic."

"Ah yes, the Clinic," Peter echoed. "Unwashed necks and ratty underwear."

"Facile generalizations about poor people, Mr. Joshua," Nick said sharply, "are hardly why we're here tonight. We are trying to give the poor something at the

Clinic . . . a chance. A chance they wouldn't get otherwise because nobody wants to know about poor people."

"Except you. Dirty—"

Nick glared at him. "Some people are clean, others are dirty. What the hell does that have to do with anything?"

"Quite right," Peter said and lifted his glass to drink. "Well, okay, it's your choice and I concede your Clinic probably does some good. Enough good so I can sign eleven forms, in triplicate, so you can get your grant. So you can keep trying with the poor bastards."

"Does that mean we get the money?" Grady asked.

Peter looked at him, his pale eyes measuring the impatience on Grady's face. He looked thoughtfully at Grady, seeing the shrewdness behind the innocent eyes, the spirit behind the words. "You get it," he said finally. "Courtney Ames will make out the forms with me. That takes about a week, off and on," Peter said slowly. "And it takes four weeks to clear the Washington office. It takes another four weeks for a check to be drawn, and then it's yours. It's a two-year grant, renewable at the end of that time for another two years. Providing everything's in order, of course." He smiled. "That's to say providing you haven't absconded to Buenos Aires with our funds, providing you haven't bought a Rolls Royce . . . providing nothing suspicious has happened. But all of you are above that." He smiled again. "We ask little in return. At some time we'll send a film crew to the Clinic to get some shots of the facility. For use in our own promotional campaigns. One of you may have to speak at one of our dinners. In other words, as soon as you get the money, you become a party to our own fund-raising efforts."

"Is that standard procedure?" Nick asked.

"Scratch my back and I'll scratch yours. A principle without which no charity could survive. You see, fund-raising is big business. It's like politics. That we support many institutions is incidental; what's important is that a few dozen or so men live very well, very well indeed. Salaries, fringe benefits, trips, the company of the Washington power boys. More than one man has been known to get rich on charities."

"How do you stand it?" Courtney asked, annoyance in her look.

Peter didn't answer for a moment, then laughed abruptly. "I've shocked you all. No, not you all, I haven't shocked Nick . . . and probably not Mrs. Clinic either. They know the ways of the world," he said amiably, smiling at Tessa. "Courtney Ames, what big eyes you have . . . but it's all right because you're such a *pretty* girlchild. It's an ugly green world, girlchild. And it doesn't rain but it pours, and that's a fact," he said and drank the rest of his drink in one gulp.

Grady took his glass and refilled it, silently handing it back to him.

"Thanks," he said and took a sip. "That's what's so funny about this. About the Clinic. Good Nick, so concerned with the poor, with the starving, huddled masses. Yet look around you. For someone so concerned with the poor, with the starving, huddled masses, you're surrounded by money. The Cabots on your wife's side. Grady on the Malory side. You will admit the irony."

Tessa was about to speak, but Nick patted her hand and turned to Peter. "I'll admit it. You're not the first to point it out. The Cabot Foundation has given us one of its grants. The Malorys also made a substantial contribution. I'm not pretending anybody here is poor, but I am saying we are serving the needs of a poor community."

"Oh, I know all that. We have a file on all of you. I know who's given what to whom."

"Then what's your point?"

"Point? I'm not sure I had one. I don't always," he said and smiled at Courtney.

"What's this about filling out forms?" Grady asked.

"Eleven forms. Some long, some short. Lots of information, lots of signing. Everybody is protected against everything in every contingency. Sensible precautions when one is dealing essentially with public monies. That way we don't get our delicate arses hauled up to some Congressional committee."

"Don't you think Nick . . . or someone at the Clinic should do those forms with you?" Grady asked.

"No, I do not. I have my reasons, Grady. One of them is that Courtney Ames already appears as the request source on eleven forms, in triplicate."

"She's not actually connected with the Clinic," Tessa said.

"She is my contact," Peter said coolly, and quickly the mirth was gone from his eyes. "She came to my suite to present a case for a grant. If she's not connected with the Clinic, then why was she there? With whom is she connected? Does she represent the Boy Scouts? The ASPCA? The Harlem Globetrotters? Was she there under false pretenses? You'll allow me, I hope, the liberty of doing things my way."

"Of course," Tessa said, "but it seems arbitrary. You'll allow me, I hope, my curiosity."

"Touché. Courtney Ames should have told you I'm arbitrary. It's my security blanket. To each his own blanket. Right, Grady?"

"Why not?" he said and got up to refill his own glass.

"Indeed, why not. Tell me, Grady, how does a good old boy from Texas like working with our dark-skinned brethren?"

Grady left the sideboard and resumed his place on the bright, polished wood floor. He pushed a square, needlepoint footstool out of the way and stared up at Peter.

"Our dark-skinned brethren," he said slowly, drawing out the words. "You mean what you call your spooks?"

"Grady!" Courtney said, unsure now if she was more upset with Peter's behavior or Grady's.

"C'mon, Courtney." Grady smiled without humor, "That's what he's been waiting to hear all night. Ask him if that isn't so. He's been waiting for me to say how there's your good spooks and there's your sum-bitch spooks, but how I figure as how everybody deserves his chance to be a good spook. Now isn't that right, Peter?"

Peter's lips twisted in a wry smile. "Absolutely right. I've been waiting. It amuses me to think there's actually such a place as Texas. Such a thing as a Texan. Texans should be mythical, like unicorns."

"Yeah," Grady drawled, "ole, dumb-ass Texans."

"I see now. I misjudged you," Peter said and drank. He was quiet for a while and then smiled slightly. "I'm from Iowa, myself. Iowans, too, should be mythical."

"Maybe they are," Tessa said softly, and they all turned to look at her. Nick and Grady smiled, but Courtney looked uncomfortable, for she feared that soon they'd all be sniping at each other. Silently she cursed herself; it was she, she knew, who should put a stop to it, she who should escort Peter Joshua to the door. But she couldn't; she was fascinated by the man.

"Is this a private game or can we all play?" Nick asked pleasantly.

"You're right, noble Nick, I'm being bad. I've always been bad. After a while it grows on people. Doesn't it, Courtney Ames?"

"Anybody ready for another drink?" she asked.

"No, thanks. We'll have to be leaving soon, it's getting late. Peter, do you need anything more from us?"

"No. All the rest is formality. The girlchild and I will muddle through." He smiled. Courtney looked away from him and moved closer to Grady, her hand reaching absently to his neck, toying with the soft curls at the nape. She needed closeness to Grady, needed to feel him near. Grady quietly took her hand and held it in his.

"Won't we, Courtney Ames?" Peter persisted. "Muddle through?"

"I've muddled through worse," she said tersely and glanced away from him.

Peter laughed. "Gracious to the end, that's Lady Ames." He looked elaborately at his watch and then put his glass down. He stood. "Nick is right, it's getting late. The first thing a fund-raiser learns is never to overstay his welcome. That's so he gets invited back. Will anyone see me to the door or shall I slink out in shame and regret?" He smiled.

"We'll leave with you," Nick said hurriedly. "The car's downstairs, we'll drop you where you're going."

"Thanks," Peter said and went to the door. Grady climbed up off the floor and pulled Courtney up beside him. He looked at her briefly, smiling tentatively down into her eyes, and then put his arm around her shoulder as they joined the rest of the group.

"The meal was excellent. As was the company. Thank you," Peter said.

"We . . . enjoyed it too," Courtney said.

"Yes. Well, Courtney Ames, I'll be in touch. About the forms. We'll make a time for us, yes we will. Grady, good night," he said and held out his hand.

Grady shook it and then turned to Nick. "See you tomorrow."

"I'll be a little late, I've got a house call."

Tessa looked back at Courtney. "I'm sorry to leave you to finish up."

"It's okay, Grady'll help."

"Of course he will," Peter Joshua said. "Let's go, children . . . hurry, before we turn into pumpkins." He waved once, over his shoulder, and started down the stairs. Nick and Tessa followed him with their eyes and then looked at Grady.

"Tomorrow," Nick said and then took Tessa's arm and followed Peter down the stairs.

Grady closed the door and leaned against it, exhaling a deep breath. "Christ, I thought this night would never end. Time sure goes fast when you're having a good time."

"At least we got the money."

"He doesn't care about the money. He wanted to get a look at us."

"I know that, I saw that," Courtney said. "The only real question he asked was the projected rate of increase over six months."

"A cat knows a mouse and a mouse knows a cat."

"Don't you start getting oblique, Grady. He's enough of that for everybody."

"That's not oblique, not oblique at all."

Courtney raised her head and looked at him and the words she wanted to speak stuck in her throat. "I think . . . I'll take a bath," was all she said.

"I'll start the dishes," he said and then grabbed hold of her shoulders. He looked at her intently. "But he's got a kind of charm, hasn't he? With it all, he's still got a kind of charm?"

"He's . . . he's . . . Grady, I don't know, he isn't like anybody I've ever met before."

"Say it, Courtney, say it. You think he's charming. You feel like reaching back and hitting him full in the face, but you don't, because despite everything, there's something about him. That's true, Courtney, isn't it true?" Grady insisted in a loud, dark voice.

"I . . . suppose. In his way. Grady, I don't care if he's charming. He's strange. I want to forget about him, please."

Grady stroked her hair and then he sighed, the smallest noise in the quiet room. "Okay, I don't even know why I asked. Go get your bath and I'll start in the kitchen."

She took a few steps and then turned. "Would you turn up the air conditioner? It's so warm in here."

"It's not warm. You're flushed," Grady said and turned away from her. He heard her walk into the bedroom and close the door. He stood where he was for a long moment and then slowly, leadenly, he went to the desk in the corner and opened the lower drawer, taking out the manuscript Courtney had left inside. He opened the folder and again saw the note, again forced himself to read it. "This is what we should write. Together. In some special place where no one has been before. Peter Joshua." He stared at the note, his face drained of expression, hurting, until he could stand its sight no longer. Slowly he closed the manuscript and replaced it in the drawer. He stepped away from the desk, seeing nothing.

"Man," he said in a quiet, choked whisper, "man, don't do this to me. Don't do it."

He walked to the couch and sank down, his face in his hands.

"Don't do it," he said once and then twice and then over and over again until he'd lost all count.

Tessa paced up and down the length of the blue and white living room. It was a long, narrow room, filled with the furniture of her former apartment, and she moved about with the accuracy of a sleepwalker.

Nick sat in a large blue armchair and watched her, shaking his head back and forth. "There's nothing we can do about it now, I tell you."

"How could I have been so stupid?" Tessa said angrily.

"It's not your fault. But I don't like the looks of it, I'll say that much."

"Not my fault? Then whose fault is it? Of course it's my fault! I should have known. . . . I should have had her working inside . . . the paperwork, while I went out and dealt with the people."

"Tessa," Nick said, trying to calm her, "Courtney is an adult, you can't expect to supervise what she does. Besides, how could you have anticipated a Peter Joshua?"

"Damn it all, I should have found out. I *knew* what kind of mood she's been in. I *knew* her feelings. Knew them better than she did. She's ready for someone. Especially someone like Joshua, don't you see?"

"No, I don't. I don't like him. He's always just a millimeter away from being rude, offensive. He's abrupt. He's arbitrary. He's opinionated. He's—"

"Oh, Nick," Tessa sighed and sat down in a white side chair. "You wouldn't understand about him . . . a man wouldn't. There is something very . . . *compelling* about him to a woman. I saw it myself. To a confused woman, a woman going through a bad phase, he's . . . especially compelling. I am sure he hasn't one male friend, and I am sure he has no trouble at all fascinating women. Don't you see? Well, why should you? Even she doesn't see yet. Grady sees, though. Five minutes with Peter Joshua and he saw exactly what that man was up to. And he saw Courtney, one nervous package of confusion. *Forms*. Damn him, anyway. *Forms*!" she said and reached for a cigarette.

Nick left his chair and walked over to Tessa. "There's nothing to do about it now," he said quietly.

"Oh, I know, I know that. Courtney and Grady . . . they sit there like The Sun and The Moon, as if the world was created for their moods. Being lovely, being careless, because that's all they know how to be. They didn't protect what they had, and now it's going to catch up with them."

"Would it help to withdraw the request for the grant? It'd be a blow, but I'd go that far if I were absolutely certain it would help."

"No, we're well past that stage now. He doesn't need the grant for access to her and he knows it. She's fascinated half by him and half by that writing thing. I see what he's doing, he's a canny fellow. He's giving her an image of herself. Her own image is damaged right now, it's off-center . . . he sensed as much or he saw it and he's using it. He's assessing what she thinks she needs and offering it to her."

Nick stared at his wife. He tipped his face to hers. "I wish you'd calm down, I don't like to see you this upset."

"I feel so responsible. Two charming, spoiled children, and I put them together with the bogey man."

Nick shook his head. "Something like this was exactly what I was afraid of. Something happening with Courtney at a time when Grady's got the Carlino kid on his mind. The dam's going to break. I'm going to have to sit on Grady now . . . I'll have to watch him like a hawk . . . and *hope* I'm around when he needs me to be around. I've seen more good doctors screwed up by personal problems. Grady is an A-number-one candidate."

"And poor Courtney," Tessa said quietly as she unpinned her hair, sending it spilling onto her shoulders.

"Courtney," Nick said, impatience in his voice.

"This is not all her fault. You can't blame her for everything."

"Who says I can't? I don't like what she does to Grady."

"She doesn't—"

"I mean how important she is to him. How she affects him."

"People who love each other affect each other, I hear."

Nick looked at Tessa and smiled, taking a long strand of her hair and curling it around his finger. "Yes, I know. I didn't mean us. I meant . . . sometimes it's not a good kind of affecting."

"It's too complicated, Nick. It's all too complicated."

Nick walked over to one of the windows and looked down at Tessa's windowboxes, staring at the small shoots that would soon blossom. He looked then at the window and drew the bamboo shade aside. "Summertime," he said. "Last January, at the party for the Clinic, I thought by this time we'd all be on an even keel. By summer. By summer, I thought the worst of the problems would be past. Well, it's summer, God help us."

13

On Monday a fine, misting rain fell over the city. Tall towers disappeared in fog, traffic stalled, and people would be glad when the day was finished . . .

CLOVIS bounced through the door of the Clinic and shook himself impatiently to get rid of the wetness settled in his hair and on his clothes. "I think I need a towels," he called to Jean, who came to him with a handful of paper towels. He swiped at his face and his neck and then stuffed the wet papers into his pocket. "Cowboy upstairs?" he asked.

"He's still down here with patients. Do you want to see him?" She smiled.

"You just tells him I got a toy for T.K. For his cage," he said and took a small, blue plastic gadget from his pocket. "When he jump on it, the bell ring."

"I'll tell him."

"Yeah," Clovis said and walked off to the stairway. At the top of the landing he was stopped by Frankie, coming from the second floor.

"How's it goin', Clove?"

"My name Clovis, you knows that."

"And your bird's name is T.K., ain't it?"

"So what?"

"So nothin'. Grady likes T.K., don't he? I seen him feedin' it some kind of seed shit."

"How I know what Cowboy likes?" Clovis said and made a move to continue up the stairs. Frankie grabbed the boy's small shoulder and pulled him back.

"You ain't being friendly, Clove. Everybody's supposed to be pals around here."

"I being no pal of yours. Maybe and you got Cowboy trickered, but you ain't got me. Why for this all about? Cowboy say sit, you sits, Cowboy say smile, you smiles, Cowboy say jump, you jumps. . . . You behaving better than my bird. She-et, who you kidding?"

"You shut your mouth, Sambo. Who do you think you are, all of a sudden? You ain't nothin' but a nigger, Sambo. Don't open your Sambo mouth to me," Frankie said, his eyes narrowed into mean, black slits. Clovis stared at him without expression for a moment, then kicked him squarely in the ankle. Frankie cried out and lunged. He had his hand only inches away from the boy's face when abruptly he stopped, his hand freezing in midair. He looked around, over his shoulder, and then moved away from the child. He spit at Clovis, but Clovis jumped away quickly and ran up a few steps.

"You plain no good," he said, making his way up the stairs. "I don't care how you haves Cowboy sucking."

"Nigger bastard!" Frankie said under his breath as he headed downstairs. "I'll get you too, fuckin' nigger."

"What? You talking to me?" Jim asked as Frankie reached the ground floor. Frankie looked up until he saw Jim's brown eyes staring at him.

"I was talkin' to myself," he said quickly and walked away, relieved with each quick step to be farther from the mountainous man. He stopped for a second, his mind caught by a sudden thought, and then covertly, he sneaked a look over his shoulder at Jim before he continued on his way.

"Have to figure out about Jim," he muttered. "Have to figure on that," he said to himself as he planted himself by the desk.

"Where's Mal—Grady?" he asked Jean.

"With a patient."

"He goin' to be long?"

"I don't know. Is it important?"

Frankie shook his head. "Naw. I'm finished here, I wanted to ask was there somethin' else he wanted me to do before I beat it home?"

"I'm sure there isn't, Frankie. You're here overtime as it is."

"Yeah, okay. Then give him this list," he said and handed her a wrinkled piece of paper. She glanced at it briefly and then put it on a pile of papers sitting in a large box marked MALORY.

"S'long," Frankie said.

"Good night, see you tomorrow," Jean called as Frankie hunched his way to the door and left the Clinic.

Outside, Frankie paused on the Clinic steps and cupped his hands together to light a cigarette. He inhaled deeply and then walked on, his eyes darting around him as he walked. He lowered his dark head against the rain and jammed one hand into his pocket, passing four old brown tenement buildings before reaching his own. He pushed the door open roughly and began climbing the filthy tiled stairs, his hand dragging over the rusting metal rail. At the third floor he stepped nimbly over a circle of yellow vomit and then kicked a dented Pepsi can down to the end of the hall. He turned and put his key in the lock of the Carlinos' apartment. He leaned on the door, cursing when he saw the chain was on.

"C'mon, open up. Open up already, hey."

"Coming, I'm coming," Marie said and hurried to the

door. She slid the chain back and opened the door to her brother.

"What are you so ascared of?" Frankie sneered at her. "You ascared some nigger boys'll come bust you one?"

Color raced to Marie's cheeks and she pulled her robe tighter about herself. Frankie stood where he was, watching the rise of her breasts under the cheap fabric. Marie saw his eyes and turned away.

"Do you have to be this way, Frankie? Jeeze, I'm your sister, can't you be nice?"

"Shit." He spat out the word and walked down the railroad apartment a few steps until he reached the kitchen. He opened the refrigerator door and removed a can of beer. "Where's Ma?"

"She went to bingo."

"Bingo. Somebody should bingo *her*. She leave somethin' for supper?"

"She said to give you two dollars. She said you could eat Chinks."

"What if I don't want no Chink food?"

"Then you could get some heros at Ciappa's place."

"Yeah, I bet she gave *you* supper. I bet that cunt made you a good supper before she left."

"I was home, you wasn't . . . weren't. And don't call Ma those names."

"Oh, I'm sorry, I'm sorry, forgive me for livin'. I forgot she was the Blessed Virgin," Frankie snapped and took another beer from the refrigerator. He carried the cans into the long, narrow living room and sprawled on the couch, reaching out with the tip of his boot to press the *on* button of the television set.

Marie sat at a table in a corner of the room, her face pale and tense, her eyes concentrating on the book before her. Frankie drank his beer and paid no attention to her, looking for a while at the television screen, then looking absently around the room. His mind was off in thought and he saw nothing of the familiar room, not the metallic aqua curtains on the windows, not the worn linoleum on the floor, not the large, old-fashioned furniture covered in clear plastic, not the crucifix on the wall. His thoughts remained elsewhere for a long while, and then finally his expression cleared and he glanced back at the set. He watched the program, boredom etched on his face, and then crumpled the beer can in his hand and threw it at Marie. The can glanced off her shoulder and fell to the floor.

"I asked you before, don't do that. It scares me."

"Scares, scares, scares. How come you're always so ascared? What you got to be so ascared of? You got Ma lookin' over you shoulder like the guardian angel. She's even sendin' you to that fancy school."

"It's not fancy. It's just to be a secretary."

"Yeah, you'll be some secretary. You going to let your boss play with your tits while he tells you his letters?"

"Don't talk like that, Frankie, please. I asked you already."

"You ain't got bad tits, considering you're such a ghost. C'mon, show me your tits."

"Stop it!" Marie yelled and jumped up from her chair. She took a few fast steps, but Frankie was faster; he caught her and whirled her around by the shoulder.

"I said stop it, Frankie," she said and tried to free herself from his grasp.

"And I said I want to see your tits," he said roughly and pulled her robe apart. She struggled against him, but he slapped her hard across the face and she staggered back against the wall. He held her arm, his eyes intent on her breasts; he used his other hand to pull her slip down.

"Yeah, you got a mouthful," he said. "A mouthful. And nice nipples. How about a handful? You got a handful?" He leered and cupped a breast with his fingers.

"Stop it, stop it, *stop it*," Marie cried, sobbing now, deathly pale. "*Please*, stop it."

"What's the matter? Don't you like a guy to play with your tits? C'mon Marie . . . c'mon, c'mon, c'mon," he repeated again and again until finally he freed her.

She bolted away, her cries echoing loudly as she ran, but Frankie's attention was gone from her. He threw himself on the couch and unzipped his jeans.

"Frankie said to give you this," Jean said, handing the paper to Grady.

He looked at it and grinned. "It's his idea to get some games for the basement. He made up a list of the games to get."

"Games?"

"Sure. The kids around here see new games advertised on television, but nobody can afford them. He thinks if we had more things to do, we'd get more kids to come here at night."

"What do you mean, games? Like . . . monopoly? *These* kids?"

Grady laughed. "No, not monopoly," he said and looked down at the list. "Like Skittle Pool and Quarterback and Three Hoop. It's a good idea, don't you think?"

"I suppose. He cleaned out the storage closet in the basement, by the way. And sterilized all the test tubes again. You're doing a great job with him."

"I'm beginning to believe I belong, after all," Grady said quietly. "Every morning Frankie comes up to the office and we have a little talk. It's amazing how well he's responding," he said and looked again at the list. "Is this all?"

"This too," she said and handed him a deep stack of papers. "And Clovis said to tell you he got a toy for T.K."

Grady smiled and walked away, going leisurely up

the stairs to the office. He met Brian at the second floor and they walked the rest of the way together.

"Have you seen Nick?" Grady asked.

"I just lost a patient to him."

"Oh?"

"The Ganter family. Do you know them?"

"No, I don't recall a Ganter."

"I've been treating the girl. Fifteen years old, pregnant, unmarried. She has a brother, eleven years old. The boy gave me the surprise of my life," Brian said calmly.

"What?"

"Odd symptoms. Liver slightly inflamed, morning sickness, headaches, loss of balance, bruises on his legs and arms that he didn't remember getting. I found nothing to tie it all together, he had me back hitting the books," Brian said as they walked up the last flight of stairs. "Then one night I realized it was alcohol, had to be."

"Alcohol? You mean the boy—"

"The boy's got a drinking problem. I never saw it because he never drank the night before he was due in here. His blood tests were clean. And I didn't think of it because he's eleven years old."

They turned into the office and Grady sat at his desk. "Bad?"

"Liver function's already started reducing, but not so bad we can't reverse it. If he quits drinking wine like it was soda pop," Brian said and looked off toward the window. "I had, and I have a mind to start some kind of letter-writing campaign about the liquor industry. They make wines that taste just like soda so the kids will drink it. And they do. It's sweet, it's cheap, and it gives them a hell of a kick. We've got teenage alcoholism in growing numbers and the liquor people are making a profit on it. It's wrong. This boy's been drinking that junk for over a year."

"What's Nick doing?"

"I told him my suspicions. He came charging into the room, gave the boy one of those looks, stood him up, dressed him down, and hustled him off to City. They've got a new teenage alcoholism clinic, I understand. I think Nick will handle the boy from now on. The man's amazing, really is. In less than ten minutes he had Billy begging to be helped. That boy startled me; he's the youngest drunk I've seen here."

"How do they get it? I know all about phony I.D., but eleven is going to look like eleven."

"They get it, that's all I know. Billy admitted to Nick that a lot of kids take the stuff to school with them, drinking all day. The drug problem eases a little and alcohol comes along to take its place," Brian said and then was quiet. After a moment he looked back at Grady. "I saw the notice on the bulletin board. Does it mean that we can all make our recommendations on allocations?"

"What are you talking about?"

"The new grant. From Joint Charities. The notice says he's accepting recommendations on allocations for ten percent of the first year's grant."

Grady was silent. He looked at his desk, searching around for his cigarettes. He found a squashed package and shook one out, lighting it slowly. "I suppose that's what it means. All of us," he said.

"Good news. Courtney must be proud."

"I suppose."

"Grady, I'm supposed to be the unenthusiastic one, not you."

"Hmm? Oh, oh, yes. Well, sure it's good news. Sure it is. Maybe we'll be able to get our camp program going for next summer."

"That's going to be my recommendation," Brian said and looked closely at Grady. "Something wrong?"

"Wrong? No, nothing. I was thinking how much paperwork there was to do on the grant. Courtney . . . Courtney's going to it. She should be hearing about it any time now."

"That's good. It'll free your hands."

"It'll free my hands all right," Grady said and drew on his cigarette. "Not that anybody asked me," he added in a voice hardly louder than a whisper. He rose from his chair and took a few steps across the room to a small, round table that held the bird's cage. He bent to it and stared inside.

"Hello, T.K., hello bird. Can you say T.K.?" Grady spoke quietly to the bird and then opened the small door and withdrew him. T.K. flapped one wing but held the other close to his tiny body as Grady held him in his hand.

"He won't fly again, will he?" Grady asked, stroking his feathers.

"The wing won't heal properly, no," Brian said.

"Poor T.K.," Grady murmured. "Poor bird."

"He's got a good home now. Clovis loves him, you're always fussing over him, Nick gorges him on sesame seeds. He'll be all right."

Grady petted T.K. a while longer and then returned him to his cage. "He looks lonely," he said.

Brain almost smiled. "How does a bird look lonely?"

"The same way a person does," Grady snapped abruptly and went back to his desk. He removed his white jacket and put it in the laundry bag and then grabbed the cigarettes from the desk and stuffed the package into his pants pocket. He looked over at Brian.

"Sorry, I didn't mean to be curt."

"It's all right."

"It's not, but that's the way it is, sometimes. Well, I think I'll be getting home."

"Say hello to Courtney for me."

"I will. If she hasn't already started her . . . paperwork," Grady said.

"Courtney? Courtney?" Grady called out at the doorway of their apartment.

"Here. I'm here."

"Where?"

"By the radiator."

Grady put his packages on the table by the door and crossed the room to the windows. He saw Courtney on the floor, her head bent over the side of the radiator. He smiled suddenly and felt a kind of relief, an easing of his mood.

"What in hell are you doing?" he asked.

"There is an enormous, *vicious* bug down there."

"How'd he get there?"

"Well, he was flying around, *menacing* me, so I got the Raid and had a little ground-to-air combat," she said and looked closer at the space between the radiator and wall. "Bang, bang, I shot him down, except he fell behind the radiator."

"Then what's your problem?" Grady laughed.

"I don't know if he's dead. I don't want him sneaking out and attacking me again. He is a *vicious* bug, Grady."

"Come away from there, I'll look," Grady said and took her position on the floor. He looked into the space and then reached out with his hand. "Got it," he said and stood up, his hand closed.

"Throw it away." Courtney grimaced.

Grady opened his hand and held the insect close to her. She squealed and took a few running steps from him.

"Don't," she laughed. "Just throw it away."

"No, you killed him, you're going to see your victim in clear, cold light. Be lots fewer murders if people saw their victims in clear, cold light."

"No, Grady." She laughed again and ran toward the kitchen.

Grady looked at the bug and then exploded in a shout of laughter, following her into the kitchen. He backed her into the corner between wall and refrigerator and held out his hand.

"No, no, I won't look. You can stand there all night and I won't look. And I'll hold my breath, Grady, I'll turn blue, see if I don't," she giggled.

"Look at him. It's just a bitty little thing, you sissy," he laughed. "Come on, you're going to look or I'll put it down your shirt."

"*No*, no. Okay, I'll look," she said and opened her eyes. "Well," she said after a moment, "he looked vicious before. All those legs looked enormous when he was flying around. And he flew right at me."

"A bitty little summer spider. Sissy, that's what you are. He looked big because he was casting a shadow."

"Okay, I'm a sissy. I plead guilty to being a sissy. Now will you throw it away?" she laughed.

Grady went to the sink and opened the drain, flicking the insect into it and running the water. He washed his hands and then turned to Courtney. "Burial at sea."

"Very dignified," she said and smiled. "And you needn't look so pleased with yourself. You know how I hate bugs."

"Sissy," he said and kissed her. "Hello, Courtney, yes, I had an okay day. No, I'm not tired. Yes, I wouldn't mind a little thirst quencher."

She hugged him and kissed him lightly. "You think you're so smart," she said, opening the refrigerator door to remove a tray of ice cubes. "If you're so smart, how come you're not Robert Redford?"

"You talk like that and I won't fish out any more spiders for you. Bury your own spiders if that's how you feel." He grinned.

"You win. Forget Redford."

"Thanks."

They walked into the living room and Courtney went to the sideboard and dumped the ice cubes into a bucket. She made a drink for Grady and took it to him, settling herself on the couch.

"What are those?" she asked, looking at the packages on the table.

"Games."

"Games?"

"Games for the Clinic. All kinds. Want to play?"

"Sure, I'll show you I'm no sissy. I may be a bug sissy, but I'll ruin you at—" she leaned over the back of the couch to look at the boxes "—at Three Hoop."

"You're on," he said and stood up. He took a long sip of his drink and walked to the table. "Want to make it interesting?"

"Okay, what do you bet?"

"Umm, loser washes *and* waxes the car this week."

"Don't throw your squeegee out," she said, joining him at the table, "because you're going to need it."

"Yeah? Well, we'll see about that. You're playing with a pro here." He smiled and carried the large, boxed game to the dining table and quickly undid its casing. He glanced at the instruction sheet, nodded a few times, and in minutes had the game assembled, ready to play.

Courtney read over the instructions and moved closer to the table. She took the first shot and missed. Grady took over. They played, laughing and needling and calling small noises into the room for the better part of an hour.

"You're only one up," Courtney said. "I can still take you."

"No chance. I told you, you're playing with a pro."

"Stand back, pro, and see me become M.V.P."

She pulled her hand back, and as she was about to release the ball, the telephone rang. "Damn."

"Now I've really got you," Grady said. "You'll answer the phone and you'll lose your momentum."

"Talk is cheap." She smiled. She took the call in the living room, keeping her eyes on Grady.

"Hello . . . oh, yes, hello . . . well, yes, you did . . . no, that's all right . . . oh? . . . oh, okay . . . yes, yes, that's fine I'll . . . see you then, good-bye." When she returned to the game, her eyes were preoccupied and nervous. Grady said nothing. He didn't have to ask her who the caller was, for he knew from the expression on her face that it was Peter Joshua; he'd seen the same look whenever Peter Joshua was mentioned—a look a little tense, a little vague, and a little excited.

Courtney took her place at the table and again pulled back her hand and released the ball. She missed the shot but seemed only barely to notice.

"Okay," she said after a moment, "can I borrow your squeegee?"

"I guess we've had enough game for one night."

"I guess," Courtney said and walked away from the table. She went to the sideboard and poured some wine, sipping it in silence. After drinking half the wine she turned to Grady. "Don't you want to know who was on the phone?"

"If you want to tell me, you'll tell me."

"Terrific. It's your phone, I'd think you'd be interested."

"It's your phone too," he said quietly.

"*Your* phone, *my* phone, why the hell isn't it *our* phone?"

"You're picking on words."

"All right, I'm picking on words. I just don't understand why you can't be interested in who calls me up."

Grady looked steadily at Courtney. He knew their mood was gone, the fun and the laughter that was so easy. "I didn't say I wasn't interested. I don't want you to feel like I'm prying, that's all."

"*Prying*? That's wonderful, Grady, wonderful. After all these years you feel like you're *prying*. The other word is sharing, but we don't use that word. No, we use *prying*."

"Why do you want to have an argument?" he asked softly.

Courtney looked quickly at him and then looked away. "I'm doing that, aren't I?"

"Seems like."

"I'm sorry."

"I don't want you to be sorry, Courtney, not with me."

She put her hand back through her yellow hair and then went to the couch and sank down beside him. "I'm weird. I'm really convinced of that. We were having such fun and then . . ." She let the thought trail off.

"And then the phone rang," Grady said.

"It was Peter Joshua. I don't know why, but he makes me nervous."

Grady slipped his arm around her and drew her head onto his shoulder. "I'm here, just know that, Courtney."

"I do," she said and reached up to kiss him on the cheek.

"Maybe I'll grow out of it . . . being weird. Do you think?" Grady didn't reply and Courtney was silent for long moments before she smiled brightly up at him. "I could have made that shot, you know. I just didn't want to show off."

"The hell."

"Really."

"You still get to wax the car." He smiled. "But if you behave yourself, maybe I'll help."

"I'll behave. I'll be very, very good," she laughed.

Her tone returned to normal and the vagueness in her eyes disappeared, but Grady couldn't relax. In a while they'd be back where they'd been, in a while they'd be back to laughter and teasing and enjoying, he knew that. But he knew as well as he knew anything in the world that as much as things would soon be the way they'd been, that this was the beginning of the time when things would never be quite the same again. He felt the pain then, something dull and insistent and threatening in the deepest part of him. He felt the pain.

14

Tuesday was a long gray day. The rain had gone but still there was no sun . . .

COURTNEY rang the bell to suite 911-12 and waited, her eyes looking down at the carpet. She had a large notebook in one hand and a small, black patent leather purse in the other, its slim gold chain scraping at the tan slacks she wore. If she was early or if she was late she didn't know, for she'd forgotten her watch, and she thought that symbolic of the way the day had been so far—confused and forgetful and uneasy. She wished very much that she was not standing at this door and yet she wanted as much to be there, and her indecision made her impatient. Her notebook slipped from her hand, and as she bent to pick it up the door opened.

"Courtney Ames, hello."

"Hello, Peter," she said and entered quickly into the suite. She chose a small, tufted, gold chair for herself and sat down, glancing back at Peter. He wore deep charcoal gray—his slacks, his turtleneck, the socks on his unshod feet, all the same brooding color. The dark tones made the silver in his hair more prominent and emphasized the spareness of his body and face; he looked more angular than she remembered. He looked tired, wan and used, though his pale eyes were very bright. There was a tall, half-full tumbler of whisky in his right hand. He lifted the glass to her.

"Wine, or some of the real stuff?"

"Nothing. Really nothing."

"You've come prepared to be unsociable," he said and walked over to her. He sat on the couch, opposite, and stared at her.

"What are you doing," she asked finally, "trying to wear me down? I don't understand you . . . I get the feeling that some very tense game is being played."

"That's a contradiction, you know. Tense game. Game is defined as sport or diversion, fun. Tense is tense, neither sport nor diversion nor fun."

"I'll remember that."

"You should. You're often making little mistakes like that in your writing. We don't want that to happen in our book."

"Peter . . . perhaps you've noticed by now, you make me very nervous. You make me feel . . . unprepared in some way. Tessa said you play with people, toy with them. If that's what you're doing with me, I wish you'd stop."

Peter gulped at his drink and then smiled tiredly at her. "The loneliness, you don't understand about that. And your Mrs. Clinic, maybe she understands too well."

"I don't know what you're talking about. I seldom have, since I met you," she said in exasperation.

"Open your eyes, your mind. You'd understand, you'd know. I'm lonely. You're lonely too, but you can't see it for the protective wrapping you've got over your eyes."

"Nonsense."

"It's not your typical wrapping. It's not canvas, it's

not aluminum foil, not waxed paper, not plastic. It's unique to you, it's called Grady."

"I'd like to get to the Clinic business," Courtney said suddenly. "That's why I'm here."

Peter stared at her and then leaned forward. "Why so sensitive on the subject of Grady?"

"Why are you always making remarks about Grady? Why don't you like him? Everybody likes Grady."

"How fortunate for Grady," he said quietly. "That's one thing they'll never put on my headstone. Everybody doesn't like Peter Joshua, you see."

"You don't let them. You deliberately make people uncomfortable."

"Do I? Yes, maybe I do. If I can't make them love me, I suppose I can make them uncomfortable. They shouldn't feel nothing at all, is my point."

Courtney shook her head. "Can we please get to the Clinic business?"

"Clinic business?"

"Are there really forms to be filled out, or did you make that up?" she asked impatiently.

"Forms? Yes, Courtney Ames, there are forms. Do I really need you for them? Yes and no."

"Then why am I here? What is this all about?"

"I want to know you, I think it's important. You haven't mentioned my *screenplay*, that's important too."

Courtney looked down at her lap and then back at Peter. "It's beautiful, but you know that."

"Do I?"

"Yes."

"Well, you're right. I do know it. And I want you to know it . . . because that's us. The work we'll do together. Not this one maybe, but *some* one. Your book, my screenplay, and in the end something that is ours. Is that so hard to understand?"

"Yes, it is. *You* are very hard to understand."

Peter went to the tray of liquors. He refilled his glass and returned to the couch. "You'll feel better if you do some Clinic business, won't you? Less guilty? All right, whatever you say or the king will cut off my head." He handed her a group of typed sheets and a pen. "Sign wherever you see the big red X," he said.

"I should read these first."

"Courtney Ames, Courtney Ames . . . I'm giving *you* money, not you me. *You* can't be cheated," he said and then laughed. "It's not a bondage agreement, merely a set of forms duly noting the need of The Gorlin Clinic, and therefore the request of The Gorlin Clinic, for a grant of one hundred thou. In small, unmarked bills." He smiled.

"You see what I mean now, you confuse me and then I say stupid things."

"I like the idea of that, confusing you. Confusion is a step to ruination, and it's my intention to be your ruining," he said, watching her calmly, though she looked sharply at him.

"Is there a translation of that?" she asked.

"To write. To write, Courtney Ames, you have to be ruined a lot more than you are. Especially to write what you're going to write."

"No, thanks, I think I'll pass on that," she said and lowered her eyes to the papers. She signed each one, her large, careless writing filling the spaces. When she reached the last one she looked again at all the sheets and then handed them back to him.

"A copy of each of these will be sent to the Clinic from Washington. For your files, do you have files? Anyway, the good doctors will be provided copies," he said.

"Is that all?"

"No, not quite. There are three, lengthy forms. The guts of the matter, as it were. Our master forms."

"Then may I have them?"

"My office is forwarding them. Tomorrow, the next day, I'll have them then."

"So you really didn't need me here today at all?"

Courtney asked, though she wasn't sure what answer would be satisfactory to her.

"But I did. I do. You, not a Lower East Side executive."

"Again, you're doing it again." She frowned. "Making yourself unintelligible."

"How foolish will it sound to say I need you to be my friend? Very foolish, I agree, but that is the way the wind blows. I know you will be, I've read your stories, I know your mind," he said in a soft voice. He smiled. "I'm alone. Not literally, but in my mind, where it's important, I'm completely alone. There isn't another person who will come into my mind, get comfortable in there. And none I'd have. But I want you there. Courtney Ames, I won't spend the rest of my life raising bucks for good causes, bad causes, whatever causes, because I don't have any causes anymore. They took them away. They came in the night and they stole them. One by one. I woke up as they were fleeing through the window and I thought they wouldn't get far, but they did. They flew and flew until I couldn't see them anymore. And all my causes were gone. Just like that." He snapped his fingers. "Later on people would say to me, fool, you should have kept them in the hotel safe, where they'd have been protected from theft and fire and the plague of the locust."

"God," Courtney shook her head, "you are something."

"No, I'm not, not yet, and that's my point. Because I can be. What I write can make me something."

"You don't need me for that. If I wrote the way you do I wouldn't need anyone to help, I'd just do it . . . because it's beautiful stuff. It may wind up being great stuff. Peter, I write little stories, nice little stories. Once in a while I write a line that is very good, that pleases me . . . a phrase. But mostly I just write little stories, nice little stories that happen to suit the market. We're different leagues, you and I."

"Don't you care about what you write?" he asked with new, sudden fervor in his voice.

"Of course I do. When I started . . . oh my, when I started I wanted to be Fitzgerald. I wasn't."

"I'm Faulkner. 'Perhaps they were right putting love in books. Perhaps it could not live anywhere else.' I understand that," Peter said quietly.

"You don't need me. You have all the beautiful words, all the strange emotions, and you let them languish in a drawer somewhere. So-called writers run around hustling their books like so many pounds of herring while someone who really can write, you, leaves his work unread, unknown."

"Should I take notes at this lecture or will there be a review at the end of the term?"

"You asked me, that's my answer."

"There's no compassion in your answer, Courtney Ames, where's your compassion? I can't do it alone, don't you see? I have never been able to do it alone. . . . Alone, all I can be is Peter Joshua and I need so much more than that. You have to help me."

"I can't."

"Are you that absorbed?"

"I'm absorbed enough," she said, looking toward the windows of the suite. "My work, the Clinic work. Grady."

"What is so magical about Grady?"

She looked back at him sternly. "Stop being so snide about him."

"I'm not being snide, not now," he said quickly. "I've thought about it since the day we met. Why Grady? What's so extraordinary about Grady Malory? It's been such a long time, the two of you . . . I wonder about relationships like that. I have to know about them. I'm not being snide, Courtney, I want to know."

"Some people fit together, that's the only explanation I know."

"And keep on fitting?"

"Yes, I guess."
"Forever and ever, amen?"
"I guess," she said curtly. "Grady and I never really plan a long time ahead. I . . . it is a long time, yes," she said, and suddenly there was something very still and remote about her; she was remembering. "I had my own apartment once. When I got out of school. It was a fine little place . . . I fixed it up as best I could, got in all sorts of liquor, imported cheeses, good brandies . . . I was ready for the wonderful people to come. And some of them did. Bright young lawyers and brokers and editors and actors and advertising people. Filmmakers. There were lots of parties, and I had my share of involvements," she said quietly, "but I began to notice something . . . it always came back to Grady. The only thing that ever lasted was Grady. If I missed someone, it was Grady I missed, if I needed someone, it was Grady I needed. If I was crying I called him, if I was laughing I called him. Finally I saw it had been Grady all along . . . the hell with the bright young New York people, it was Grady Malory I called at four o'clock in the morning."
"And you lived with him and were his love. Fade into long shot of girl and boy running through park on sunny day. Laughter. Balloons. A field of daisies." He paused. "You moved into a shampoo commercial."
She felt color rush into her face. "For God's sake, I don't know why I bothered to say anything at all! I might have known you'd make something decent sound trivial. Things can be simple and still mean something. Grady's been my security for as long as I can remember. I feel safe as long as he's there. We have something you couldn't understand."
"Are you sure?"
"I am. Besides everything else, he's as complete a person as I've known."
"Really?"
"Really!" she said loudly. "He's so . . . competent.

There's nothing he can't build or cook or mend or grow or photograph. He plays super tennis, he rides, he sails like a Kennedy. There's no subject he can't discuss, if he feels like it. Most important, he's as kind a man as there is."

"Anything else?"

"He knows every line A.J. Liebling ever wrote."

Peter laughed, though his eyes were chilly, their faint color lusterless in the afternoon shadows. "And you need him?"

"Yes," Courtney said and left her chair. She wandered over to the windows and looked down, staring at the widening ribbons of people around the Plaza Fountain. She studied them for a while and then looked to her left, to the line of hansom carriages, the sad, tired horses nodding into their feed buckets. She and Grady had taken a hansom ride once. She smiled, remembering how they'd taken the reins from the driver and directed the horse halfway to Harlem before a policeman stopped them, the driver sleeping peacefully in the back all the while.

"And he needs you?" Peter Joshua's voice came at her.

"Yes, he does," she said softly, her mind still on that evening years before.

"Then why haven't you married? Sealed the deal?"

"Oh, Grady will never marry. He'd never let himself get that close to . . ." She stopped, hearing her words, stunned by the truth of them. "Get that close to another person. He is afraid of being hurt," she finished and her voice was stone. She gripped the windowsill as hard as she could, for all of a sudden she felt lightheaded, foggy; as she'd recognized the truth about Grady she'd recognized her own: she needed his commitment now and that was the only thing he could not give her.

"What . . . difference does that make anyway?" she asked. "Marriage? It doesn't make what we have any . . . *less* what it is."

"You're protesting too much. You've been protesting too much all afternoon. Grady this, Grady that. Grady sails, Grady plays tennis, Grady cooks, Grady and A.J. Liebling. What you'd give your soul to say is, Grady loves me, he needs me, he wants me, he gave me his ring as token of all that. But you can't say that, Courtney Ames, can you? There's no token . . . and in fact, you have an idea he'd survive very well without you. Does he need you? You're not so sure at all. How would his life be different if you weren't there? How really?" Peter asked mercilessly.

Courtney grasped the sill harder. She knew she had to leave, had to get out of this room, away from Peter Joshua before she heard his words too well. But she couldn't move; she was trapped, immobilized where she was, feeling only the sudden trembling in her hands. "You . . . you don't know anything about it," she managed to say.

"I do know. I've read what you write. I've read the loneliness, the hollowness. What are you hollow about, Courtney Ames? About Grady, because what you have doesn't do it anymore? It's not enough, but you know that's all there is. All there is to be had from Grady Malory."

Courtney ripped her hands away from the windowsill and glared at him, the muscles of her face stretched tight. "Don't you dare. Not another word."

He regarded her silently for a moment and then slowly left the couch and went to her, standing over her. "He doesn't need you for his life. He has his work. What have you got? Work that doesn't satisfy you, a relationship that isn't enough. I will need you, Courtney. We will mean something. And I will need you."

"You're insane. If I didn't know it before, I know it now. You would be this cruel just to involve me in your *writing*?"

"We have the chance to do something important together. We—"

"*We* have seen each other exactly three times. And I'm already doing something important, thank you." She turned and looked levelly at him. "And now I think it's time to go."

"I was bad. I was bad again," he said and took her arm.

She wrenched away from his grasp and stepped away. "Please, stop it."

"I was bad, I admit it. Don't be mad at me . . . don't you see, I can't have you mad at me."

"I have to go now, Peter," she said in a small voice. She walked over to her chair and picked up her purse, slipping the chain over her shoulder. She picked up the notebook and then looked back at him. "I'm sorry about . . . all of this. I don't know what to make of it, I really don't."

"I have to see you again."

Courtney didn't reply. She walked in silence to the door and then looked at him again. "Why do you make yourself so unhappy? Why must you make me so unhappy? Why?" she asked sadly. "I have to go," she said distractedly and left the suite.

The walk down the corridor, the moments in the elevator, the steps from the hotel to the street, the steps to the corner and a taxicab—all that time she heard nothing, saw nothing, felt only the drumming in her head. Her mood shifted from rage to sadness, blue and empty and bereft. Thoughts spun and whirled in her mind, and it was a moment or two before the dizziness passed. She didn't know why suddenly, today, her knowledge of Grady left her feeling as if she'd been hit in the face, why she felt doubled over by a curious pain that came out of nowhere viciously and all at once: the pain of recognition that she now needed more from Grady than Grady could give.

She opened the door to their apartment and poured a glass of wine, drinking it down in long, hasty swallows. When, she wondered, had it happened that she needed more? Had it been a certain day, a certain hour, a certain season of the year? And how had Peter Joshua seen that need?

Courtney walked listlessly to the fireplace and draped her arm over the mantel, staring around her. It was empty in their apartment and she hated the stillness. She began to pace back and forth and then she sank down tiredly into the rocking chair, absently rocking herself while she thought over the past few months, the months when she first knew she was not happy, not entirely. It was coming clearer now and her face grew darker as she sorted through her thoughts. It was no good, she told herself, pretending that things would work themselves out and be well, for the extent of her need was too great. She needed a closeness Grady could not give, could not share; she needed commitment, because now, in her thirty-first year, she felt futility, knew what they had between them wasn't enough.

The phone rang, but she did not answer. She continued to rock herself, continued to think the thoughts that for too long she'd kept back. She sat that way for a long time, until outside the sky turned a deeper gray, until shadows lengthened inside the room.

"What are we going to do, Grady?" she asked aloud. "What are we going to do when you won't understand?" she asked.

15

Friday was cool. Large, dolorous clouds hung in pale sky . . .

NICK GORLIN walked into the Clinic, large, bulky packages in his arms. He glanced around at the ground floor, now lit by only one overhead light, and walked back to the elevator. He heard a door slam shut and turned to see Grady coming toward him.

"I thought you might still be here when I saw Mr. Benke outside. What's he got now?" Nick smiled indulgently.

"We covered heart disease so well last month it looks like we've moved on to cancer." Grady shook his head. "I wonder what he did to pass the time before there was this Clinic."

"Well, you encourage him, you know."

"It's harmless enough. The old guy's lonely. I'll be a lonely old guy myself one day and I hope someone pampers me." The elevator door opened and the two men walked inside, Nick smiling at Grady.

"He is all right, isn't he?"

"He's fine. He heard about John Woods and *his*

cancer. Mr. Benke has a cough so he decided . . . well, you know how he is."

"Cough?"

"Hell, Nick, a man his age smoking three packs of cigarettes a day is going to have something. I tell you, he does everything wrong . . . eats wrong, drinks too much, smokes too much, Lord knows what else, and he's perfectly healthy. I'm beginning to think health's a matter of attitude. The hell with what they teach us in med school, if a man's got a good attitude he's going to live to be a hundred," Grady said as they reached the fifth floor. They walked down the hallway and into the office, Nick tumbling his packages onto his desk, Grady going to the coffeemaker.

"Look at Mr. Benke," he went on. "He should be dead, and there he is, smiling like Happy Jack. Whenever I see him all I see is that great big, toothless grin." He took the coffee to his desk. "What have you got there?" he asked, looking at Nick's packages.

"Boating clothes."

"*Boating* clothes?" Grady smiled. "If that doesn't beat all."

Nick unwrapped the paper and began unfolding the garments from their boxes. He held up a blue denim blazer for Grady to see. "And I got white ducks and a sailor shirt the salesman said is Breton-striped. Don't laugh, I want to be ready if Jason Cabot invites two or three hundred of his closest friends on the boat to meet his son-in-law."

"How big is that boat, anyway?"

"It could be the Staten Island Ferry, if it wanted to be."

Grady laughed. "Nick, you'll knock 'em dead. You're set for September then?"

"Yep. But Klein's was having a sale, so I decided to shop now."

"Class, class is what you've got." Grady smiled.

"Only a very classy guy would wear Klein's specials on Jason Cabot's Staten Island Ferry."

"It's a little late in the game to get fancy. These are okay, don't you think?" Nick asked, looking down at the boxes.

"You and Tessa just have a good time. Screw the rest of the world," Grady said, the tone of the last few words very sharp indeed.

Nick looked at him carefully. "Bad day?"

"No, it was all right. Courtney said . . . to tell you the last of the Joint Charities forms went to Washington today."

"It's been time-consuming, hasn't it?" Nick asked quietly.

Grady shrugged. "I haven't seen much of her the past few days."

"I'm glad it's over with."

Grady was silent for a moment. He lit a cigarette and looked off. "I wouldn't say it's over with exactly," he said slowly. "I mean, the forms part is over with but . . . it seems Mr. Peter Joshua is planning on staying in New York another week or so."

Nick sat down behind his desk. "When did you hear that?"

"Today. When Courtney phoned. It was very casual . . . like, 'Oh, Peter may be staying on a week or so. There's a writing project we may do together.' "

"Jesus Christ."

"Yeah," Grady said, staring straight ahead. "Nice, huh?"

"What kind of writing project?"

"It seems Mr. Peter Joshua is a writer. It seems he has a *screenplay*. It seems the idea is to turn the *screenplay* into a book." Grady paused. "It seems her own work's no good, not good enough, could be better. She explained it all very clearly. According to Courtney, this might give her an opportunity to . . . develop."

"What are you going to do about it?"

"Do?" Grady looked over at Nick. "There's nothing for me to do. I've no right to interfere with what she wants to do. If she wants to . . . *develop*, I think that's up to her. I'm only telling you about this so you don't hear it from Tessa and come running to me with advice. The fact is I really don't want to talk about it."

"Grady, you—"

"No! Let's understand something right now. We don't, it's going to be hard times working with each other."

"Go ahead," Nick said quietly.

"We both know Courtney's been . . . on edge lately. We both saw . . . well, we saw how it was when Joshua was over for dinner. Now this new thing. Okay, it's in motion, it's the way it is, and I don't want to talk about it at *all* after tonight. Not even indirectly. I can't take any pushing right now. I really can't. I guess what I'm asking is to please bear with me," he said softly, looking at Nick. "I don't know what's going to happen. I only know he's sending her sugar notes and talking up this . . . writing project . . . and that it's out of my hands."

"It's not out of your hands. Your whole attitude of out-of-your-hands is probably what put Courtney on edge in the first place."

"Courtney's a free agent. There's nothing holding her if she doesn't want holding."

"That's exactly what she does want. How many kinds of fool are you? She *wants* something holding her."

"Tend your own garden, Nick. Leave me with mine."

"You're part of the garden."

"What's that supposed to mean?"

"It means I'm your friend. And it means I have a Clinic to worry about."

"You think I'm going to fall onto hard times, fall to pieces? Well, maybe I will, but I'll do it on my own time."

"There's no such thing. What affects you at home will affect you here."

"I'm a doctor," Grady snapped. "Before everything else, I'm a doctor. Nothing's going to interfere with that. That's the only real thing I have and I *will not lose it*," he said harshly and looked away. "Maybe I'm a zero at home, but when I'm here I . . . I begin to feel like somebody for the first time in my life. And do you know why? Because I'm helping a kid to straighten out his life. *Me*. I'm doing it. Not you and not Brian and not anybody else. *Me*, by myself, no help from Daddy Lucas. I'm not going to throw that away, Nick, so don't worry so damn much about your Clinic, I'll be all right. I'll have to be."

"You shut everybody out," Nick said quietly. "You probably shut Courtney out too, so a guy like Joshua, who invites her *in*, suddenly looks attractive."

"I am what I am, I never said I liked it. I never said you had to like it."

Nick's head shot up. "I thought we were friends."

"I thought so too," Grady said in a low, quiet voice. "So let's not argue." He reached for a package of cigarettes. Nick stared at Grady and then suddenly both men looked up when they heard the night bell ring downstairs. "We have a customer," Grady said and stood up. Nick rose from his desk and they walked to the door and into the hallway. They went rapidly down the stairs, their faces taut and strangely unresolved.

"Just keep in mind, you start pushing me, you might push me over the edge," Grady said as they reached the ground floor. Nick glanced quickly at him but said nothing, looking around then at the deserted ground floor. Suddenly they heard a noise in the emergency room and went to it, walking quickly inside.

Nick saw the man first and recognized him immediately; it had been a year, perhaps two, since he'd last seen Steven Kadik; the time in between hadn't been good to him. Heavier by ten or fifteen pounds, his once thick, fair hair was now dim and thinning, his face lined and old beyond his thirty-five years. His eyes were hard and his mouth had a new, tired cruelty to it. Nick saw Grady rush to the man and he followed, seeing then a darkening circle of red spreading through his light, tan jacket.

"Nick, get rid of him." Steven Kadik nodded at Grady. The effort of speaking made him grimace and grasp his shoulder tighter. Nick shook his head at Grady, but Grady made no move to leave.

"Go on, I'll call you in a minute," Nick said, and Grady, after hesitating for a moment, left the E.R.

"Hello, Steve," Nick said quietly. He looked down at the dark red moisture and then turned to the cabinet behind him, extracting a pair of surgical scissors. He cut away the cloth of the jacket and bent to the wound.

"Nick, this is between us, right?"

Nick went to the sink and soaped his hands once, then twice, letting hot water play over them until they were bright red. He reached up to a shelf and removed a sealed package, broke the seal, then put on the thin, sterile gloves. He returned to Steven.

"How?" he asked again.

"Nick, I asked you, this is between us, right?"

"That depends, Steve, you know that. We'll talk later, after we fix you up. I'm going to need help, I'll need Dr. Malory."

"That guy was with you?"

"Yes."

"I can trust him?"

"Yes."

Steven Kadik looked down at his bleeding shoulder and then up at Nick. He nodded and Nick looked to the doorway.

"Grady," he called, and in seconds Grady was at his side. He looked at the gaping tear of skin and quietly opened the cabinet door, removing a clear liquid and a syringe. He swabbed the man's arm with alcohol and plunged the needle in, holding it while the liquid emptied. Grady threw the needle into a basket and wrapped a blood pressure cuff around the other arm while Nick poked around in the ripped flesh.

"It's deep," he said to Grady.

"Pressure one-thirty systolic."

"Good." Nick nodded. "Get some swabs over here," he said, and Grady filled a tray with wrapped, antiseptic cotton swabs. He placed a bottle of alcohol next to them and left the tray, washing his hands before he returned.

"This will hurt," Nick said as he applied an alcohol-soaked swab to the wound. Steven winced and then cursed and perspiration gathered on his forehead and above his thin lips. "Sorry. We've got to get this cleaned out. I'm going to have to stitch it."

"Yeah, Nick," Steven gasped, "you do what you got to do."

"Get that light over here," Nick ordered, and Grady moved a tall lightstand into place, flipping the switch to make a strong circle of light on the bloodied area. Nick worked away for five minutes, cleaning the torn flesh, as Steven cursed and Grady kept his gloved hands in readiness over a small surgical tray. Nick threw the last bloodied swab into the basket and stepped back, looking hard at Steven.

"It has to be stitched, Steve. We'll give you something, but it's still going to hurt like hell."

"Yeah, yeah, just do it."

Nick inclined his head toward Grady and Grady prepared another syringe and again injected Steven. He tossed the needle away and put his stethoscope to the man's chest.

"About eighty," he said to Nick.

"All right, we'll give it a couple of minutes to take effect," Nick said and looked over the instruments on the tray.

"Stretch out and make yourself as comfortable as

you can," he said to Steven. "I'll need you as still as you can manage. . . You're lucky this time, Steve, nothing severed, just a bad flesh tear. If the knife had gone in another inch it would have cut a nerve."

"Sure, Nick, I'm a lucky guy. I always was a lucky guy," he said bitterly, and an enormous sadness filled Nick's eyes. Steven Kadik, he thought to himself. The Steve from the old days? The leadoff man on our old team, the three-sewer guy? For a moment he saw the boy of those years ago, tall and fair and strong as a tree, swaggering the Lower East Side streets in a jacket that said New York Giants on the back, practicing catches like his hero, a rookie named Willie Mays. Steve, the kid who sat behind him in school, who sat next to him on the subway the first day of his first year of college. Nick's face was quiet with sadness, and he looked away from the man, the man who once had been his best friend and who had not been his friend at all for so many years. Nick had gone on, but Steve had stayed, stayed on the streets until the streets finally got him, until the two men had nothing to say to each other. He didn't know this Steve, the small-time hood who'd been in and out of jail since his nineteenth birthday. Nick shook his head to clear the wetness from his eyes. He looked back at Grady and knew that Grady had been watching him, for compassion glowed in his eyes. Nick held his glance for a moment and then turned back to Steve.

"How are you, Steve?" he asked in a troubled voice. "Feel a little foggy yet?"

"Yeah, like a good drunk."

"Okay, I'm going to start now. Hold on," Nick said and took a breath. He nodded then at Grady. "Clamp," he said, and Grady slapped the clamp into Nick's outstretched hand.

Tessa made a notation in her folder and then snapped it shut. "That's it for tonight."

"I think we're in good shape," Courtney said and stretched.

"Everything's paid up. Our shoestring's getting a little longer. We're in the clear for the next four months." Tessa smiled.

"And with the new money coming . . ."

"I personally am very sorry I ever thought about Joint Charities," Tessa said slowly. "We would have gotten along without it."

"It's done now."

"Yes, it's done," Tessa said and rearranged herself on the couch. She looked around the room absently, not so much seeing as feeling the presence of Grady in every piece of carefully chosen furniture, in the paintings, in the shelves and shelves of books. "I wish you'd reconsider what you're doing."

"All I'm doing is trying to catch up with a part of myself that's been missing for a while. I've been . . . idling, you might say, and now that I've realized that, I'm—"

"Going to make a mess of things."

"I'm not. Is it so wrong to get involved with something that will provide a little meaning? Something I can care about?"

"This *book* thing with Peter is going to do that for you?"

"I think so, yes. His screenplay will make a beautiful book, and he actually *needs* me to work on it. It's very nice to get involved with something knowing you're needed for it, that not anyone would do. And I think it'll work. Peter and I got off to a few bad starts, but at lunch today we talked the whole thing out. I . . . I think it will work."

"And Grady? Does Grady think it will work?" Tessa asked quietly.

"This has nothing to do with Grady. Or with anybody else. Look, my Clinic work takes one day a week, my own work takes a few hours a day . . . I have all that other time to play with, and nothing to do with it. Why not this project with Peter? I mean, would Grady think twice about starting some new project at the Clinic? No, it's his work and he'd do it. Well, this is my work, or it will be."

"The two situations are a little different," Tessa said impatiently. "Courtney, work is work and play is play."

"*Play*? There's no playing involved here. I'm not looking for an affair. I'm looking for something much harder than that . . . for something to commit myself to." Courtney rose from her chair and went over to the window, sitting on the window seat. "All my life in New York, leading a very New York life . . . and loving it, but I'm not twenty-two anymore, I don't love it so much anymore. I want . . . to be a serious person, can you understand that? I want some stability. Something I can depend on. There's nothing in this apartment I can depend on. Not Grady, not my own work. I am going to try this book, Tessa, I need to try this book."

"And Peter?"

"Is the vehicle."

"Is he looking for an affair?"

"I don't know, I don't care. I love Grady, that hasn't changed. But goddamn it, I need more than Grady."

"Peter is using you to face the work he can't face himself. A couple of years working on that *screenplay*, you said, and it's still unfinished. Obviously he'd rather talk than do, dream than do, except now he's got you to do the doing for him. He won't let that go, he'll never let you go."

"You're dramatizing. Lots of writers collaborate, it's not that unusual. He has things I don't have and vice versa. I've got the discipline he doesn't have. Tessa," she said urgently, "this may be the *only* way to keep together what Grady and I have. You have to see it from my view. I want something . . . completeness. I can't have that with Grady, but maybe I can find enough of it in work not to care about it in us. Limbo. Limbo is what we've had for five years. It was all right for four and a half of those years, it's not now. So what to do? Go on and on, getting more and more nervous until I crack or become bitter about Grady? No, I'm going to throw myself into something for which I am needed, which occupies me. I won't have time to brood."

"Did this all come to you when you were with Peter?"

"I guess it did. What's the difference?"

"Vast. Anyway, it isn't even practical. I assume Peter Joshua will have to go back to Washington, to his high-paying job, *some* day soon. Washington's not far, but it isn't around the corner either. How will you work together?"

"I . . . I might go to Washington for a few days at a time. We talked about that. I'd stay in a hotel or something," she put in hurriedly, "and we'd work together in the evenings."

"Go to Washington," Tessa repeated wearily, "and leave Grady?"

"Only for a couple of days at a time. Only until I got rolling."

"It's a mistake, it's all a mistake."

Courtney was silent for a long while, her eyes tracing the reflected light on the shiny, polished wood floor. She played idly with a loose strand of her pale hair and then glanced at Tessa. "I notice Grady hasn't said it's a mistake," she said very quietly. "I notice he hasn't said, 'Don't do it' . . . hasn't said, 'I don't want you to do this' . . . hasn't said, 'Don't see Peter Joshua.' Tessa," she said, biting on her lip, "he didn't say a word, not one. All he had to say to me is 'don't.' No speeches, just a word, 'don't.' To declare himself on the side of us."

"Are you playing Peter against Grady? Is that it?"

"No, at least not consciously. But I would drop it all if Grady would only take enough responsibility for us to say, 'Don't get involved.' " Courtney left the window seat. She fell into the chair opposite Tessa. "But he won't do it. Not even that little thing. What am I supposed to do, Tessa? Tell me what?"

Tessa sighed and spread her arms apart in a gesture of helplessness. Poor Courtney, she thought, saying love me, love me, pleading to Grady. Poor Grady, she thought, for he refused to hear.

Steven Kadik sat on the examination table, his shoulder propped against the pillows hastily provided by Grady. He sipped his coffee slowly, in silence, as Nick and Grady sat in chairs by his side and were quiet too. Steven's eyes wandered around the room, staring here and there at a baffling piece of medical equipment, looking with curiosity at the cabinet filled with shiny metal objects and vials of colored liquids. After a while he rested his cup in his lap and looked at Nick.

"It's a nice setup you got here, Nick."

"Why'd it take you so long to come around? You didn't have to wait until you needed a doctor. I hoped you'd be here the first day."

"I was going to . . . you know how it is, Nick. A guy gets busy."

"What are you doing these days, Steve?" Nick asked quietly. Steven began to reply and then stopped, his eyes darting to Grady and then shyly back to Nick.

Grady stood and smiled at Nick. "I guess I'll wander up to the office, you don't need me here anymore."

"Why don't you go home? It's getting late."

"No, I'll hang around a while. Tessa and Courtney are there, working on the Clinic budget. I'll give them a chance to finish without interruption from me," he said and turned, on his way out.

Nick watched him leave and then looked at Steven. "I have to know how that happened," he said, nodding his head toward the bandaged wound.

"We were playing some cards . . . the money got big. Tempers, you know how it is. There was Rodrigo there, you know how the PR's can be. We had some words, and the next thing I know he's flashing his blade and chairs are falling on the floor and guys are backing off. He got me in the shoulder, that's all. Ran like hell when he saw. Nick, the problem is . . . well, shit, both of us, Rodrigo and me, we're both on parole right now. Was nothing big, I lifted a car no one was using. Rodrigo, I don't know what he did, I think he hit a liquor store. Anyway, we're both on the leash, shouldn't be together in the first place, and he shouldn't be carrying any knife. If I went to Bellevue, there'd be cops and questions and the next thing I'd be back at the Tombs. And Rodrigo, he doesn't like anybody opening their mouth about him. I was to say anything, I'd be looking over my shoulder the whole time." Nick stared into his coffee and Steven went on. "You won't call the cops, Nick? I figured . . . well, from the old times, you were never a squealer."

"Steve, is this straight? What you told me?"

"On Poppa's grave, Nick. I swear. No one was hurt but me, and I'm not really hurt. No harm done."

"You didn't fight back? You've used a gun before, I hear."

"Since I got out I have the piece in cold storage. Better that way. A cop decides to shake me, I don't want to give him a reason to shake me good. Like I said, I'm only out a short time, a few months. I got things to do, I'm in no hurry to go back. . . . Nick? No cops, okay?"

"I have your word that's all it was?"

"Like I said, on Poppa's grave."

Nick looked evenly at Steven and then nodded once. "Okay. No cops."

"What about the other guy?"

"He's okay."

"Thanks, Nick. I knew you wouldn't of changed. Some people around here are saying you changed, I knew you didn't," he said and picked up his cup. "I guess you're thinking I changed, though."

"What happened, Steve? How did . . . how did it turn out this way?"

"Aw, who knows? I think about it sometimes. I thought about it a lot when I heard you opened this Clinic. I came by one night, didn't come in or anything, just stood outside and looked at it. The Gorlin Clinic . . . on that shiny plaque and all, I was proud of you, Nick, I mean it. Yeah, I thought how a thousand years ago we used to be pals." He stopped abruptly for both of them heard the phrase, "used to be," and were saddened by it.

"You always wanted to be a doctor," Steven continued. "I remembered that day the woman—Mrs. Finnegan was it?—the day she got her throat ripped by that rat and died there, bleeding to death. I remembered how you talked about it, you kneeling with her, trying to put her skin together. You cried when you told me about it. I never forgot that because it was the only time I ever saw you cry. . . . I guess from that day on you were set on being a doctor. You had . . . like a goal. Me? What did I ever want to be?"

"You wanted to be a ballplayer."

"Kid talk. Mays, I wanted to be Willie Mays, but that was kid talk. I didn't plan to become what I become, I don't know, it just happened. I got in with some guys who had a few ways to make a few quick bucks. It got to be a habit. Before I realized it I was in deep. Aw, what the hell, it hasn't been a terrible life, there's people who had worse than me. And I never killed anybody, never fooled around with dope. I hurt a couple of people but I never killed, never got them on the needle, and that's *okay*. Like I said, it could be worse. . . . But you, I'm glad you made it, Nick. I feel, well, I feel like maybe even I had something to do with it. When all the kids were making fun, saying you'd never make it, I was the one said, 'Go ahead, you can do it.' So maybe I did a good thing there."

"Steve, it doesn't have to go on this way, more and more trouble. You're young yet."

"Naw, I'm thirty-five years old, and in my kind of life that's not so young. I never expected to live to be an old man, remember I used to say that? Nick . . . you and me sitting here, we're thinking of how it was, and it was pretty nice. We had fun and I'll never forget it. How it was. But like I said, that was a thousand years ago. I've done a couple of things . . . well, if you knew, you wouldn't like me so much. And that's my life. No turning back now. I'm not kicking. It's too bad I wound up what I wound up, I guess . . . but one of us made it, Nick. That's batting five hundred." Steven carefully slid himself off the table. "I should be moving on. I want to thank you for taking care of me tonight. I mean it." He held out his hand.

Nick clasped it tightly. He stood and looked into Steven's eyes. "You'll . . . you'll have a little pain tonight. You want some pills?"

"I got some Canadian that kills the pain. It's been killing the pain for years now."

"I'll want to have a look at that arm in a couple of days."

"It'll be okay. These are the dissolving stitches, aren't they? That's the kind Johnny Murphy got when he got shot up."

"Yes . . . but I want to . . . Steve, I want to keep in touch, dammit. I'm married now, I'd like you to meet my wife."

"Yeah? You married now? That's swell, Nick. I was married too, till she started on the sauce . . . drank up all my Canadian. All the luck to you, Nick."

"I'd like you to meet her."

Steven smiled, and for a brief second it was the large, open smile of twenty-five years ago. "Naw, Nick, we got different lives now. I'm glad I saw you, really glad. But it's better we remember things the way they were, not the way they are. . . . Batting five hundred, Nick. Remember that." He walked toward the door.

Nick stood where he was, wanting to say something yet not knowing what; he knew there were no words that would make things different—but the old times, he couldn't let them go. "Hey, Steve? You still follow the Giants?"

Steven stopped at the doorway and turned. "Naw. When they moved to Frisco the heart kind of went out of it. But Willie . . . I always followed Willie. He was my man. Nick . . . you remember how we used to call them the Jints? Yeah," Steven smiled and shook his head, "it wasn't so bad, you know, being a kid in those days. Remember the bleachers at the Polo Grounds and Willie would—" He stopped and for a moment looked anxiously at Nick, looking for all the world as if Nick had something he was trying to find. And then, in the next moment, Steven Kadik was gone and Nick heard the Clinic door slam shut. Nick looked down at the floor, kicking at it, his hands deep in his pockets. When he looked up again, Grady was standing there.

"I waited on the landing until I saw him leave."

Nick was silent and Grady took another step inside.

"What do you say to a drink?"

"A drink?" Nick said vaguely.

"Why not? We're sure not doing much business tonight. Besides, Sturgis will be in in fifteen minutes or so. When he comes we can take ourselves over to Hagen's."

Nick walked out of the E.R. and to the stairway. Grady followed.

"What about it?" Grady asked.

"Hagen's? The old City hangout?"

"It was Bellevue's hangout too, I spent my youth there," Grady said, trying to sound cheerful.

Nick leaned against the banister and looked at Grady. "Youth. And then we turn around and see we're thirty-five . . . forty, forty-five," he said and sat down on a step.

"Yeah, I know," Grady said and sat himself next to Nick on the stairway.

"That's no answer, 'Yeah, I know.' "

"What do you want me to say?"

Nick was silent for a moment, then he spoke. "A drink's a good idea. I don't want to see Tessa while I'm in this mood."

"Are you going to tell her about. . . ?" Grady asked, inclining his head toward the door.

"Steve? No, I don't think so. She tries so hard to understand everything that concerns me, and she usually does . . . but how could she understand about Steve? I feel very old. And very sad."

"Nothing lasts. I always knew that."

Nick turned to look at Grady but didn't have the strength to answer him. He felt drained in a way he'd never felt before and he leaned back against the stairs, stretching his legs in front of him.

Time passed quietly, five minutes, ten, fifteen, and there was only stillness; phones didn't ring, patients didn't appear at the door, and there was no conversation between the two men, for both of them were dealing with their own thoughts. Nick was startled when suddenly there was a noise at the door and Dr. Sturgis burst in.

"Only three minutes late, only three minutes," he said, gesturing wildly at the clock on the wall. Nick and Grady looked at him without comment and then stood up.

"Don't forget to feed T.K. before you put the cover on his cage," Grady said to him.

"Okay."

"Mr. Martinez will be in after his night shift. His pills are on my desk, be sure he gets them," Nick said.

"Okay."

"Ready?" Grady asked Nick.

"Yep, let's go."

They walked to the door without another word to Dr. Sturgis, who watched in confusion as they left the Clinic.

"Good night," he called out finally, but the door had already closed.

Outside, Nick and Grady walked to the corner, stopping once or twice to say hello to the few old people who sat outside on old folding chairs. They turned and walked north. After a while they came upon an empty cab leaving the East Village and they hailed it, Grady giving the driver the address. On the way uptown their moods dipped farther, deepening and darkening until they both felt as if the world had been unkind indeed. There were no smiles, no words, as both men felt their own melancholy and yielded to it without resistance.

"This is it," the driver mumbled at them finally, and Grady fumbled in his pocket and paid him. They left the cab and went inside to Hagen's—for thirty-one years a gathering place for the young doctors of City and Bellevue. He'd seen them all, Hagen had, all the interns, hundreds, thousands of them, from all over the country, all over the world—all of them came back to Hagen's sooner or later, usually when times were bleak.

Nick made a path for them through a crowd of white-jacketed young men and women. It was dim in Hagen's, hard to see, but Nick saw the eight leatherette booths were occupied and so he found places at the long bar. In the background a jukebox played loudly, above the bar a television set offered a ball game, but Nick disregarded it all, screaming over the noise to get Hagen's attention.

"Nick Gorlin, isn't it?" John Hagen asked, after squinting at him.

"Right. Scotch and water."

"Coming right up," Hagen said and looked at Grady. "And Dr. Malory. Well, well."

"Hi, Hagen. Jack Daniels and a splash."

"You want something to eat?" Grady asked Nick while Hagen mixed their drinks.

"No . . . goddamn hamburgers," Nick muttered, for it was true that morning, noon, and night, Hagen served only one dish, hamburgers with home-fried potatoes.

"There you go," Hagen said and put their drinks in front of them. He watched while they sipped them and then smiled at Grady.

"The Mets're getting it all together," he said, beaming. "First place all the way."

"They say the Lord's a Mets fan," Grady said tonelessly.

"And what else would He be?" Hagen said aimably. "Listen," he said to Nick, "there's one of your old City boys here."

"What?" Nick shouted.

"A pal of yours. Over there," Hagen shouted back, pointing down to the end of the bar. Nick stood up from his stool and leaned over, narrowing his eyes in the meager light.

"It's Brian," Nick said to Grady. "Tell him to come over," he said to Hagen. Hagen walked down to Brian Morgan, gesturing back in Nick's and Grady's direction. Brian looked up and then left his spot, elbowing his way through the young people, carefully balancing his glass high above his head.

"What are you doing here?" Grady asked when Brian was settled next to them.

"I just took my date home."

"This early? It's just past ten. No good, eh?" Nick said.

"D-O-G."

"Yeah," Grady said. "I don't know . . . by this time we were all supposed to be in clover. This time *last* year we were saying how this time *this* year, everything was going to be peaches and cream. Now look at us . . . just look. Pitiful, that's what it is." He shook his curly head. "Pitiful."

They settled down to their drinking then, and it wasn't long before they shared a certain glassy fuzziness, their faces a little slack but very, very somber. The troubles they had now seemed insoluble and they each decided to get methodically, deliberately, very drunk.

"D-O-G," Brian said.

"Pitiful," Grady said.

"Well, I'm depressed," Nick said.

"So am I."

"El paino in asso."

"You tell 'em."

"Yeah, tell 'em."

"Men and women," Grady said and lifted his glass high to the people around him, "men, women . . . I got one thing to say . . . it's important . . . el paino in asso. Just remember that."

"Yeah, give it to 'em good. Damn interns never pay attention." Nick weaved a little on his stool.

"Thas right."

"El paino."

"In asso. Thas right, thas right. Tell 'em good."

"Where could they be?" Courtney asked Tessa. "They're not anywhere, and it's past twelve."

Tessa moved away from the windows and looked at Courtney. "I'm beginning to be little worried myself."

"Should we call the Clinic again?"

"They're not there. Dr. Sturgis would have called us. They couldn't be on a house call this long either."

"God, Tessa, maybe there was an accident. In that neighborhood, maybe—"

"Stop it. *That* we would have heard about. Everybody knows them in the neighborhood *and* at the hospitals."

"Grady always calls," Courtney said anxiously. "He never not calls."

"Maybe they stopped to eat."

"Grady always calls," Courtney persisted.

Tessa lit a cigarette and went back to the window. "Maybe there was an emergency and there wasn't time to call."

"Grady *always calls*," Courtney almost yelled, and Tessa saw the deep, worried lines fanning out from her eyes.

"Come, let's sit down. It only makes it worse to watch by the window."

"I don't want to sit down. I want to wait for Grady."

"You can wait for him sitting down," Tessa said firmly and took her arm. "Courtney, get ahold of yourself, you're working yourself up to hysterics, I hear it in your voice."

"I don't know why you're so calm, Nick's unaccounted for too."

Tessa's face tensed and impatiently she pushed her hair from her shoulders. She poured a glass of brandy and took it to Courtney. "Drink this," she ordered, but Courtney only stared at it, twisting the stem of the glass in her hand until some of the liquid spilled onto her long, cream-colored shirt.

"Damn."

"I'll get a cloth," Tessa said hurriedly, but as she turned toward the kitchen they both heard a loud, bumping noise at the door. The noise grew louder and they heard the sound of laughter and the scraping back and forth of a key as it missed the lock.

Courtney rose and went to the door. She opened it a tiny crack and then exhaled a deep breath and swung the door open. Grady and Nick and Brian stood there, their arms draped around one another, their bodies weaving and tottering. They stumbled inside, large, foolish grins on their faces, and the two women exchanged quizzical looks. Tessa's mouth dropped open at the sight and Courtney laughed, laughed out loud at her own relief.

"They're smashed, all three of them," she laughed again.

"A fair appraisal." Tessa smiled.

The men looked at the women and then continued into the room. They held on until they reached the couch and then they fell onto it; their short fall struck them so funny that they laughed until tears came into their eyes.

"Maybe some coffee?" Courtney asked Tessa, but Tessa shook her head.

"They won't want coffee, they're having too good a time."

"You don't have . . . have to talk 'bout us like we're not here, y'know . . . we're here . . . an' if we can see you, then you can see us," Grady said, thumping his chest with his thumb.

"Thas ab . . . ab . . . absolutely cor-rect," Nick said, and Brian nodded his agreement.

"What we need is . . . what we need is, we need a drink," he said.

"I don't think so," Tessa said, suppressing a smile.

"Oh no? Why not?" Nick rolled slightly from side to side. "My old fren here, my old fren, Bri . . . Brian, is cor-rect. What we need is a drink. I'm sure . . . we need a drink."

Grady patted Nick on the shoulder. "Tell 'em," he said and looked at Courtney. "We're phys . . . phys . . . we're doctors, y'know. We should know what's good . . . for us. What do you know about it anyway?" He turned to Nick. "Anyhow, what do they know? They don't know nothing. They think we're drunk . . . thas how much they know." He laughed, Nick and Brian joining in, punching each other on the back.

"Well, we're definitely not drunk," Nick said after a while.

"Definitely not. I could walk a . . . straight line anytime," Grady said and struggled up off the couch. He took three steps and then wavered. He took another step and then held his arms out in front of him, bracing himself against the mantel. "See that?" he smiled at them, "That was a straight line if I . . . if I ever saw a straight line."

"Thas right . . . he's right," Nick said and hiccuped. "Let's hear it for him," he added and clapped his hands together. Grady began to applaud too, but the movement threw him off balance and he lurched back toward the couch. He fell over against Nick, pushing Nick back against the arm of the couch.

Courtney and Tessa both stood with their hands on their hips, looking at each other speculatively. "What do you think?" Courtney asked.

"Bedybye, I think. Boys, it's time for bed, aren't you tired?"

"We're sleeping here . . . all of us is going to sleep here . . . 'cause . . . because thas what we're going to do. Thas what we decided . . . 'cause, y'know, we were interns. All of us," Grady said and waved his finger around. "We were interns once," he said and cocked an eye at Courtney. "You didn't know that, did you? Thas why we're going to sleep here . . . to celebrate that once . . . we were . . . twenty-five goddamn years old. We had long white coats," he added, to no one in particular.

"Time for a show of strength," Tessa said. She left Courtney's side and went to the couch, bending over Nick.

"It's time to go home, Nick. Don't you want to go home with me?"

"I don't want to go home . . . I'm too old to go home."

"Thas right . . . we're too old . . . too goddamned old," Grady chimed in. "We'll stay here . . . 'cause, because it's young here . . . it's always old at home. Old, old, old," he said and then repeated the last words again and again until he was singing them to a small, plaintive melody.

"Nick, it's young at home and it's young at Brian's house too," Tessa said briskly. "We didn't have time to tell you before, but we fixed it so it's young."

"Really? Did you do that?" Nick smiled at his wife and patted her hand. "Did you do that for us? Bri? You hear that? Tessa fixed it . . . fixed it all up."

"You're a good person, Tessa . . . such a good person," Brian said, sounding as if he were about to cry. "Nobody ever fixed it up for me before."

Courtney spoke rapidly to Grady: "Come on, let's help Nick and Brian to the door. They want to go home," she said, tugging on his arm.

"Yeah. What about our . . . party?"

"You can have a party another time," Courtney said.

"You think so? To—tomorrow? Shit, you think we're drunk. Bri? You want to go home?"

"Tessa fixed it up for me . . . she's . . . really a wunnerful person."

"Okay, okay, you all want to leave me. Everyone wants to leave me. I don't know why. I try to be a good person, I really try, y'know? But everybody goes away . . . bye, bye, Grady . . . everybody leaves Grady."

Courtney's face froze. "Never mind, stay where you are," Courtney said to Grady. She went to Brian and pulled at his arms until he was in a standing position. Next to her, Tessa got Nick to his feet, and the two women guided the men to the door.

"How do we get them downstairs?" Courtney asked.

"I'll manage. The car's right downstairs, I'll manage. Stay with Grady."

"Are you sure?"

Tessa reached out her hand and opened the door. Courtney eased Brian's weight onto Nick, and Tessa stepped behind them, holding fast to both their shirts.

"Okay, take it slowly, one step at a time," she said and propelled them to the stairway. They went down two steps and then Nick turned around and looked back.

"It was a very nice . . . party. Thank you very much . . . for the very . . . nice party."

"Good luck," Courtney called out and closed the door. She went to the window and waited until she saw Tessa get the men into the car. She turned away then, turned to Grady, but Grady was on his way into the bedroom and in moments she heard water running in the bathroom and she heard Grady being sick. She sat down on the couch and stared off.

16

Saturday morning came. Too sunny, too hot, too still . . .

GRADY walked out of the bedroom carefully carrying a bottle of aspirin. He put the bottle on the dining table, next to the other remedies—a pitcher of orange juice, a bottle of club soda, two cups of hot, black coffee, two jiggers of bourbon. He put two aspirins in his mouth and swallowed them with a swig of orange juice, then continued on down his line; a large glass of club soda, swigged thirstily, a gulp of coffee, a sip of bourbon, and then back to the orange juice. He finished one tall glass and was pouring another when Courtney came out of the bedroom and swept toward him, her pale robe billowing about her.

"Good morning, good morning. Isn't it a beautiful morning? Isn't it a marvelous, clever morning? What a wonderful morning," she thrilled.

"Don't." He grinned and held up his hand. "Don't."

"And what wonderful sunshine. Did you see the wonderful, clever sunshine?" she laughed. Grady groaned. "How about some breakfast?"

Grady made a face and shivered. "You can say that to a man who's going to die?"

She shook her head at him teasingly and pointed a finger at the array on the table. "And today is the first day of the rest of your life, poor fellow," she laughed.

"Yeah, that's it. Pour it on. Let me have it."

"Poor Grady." Courtney smiled and went to his side. She moved behind his chair and slipped her arms around his neck, resting her chin on his head. "Is it really bad?"

He drank more of the juice and grimaced. "Man oh man, el paino in heado. And gut-o. Especially in gut-o. Man, I feel like someone stomped me. Even my ribs hurt."

"You really had a few." She hugged him.

"A few? I drank up a whole East Side of Jack Daniels. I wouldn't be surprised if there was a Jack Daniels famine today. I didn't leave *nothin'* for *nobody*," he said and poured the jiggers of bourbon into his coffee cups. He mixed it around with his finger and then sipped from the first cup.

"What's that for?"

"Courtney, there's only one cure for booze and that's booze. That's a doctor telling you."

"Don't you think you should eat something?"

"Eat? I don't expect to be able to eat until next December," he said and drank again from the cup. Courtney straightened up and went around the side of the table, sitting down opposite him.

"I've never seen you drunk before, Grady. Why last night? What happened?"

"Nothing happened. Nick and I felt like having a drink, we went to Hagen's. We ran into Brian . . . hell, I don't know. The three of us went at it, is all. It was fun, in a way . . . what I remember of it, and I don't remember much. Were we terrible last night?"

Courtney smiled. "You were funny or you were sad, depending on how you look at it."

"Don't ask me to look at anything, I'm still seeing double."

"Nick and Brian were pretty bad off too."

"No worse than I, they had the hundred drinks of Cutty but I had the hundred drinks of Jack Daniels," Grady said and drained his cup. He drank what remained in the pitcher of orange juice and then looked at his watch. "Got to go."

"In your condition?"

"Hell, I'm sober. If I don't die, I'll be fine," he said and got up from his chair. He went into the kitchen and returned moments later carrying a large bottle of club soda and a paper bag. "I'm going to take this along. My mouth feels like the Sahara Desert."

Courtney stood up and reached for Grady's hand. "I still want to know why all the drinking," she said quietly. He stared at her for a long moment and then dropped his head.

"I was in a mood, that's all. God knows we're all familiar with Grady's moods."

"We should talk about it."

"You always want to *talk* about things. As if there's something to say. People are going to do what they're going to do. Me, you, everybody. Do you think words are going to change that?"

"I think words are important, especially between us. We need them, don't you see how we need them?"

"I'm going to be late."

"That's no answer."

"I have no answers, Courtney, none. I'm fresh out. People have a right . . . to do exactly what they want to do and nobody has a right to step in and mess with that."

"Is that as close as you're going to get to the subject?"

"I don't know what you mean."

"Oh Grady, you do. I'm trying to figure out what to do with my life, what to add, what to subtract. Suddenly you're getting drunk. But you stand there and tell me you don't know what I mean. You know very well."

"It's your life, Courtney, I can't tell you how to lead it. I can't ask you to lead it a certain way," he said very quietly.

She turned away from him and he saw the sudden sag of her shoulders.

"I wish we could consider it *our* life," she said softly. "But we always have to have the separation of pronouns. I wonder how many people are done in by the separation of pronouns."

"Courtney. . . ," he said and went to her. He took her in his arms, wrapping her round, holding her close. "Courtney, I'm doing the best I can," he said in a tight, low voice.

"I know. I know," she said and said no more, but when he left she felt the tears start in her eyes.

Grady arrived at the Clinic in time to see an ambulance pulling away, its siren wrecking the Saturday quiet. He watched after it until he could see it no longer and then looked absently up and down the street. There were few people about; two boys hardly into their teens nodded in a doorway, their eyes sleepy with drugs; an old, old woman dressed in black carried a torn shopping bag out of a building; a black man, baseball cap tilted back on his head, sat on a peeling wooden chair outside a tenement; a cat nosed around in a pile of garbage scattered near the curb. Two teenagers sat on a rusting fire escape three stories above the street to his right, their transistors blasting hard rock music, the rhythms contrasting harshly with the moody soul and rapid Spanish music that came from a hundred different open windows. In the terrible heat of the day he could hear the sounds of the shabby, ruined apartments around him; he heard the irregularity of the plumbing and the crashing of voices as arguments began anew, the shouts of Saturday morning television cartoons and the slap of metal as frying pans were slammed onto old, broken ranges. The sun was bright, cruelly bright, and it hurt his eyes, hurt them all the more, for in that sun the dirt, the uselessness of the neighborhood was not to be hidden. He went rapidly into the Clinic, relieved to be in the coolness of the air conditioner, relieved to be in the clean, plain whiteness.

"Morning, Grady," Jim said, shuffling papers at the desk.

"Hi. What's doing?"

"Brian's got his hands full, but otherwise it's pretty quiet."

"I saw an ambulance."

"A woman collapsed three steps inside the door. Overdose."

Grady nodded. "I'm going up to the office. When's my first appointment?"

Jim looked down at a long, handwritten list. "A half hour. Drew Martin. Hey, try some of these, they're delicious," he said, pointing to a tray of big, square cookies.

Grady looked at them suspiciously and felt his stomach turn over. "No, thanks. What are they?"

"Mr. Benke brought them in. He came to fill a prescription and he dropped them off. He made 'em. Ukrainian sugar cookies, he said they were."

Grady smiled. "That was nice of him, but I'll pass. It took my stomach a month to get over the stuffed cabbage he brought last time."

"Suit yourself, but they're delicious," Jim said, and an entire cookie disappeared into his mouth.

Grady waved at him and walked to the elevator. He stepped inside and pressed 5, whistling impatiently through the short ride. When the door opened he hurried out and took long strides toward the office, only barely noticing Dr. Sturgis, who stood in the lab running tests, and the aide who left the supply room with two huge rolls of paper towels.

Grady saw Nick already seated at his desk and grinned sheepishly. "Our fearless leader's not feeling so fearless this morning, I'd bet."

Nick looked up at him and smiled. "The worst part was taking a shower. The noise of the water nearly split my head in two," he laughed.

"I know what you mean. We really did it," Grady said and took the club soda from the bag. "Want some of this?"

Nick shook his head, gesturing toward a large pitcher of ice water. Grady went to the coffeemaker and poured out a cup. He took it to his desk and set it down, turning his attention then to the soda, twisting off the cap. He poured a full glass and drank it down at once.

"You feeling as grim as I'm feeling?" he asked.

"Worse. Tessa kept talking about breakfast. I thought I'd die."

"Female revenge is what it is. How's Brian doing?"

"I feel for him. He's got a dozen squalling, squirming children to contend with this morning. I offered to help," Nick smiled, "but he said it was his punishment and he'd take it like a man."

Grady laughed. "D-O-G," he said. "Brian can be very funny. . . . Did I miss anything this morning?"

"Nothing. Except for the second floor, it's a slow morning, but everyone's booked solid this afternoon. You may have to take a couple of my patients, by the way. I just spoke to John Woods, told him I'd go see him today."

"How's he doing?"

"Badly, in terms of pain. The rough stuff's beginning. But he's made his decision to stay out of the hospital until the very last . . . until it's absolutely necessary. It's a decision I'm going to go along with."

"He'd be more comfortable in a hospital, Nick."

"He wants to use what's left of his life. He wants to enjoy what he can. The problem will be pain. I'm going to order a supply of morphine. I'll treat him myself and teach him how to treat himself in case of emergency. That is, he'll come into the Clinic every day, but he'll have a one-day supply of morphine at home . . . for the nights, if he needs it."

Grady's face clouded as he thought of the good, gentle man being devastated by his cancer. "How long do they figure?"

"City says three months and that's optimistic. More likely two, and the last month will probably require hospitalization."

"It's a shame, just a damn shame."

Nick sat back in his chair and stared at Grady. "Did you ever watch anyone die slowly?"

"I worked the death room at Bellevue one rotation. People lingering on, clinging to life . . . meanwhile suffering hell on earth. Hooked up to machines, screaming in pain. But it took a long time to die, no mercy in it at all. I understood what the law doesn't understand, that people have the right to die."

"I didn't handle much cancer at City. I'm a little leery about this. Because it's John, I think. He's such a good man."

"Well, he's got his church, and that's something at least. I've seen people who had their church go through an awful lot and not really suffer the way they might. I imagine John's thinking this is just the Lord calling him."

"Yes, he said something like that."

"I saw that a lot in Texas. The Baptists, especially the black Baptists. Amazing."

Nick took a drink of ice water. "I agree about the right to die. I hope to God John isn't kept alive on machines. Just to suffer. Just to endure," he said. "It used to be that machines existed to serve patients, now it's getting to be the other way around." He returned to his papers, his black eyes darting over each page. After a few moments he put his pen down and stood, massaging the muscles at the back of his neck. "Do you think you'll have the A.M.A. paper soon?"

"A couple of days should do it. Why?"

"I'm going to review your draft with the whole staff. I want them to add any ideas they have. Now that we have some breathing room I want to try involving the staff in more and more of our projects here. We have to keep them feeling involved."

"Okay, sure," Grady said. He ran a hand over his eyes and gulped some coffee. He swiveled around in his chair and looked toward T.K.'s cage. He smiled slightly and opened a desk drawer, searching around in it until he found a small, round cracker. He stood up and walked to the cage.

"Hello, bird. I didn't forget about you, T.K.," Grady said, breaking off small pieces of cracker into his cage.

"Grady, I told you no food here overnight."

"It's just a cracker."

"I don't care. This is an old building, I don't want any small creatures moving in. No food here overnight."

"All right, don't—"

The page sounded in the office. "Dr. Malory to one. Dr. Malory to one," Jim's voice called, and Grady looked at the speaker on the wall. He went to the closet and removed a clean white jacket, slipping it on over his thin, tan turtleneck.

"Later," he said and left, taking the stairs to the ground floor. He recognized Drew Martin—big, lumbering Drew Martin, handsome with his dark brown hair, his freckled skin, his very white, big teeth.

"Good to see you, Drew. Go right in there," Grady said, and Drew smiled, a wide, shiny smile that was also somehow shy. Grady took his chart from him and followed him into the examination room.

"How are you feeling?"

"I can't get rid of these headaches."

"Sit up there," Grady said, nodding at the table.

Drew jumped on the table and Grady brought his small flashlight closer. He looked into the young man's eyes and then stepped back. "What the hell is this, Drew?"

"What's what?"

"Your eyes, that's what. What the hell are you on?" he demanded.

Drew looked away. "Nothing."

"Don't tell me nothing. You come in here with your eyes glazed over like frosted cupcakes and expect me to believe that? What are you on?"

"We had a little coke this morning. Nothing special, no—"

"*We* had? You mean Ellen Train's fooling around too? What the hell's the matter with you? You're both too smart to start that nonsense. You don't need it," Grady said angrily. "How long has this been going on?"

"We're not . . . addicts, or anything. We just snort a little coke once in a while . . . smoke a little hash, no big deal."

Grady took a couple of steps away and sat himself on the desk. He crossed his arms over his chest and glared at Drew. "Coke is a big deal."

"We don't do it often, Grady. C'mon, I thought you guys live and let live around here."

"Oh sure, live and let live. There's not much we can say to some poor hype who's *been* a hype since he was a kid. There's not even much we can say to a kid who gets drawn into the drug scene around here by his pals, by his mother, his father, his brother. But there's a hell of a lot we can say to someone like you and Ellen. I'm not talking about hash, I'm talking about coke. Stupid! How stupid can you be? Do you know what that shit does to your head? To your nervous system? To your liver, your blood system? Your circulatory system? You and Ellen are young and bright and educated and have no excuses. But you think it's a game, don't you? A little coke, a little wine, turn the stereo up, jump in the sack. You will not know beforehand the day you're going to wake up and find your system's *demanding* drugs. Not asking, *demanding. It just happens.* And you'll open your eyes wide and say, 'Oh, we were just fooling around.' You horse's ass, I'm transferring you to Nick Gorlin today."

Drew didn't say anything, just stared down at the floor. Slowly he lifted his head and looked at Grady. "I'm over twenty-one. So's Ellen."

"Smart guy, over twenty-one. I'm not going to say anymore. Nick'll handle you. He's done it before. And don't think you can just stop coming to the Clinic and forget the whole thing. He'll stick on your tail like glue. He gives a damn about people screwing themselves up."

"Okay, okay, you don't have to sound like my father. I've heard the speeches before."

"Not well enough," Grady snapped. "As for those headaches, I suspect it's really an eye problem. All your tests have been negative," he said, looking over the file. "Monday night you come in here and see Dr. Jonas, he's our eye man. Any time between seven o'clock and nine. And make an appointment to see Nick on Tuesday sometime. I'll hand your files over to him."

"That's not really necessary."

"I think it is. He deals with horse's asses better than I do. And Drew . . . you be here Monday and Tuesday or we'll come knocking on your door." Grady grinned. "And maybe we'll bring the heat, smart guy."

Drew Martin smiled. "I'll be here. I want to hear the next lecture."

"Nick's a pro. Now get out of here, I've got sick people to see."

Drew slid off the table and walked toward the door. He opened it and then stopped.

"Ellen said to ask you if you and your girlfriend will come to our show. It's going to be in two weeks."

Grady's face tightened suddenly and he felt his own head begin to throb again. His eyes grew very quiet.

"Send me an invitation. I . . . I don't know what's going to be happening in two weeks."

"But you'll try?"

Grady slumped tiredly into a chair and turned away from Drew. "I'll try," he said very softly.

"I said I got to go to work, Ma. I ain't got no time," Frankie Carlino said, his mouth thin with anger.

"You got to go downstairs to go to work, you could still take the garbage."

"I told you I ain't taking no garbage. Take your own garbage. Or let Marie do it. She ain't doin' nothin' but readin' them fuckin' schoolbooks."

"I told you shut up about Marie and I told you take the garbage," Mrs. Carlino said, thrusting a brown bag of garbage at him.

"You want me to take the garbage? Okay, I'm takin the garbage," he said and ripped it savagely from her hands. He ran into the living room, and before she could stop him he heaved it out of the open window. "There. I took the garbage. You satisfied now, big deal Anna Carlino?"

Her hand shot out and caught him in the face, hitting him so hard that a big, red splotch came instantly onto his cheek.

Frankie touched his face and then drew his hand back and slapped her as hard as he could, quickly, before she could raise her arm to defend herself. She cried out and Frankie stood his ground, smiling. "I told you before, keep your hands off me."

"You sonofabitch, sonofabitch, that's all you are," she screamed at him.

His soft, full mouth drew back in a wider smile. "I'm the son, you're the bitch," he said calmly, and she went for him, grabbing him by the hair until he lashed out with a powerful kick and she staggered backward, nearly falling.

Marie Carlino rushed into the room then, pale, gray-pale, and ran to her mother.

"Mama, Mama, please, are you all right? Are you hurt?"

"The both of yous can go to hell." Frankie spit out the words and turned away from them.

"Frankie," Marie sobbed, "why do you have to be so mean to Mama? Why do you have to—"

"Shut up!" Frankie roared. "Shut your mouth before I shut it for you. Mean to Mama. Shit, shit on Mama. Mama who hated me all her life . . . and you, Mama's little favorite, so she could move out of the neighborhood, forget she ever had a son. Shit on both of yous. On all the shitheels. I'm goin' to take care of all the shitheels, wait and see," he shouted. "All the ones got in my way, looked down their noses at me, *helpin'* me, they call it. I'm goin' to take care of all of you. My shit Mama and my shit sister and shit Malory. Just wait, just wait, I'll cool your asses good!" he yelled at them and stomped out of the room. He went out the door, slamming it violently behind him.

Marie wiped the tears from her eyes and then bent again to her mother. "Mama, are you all right?"

"That rotten, no-good kid. I should of drowned him when he was a baby."

"Mama, I asked you, I begged you, don't argue with Frankie. You argue with Frankie and he gets . . . crazy. Sometimes I think . . . sometimes I think he could . . . kill somebody."

"That rotten, no-good kid. I should of drowned him, I should of drowned him."

"Venereal disease, Petey, that's what I mean," Brian said quietly to the boy sitting by his desk.

"Yeah, but what is that?"

"V.D., gonorrhea."

The boy shrugged, looking blankly at Brian.

"Clap."

"Oh, oh I get you now. I got the clap-o-yo-hands, hah?"

"What?" Brian asked, his eyes showing rare surprise.

"That's what the niggers call it. They call it the clap-o-yo-hands . . . I ain't never heard it called nothing else."

Brian looked down at the boy's chart and then away, concealing the small smile that had come to his lips. "Well," he said. "Well, we'll start treating it right away. Get up on the—"

"Calling code one. Calling code one," the page called urgently, and Brian stood.

"Petey, you stay here. I'll be back as soon as I can, don't leave," he said and went quickly from the room. He stopped in the corridor and called out to the waiting patients. "Everybody please just stay put where you are. Stay in your seats, I'll be back in a few minutes." He rushed down the flight of stairs to the ground floor. He saw what the code one was immediately: before him, all around him, were young, bleeding boys, blood spurting from faces, from arms and shoulders, from open, slashed skin. The Clinic aides and nurses were employing the emergency procedure they'd used only once before—equipment and bandaging and medications were being supplied to each of the ground-floor examination rooms; other patients were being ushered upstairs; the injured, bleeding boys were being helped to lines of chairs and tables hastily moved into place in the corridor and the emergency room.

Brian was the first doctor there and he rushed to Jim.

"Gang fight over at Tompkins Park. I counted twenty kids, probably more coming in. The cops are on their way. I'm holding an open line to City and Bellevue for ambulances."

Brian nodded and went quickly to the first of the dazed, battered boys just as the other Clinic doctors converged.

Nick stepped into the middle of the corridor and

took charge. "Okay," he said loudly but calmly, "we separate the ambulance cases from the rest. Ambulance cases into the E.R. The rest into exam rooms. Grady, take room one, Hank, room two, Brian, you stay with me, Sturgis, take room three. Let's go," Nick said, and with Brian at his side, he walked down the line of casualties; half a dozen aides followed, prepared to help the badly injured into the E.R.

"This one into E.R.," Nick barked, "this one to room one."

"This one into room three," Brian said, working from the other end.

"Four ambulances, Jim," Nick shouted. "We may need backup."

"Nick," Brian called, "this one needs a surgeon. Stat."

"I need a blood type over here, stat."

"C'mon, c'mon, move it."

"Tell City to stand by on E.R."

And so it went all the rest of that morning. The doctors and nurses tended twenty-four boys, not one of them older than sixteen, nor younger than thirteen. They treated them for cuts and contusions and breaks and fractures and severed veins and cracked jaws, and they did so with a grimness that was unusual at The Gorlin Clinic. They treated them and they were sick themselves, for twenty-four boys, no older than sixteen, no younger than thirteen, had been fighting with chains and rocks and knives and broken bottles and cement-filled bottles and trash-can covers and one of their number was already dead.

When the last of the boys had left, when the last of the ambulances and police cars and press cars had pulled away, Nick and Grady sat in the E.R. with Sargeant Mendez. They were tired, each of them; they drank coffee and said very little.

"Nice," Sargeant Mendez said after a while.

"In the middle of the morning?" Nick said. "That never happened before."

Sergeant Mendez puffed on a cigarette. "The Gang Squad's sorting it out. Looks like one gang was transferring their weapons, you should excuse the expression, to another place, and a rival gang intercepted them. Sweethearts, real sweethearts. A couple of sweethearts start sounding off and some more sweethearts join in and then all the sweethearts are making war on each other's heads. You know the part I like best? Nobody called a cop. You know who called a cop? Jim at this Clinic called a cop when the first sweethearts started falling through the door. So then we put two and two together and we race our butts to Tompkins Square . . . where nobody's calling a cop. The sweetheart that bought it? He choked to death, something about his windpipe. At Bellevue they told me if he'd had help right away he'd—what the hell's the use? It's a sweetheart world."

"And it's summer," Nick said.

"This makes it official," Mendez nodded. "Summer's here. Long and hot."

17

Summertime in New York, a hundred million colors and sounds and smells and sights. There would be tourists, Japanese and French and German, Americans from all over. Atop the Empire State Building, sunny, sturdy, pink-cheeked California children would stare at the city through telescopes. City children would splash in city pools, brown and black and yellow and white bodies. A helium balloon would get loose over the monkey house in Central Park. On East Fifty-seventh Street people would pack for Southampton and across town subways would head for Orchard Beach. Somewhere a storekeeper would go berserk and turn a gun on his customers, somewhere bombs would be planted in banks, and somewhere there'd be a shoot-out. There would be couples, for two is the number of summer—uptown couples. West Side couples. There would be sirens and horns and leaden lines of traffic; there would be fights and muggings and killings and cops would sweat and have nervous eyes and hate the summer. There would be birthdays and anniversaries and funerals and christenings and divorces. People would laugh and cry and make love and get lost. It would be very hot in the city.

The late August heat of the streets was sealed out of the Clinic, windows closed and shades drawn against the air conditioning. Nick and Grady stood in the supply room before an open floor-to-ceiling cabinet, written lists in their hands.

"Man, we're ordering just in time, we're low on almost everything," Grady said.

Nick's eyes roamed the shelves and he nodded. "We're dispensing more than I expected we would. Way more sleeping pills and tranquilizers. I don't know what to do about that," he said and sat down wearily on the only chair in the narrow room. "This isn't a psychiatric clinic, Grady, but we're dispensing as if it were."

"You see the files, none of the prescriptions is unnecessary."

"No, but some of them are becoming habitual. I think we should have a look into some kind of referral system, psychiatric referral. We can't just keep doling out sedatives. Thousands and thousands of pills."

"We treat hundreds of people a week, it adds up. And look at some of the cases. That Mrs. Royo? Her nerves were so shot she couldn't even walk to the corner. On chemotherapy she's taking care of her family again . . . she's even got herself a job at the Woolworth's on Fourteenth Street. It's the difference between functioning and not. We have more cases like that than not. The state inspector was around and didn't blink an eye, just looked at the files and passed us a hundred percent."

"I'm still going to look into a psychiatric referral system."

"Okay, but in the meantime we've got to order our full supplies. Since we only order every three months," Grady smiled, "we can't afford to get caught short."

"It saves us money, ordering in large quantity."

"Yes, but it's something to see. All those drugs pouring in. We could be a branch of the Mafia."

Nick stood up and went to the cabinet, slamming it shut, locking it with a key from his pocket.

"Do you have John Woods's morphine on your list?" Grady asked.

"Yes, I've got everything. I'll put it in today, we'll have everything delivered . . . let's see, this is the eighteenth, we'll get our delivery on the thirty-first."

"Good."

In the lab next door, Frankie Carlino nodded his head; he'd been patient in his weeks at the Clinic and he knew he'd been rewarded—he now had the information he'd been waiting for, and he smiled to himself. It was time to fill out his plan. Frankie heard the men leaving the supply room and he hurried over to the sterilizer, dropping a tray of test tubes into the steam. He held them there, his back to the door, his shoulders hunched over in what he thought would look like concentration. Grady and Nick saw him bent over his work and they proceeded to their office without stopping.

Inside, Grady put his list on Nick's desk and poured a cup of coffee. "When are you going to congratulate me about Frankie?" he grinned. "When are you going to give in?"

"When I'm sold."

"Not yet? There hasn't been a whisper of trouble about him in the streets. He hasn't hassled anybody, hasn't gone marauding, hasn't even been running with his gang so much."

"That hasn't stopped his gang. They hit old Mrs. Jacoby in her store the other night. Not only took all she had, but took the store apart."

"I heard. But Frankie wasn't with them."

"And that's what's so damned strange. Because Frankie is their leader, he does their thinking for them. It doesn't add up."

"What does the kid have to do to convince you he's changing?"

"I don't know," Nick said quietly. "That's a pretty sharp haircut he's wearing these days, by the way. What'd you have to do with it?"

"I gave him twenty bucks and sent him uptown. Hell, he's earned a little bonus here and there. I wanted to soften him up a little too."

"Why?"

Grady hesitated for a moment, then stared directly at Nick. "I got the catalog from the remedial tutoring school"

"Grady, you're dreaming."

"He's smarter than the other kids around here, Nick, you said so yourself."

"That's what makes him dangerous."

"He's smarter than the rest but he's had a lousy education. If . . . if he were interested, really interested, I wouldn't mind sponsoring some education for him. It wouldn't cost that much, it's an investment in a human life."

Nick shook his black head. "What is this all about?"

"It's about helping a kid who's responded to help."

Nick was silent, staring at Grady as if he were measuring something. "I don't think so," he said finally. "I think it's about you. Sometimes . . . sometimes I think you're . . . rebuilding Frankie, stage by stage, and when he's finished, you're going to trot him around to show people what you built."

Grady's eyes flashed suddenly. "Thanks for the confidence," he said coolly.

"*I* have confidence in you. It's you who doesn't have confidence in you. I think that's what Frankie Carlino is all about. He's proving something you need to prove about yourself."

"You won't give up crawling around in my head, will you?"

"Your confidence should be based on what's real, like the fact you're a damn good doctor. Frankie's flunking out of vocational training school, for God's sake, and suddenly you're talking about tutoring schools. It's a slender thread you're clinging to."

Grady stood up. "I should be getting back downstairs."

"Tessa and I are going to a movie tonight and to Rocky Lee's for pizza. Why don't you and Courtney come along? I haven't seen her in a while."

"Nobody has. She's either holed up with Tessa or holed up with her typewriter, working on Joshua's stuff," Grady said quietly.

"Then she could use a night out. How about it?"

"No, thanks. We're going out, as a matter of fact. We're going to the feast. Over on Avenue B."

"In this heat?"

"It's the last night. Courtney likes those street things. Anyway, that's where we're going," he said and then reached for the telephone. He dialed his home number and waited. Finally, with a frown, he hung up. "If she hasn't run off off with the young Hemingway, that is," he said bruskly and left the office.

Courtney sat in the back room at P.J. Clarke's, nervously tapping a pile of typed pages which sat on the table before her. She relaxed a little when she saw Peter Joshua hurrying toward her.

"I'm sorry," he said, sitting down. "My plane was late."

"Where are your bags?"

"Back in Washington. That's the other part of it, I have to go back right after lunch. I'm going to try to make the three o'clock shuttle."

"Go back? You said you'd be able to spend a few days here."

"I thought I'd be able to. Then one of the gray eminences called a meeting for this afternoon and scheduled meetings for the rest of the week and part of next. The bottom line . . . as we say in Washington, is that I have to be there for a while."

Courtney looked away in irritation. "I've worked very hard on this outline and we have to go over it together. It's a little different from the *screenplay*," she said and looked back at him, "and I can't proceed without you."

"We're ready to start writing it."

"I'm ready to start writing it, you're ready to get back on a plane."

"What did your agent say?"

"It's a substantial outline, we can start writing it. But if you're going to keep flying away, then—"

"Just a minute," he smiled at her, "I'll get some drinks and let you be huffy in peace."

"This isn't a joke. I'm rearranging a lot of things to work on this. In my own way I've begun to count on it, Peter."

He motioned to a waiter and gave his order. He turned back to her. "I have a job because I have to have a job. I carry a big overhead, Courtney Ames. Throw in some ex-wives, add a few children, a dash of sick old Mom, and I'm up against it. You and Grady in your shampoo commercial don't understand about such seamy necessities as money. And you, child, don't know the temptations."

"Meaning?"

"To run. To run, my dear, hell-bent with a blonde in my arms. To a beach somewhere. There to write all day, to listen to the crash of the waves at night. The fantasy of a thousand different desperate men, of Everyman. The far side of that fantasy is grief, however, because I have a lot of people telling me the rent's due."

The waiter, big, red-faced, a white apron stretched across his middle, put their drinks down and left. Peter took up his glass and drank in quick gulps.

"You see my plight?" he asked after a moment.

"Yes, I'm sorry, I didn't mean to sound thoughtless. But where does that leave our book?"

He looked at her, considering, then he spoke: "It's time to fly away, little bird. Time for you to come to Washington. You can't put it off anymore, because I can't be here anymore, at least not for a while. I have to be in Washington so I can pay everybody's rent, and you have to be in Washington so we can write our book. You can stay at my house, I have—"

"No," she said quickly.

"As I was saying, you can stay at a hotel, they have plenty of room." He smiled. "We'll work in the evenings. During the day you can get a start on the next pages."

Courtney sipped her wine and was silent. Peter watched her for a while and then looked away, glancing around the room. He saw the young, sleek models with their slim hips and delicate wrists and fine bones, the graying television men in their modish clothes and long hair and dreams of youth no longer theirs. He felt a kinship with the men, knew they saw the same things as he when they looked into mirrors—faces smiling, faces clever; faces very sad and tired if someone would only look.

"I'm just not sure about that," he heard Courtney say, and he turned to her.

"About what, Washington? Well, no one ever is sure about Washington."

"I told you that Grady got drunk a couple of weeks ago."

"I got drunk last night. What has that got to do with anything?"

"Grady doesn't get drunk."

"He did, though. And you're worrying that it's your doing. Courtney Ames driving good Grady to drink."

"Stop it."

Peter's eyes narrowed slightly, their paleness even paler in the odd half-light of the restaurant. "There's a grace period. I'm going to have to make a couple of quick trips . . . Georgia, North Carolina. I'll be back in

Washington to take root in September, the first or second. That gives you a couple of weeks to bind Grady's wounds, if that's what he likes done with them."

"I can't just . . . run off. I never have before."

"Courtney Ames, Courtney Ames, we settled that. If good Grady objects—"

"If Grady objects I'll never know about it," she said sharply. "That's not the point."

"What is?"

She sipped some more wine and then looked down at the typed pages. "I . . . I couldn't stay . . . very long."

"A month will be as a year to us because our hearts are pure."

"No, not a month, not all at one time."

"Three weeks then."

"Maybe," she paused, "maybe two weeks wouldn't be too bad."

"Let's be flexible," he said confidently, "let's be flexible in all things."

Courtney and Grady got out of the cab at Thirteenth Street and Avenue B, the tail end of the Feast of San Phillipa. The street festival was smaller than San Gennaro, only half the size, but it was every bit as gaudy and crowded and noisy. As far as they could see, there were high curlicues of colored lights, reds and greens and blues and whites and yellows and purples strung on pole after pole. The streets themselves were closed to traffic, and in place of cars and garbage cans and debris were brightly draped stands offering food and games, and amusement-park rides and statues of the saints. People were everywhere, three and four deep at the stands, singing or humming along with the Italian songs that played on the loudspeakers.

Hand in hand, Courtney and Grady strolled through the crowds, attracting no special attention at all, for on this evening black and white and brown and yellow faces mingled and shared a childlike pleasure. There was no hostility anywhere; old black-clad Italian women drank cocoanut milk at Puerto Rican stands, black men in Afros lined up for thick sausage sandwiches at the stands of Sicilians, young men and women in beads and long hair and peasant blouses and sandals bought lichee nuts at Chinese stands, expensive people from Gramercy Park and Turtle Bay ate spare ribs and chitlins, wiping fingers on Ruffin sundresses and Cardin slacks, everybody rode the tiny carousel and pitched pennies and threw balls at milk bottles and had fortunes told by a sallow-skinned woman from the Bronx. Courtney and Grady wandered these blocks, and they were happy. Grady's curly head popped up at the wheel of chance, and on his seventh quarter his number won and he pointed to a black and white panda. Courtney bought a balloon in the shape of an elephant and gave it to a small girl in a dirty dress; she bought a doll on a stick—all feathers and sequins and beads—for Tessa, and a shiny black cane for Nick; they ate and ate and ate. Cannolis, thick with cream and confectioners sugar, pizza, glazed chicken wings, cotton candy, all passed between them, and they shared a sausage hero, chunks of oily, fragrant sausage and sweet onions and peppers. They walked around for hours, stopping here and there, smiling at people who smiled back, dropping at ten-dollar bill into a basket held by the man who guarded the statue of Saint Phillipa, a ten-dollar bill he affixed to the long strips of money pinned to the statue. It was hot, and if it hadn't been a festival the smells would have choked them, but festival it was, and when finally they'd seen all there was and tasted all there was and played all the games, they headed away with smiles that were bright as the lights around them.

"I hope we've got a lot of baking soda at home," Grady laughed.

Courtney transferred the stick-doll and the cane to her other hand and slipped her arm inside Grady's. "I prepared for tonight, I brought Bromo *and* Alka-Seltzer. And two quarts of club soda for the big thirst at four a.m."

"What would I do without you?" Grady asked, smiling, but then, hearing his own words, he lost his smile. Courtney looked up at him and saw the change in his expression and wondered how she could tell him that soon she was going off without him.

Grady found a cab on First Avenue and held its door open for her. She sat close to him, resting her head on his shoulder. "I didn't feel the heat when we were there, but God, it's hot," she said.

Grady was quiet, running his finger idly over her hand. "When are you going?" he asked softly.

"Going?"

"When I got home this afternoon . . . I can't explain it but I knew you're going. You are, aren't you?"

Courtney felt her head throb suddenly and her stomach turn. She reached across Grady to roll down the window.

"The first week in September, if I go. Grady, why do you always know things before they happen?"

"That's soon."

"It doesn't have to be the first week in September, it doesn't have to be at all. I picked it because I thought if I'm . . . going to do it, I might as well do it . . ."

"Yes."

"It doesn't have to be, though," she said anxiously.

Grady turned his head and looked out of the window. They were driving up First Avenue, making the lights, flying along, and there was a blur, Stuyvesant Town, Peter Cooper Projects, Bellevue, the U.N., shops and apartment houses and restaurants blurred from sight. They passed the long row of singles bars, young people and people not so young, laughing, looking like they were having fine times, though their eyes roamed and searched. Sad, Grady thought, and then he thought, shit, it's all sad.

"Grady," Courtney shook his arm, "I feel like I'm being forced to go because . . . there isn't enough in us." Grady took her hand but said nothing. She sighed. "Please, let's talk about it just once."

"I can't change us."

"We can be more. Grady . . . *you can tell me not to go*," she said so loudly that the driver, behind his plastic, bulletproof partition, turned around to look at her.

"No," Grady said after a while, "I can't."

They sat again on the roof of Frankie's tenement, three bare-chested boys in jeans and sneakers. They sat in a row, their backs against the rough, dirty brick of the building, their legs stretched out before them. A cigarette dangled from Frankie's lips; in his hands was a half-gallon bottle of Gallo wine, one-third empty. It was late, past two in the morning, and the streets below them were quiet. Occasionally there was the sound of a television set, its dial turned the wrong way before being turned off, or the sound of something falling, being knocked to the floor, or the sound of voices raised and then hushed, or the sound of a baby crying; that was all. There was no traffic and only a few lights shone around them. They were alone.

"I'm out," Joe said.

"Okay, you're out," Frankie said impatiently. He dropped his hand to his side and picked up a small plastic bag, holding it before him. There was a handful of pills in the bag, capsules of red and yellow and blue.

"How much you lay out for these?" he asked Charley.

"The reds fifty cents. The others a buck."

"A buck, fifty cents. *Each*. You know how many of these the Clinic's gettin' in? Thousands and thousands. I heard Gorlin say so today. Plus other stuff. Plus morphine. We lift the stuff, we sell it to Big Skeeter on Tenth Street, we make . . . maybe fifteen thousand for us. Street value, that's what we got to figure. How much it's all worth to Big Skeeter on Tenth Street. It's worth plenty . . . maybe not so much as if we peddle the shit ourselves, but this way we don't get no hassle and we wind up with good bread for ourselfs. Charley, you in or out?"

"Hey man, I'm all for we rip off the shit, but how come we got to cut up on the bird? I don't mind we cut on Malory ... but why mess on T.K.? I don't know. What you got against that bird you want to cut on him?"

"That's my business. This is my deal, it's my brains, my ticket. We do it how I say. We get maybe ten thou from Big Skeeter, that's five apiece. Travelin' money, but I ain't travelin' nowhere before I give it good to all the sonsabitches who gave it to me. Malory, I want to see him *cry*, man. Cry like a baby. What's he goin' to feel when he sees I cut up that fuckin' bird? Man, it'll blow his mind. Head of bird, and neck of bird, and heart of bird, and wings of bird ... cut him up like in the butchers. And we leave the pieces on Malory's desk . . . spread out." Frankie's eyes were pinpoints of pleasure. "We'll spill so much bird around that Malory won't forget me as long as he lives. If he lives."

Charley looked sidelong at Frankie and then sat back against the wall of the roof once more. "Why we don't just cut on Malory?"

"You ain't hearin' me, Charley. I said I want to see Malory cry. I want him to see what Frankie Carlino really thinks about him. You hearin' me now? You understand where I'm comin' from?"

"Man, I never cut on no bird before. I don't care none about cutting on people ... man, people is bastards anyways, but no bird never did nothing to me."

"A bird's a pet, ain't it? Like a dog or a cat? Everybody takes good care of pets ... feed 'em good, love 'em, take care of 'em ... same people don't give a shit for you and me. I seen it, I know. My old lady had a cat once ... nothin' she didn't give to that fuckin' animal. Me, she spit in my eye. That's the way it is, Charley, people is nice to the animals and shitheels to their own. We don't need no more pets."

"I don't know," Charley said unhappily.

"You want to make yourself five thousand? Where's a spade goin' to get five thou anywhere? Nowhere, man, that's where, except for my plan. You want in, then you do it how I say; if not, then fuck off. Maybe I should of picked me another dude anyhow, a dude ain't a spade."

Charley looked sharply at Frankie and then drew his legs up against his chest, hiding his head. His color embarrassed him, it always had, and as much as it twisted him inside to be called spade and nigger and spook, he felt he could expect no less.

"Okay, man, I'm in. But how we get to do all this? We just bugaloo our asses in or something?"

"I'll pick the night, I still got to do that. And I'll pick the time, tha's important. Got to be a time when Malory's in the Clinic by himself . . . when that fuck Jim is gone home . . . when all the other doctors is gone. Then," Frankie said and smiled, "we got to have a *di*-version. Somethin' got to happen that calls Malory out from the Clinic . . . that gives us time to get in, get the shit and slice the bird. Then when Malory gets back . . . there's no shit on the shelves and old T.K. is parakeet stew."

Charley's palms were wet now and he rubbed them hard against his jeans. He lit a cigarette and reached over for the plastic bag, taking one red and two yellows, washing them down with wine.

"What's your diversion?"

Frankie laughed loudly and punched the boy next to him in the ribs. "Man, that's the best part. That's the part I take care of my fuckin' old lady and her lousy Marie."

"Yeah, how?" Joe asked.

"All of a sudden you're so interested," Frankie sneered. "I thought you was out."

"I'm out."

"Then shut up."

"C'mon, Frankie," Charley said, "how?"

"You know the Devils? Over from Avenue D?" he

asked, and Charley nodded. "You know they always like a little fun. I'm gettin' the word out the day we go. That day the word goes out they can use my sister. That night, she goes to class like usual, but it ain't like usual, 'cause the Devils is goin' to be waitin' for her. Man, man, when they get through with her . . . Then you call the Clinic and say, 'Help, help, help, a girl is dyin' in the street.' So big shot Malory gets the call and goes runnin' . . . and," he spread his hands, "we make our move. You and me, Charley, you and me inside the Clinic."

Charley whistled and shook his head, "Man, you got the action figured."

"I been eating shit for two months, waiting for the night we make our move, sure I got it figured. The old lady and Marie . . . man, I want to see their faces when it's over. The old lady, she'll go nuts, or have a heart attack. And I want to see Malory's face. For the rest of their lives they won't forget me. And meanwhile I'm somewhere else, enjoyin' the bread. Florida maybe, maybe California. I hear a guy can score in California."

Charley looked briefly at Joe nodding now from the pills and the wine, and then at Frankie. He slapped his moist hand against his knee. "Okay man, I'm with you. How we get to the shit? It's locked up, ain't it?"

"There's two keys. Gorlin keeps one in his pocket. Malory the big shot keeps his in his desk. It's a cinch. Nothin' ain't goin' to go wrong."

"What if it does? What if the Malory dude comes in before we's done?"

Frankie looked over at Charley and smiled, a smile that was evil and vicious and strangely old. He smoothed his dark hair and then stretched his arms out. In one hand he held his switchblade knife, its blade sheathed. There was a sharp click and the blade shot out, glinting metal in the thin light of the moon. He took the blade to his cigarette and sliced it in two with a single quick motion of the blade. He smiled again.

"Man," Charley said, "you a *bad* dude."

18

A heat wave came to the city and lingered on, temperatures rushing into the nineties. Machinery broke down, and people gave in; they had no more strength . . .

"WHERE in hell is Jean?" Grady asked in annoyance.

"I haven't heard from her." Jim shrugged. "Anything I can do?"

"She insisted on taking some charts home with her last night. To organize them, she said. Now I'm missing my charts."

"I'll get the duplicates, only take a minute. Which do you need?"

"Hell, you better pull the whole A file and the G . . . and the R."

"Okay, give me a minute," Jim said and moved his huge body away from the desk. He was at the stairs when he heard the dazed, wailing voice at the door and he turned around.

Grady ran to the door. It was Jean, whiter than the walls around her, deathly white, her eyes glazed.

"I saw it, I saw it, I saw it," she said, stunned.

"Jean? . . . Jean!" he said and shook her.

"I saw it, I saw it, I saw it."

"Get Nick," Grady barked at Jim and then led Jean into the E.R. He eased her into a chair and leaned over her, his fingers on her pulse. "What did you see? Tell me," he said quietly.

"I saw it, I saw it," she cried, repeating the words as if in litany.

Grady looked into her eyes with his light, his brow wrinkled with concern. "Shock," he mumbled to himself and then fell on his haunches, holding Jean's face level with his own.

"Jean, Jean . . . listen to me. . . ," he was saying as Nick rushed into the room.

Nick moved Grady aside quickly and peered closely at Jean, his face somber as he listened to her repeating the same words. He stepped back a little and then raised his hand, slapping her hard across the cheek. She blinked and looked at him, at first as if she didn't know him, then slumped back in the chair. She began to cry.

"What is it, Jean? What happened?"

"I saw them die . . . right in front of me . . . not . . . not two feet away . . . Mr. Benke . . . I saw . . right in front of me . . . I saw—"

"Mr. Benke? Is Mr. Benke dead? Did something happen to him? Easy now, Jean, take a breath and tell us."

"I was walking along the street . . . here, coming here. I was . . . a . . . a step away from Mr. Benke's building and all of a sudden . . . all of a sudden Mr. Benke came . . . came running out. He had . . . a gun," she said, and Nick and Grady exchanged worried looks. "He had a gun and he started . . . shooting . . . just anybody . . . he was shooting people. There . . . was a man, right in front of me, the bullet . . . he fell down and his head was bleeding . . . and then . . . I looked around and another man was down on the street, bleeding, more blood. I . . . I . . . ," she said and then stopped. She looked faint and Grady bent to her with a small bottle, moving it back and forth under her nose. After a moment she looked up.

"Didn't you hear . . . the sirens?" she asked, and the tears began anew. "Somebody called . . . the police . . . and suddenly they were there . . . and Mr. Benke was taken away and . . . then there were ambulances . . . and, and the men in the street were . . . *dead.* They were *dead*, Nick, they covered the bodies with . . . with sheets. Didn't you *hear*? Didn't you *hear* the sirens?" she asked desperately, and Nick thought, yes, we heard them, but we always hear sirens, we pay no attention anymore.

"We heard, Jean, but we didn't think, we didn't know what it was," he said gently. He too was stunned. *Mr. Benke*? Not Mr. *Benke.* He turned and went to the cabinet. He removed a small capsule and then went to the sink, filling a cup with water and wetting a bunch of paper towels. He took the pill to Jean and watched as she swallowed it, then wiped her face with the cool towels.

"Do you know what happened?" he asked softly. "I mean did Mr. Benke say anything?"

"He . . . he told the policeman . . . I heard him. He said he left his building and . . . a kid, a junkie, he said, forced him back into the hallway and took his money. He . . . said it was the . . . fourth time in two months some junkie took all his money. He said . . . he couldn't take any more. That he went back into his apartment and . . . got his gun. He said he . . . didn't care, nobody was going to take his money anymore. He said he was an old man . . . that it wasn't nice to take his money from him." Jean put her head in her hands, sobbing. Nick put his hand on her head and stroked her hair gently, his eyes on Grady.

"Mr. Benke? I don't believe it."

"A gun?"

"Everybody has a gun around here," Nick said, "I guess they pushed him too far, finally."

Grady ran his hand over his face, rubbing his eyes, and then moved over closer to Jean.

"Help me with her," Nick said, "let's get her on the table." And together they lifted her up and settled her on the examination table. They pulled up the crib sides and then stepped back.

"Maybe a shot?" Grady asked.

"I'd rather not. I'd rather she get it out of her system."

"Maybe I should take her home."

"She lives alone, she's better off here, until she's calmer. Jim?" Nick shouted into the corridor. "Get an aide in here . . . Grady, we'll let her rest here, the aide can watch her. I've got a floor full of patients waiting," he said, looking at his watch. "I'm going to call Mendez and get the story."

"I'd like to help Mr. Benke, if I can."

"He must have been insane," Nick said wearily. "Why don't you call that lawyer . . . the one who donates some time here. Find out about procedures and everything," he said and then turned to the door. "Oh, Frankie, I want you to stay here with Jean. She's had a bad shock, she needs to rest. If she needs anything, wants anything, call Grady, he'll be down the hall."

"Sure, Nick. What happened?"

"Two men were . . . killed, apparently, right in front of her eyes. At least I think that's what happened."

Frankie looked sincerely sorry; he shook his head. "Terrible things around here, ain't they? Sure, sure I'll take care of her. I'll watch her."

"Thanks," Nick said. He nodded to Grady and they walked out of the room. Nick stopped at the doorway and looked back. He saw Frankie patting Jean's pale face with the damp towels, smoothing the paper sheet underneath her, and, satisfied, he returned to his patients. Frankie waited until they were gone and then he threw the paper towels across the room and slumped into a chair, stretching out his legs. "Terrible things around here, ain't they?" he heard himself saying and he laughed out loud.

Courtney stopped typing and looked toward the door. The knock came again and she left the desk, frowning as she crossed the room.

"Who is it?" she called.

"Me. It's Mother."

"Mother?" Courtney said, startled. "What in the. . . ?" She opened the door, smiled and reached to hug the woman standing there. "What a surprise. I didn't know you were coming down today. Something wrong at the Cape?"

"No, everything's lovely," Joanna Ames said and walked into the apartment. "Your father wanted to check the apartment and I decided I could do with some shopping. We flew down this morning," she said and sat down. "We've been phoning you all day but the line's been busy."

Courtney looked at the phone, the receiver lying on its side on the desk. "I took it off the hook. I've been working."

"Is this a terrible time to come? I won't stay long."

"I want you to stay. I wasn't expecting to see you again until fall."

"Well, we've been at the Cape since May, we got a little lonely for the city. We'll stay the night and fly back tomorrow. Of course we didn't know how hot it was here. It's dreadful."

"It's been this way for a week. How about some iced tea?"

"No, don't bother. Your father and I just had a long, long lunch," she said and looked carefully at her daughter. Joanna Ames was a graceful, attractive woman in her early fifties. Slim, on the tall side, her pale blue eyes missed very little. "You look awfully tired," she said.

"I haven't been sleeping too well."

"Why not?"

Courtney sat in the rocker and looked away. "We got trouble right here in River City." She tried to smile.

"Can I help?"

"No one can."

"Don't be dramatic," Joanna Ames said lightly, though she didn't like her daughter's color or the way her hands fidgeted nervously in her lap. "Is it Grady?" she asked after a moment.

"It's Grady and me together," Courtney said. She paused, weighing her words, but then all the words came out, the thoughts, the fears, the doubts that she hadn't expressed to anybody before tumbled from her. She told her mother about Peter Joshua and about the book; she told her about Grady and about how alone and useless she felt. Joanna Ames listened quietly throughout; her expression didn't change though her eyes went quickly from surprise to concern.

"And that's the story," Joanna said when Courtney had finished.

"That's it. My miserable little story. I sound like a whiner, don't I?"

"You sound like an unhappy girl. And you've been keeping all this to yourself, and that never helps. Your last letter was so cheerful, I had no idea."

"I know how much you and Father care for Grady."

"We do, but you're our daughter."

"Anyway, it would have sounded strange, in a letter. Grady shuts me out . . . how would that have sounded?"

Joanna sat back on the couch and spoke quietly. "Everybody wants to leave somebody at one time or another. They need to leave to learn about themselves, or so they think."

"You never left Father."

"Which doesn't mean I didn't think about it, or that he didn't. It's different, though, when there's a child involved. It's even different when there's a marriage involved. And then it was different in my day, times were different. People didn't always rush to suit themselves."

"Is that what you think I'm doing, suiting myself? It sounds awful. It sounds cold."

"Leaving isn't easy under any circumstances. Leaving Grady . . . well, that seems a terribly hard thing to do. He's such a sweet boy."

"That may be the crux of our problem. Boy. He's determined to live as a boy while I need us to be man and woman. I don't want to play house anymore, I want Dick and Jane to grow up."

"And if Dick can't?" Joanna said and leaned forward. "Courtney, your father and I always gave you a lot of independence, freedom. You were a bright child and we knew we couldn't make your mistakes for you, we couldn't grow for you, you had to do that all by yourself. When you and Grady decided to live together we knew that in time just living together wouldn't be enough for either of you. You're both deeply sensitive people, you're caring people. We didn't raise our eyebrows and deliver lectures or look sad or any of those things, because we knew you and Grady would work it out on your terms."

"There's a 'but' in there somewhere."

"Only that now maybe it's time for a few words from a parent. I've had more than thirty years of marriage to your five of hanging around with Grady, and I've learned a few things. One of them is that two people seldom realize something at the same time. You've just come upon these feelings you have and you're impatient, you want Grady to understand at your speed. Darling, that isn't taking Grady into account, nor his fears. Time and understanding, both are necessary. Maybe if—"

"Maybe. Maybe I'll win the lottery, maybe I'll run for Congress, maybe I'll meet Marjoe and he'll ask me for a date," she said wearily. "That's all possible, but it's not bloody likely, Mother. I need something to happen *now*. I have no more time, I can't stay in this house the way things are. And Grady won't even talk about it. All he says is he's doing his best, and his best isn't enough."

"People don't grow all at once, you know. They grow in stages, and they need help."

"I can't. I've tried."

Joanna sat back. "All right. Then let's say you do go to Washington for a few weeks, perhaps you should. But why do you hesitate so if that's what you want?"

Courtney looked at her mother and then looked quickly away. "I . . . have a . . . feeling that if I go . . . it really won't just be for a few weeks. It'll be the break."

"And you don't want that?"

"I love Grady, I adore him. But obviously not enough to put aside what I need. If Grady and I can't be what I want us to be, then I have to go away and be somebody else. Obviously I don't love him enough."

Joanna Ames smiled gently. "Or enough that you realize now."

Courtney was about to speak when something on the radio caught her attention. She left the rocker and went to the radio, leaning down to listen. She heard only the tail end of a news broadcast—something about murders on East Fifth Street—and she hurriedly went to the telephone. She picked up the receiver and cleared the line, dialing the Clinic's number.

"What's wrong?" Joanna asked.

"I don't . . . Dr. Malory, please," she said into the phone. "Grady, I just heard the news, what? . . . That's terrible, are you all right? . . . Grady, I'm scared, I don't want you down there . . . No, no, I'm not getting hysterical, I don't want you down there. Come home, please. Please, I want to see you . . . but . . . Grady, I want you to come home . . . not later, *now* . . . *Grady,* I . . . All right, all right, if that's the way it has to be, that's the way it *has to be*!" she said and slammed down the receiver. She stood over the desk for a moment, her head bent, and then turned and went to the sideboard. She poured a glass of wine and drank it hastily, then turned to her mother. "That does it, that really does it."

"What does? Courtney . . . ," Joanna said and then went to her daughter, for she saw she was trembling. "Courtney, what is it?"

"People were killed down there today . . . about ten steps from the Clinic. *Killed.* I just wanted Grady to come home," she said and began to cry. "That's all. But he can't even do that. That damn Clinic, if you think that hasn't been a strain too. Day and night, worrying if Grady's going to be all right down there."

"Courtney, sit down," Joanna said, leading her to the couch. "Grady was right about you getting hysterical."

"I'm okay," Courtney sniffled. "I'll be okay now. It's just . . . he's made more of a commitment to that damn Clinic than he's made to me. The Clinic, the Clinic, the Clinic, it makes me sick sometimes. And just try to say something about it and you get lecture number one hundred and twelve . . . the starving children, the oppressed minorities, the garbage in the street . . . *whose* goddamned garbage is it anyway? People don't come for miles around just to dump their garbage on the starving children."

Joanna smiled slightly and reached into her pocket for a handkerchief. "Here."

"Thank you," Courtney said and blew her nose. She dabbed at her eyes and then took a deep breath.

"You don't really mean that, do you?" Joanna asked.

"No, no I don't," Courtney said dully. "I get so angry with him, though . . . What do I have to strike out at? The Clinic. I do worry, though," she said quietly. "I meant that part, it has been a strain. Anyway, I just made up my mind, I'm going. Damn the torpedoes, I'm going."

"To Washington and Peter Joshua?"

Courtney threw her hands in the air. "*Carpe diem.*"

"Must it be right now? Anything would have set you

off, in your mood. Why don't you think about it some more?"

"I haven't the strength. I just haven't the strength. And I don't want to talk about it anymore, I'm talked out, let's change the subject. How's Father?"

"Taking a long walk around the city, I'm sure," Joanna smiled. "He was hoping you and Grady would join us for dinner. He brought back mounds of sweet corn, picked this morning. And tomatoes. And fresh shrimp and scallops, caught this morning, according to Lobster John. Of course we had no idea what was going on here."

"We'll join you," Courtney said.

"Really?"

"Now that my decision's made, I'm not going to sit in the corner and cry anymore. It's going to be a new Courtney, how about that? Courtney faces life," she said and went to pour more wine.

Joanna shook her head sadly. "I'd forgotten how confusing it was to be young," she said softly, as if to herself.

"Fie on young."

"It goes quickly."

"None too quickly for me."

Joanna laughed. "Come sit down and calm down and let's talk quietly. Can do?"

Courtney sat next to her mother on the couch. "Okay, but not about all this stuff. I hate all this stuff. I just hate it."

19

Saturday was tall and cool, an early taste of fall that would not last . . .

NICK sat at the long metal table in the Clinic basement. Jean across from him. She was edgy, the way she'd been since the day of the Benke killings, as they were called now, and she avoided Nick's eyes.

"You can change my mind, Nick. I want you to change my mind."

Nick shook his head, his black eyes were very serious. "I wouldn't do that. I want people to be happy here. I want people to be comfortable. You're neither, anymore. It's not surprising, what you saw would have affected anybody that way."

"I loved it down here, Nick. I loved the work, the people. For the first time I felt like I was doing something worthwhile. At the hospitals I worked at . . . well, you know how it is, I was just one of five hundred nurses doing what any other five hundred nurses could have done. It was different here, you made it different. I used to go home and feel like I'd done something worthwhile, like I'd contributed. I don't know where you got your reputation for being mean to nurses . . . I loved working for you."

"You're a good nurse, I never had any patience for the bad ones. You *are* good, and that's why I thought about this a while before speaking to you. I hate to lose you, but I'd rather lose you than have you spend your time looking over your shoulder. I know I could change your mind, but you'd still never feel at ease again around here. I care about my staff, Jean, I want them to be happy. I agree with you, I think you should leave. And you don't have to give notice, you can leave today."

"No, I wouldn't leave you shorthanded."

"I'll manage, I've managed worse. Fear makes people vulnerable, and I don't want a vulnerable young woman on these streets alone. I've given all the nurses their release if they want to leave."

"I'm the only coward."

"You're the only one who *saw* it. Cheer up," Nick smiled, tilting her chin to him. "I've got some good news for you. I've been on the phone . . . I made arrangements for you to be the E.R. head nurse at City, if you want it."

"If? Nick," Jean smiled, "that would be a little bit like working here. I'd love it."

"Good. Get in touch with Sam Matthews, he'll set it up."

"Nick, I—" Jean began when Grady appeared at her side.

"Is this private?" he asked.

"No, sit down," Nick said. "Go along, Jean, I'll see you later."

She stood up. "I . . . thanks, for understanding," she said and hurried away.

"What's that all about?" Grady asked.

"We're losing Jean."

"Figures," Grady said, in the throes of a deep, dark mood that hung heavily on him.

The two men were quiet then, toying with their lunch plates, while around them nurses and aides wandered in and out, making sandwiches and taking them back upstairs, for they were not at all anxious to be around either doctor. Nick and Grady had been curt during the last few days, snapping and frowning, and as unusual as it was, the staff understood. It hadn't been an easy few days; there'd been the shock of Mr. Benke and then the awful, confusing hours when they'd sought to offer help but had run into a tangle of legal maneuvering and been forced to withdraw. There'd been the mumbling in the neighborhood over Mr. Benke, the mumbling that he was a Gorlin Clinic patient and why hadn't the doctors spotted his mental condition. There'd been the distraught wife of one of the dead men; she threw a bottle through a Clinic window, she'd been abusive, they'd had to call the police. And of course there'd been Jean, the talk of her quitting. The staff thought it understandable that the doctors were in bad spirits, and yet they sensed something more than the events of those few days as the source, especially in Grady. Whatever it was, they'd decided to stay clear of it. They kept their distance where they could, cleared paths, spoke only in the course of business. Nick was aware of all of this but let it go; if Grady was aware he showed it not at all.

The two men were troubled, quiet, tired when Brian walked into the basement. He stopped to pour a cup of coffee and then joined them at the table.

"Hi."

"Brian," Nick said.

"I thought you might want to know . . . Clovis was in for his checkup and I noticed it's his birthday."

"Today?" Grady asked, and a certain eagerness returned to his voice.

"Today."

Nick saw the trace of a smile on Grady's face and decided to use the opportunity. "Why don't you arrange something for Clovis?"

"Like what?" Grady asked. "Like a party?"

"Why not? We've got about twenty bucks in the miscellaneous fund, and I'll be happy to kick in another ten."

"Ten from me," Brian said.

"What about it, Grady?" Nick prodded.

"Well, yeah, why not? We could have it down here, invite his friends . . . who are his friends, Brian?"

"I don't think he has any. A loner. T.K. is the only friend I know of."

"Well, sure, we'll have T.K. here. Hell, he really has no friends?"

"I've never seen him with anyone. He doesn't hang around with anyone."

"Then it'll be just staff. We'll get some paper hats and things, some ice cream. A cake. And presents . . . I wonder what he'd like?"

Brian looked at Grady impassively, his long golden lashes shadowing his cheeks. "He could use anything, he doesn't have anything."

"He will when I get through," Grady said and stood up. "Toys. I'm going to buy out the toy department. Ever see a Texan shop?" he asked and grinned suddenly, the first real smile they'd seen on him in days. "Man, he just points and keeps on pointing. Nick, can I leave for a while?"

Nick smiled and nodded. "Go ahead, I'll send an aide out to get the food and decorations, you just worry about the expensive part. How's your patient schedule?"

"Four coming in that I know of."

"I'll take care of them."

"Where's Clovis now?" Grady asked.

"In the office, playing with T.K."

"Good, he'll be busy up there for two, three hours. When he's leaving, we'll lead him down here and he has his party."

"Well," Nick smiled, "get going if you're going. An hour is all I'm giving you."

Grady searched around in his pockets and pulled out a crumpled bunch of bills. He counted them, then cursed and impatiently pulled out his wallet, flipping through the cards. "Good thing I've got charge cards," he said. He took off his white jacket and handed it to Nick. "Hold on to that, will you, I've got some notes in the pocket," he said and then rushed from the room.

"Just what the doctor ordered," Nick said when he was gone.

"I thought it might be."

"It was nice of you to notice."

"Coincidence. I know Grady would like to break through to the boy and Clovis's birthday obliged."

"Timing's perfect for Grady. He needs something to bring him out of this mood, or did you notice that too?" Nick smiled.

"I did, yes. He's seemed terribly depressed. The Benke killings were awful, but it seems more than that."

"You amaze me."

"How so?"

"You walk around here as if you were in another place, you don't seem to have . . . contact with anything. With anybody. Yet you notice everything, you notice as much as I do, which is quite a lot."

Brian sipped his coffee and glanced at Nick. "People who aren't good conversationalists become good listeners. People who aren't themselves involved, notice everybody else's involvement."

"That simple?"

"I think so."

"You're a strange bird, Dr. Morgan," Nick smiled warmly, "and every bird has his day."

"Then I'll wait."

Nick looked at his watch and then stood up. "I'd better get moving if we're going to run a Clinic and a party too. See you later," Nick said and strode to the door. He stopped and turned around. "And Brian, thanks."

"Anytime," he said.

As children's parties go, the party for Clovis wasn't much of a success. The guest of honor wasn't too interested, eating none of the cake or ice cream, only reluctantly drinking a cup of Coca-Cola, saying "she-et, no," when Jim suggested they play a round of pin-the-tail-on-the-donkey—one of the games purchased by an aide in a surge of enthusiasm. There were presents, dozens, for Grady had found a sudden release in the toy department of Macy's. The games he'd seen advertised on television, the kits, he swooped up eagerly—so eagerly that it hadn't taken him long to admit he was doing it at least as much for himself as for Clovis; because he needed to, needed to do something, needed to do anything. All of these packages Clovis dutifully opened, looking hard at their contents but never, not once, reacting to them. It was only when he got to the last package that he smiled, and Grady and the others knew the child was pleased. It was a camera, a Polaroid, with boxes and boxes of film, and once the workings were explained to him he wasted no time in clicking off a score of photographs, T.K. hopping around in his cage the favored subject. Clovis put a new packet of film into the camera and again raised the viewfinder to his eyes when Grady tapped him on the shoulder.

"Let's get a shot, you and me and T.K."

"I ain't got too much films left, Cowboy."

"There's a twenty-dollar bill in there, enough to keep you in film for a while. We can use up what's here. C'mon, Nick'll take the picture. He'll take two, one for you, one for me."

"What for you want a pictures of me? You knows what I look like."

"I'd like to take it home. T.K. and T.K.'s friend."

"Well . . . for you lady?"

Grady swallowed hard; he felt his throat catch. "For my lady."

"Okay, then. If it for you lady," Clovis said. Grady arranged himself next to T.K.'s cage. He drew the child closer and put his hand on his shoulder, but the boy shook it off. "You don't got to touches me, Cowboy," he said bruskly and Nick shook his head at him.

"This party was Dr. Malory's idea, you know. It wouldn't kill you to stop fighting him."

"Like a pickaninny boy?" Clovis grumbled.

"Clovis!" Nick said sharply. "That's enough. Has Dr. Malory ever been anything but nice to you? Answer me," Nick demanded. "Has he?"

"Nick—" Grady tried to intervene, but Nick held his hand up.

"Answer me, Clovis. Has he?"

"No," the boy said, looking levelly into Nick's angry eyes.

"Then let up. Get the chip off your shoulder, you can't go on battling the whole world."

"You ever been called a woolhead, Docker Gorlin? They's ever spit on you 'cause you was a nigger boy?" Clovis asked, suddenly stiff with his own anger. Hate, as much as his small body could hold, exploded from him, and Nick stood still where he was, his eyes wounded, as if he'd been hit. He hadn't known that such a small young body could hold so much hate. Hank Mitchell, standing nearby, was very pale, and Brian's mouth was parted slightly in surprise. Grady, his mouth inverted with sadness, instinctively reached out to the child, and this time the child allowed himself to be held, unmoving while Grady grasped his shoulders, trying by his grasp to tell the boy that the wrongs done to him would be put right; how, he didn't know.

People around them drifted away knowing the small scene was over, knowing the party was over, knowing the funny feelings in their own stomachs. They left, returned upstairs; Grady and Nick and Brian and Hank remained with Clovis.

"Okay, let's we take the pictures now. Now you see what I means," Clovis said in a clear, firm voice. Nick hastily complied. He took one more, and that was the last of the photographs. For the next few minutes they went around the basement, gathering up the presents, stuffing them into two large shopping bags. Grady checked the room with his eyes one more time and then, satisfied, handed the bags to Clovis. "That's all of it."

"What you be doing with all the cakes and stuff?"

"Why, nothing, you want it? We'll wrap it up and—"

"I don't want it. They's a man lives in my building. Maybe he wants it. He don't never eat nothing but corn flakes and potatoes and tuna. He ain't got no money. Maybe he wants it. I wrap it up myselfs."

The doctors stared at each other, grimmer now than before, and then Nick spoke to Clovis. "We always have food in the refrigerator. You're welcome to take whatever you want for the man," he said very softly.

"I don't never steals, Docker Gorlin," Clovis said, almost formally.

"You have my permission, it's not stealing."

"Then I be taking some of that meats inside there. I sees you has some baloneys, I be taking that and some hams. With you permission."

"Take whatever you want. Take it all," Nick said tiredly. "Every day. You have my permission to take what you want," he said and turned back to the circle of doctors. "Hank, try and find out who that man is, you know that building better than we do. Maybe there's something we can . . ." He rubbed his eyes. "Let's go."

"I see about that," Clovis said. "Maybes it's not such a good idea to take ever'day. Start feeding one man, and next thing you turn around you got a whole street to feeds. Not nobody got any money."

They had heard enough, the young men, and Nick

saw it; he took Grady's arm and then pushed Hank toward the door and nodded at Brian. "C'mon, there's work waiting."

"My God!" Hank said, the distress of it all on his face.

"Let's go, Doctors," Nick said firmly.

"Hey, Cowboy?" Clovis called.

"Yes?"

"I want you take the camera and holds it for me. Here. I brings it home, and next thing you turn around my mother goes and hocks it. She a bitch," he said and held the equipment out to Grady. He took it and turned, wordlessly leaving the basement, the other doctors behind him.

Grady waited until they reached the desk before he spoke, his hand rubbing his forehead. "It's enough to drive you crazy, all of it. What the hell's going on? Spitting on kids, old men living on damn *corn flakes* . . ."

"Get going," Nick said to Brian and Hank, Hank still pale. They didn't move, looking at Grady until Nick pointed the finger at the stairs. "Get going," he ordered, and they left.

"I'm going to go out of my mind, Nick, I swear. That was just too much. I can't take it anymore."

"Calm down, it—"

"Calm down?"

"I said calm down and I mean it," Nick said sternly. He dragged Grady into the E.R. and pushed him into a chair. "The answer is for everybody to do what they can. We're trying. It's not enough, but we're trying."

"How much are these people supposed to take? How much is anybody supposed to take," he said quietly and rested his head on the examination table.

Nick watched him silently for a moment and then leaned against the table. "It's ugly out there, Grady," he said softly. "That's why this Clinic exists. Call it shelter, call it an option, but that's why we're here. We'll take care of Clovis's man, but there are a thousand, ten thousand, just like him we'll never know about. We could chuck it all and say, no, it's too much to think about. Or we could do what we're doing. What do you think, should we turn tail?"

"I didn't mean that, you know I didn't . . . the whole damn world is falling around me, Nick."

"Courtney?"

"It seems so sudden, yet I've always known it would come to this."

Nick looked curiously at Grady. "Always?"

"People always leave me, it was only a matter of time."

"That's ridiculous."

"It's the truth."

"Why would you—"

"Why? Why, why, why, why, why. Because I'm me, because I'm not Lucas Malory. And I learned that at my mama's knee," he said and stood up. Nick stared at him. "It's too much . . . sometimes it just gets to be too much."

"Grady, you have to get yourself in hand, you keep up like this and you're heading for trouble."

"You'll keep me together, Nick. You'll take Humpty Dumpty and keep him whole . . . just like you've kept all the Humptys together before."

"I could use a little help from you."

"I'm out of my hands."

Jim stuck his head in the door. "Nick, they're calling for you on three. Grady, you have a patient waiting."

"Is that the last of them for today?"

"Uhuh."

"Thank the Lord," he said and walked out without a word to Nick. He passed Jim and went through the corridor into the first examination room. He sat down and put Clovis's camera on the desk. He still had the photo in his hand and suddenly he felt like crying—crying for Clovis, for all the Clovises, for all the old men who lived on corn flakes and tuna fish; and for Courtney, for his lady.

20

It was the fifth evening of September and the night was pale, the color of an old, forgotten dream . . .

COURTNEY stood at the window, watching summer go away. She had never liked September, its temperament, its vagariousness, still a season yet marking its end, and she liked this September least of all. She was leaving this month—on this night—and while a part of her demanded belief in what she was doing, another part of her, the greatest part, was feeling only empty sadness. It was tearless, wordless, the pain was not acute, and yet it was the worst sadness she'd ever known, for she was opening a door that led away from Grady and even as she stood there, ready to go, she fought against that thought. Away from Grady? Grady of so many years? It was not possible.

"Courtney," Tessa called to her. "I'll have to take all these files with me. There's not enough time to sort through them. . . . Courtney?"

"Yes, yes I heard you."

"All right then, we'd better be going if . . . we're going," Tessa said and arranged the Clinic files in the crook of her arm.

Grady had been sitting silently in the rocker by the fireplace and now he rose and walked over to Tessa. "It's nice of you to . . . drive her to La Guardia," he said quietly.

"There's some unfinished Clinic business, we'll get a chance to go over it in the car," she said and then looked away, for she couldn't stand the look on his face.

"Courtney?" she called again, "it's getting late."

"I'm coming," Courtney said. She left the window and walked over to them. Her one large suitcase was by the door, next to it her typewriter in its traveling case. A slim leather pouch rested atop it, heavy with manuscript and notebooks. She looked at the luggage and then slowly toward Grady. Now, she said to herself, now Grady; say something, do something so that I won't leave. *Please*, please now.

"I guess it's time to be going," was what she said to him.

He nodded. "You have enough money?"

"I cashed a check."

"So did I. Here, take this," he said and handed her a bunch of bills pulled from his pocket.

"I don't need it. I—"

"I'd like you to take it. No point in getting caught short."

"Well," Tessa cut in, "I'll be waiting in the car."

"No, that's all right," Grady said softly. "I'll take this stuff downstairs." He reached for the luggage.

Courtney caught his arm and shook her head. "We'll manage," she said. She bent down and picked up the large case. She tucked the pouch under her arm.

"Well . . . Grady?" she asked, and the tone of her voice shook him to his soul. He wanted to reach out to her, to hold her, to keep her there, but he couldn't; he didn't dare. He kissed her on the forehead and smoothed her hair with his hand, then stepped back. They stared at each other, they saw each other's hurt, each other's need; they saw someting worse—impasse.

Courtney dropped her head and reached for the typewriter case. In a moment she was out the door.

Tessa looked at Grady and her face grew very still. She saw his look and she thought if it were true, as the poet said, that in this world the heart must either break or turn to stone, then Grady's heart would surely break. "I'll call you," she said to him. She picked up the last bit of Courtney's paraphernalia and walked out of the apartment, turning as she reached the head of the stairs. "You'll come have dinner with us tomorrow?" she asked, but the door had already closed.

Grady leaned against the closed door for a long while. "The lady's gone. She's . . . ," he said, and then tears came. Big, wet, sloppy tears splashed down his face and he let them come. He'd cried this way once before, when he'd been fourteen years old, and he hadn't forgotten, not for a moment through all the years that followed. He'd cried then as he cried now, and eventually those tears had stopped by themselves, leaving . . . leaving what? he asked himself. Leaving a man frightened, a man wary. He walked slowly from the door. He made a drink. Slowly, very slowly, he went to the couch and sat down.

"Courtney," he said, "oh, Courtney."

21

Tuesday was warm and muggy. A dark, heavy rain fell over the city . . .

SOMEHOW, time passed for Grady. On the first night of Courtney's absence he'd sat drinking until he saw the first rays of daylight in the sky; oddly sober, with an ache in his stomach, he'd showered and gone to work. On the second night he'd walked around the city for hours and then finally, at home, watched all of the late movies; it was past five when he lay down to sleep fitfully. On the third night he'd brought T.K. home, talking incessantly to the bird while the television set played, while he wore a path to the sideboard; there'd been four hours of sleep that night, deep, dreamless, besotted, and the next day he returned the bird and had no memory of the words he'd shared with the small, mute creature.

On the fourth night Grady was at home, stretched out on the couch, a drink in his hand, surrounded by noise and an awful brightness. The television set was turned up, as were the radio and the stereo, playing something of Paul Simon's; every light in the room was on, as were the lights in the bedroom and kitchen and bath. His mind was far, far away, and with his thoughts and the noise he didn't hear the knocking at the door until it became a pounding. He turned his head a little but didn't move. A second series of poundings came and then the third and, finally, he rolled his body from the couch and went to the door.

Tessa Gorlin stood there, a bulky parcel in her hand. "I could hear your apartment way down the street. Don't you have neighbors?" She smiled gently.

Grady shrugged. "We all live and let live."

"Can I come in?"

"Oh, sure. Help yourself," he said and stepped back. Tessa entered and walked directly to the kitchen. She returned after a moment and glanced around her. She hesitated and then went round the room, turning off four of the lamps. She turned the radio off and then went to the television set.

"What are you doing, Tessa?" Grady asked and fell onto the couch.

She switched off the television set and sat in a chair across from him. "That's better, I can hear myself."

He spoke without turning his head. "To what do I owe the honor? Did Nick send you over here to check on me?"

"Nick doesn't know I'm here. Instead of going to the New School tonight, I decided to pay you a call."

"The New School?" He glanced at her.

"I'm studying eighteenth-century Britain. I always was a history buff."

"Funny. What you don't know about people. Is that why you're so happy all the time?" he asked, staring up at the ceiling. "Filling up the time Nick's not home with . . . hobbies?"

"No hobbies, only things I enjoy. I take a few classes, I do a little windowbox gardening, I work for the Clinic, I'm on a couple of committees. I'm doing the City Hospital benefit again this year too. Those are things I enjoy. People still have lives after they marry, you know."

"No, I don't know."

"Do you know that Nick is deeply worried about you?" she asked quietly.

Grady's pale eyebrows moved up and down. "I'm deeply worried about myself. Have a drink? The stuff's over there."

"No thanks," Tessa said and looked closely at Grady. Nick had not exaggerated, she saw; Grady seemed to have aged in just these past few days. His face was drawn and there were terrible dark circles under his eyes. His fair skin was almost chalky and his eyes had the vacant, unseeing look one sometimes noticed in old people. Tessa sat back. "You're doing enough drinking for everybody, aren't you?"

Grady smiled slightly, only a bleak imitation of the real smile she knew. "Hell, I'm jes' an ole boy from Texas quenchin' his thirst. Usin' a little brother bourbon to do it," he drawled. He took a sip of his drink and wiped his mouth. He looked over at her. "What brings you here? Really."

"I wanted to see you. I wanted to see how you were doing."

"Behold how Grady is doing."

"I brought some steaks and a spinach thing I made. Hungry?"

"No."

"When did you eat last?"

"Tessa, let it go."

"When?"

"A little while ago. I had a hard-boiled egg."

Tessa pursed her lips and leaned forward. "It's a bad idea for you to be living alone. You're drowning in . . ."

"Self-pity? Say it, it's all right, it's the truth. What to do about it though, that's the rub."

"Why don't you go home for a while, a visit?"

"Texas? No thank you."

"Why don't you invite someone here? I've heard about your brothers, why don't you invite them up for a visit? Show them the town."

"All the tall buildings?" He smiled a little. "Maybe come fall, not that I'd get them here. Garth is always running to Europe, or to Chile to ski . . . and Logan, easy-going, placid old Logan, he loves the land, loves Texas. He'll never leave. All these years I tried to get him up here, no dice." Grady mused, "I remember . . . I remember once . . ." He began to laugh. "The year Logan graduated S.M.U. . . . my father, he said to Logan, 'Well, son, I expect you'd like to do some traveling, see a bit of the world,' and Logan allowed as how he might like that fine. So my father," Grady said and began laughing harder, "he says, 'Well, how would you feel about Europe?' And Logan says, 'Well, sir, I don't think so.' So my father says, 'Well, how about the Orient?' And Logan says, 'Well, no, sir, I don't think so.' About then my father starts to get a look on his face, like, speak up, boy, and he tries again. 'Well, son, how about Australia? How about South America? A boat through the Greek Isles? The Carribean? Hawaii? The West Indies?' My father is getting good and desperate about then and he throws up his hands and says, 'Well, son, there's Canada. Maybe you would like to visit Canada.' And Logan looks at him and says, 'Well, sir, what I had in mind was visiting San Antonio.' Man," Grady said, laughing hard now, "my father turned the colors of a Christmas tree. He grit his teeth and clenched his fists. Finally he said, 'Well, son, if that's what you want.' And stalked off, a discouraged man. That's Logan," Grady finished and wiped his wet eyes, his throat still caught with laughter.

Tessa laughed, but her concern was not abated. "Scratch Logan."

"Scratch Logan," Grady agreed. He reached to the table for the bottle and poured more bourbon into his glass. He took a large mouthful and then put the glass down, staring straight ahead of him.

"Grady, is it going to be all right?"

He didn't answer for a moment and then he looked at her. "I don't know. I don't think she'll be coming back. Maybe to get her things, but that's all. How am I going to be? I don't know."

"Why did you let her go?"

"*Let* her go? I have no damn right not to *let* her go. She wanted to go and she went. I always knew it was going to happen, it was just a question of when. I got the answer to my question."

"Always knew?"

"I knew, that's all. I knew our . . . how do they say that? Destinies? I knew our destinies weren't together. Friends is what we were meant to be, the rest was overreaching."

The frown on Tessa's brow deepened. She impatiently pushed her hair from her shoulders. She was still damp from the rain, she could have used a towel and some hot tea, but she didn't want to leave Grady now even for a moment. "All she wanted was for you to tell her not to go. All she wanted was to know you cared. Don't you understand that?" she asked.

"Sure I do. And sure I care. But, see . . . it was wrong, all of it. The only way I would have it was . . . free, for her, I mean. I wouldn't have her in a way that held her here . . . because in the end I wouldn't be able to hold her anyway. She'd leave anyway. I knew when she started getting restless, I knew she wanted more than I could give her. Or should. Because it wouldn't work out anyway, in the long run. As long as she wanted to stay here, that was fine. The moment she started thinking about going, it was time for her to go. Stop her now and lose her later? I couldn't take that."

"Why lose her later? What are you talking about?"

"I'm not my father," Grady said suddenly and reached for his glass. He drained it and then poured more bourbon into it while Tessa watched in deep confusion.

"What has your father to do with anything?"

"Tessa, you don't understand, nobody does. I found out . . . man, I was fourteen years old and I found out all I had to know."

"Whatever it is you think you found out . . . talk about it, for heaven's sake. Talk it out. Talk with Nick, he wants to help."

"Nick's a very strong man, like my father is a very strong man. It's hard . . . talking things through with strong men, their view is different. I go on the defensive."

Tessa was quiet. She got up and took a glass from the sideboard. She dropped a few ice cubes into it and added an inch of bourbon. She took a quick sip and made a face, then reached to the water pitcher and filled the glass a quarter of the way.

"I haven't kidded myself since then," Grady said, "and one thing I'm not going to do is present them with what they're expecting . . . spectacular failure. That's what would be with her, spectacular failure. Eventually."

"*Why*? Are you gay, is that what you're saying?"

Grady smiled slowly. "No, I'm not gay. Hell, that'd be simple, this is complicated. It goes back a long time . . . a long time of being told you're nothing. I always loved my people. What they said, what they believed was law to me, the Bible. I wanted nothing more than to grow up and be Lucas, to make a woman happy like he made my mother happy. To be the man who never failed at anything . . . business, friendships, love. Card games. I didn't grow up to be Lucas, the man no woman would ever leave. I wasn't even a shadow of my father . . . 'You better never fall in love, boy,' my mother would say, ' 'cause any woman with an ounce of sense is going to leave you straight off. You're weak, you need too much,' she'd say to me, 'like your granddaddy, Cyrus.' " Grady looked again at the ceiling. "Everybody knew about old Cyrus, he was kind of a local joke. They used to say there wasn't a woman here to Mexico who could stand him longer than a night, and they wouldn't stay that long if it wasn't for his money. Blood tells, I hear, and they tell me I have Cyrus Malory's blood."

Tessa, straining forward to hear every muted word, shook her head, trying to clear it, trying to make sense of what Grady said.

"I don't believe this," she said finally, quietly. "Not a word I'm hearing. You're saying that all these years you've written yourself off because of something your mother said to you? Because of someone named Cyrus?"

"When you've had something pounded into your head long enough, you begin to believe it. When it's been pounded into you that you're no good to anybody, and that everyone's going to catch on to you—the jig's up, kid—you begin to believe it. You say to yourself, hell, they're wrong. I know what I am and I'm better than that, but you don't *believe* it." Grady sipped his drink. "Not in your heart. Then you meet somebody, somebody you care about more than you care about anything in the world and, man, you panic. You're afraid to love at all, but it happens anyway and you do and you're really in torment. Waiting, just waiting for her to wake up one day and say she's leaving. And one day she wakes up and says she's leaving and you know the bastards were right all along. Oh," Grady said, "she stayed longer than a night, she stayed five years. But she left. Like I always knew she would."

"She left because you *made her leave*."

"No," Grady said quietly, "she left because it was inevitable."

"If I hadn't heard you say these things with my own ears . . . why did your mother say that anyway? What did she have against you?"

"Ah, that's a story. A new teacher came to town when I was about fourteen. Pretty young woman . . . and nice, you know? It was love at first sight." A faint smile came onto his face. "I would have killed for her . . . thus are the passions at fourteen. Anyway, I came back to the ranch one day . . . earlier than usual, I wasn't expected. I went into my father's den, I thought maybe we'd take a ride before dinner. I don't have to tell you what I found . . . who, more precisely. *My* schoolteacher and *my* father, right there on the big old leather couch. I was taken aback, I guess. And I was hurt . . . My father, my married-to-my-mother father, and *my* pretty schoolteacher lady. I ran. Ran and hid, and then later my mother came for me . . . found me crying. I don't know why, looking back, maybe it was the hurt, the disillusionment, but I told her the whole thing. I wanted to know why that was happening. Well, she smacked me so hard my head spun around twice. And she lit into me . . . But you know why she lit in to me? Because I was *talking bad* about Lucas Malory, a man all Texas loved and no one more than she . . . me, a kid who wasn't fit to lick his boots."

"She was hurt."

Grady nodded. "Later, much later, I realized that. Intellectually, but never in my heart. From that day on she kept on me, how worthless I was, how no one would ever love me for long . . . not the way they loved Lucas Malory." Grady paused. "She died about a year later. She knew she was dying, there was plenty of time for her to talk to me, take the words back . . . but she never did. The very last time I saw her all she said to me was, 'I pity you, boy.' "

Tessa sat back, her face very still. She said nothing, and Grady went on.

"About a year after that my father married again. He married the woman who'd been Mother's best friend. She knew exactly how my mother felt . . . and she picked up where my mother left off. When I started dating, bringing girls home to the ranch, she'd be there, reminding me that the only reason I got dates at all was 'cause I was Lucas' son." Grady sighed. "Do you think you don't start believing that after a while? Hell, after a while it's the air you breathe. So . . . you don't take chances, you don't risk getting found out, getting hurt . . . you do things for people to ingratiate yourself. . . . It's no accident, no God-given gift that I'm handier than any ten men. Want a bookcase built? Sure, I'll build it for you, because maybe then you'll like me. Want a twelve-course French dinner made? Sure, I'll make it for you. Want your TV fixed, your car tuned, your spring flowers planted, your chair recaned, your air conditioner installed? Sure, happy to, maybe then you'll like me. I *learned* to do things because it was the only way I knew to please people by myself."

"Grady—"

"And medicine," he said, oblivious to her now "I found medicine the end of that fourteenth year . . . and I grabbed at it because being a doctor would give me an identity. People would *need* me. I wouldn't be worthless to them . . . Then I meet a girl named Courtney and I was seventeen years old and the first thing I thought was, how long will it be before she walks away from me' And, 'Please, Lord, don't let me get involved because I can't stand the pain, not again.' "

"Where was your father through all of this?"

Grady smiled, his eyes very clear and fixed. "Lucas tried to make it better. . . . He was the happiest man in the world when he found out Courtney was living with . . . here. He thought she would give me confidence in myself. But I never, ever, believed for a moment that she'd . . . that she'd stay with me. Every time I let myself wonder, I'd hear my mother, my stepmother. So I never made any demands, didn't dare to, especially on Courtney. Not to fix dinner, nothing. Everything she did or didn't do was because she wanted it that way, that was my rule. For as long as it could last, might last." Grady stared down at the floor. "I couldn't stop her now to lose her later. I couldn't do it. It's what I feel inside me," he said, and the exhaustion in his voice was awful. "I know better than to feel it, but I feel it nevertheless. It'll always be with me. The fear. You don't know the fear," he said and then, without warning, he sailed his glass into the air, sending it crashing into the fireplace. Tessa rose quickly and went to Grady, sitting down next to him.

"Does Courtney know all this? Any of it?"

Grady shook his head and stood up. "No reason for her to know. No reason for you to tell her." He looked urgently at Tessa.

"I won't, if you don't want me to."

Grady went to the fireplace and knelt down, gathering up the bits of broken glass and brushing them into a small copper dustpan. "At least there's Frankie Carlino," he said and stood up again. "I look at him, improving day by day and I can still feel a shred of confidence in myself. Not much, but it's something. As long as he keeps developing I can feel I still have some identity." Grady leaned over the mantle and Tessa joined him. She took his hand and looked up at him.

"You're a very dear man, Grady."

"No, you're a soft touch."

Tessa smiled. "This soft touch has some steaks waiting in your refrigerator. Come, let's go into the kitchen and I'll—"

"I'll do it," Grady said, walking toward the kitchen, "How do you like your steak?"

The shadows were deep and dark in the alley and Frankie Carlino jumped around in them gleefully.

"Yeah, man, we go on Thursday," he said to Charley. "They got the shit in today . . . Thursday, Malory's on late duty. All alone," he leered. "And I got my friend ready," he added, sharp, shiny blade flashing. "Thursday night," he slapped Charley's palm, "and we get the bastards. The bastards, the bastards," he sang into the empty night, "we get 'em all."

It was only slightly past ten o'clock in Washington, but the town was already falling silent. Streets were dim, traffic was light and restaurants were preparing to close; all was quiet. It wasn't a nighttime place, and the enormous stillness made Courtney sad for New York, for Grady. The days had not been bad, but the nights—she'd begun to understand how bad the nights could be.

She wore a cream-colored skirt and a pale blue blouse; her hair was tied back from her face with a blue ribbon. She sat in her hotel studio, in a space separated from the sleeping area by a wide, fluted divider. Across from her, head hunched over the desk, fingers slowly striking the keys of her typewriter, sat Peter Joshua. She gazed at the back of his head and then looked hurriedly away. She didn't want to see him, didn't want to think about him or even about their work. She was growing tired, tired of his liquor, his strange fragile words and speeches and nuances—tired of their book even as she knew it was the best thing she'd ever done. She heard the steady click-click of the typewriter until she thought she would scream; she didn't want to know what he was writing, what corrections he was making, she only knew she wished he would stop, would go away, *would leave her alone.*

Courtney had arrived in Washington and gone alone to her hotel and to a tense night. She'd cried a great deal that first night, a hundred times going to the telephone, a hundred times walking away; she'd slept little and had been grateful for daylight. The next day she'd organized herself and her material and set to work, working straight through until Peter Joshua joined her. They'd worked together then, working well together, ideas and characters and emotions flowing between them and then onto paper. Peter had left, reluctantly, and she'd tossed around in bed until she gave in and swallowed a couple of pills. In the morning she was very nervous, as if every fiber in her body was standing on edge; she drank a large amount of wine with lunch and again that night when she and Peter had dinner and then got to work. Somehow she got through the twenty-four hours. The third day was all work, she didn't leave the hotel at all, and that night she was short with Peter; after he left she took a very hot bath and paced around and didn't sleep at all—she read Thomas McGuane until it was light outside.

This day—the fourth day—had come and she'd risen early, renting a car and driving into Virginia. In beige slacks and an old sweater, her hair flying free, her bare feet on the pedals, she'd driven the convertible up and down the strange streets and roads, stopping here to look at a pretty McLean farmhouse, there to look at a graceful old Alexandria townhouse. She'd enjoyed it all; the nervousness was gone, she felt a headiness that gave her a funny feeling in her chest. She'd driven back to the hotel and changed her clothes. She had lunch at the Sans Souci and hoped a senator would come in, was elated when she recognized a congressman from Missouri. She wandered through Georgetown, browsing leisurely until she saw a tiny, filigreed antique store. There she saw an old pewter penstand, which she bought for Peter. She saw a small, beautiful, Renaissance angel and bought it for Grady, and then her mood had changed. She returned quickly to her hotel, thinking what did anything matter when she still wanted to buy Renaissance angels for Grady. She called the Clinic; Dr. Malory was in a staff meeting, did she want to leave a message? No. She called her parents, but that didn't help. She called an old friend who lived in Washington but hung up before the first ring. Tessa wasn't home, and then she cried when she thought there was no one else to call. And then she began to work again, forcing the words, forcing her fingers to get the words to paper. And then Peter Joshua came, a bottle of Scotch in one hand, a sheaf of notes in another.

And now it was slightly past ten o'clock in Washington and Courtney was sad for New York, for Grady. She fingered the angel and put it down. She looked at the phone a long time, and then looked at it no more. "What?" she said absently.

"Don't you want to see this?" Peter was asking, and vaguely she heard the words, "I made a few changes in the scene where Aleda meets Johnny Tom."

"Johnny Tom?" Courtney mumbled and then looked at Peter. "No. I don't want to see it."

"I'll read it to you."

"No," she said quickly and then smiled because she saw the enthusiasm in his eyes. "Not now. Tomorrow, maybe. I don't want to do that now."

Peter crossed his long, long legs and leaned over the back of his chair. "What does the Lady of the Shadows want to do? Maybe there's a good wake in town. Could I interest you in a good wake? Or how about a good vigorous walk around the terminal cancer ward?"

His tone was light, almost casual, but she heard an anger under it all and she looked at him apologetically. "I'm sorry, I didn't mean to be depressing."

"Why are you? We're doing the work we wanted to do and it's good. It's good, Courtney and it's us, you and me against it all."

She was quiet for a moment and then shook her head. "It's not working, Peter. It's not working."

"You don't mean the book, you mean something else. You mean you're not happy."

"I mean I'm not happy."

Peter took a sip of his drink. "You're not trying."

"I don't want to try, I just want to be."

"It's a period of adjustment, Courtney Ames, not an emergency."

Courtney smiled a little and reached across the space

between them to take the typed pages from his hand. "You're right. It's not an emergency."

"Like all the rest of the world, you'll adjust," Peter said and drained his glass. He reached for the bottle and Courtney stood up.

"But I'd like you to go now."

Peter looked at her quickly, the cool light again in his eyes. "Don't be polite on my account."

"Sorry, but I want you to go. Now. I'll read the pages later. Or tomorrow."

Peter stood up. "Why won't you move your things over to my house and let us be done with all this going and coming?"

"No. This is where I'm staying and this is where we'll do the work."

He put the tip of his finger under her chin and tilted her head up to him. "Do you think I'll throw you down on my bed and ravage your hutch?" he smiled.

"Don't be rude." She walked away from him.

"The Rape of Courtney's Hutch. I think I'll write a short story and call it—"

"Go home, Peter. I'll see you tomorrow."

"Guilt. The mother of us all." He smiled broadly and went to the door. He turned back to look at her. "On behalf of all us Elks I'd like to say thanks for a—"

"Go *home*, Peter," she said and then heard the door close. She put the pages on the desk and sat down, her chin cupped in her hand. It would get easier, she told herself; she wouldn't always be running across Renaissance angels to buy for Grady, she'd learn not to mind when she saw a man and woman smiling at each other. It would get easier. Courtney rose, hesitating, looking again at the phone.

"All you have to do is call," she said to it. She stood there, watching it as if it would ring if only she willed it to. There was no sound and she walked away.

"Forget it, Grady. Forget it," she said aloud.

For a while she paced the length of the room. Then

impatiently she grabbed the newly typed pages and carried them to the bed. She sprawled across it and spread the pages before her, squinting in concentration. It was no good; she didn't care about Aleda and Johnny Tom, not then.

Courtney crawled across the bed and flipped on the television set, turning the volume up loud. She watched absently for fifteen minutes and then gave it up, crawling over to the other side of the bed to reach for a paperback Louis Auchincloss. She read, her head swiveling around every few seconds to glance at the telephone. After a while she got up and covered the phone with two large bath towels. She began to laugh, and then she cried.

Later, much later, lying in bed, the covers pulled close around her, she felt the exhaustion and, at last relaxed, slept deeply.

22

The pace of the city increased as fall neared; the doctors were busy . . .

GRADY left an examination room and walked quickly into the corridor. His head was bent, his eyes scanning a lab sheet, and he didn't see Nick, equally preoccupied, coming from the opposite direction. They walked into each other.

"Sorry," Grady said. "I was just going to find you."

"You look terrible. How many times do I have to tell you to go home?"

"Take a look at the woman in three, will you?" Grady said and handed the lab sheet to Nick. "This and what I felt in her stomach tells me she needs a hospital."

"All right," Nick said, hurrying away, "but I don't want to see you here when I'm finished. Go home!"

Grady walked to the desk. "Who's next?"

"Mrs. Nadez is waiting in room one. She asked for you. Hey, are you okay?"

"Rosa Nadez? Tony is her husband?"

"That's right."

"She's really Nick's patient."

"She asked for you."

"Well, okay, give me her—" he began, and Jim held out her chart. Grady took it, looked over it briefly, and then went to the room.

Rosa Nadez had a fresh bandage on her cheek, a small cut at the side of her mouth, and tired, troubled eyes. She played nervously with a tissue, twisting it, pulling at it, the small shreds falling into her lap.

Grady took a breath and raised his eyes up, away from the woman; he knew without asking that Tony had been at her again, and he didn't want to hear about it. He was in no mood to hear her troubles, he didn't want to go through it again. He sighed and sat down, flipping open her chart. She brought one timorous hand to his and stopped his movement, her eyes pleading.

He saw she wanted to talk and he listened to her. For twenty minutes of strained, tortured English underlining her own strain, her own torment, he listened carefully, saying nothing, his face terribly pale in the harsh light. He was deeply affected by her words, by her hurt and her fear, and he had to catch himself, force himself to keep control over his emotions. When he felt able to speak, he leaned closer to her. He talked slowly, softly, patting her hand and making himself smile. Finally he wrote a note on his prescription pad and gave it to her. She gazed at it a long time and then looked back at him. He nodded at her reassuringly and said a few words, and then she stood and he opened the door for her. He watched her walk from the room, and then he took a step into the corridor, stopping when he felt a wave of dizziness come over him. He was very pale and his heart beat rapidly; he put an arm out to steady himself against the wall.

Jim, watching from the desk, picked up the phone and pressed hard on a button. He spoke rapidly into the phone, nodded, and then left the desk, rushing to Grady. He eased him back into the room, toward the chair, and when he felt Grady stumble, he lifted him in one strong sweep to the examination table. Grady tried to speak, but Jim paid no attention; he took Grady's pulse, and then his pressure.

Nick burst into the room. "I'll take over. Get a City ambulance for the woman in three. Call Dr. Cord and tell him I'll call him as soon as I can about her. Tell him to start a complete blood workup and stand by in O.R. . . . What's his pressure?"

"140 over 80. Pulse is over a hundred."

"Okay, get going. Come back when you're finished," Nick said and turned to Grady. "You're the shoemaker's child." He reinflated the pressure cuff. He watched the needle carefully and let it drop. He put his stethoscope to Grady's chest and shook his head. He looked into Grady's eyes with his light, pulling the lids apart. When he was finished he drew a deep breath and stepped back. "How do you feel?"

"I got dizzy, suddenly. My stomach was rocky this morning, maybe I've got a bug."

"The no-sleep-no-food-too-much-booze bug. You've heard of it?"

"I've heard."

"Good. Now I'll tell you how we cure it. We shoot you full of vitamins, give you some mild sedation and throw you in bed. We wake you up for food and then it's back to sleep. And we don't listen to any arguments."

"Maybe I've got a virus."

"What you've got is a hole in the head. A doctor treating his own body so badly. Ten, twelve years of training and you don't know any better than this, what am I supposed to do with you? I could put you in the hospital, you know. I could do that right now. Is that what you want?"

"No, no hospitals, I'll do as you say. I'll go home and get some rest. I'll stay in bed today and tonight."

"And tomorrow."

"Please, Nick. If I'm feeling better I'd rather be here. I sit alone in that apartment and I get depressed. That's when I pour some bourbon. Please."

"Maybe you're right. We'll see how you feel tomorrow. But you're not leaving your place until I check you. Agreed?"

"Agreed."

"We'll bring some decent food around tonight and you'll eat it."

"All right." He was tired and a little scared; he wouldn't argue.

Jim entered the room then and Nick ordered B-12 and iron and twenty milligrams of Valium. Jim left and Grady turned to Nick.

"Can I sit up now?"

"Wait until I give you your shots."

Grady wiped his forehead, pushing the curls back from his face. "Mrs. Nadez was in. She said she was ashamed to see you, so I saw her."

"What's the problem? Tony?"

"In a way . . . I wrote it all in her chart. She's sure she's pregnant and she wants an abortion. The way Tony is she's afraid he'll . . ."

"Forget it for now. We'll take care of everything."

"I sent her to Dr. Meyers."

"Bellevue?"

Grady nodded. "He's heading the OB/GYN service now."

"Grady, would you rather stay at our place?"

"No, I'm just going to sleep, it doesn't matter where I am. As long as I can get back to work tomorrow."

Jim came in and handed two syringes and a couple of tablets to Nick. Grady rubbed his eyes, feeling a great fatigue come over every part of him; he was so weary he didn't feel the needles at all.

Clovis stood at the door of the doctors' office, waiting for Nick to look up from his desk. He shuffled his feet and then kicked at the wall. The last sound got Nick's attention.

"Clovis, what are you standing out there for? Come in if you want to speak to me."

"I hear Cowboy sick," he said and walked into the office.

"A little, yes."

"What he has?"

Nick looked up from the papers on his desk and stared curiously at the child. "What do you care?"

"I asks you what Cowboy has."

"And I want to know why you care. The way you treat him . . . I didn't think you'd care if he was sick . . . I thought you'd be glad."

"I ain't never says Cowboy should be sick. I asks you straight, what he has?"

Nick shook his black head and smiled at the boy. "If you'd only give in and admit you like Dr. Malory. It's not against the law to show you have feelings, you know." He sighed. "*Cowboy* is tired, that's all. He'll get a good night's sleep and he'll be fine. Clovis . . . do you really care?"

"I asks you, didn't I?"

"Yes . . . yes, you did. It's—" he said and stopped, seeing Frankie walking down the corridor to the office. Clovis turned around and saw Frankie; he glared at him.

"Here come the big cheese," Clovis said, disparaging eyes on the older boy. Frankie looked at him and then away, staring at Nick, and it was apparent to them that he was agitated.

"They just told me about Grady. Is it bad? How long is he out for?"

Nick sat back in his chair and crossed his arms over his chest. "The Malory fan club," he said, looking from

Clovis to Frankie. "He'll be fine, just needs a night's sleep."

"Just tonight? I mean, he'll be back tomorrow?"

"Probably."

"Not definitely?" Frankie prodded.

Nick laughed at the boy's insistence, but Clovis eyed him suspiciously. "What you care about tomorrow fors?"

"Nick?" Frankie asked again, paying no attention to Clovis.

"Probably definitely," Nick said. "Now, if you two don't mind, I have work to do. How about it?"

"He mean we should gets lost," Clovis said to Frankie, and they both took a step toward the door.

Frankie looked back. "You sure it ain't serious?"

"I'm sure. Now as Clovis said, get lost." He smiled and waved them from the room.

They walked to the elevator. Clovis didn't take his eyes from Frankie. A question stirred in his mind, and though he was unsure what question it was, he was sure of his own uneasiness, sure it had something to do with the boy who stood beside him.

"Hey," he said as they entered the elevator, "why for you so hassled about Cowboy? What you care what day he coming back? You acting strangest than usual, Mr. Frankie Carlino."

"Mind your own business, Sambo, I got things on my mind," Frankie snapped and, indeed, his eyes were dark with concentration.

"Yeah? What things you has on your mind? Whatever you be up to, it be no damn good, I tells you that much."

Frankie's hand jumped out to silence the boy, but just at that moment the door opened and he saw an aide waiting to step into the elevator. Frankie nodded to the aide and walked briskly away, forgetting the child who stared after him, suspicion etched on his small face.

23

It was the eleventh evening of September; it was Thursday. A sliver of moon hung in the sky, here and there a jagged diamond star danced. The evening was still of summer, a summer they—a few of them—would remember until they were very old and there were no more summers . . .

NICK returned to the Clinic from City at seven o'clock. He went directly to his office, to meet Grady and Brian and to review a few matters before he took a rare night off. He was in a good mood, for it had occurred to him that afternoon that despite the problems they'd had, were still having, the Clinic was functioning well. They were doing what they'd set out to do, they were serving the neighborhood. In time, he thought to himself, they'd be fully accepted as friends, as allies, but for now they were making their way, having their impact. Only that morning there'd been a call from some people in Philadelphia who wanted to form a Gorlin Clinic. "Would you help train our doctors in neighborhood medicine?" they'd asked. "Yes," he'd replied and meant it. "I'd be very glad to." There'd been a long, long letter from a neighborhood association in Cleveland—they'd read about the Clinic and wanted particulars. The check from Joint Charities was safely tucked in the Clinic account, and, most surprising of all, the elders of the A.M.A. convention board had scheduled time for Nick to present the Clinic paper. Nick saw it all forming now, taking shape as he had dreamed it could for so many years; the dream was no longer a passionate fantasy, it was a living, feeling truth.

Nick allowed himself a broad smile as he entered the office. "I have good tidings," he said and looked at Grady. "But before I get to that . . . how do you feel?"

"Better, Nick. The sleep helped."

"You're still pale, are you sure you want to take the night shift?"

"I want to. Brian said he'd stay, keep me company."

"What's the good news?" Brian asked.

"The . . . A.M.A.," Nick said slowly, enjoying every word, "has agreed to let us present our paper in convention. It's scheduled, on the agenda. *We made it.*" He laughed.

Grady smiled happily and even Brian looked pleased. They got up and went to Nick, shaking hands. "When?" Grady asked.

"Next Tuesday afternoon. That's the second day, the best day."

"You'll knock 'em dead," Grady said. "Are we all agreed this is the final paper?" he asked, rooting around on his desk until he found a copy.

"That's it. We can send it out for typing and copying. And I'll tell you, it's not going to hurt our case that we got the grant from Joint . . . ," Nick said and then stopped, regretting his words.

"Joint Charities," Grady said in a cool, hard voice. "You can *say* it, for Christ's sake."

Nick looked away and then went to his desk, sitting atop it. "All right, Joint Charities isn't going to hurt our case. It gives us a legitimacy we need for those fogeys."

"I think the report will stand on its own merits. The section on preventive medicine has got to get to them. Reducing the hospital load, reducing the welfare rolls, they'll understand that," Brian said, his gray eyes thoughtful.

"It's all there," Grady said. "Dollars and cents, pros and cons. You can talk to them and put it all on the table. How are you going to celebrate?"

"I'm spending the evening with my wife. The whole evening, for a change. What a luxury."

"Then get to it, time's flying." Grady smiled.

Nick looked at him. "You're sure you're all right?"

"Fine. Fine, fine, fine. Go home."

Nick looked at Brian. "Take care of the kid," he said lightly, but Brian saw the concern in his eyes and he nodded. Nick went to the door. "Enjoy yourselves."

"Don't you worry about that," Grady said. "We're going to have a high old time. Aren't we, Brian?"

Nick waved over his shoulder as he went out.

As Nick left the Clinic, Tessa Gorlin, twenty blocks away, put a casserole into the oven and checked that the bottle of white wine was in the refrigerator; Courtney Ames, in Washington, paced up and down the length of her hotel room; Marie Carlino, on Fifth Street, stepped from the shower and began dressing for her class, the last of the summer schedule; Anna Carlino left for a bingo game; Frankie Carlino, Charley at his side, placed a last-minute phone call to the leader of the Devils; Clovis Williams left his mother and the television set, slung his windbreaker over his shoulder, and walked out onto Avenue B; Grady and Brian went downstairs to the basement where they would stay unless and until a patient rang the night bell.

The streets were in shadows, murky cobwebs of darkness spreading spindly fingers over the blackened pavements. Threads of moonglow bounced off the few cars, the trash cans, the curbside garbage, the brown tenements of the Lower East Side. It was too dark to see the roaches, the mice, the rats, the cats who chased the rats; too dark to see more than an outline of the two or three junkies who sat in doorways, high for the night; too dark to notice the old man who wandered from garbage can to garbage can, filling his shopping bags; too dark, for the streetlight had been knocked out by a bunch of kids and a bunch of rocks three weeks before and hadn't yet been replaced by the City.

Eleven o'clock at night and Marie Carlino walked up the stairs from the subway and stepped into that darkness—tired, too tired to see it or feel it or care about it. It was only another night, another unhappy night of which the best that could be said was that it was the last of the classes that twice a week all summer had confirmed that she'd never be a particularly good secretary, perhaps not a particularly good anything. But Mama was counting on her and she'd have to try. For Mama. Though she didn't want to—God, how she didn't want to. She thought of Jimmy who was a clerk, her Jimmy . . . only he wasn't her Jimmy anymore. Not anymore at all, because Mama said so. He didn't call anymore, didn't come around; he was gone, and she wondered if she'd ever find a boy to feel about the way she felt about Jimmy. The funny way, like when he touched the back of her neck.

Such were her thoughts—tired, deprived, bereaved little lonelinesses—as she neared the end of the street. She was accustomed to the neighborhood, used to it, for she'd never known another, but this was a part of the street she passed warily, for at the end of the street, running left to right, was a small, black alley, and she passed it now as she always passed it—as far from its entrance as she could get. She walked those five steps rapidly, anxious to be away from its clouded mouth, and with her sixth step she relaxed, again walking slowly. It was on her seventh step that she felt the hand on her arm, rough, demanding, and she screamed. She screamed once, but then there was a hand on her mouth and she was swung around in one violent push. She saw them then and her eyes grew huge in her terror. There were five of them; the five and the one holding her dragged her back and into the alley, into the blackness, into anguish, into the loathsome hurt.

Only the thinnest shaft of moonlight penetrated into the darkness, but it was enough. Enough for her to see. And she saw it all, drunken, evil faces, young faces so twisted with malice that they were aged; she saw the roll of white tape one boy held and the heavy chain held by another; she saw the strange, long metal rod and she saw the box of kitchen matches. She saw their eyes, and that was the worst of all, for she knew then what was to happen to her and she wished for death, prayed for it, as every inch of her body convulsed and trembled and tried to wrest free.

They beat her first. They beat her brutally and thoroughly, until their excitement was at its peak, and then they ripped away her remaining clothing, shrieking as they threw torn cloth into the balmy evening. They did unspeakable things to her poor young body; the night was very long.

Frankie stepped away from the shadows among the buildings across the street from the alley. He nodded to Charley.

"You can call the Clinic now. We go now."

Charley looked again in the direction of the alley and turned back to Frankie. "Man, I don't dig this. I don't dig this."

"We find a phone booth now, man. You call."

"We got a bunch of trouble already. Yeah, we bought us real trouble. Them Devils, they—"

"C'mon, man. You got no choice now. You're in."

Charley followed Frankie down the street and to the

corner. There, he looked anxiously up and down the street as Frankie slammed open the door of the booth.

"Hey man, I don't know about this . . . I don't know," he said in a voice pitched high with fear. This was more than he'd bargained for, and he felt the shock of it now for the first time. He would run, he told himself; the moment he saw his chance, he'd run.

"Make the call," Frankie said, holding out a piece of paper with the Clinic number on it. "Make it!" he said viciously. "Nigger," he added slowly.

"Okay. Okay, man." He walked into the booth and dialed The Gorlin Clinic.

"Who is this call—" Grady was asking when he heard the phone go dead. He shrugged and replaced the receiver on the basement wall set.

"Somebody says there's a girl lying in the Third Street alley. I better get my bag."

"Why don't you call an ambulance?" Brian asked.

"No. Ten to one it's an overdose, and the only reason people call us is because they know we don't call in hospitals unless it's absolutely necessary," Grady said, walking to the stairs.

"Wait a minute. I'll go, my bag's right here."

"Sure?"

"Yes," Brian said, checking quickly through his bag. "You don't mind being alone?" he asked at the stairs.

"No. I wonder what happened to the kids, though . . . It's mysterious, like someone posted a keep-out sign."

"See you," Brian said and rushed out.

Frankie and Charley, coming from the opposite direction, saw the flash of a man and a medical bag round the corner. Frankie smiled at Charley. "See? Told you it'd work. Big shot Malory on his way . . . you got all the stuff?"

"I got the flashlight and the plastic bags, like you says me to."

"We're rollin' now, man," Frankie said as they stood two steps from the Clinic entrance. They saw a light in the basement, but that wasn't unusual, and they continued on their way, opening the front door very quietly, stepping lightly on their sneakered feet. Frankie entered first and went immediately to the desk, using his switchblade to cut the main telephone line. He began to walk away and then turned back, carving a great gash in the desk's surface.

"Hey, man, let's do it if we're doing it," Charley whispered.

"We're doin' it," Frankie said and walked stealthily to the stairway. They got as far as the fifth step when the flashlight slipped from Charley's wet hands and fell noisily to the tiled stairs. Frankie picked it up impatiently and glared at Charley.

"Damn nigger," he growled as they went upstairs, the flashlight guiding their way.

In the basement, Grady looked up and went to the stairs. He was sure he'd heard something, but it was a sound he couldn't identify. Frowning, he left the basement and went to the ground floor. He looked to the entrance, thinking it might be a patient who couldn't find the night bell; he heard nothing more and he shrugged. He was on his way back to the basement when he heard another sound. It was not loud, but in the quiet of the Clinic it was clear; it sounded like something bumping into something, and Grady looked toward the stairway. Still frowning, he started upstairs. He reached the second floor and saw nothing, the third and fourth, and then he heard another sound, the sound of something scraping. Grady reached the fifth floor and stopped stock still when he saw the boys at the entrance to the supply room. When he saw the flashlight, he realized what they were about. He took a few quick steps to the stairway but he wasn't quick enough, for the boys had heard him and Charley had dashed after him, throwing himself on Grady's back. Grady staggered, tried to get his elbow into Charley's ribs, and then finally, getting his balance, he managed to throw Charley off. He slammed Charley against the wall and smashed his fist into Charley's jaw; the boy slid to the ground. Grady whirled, panting, and then he saw Frankie Carlino. His mouth fell open, his eyes just stared, for he saw Frankie coming at him; he saw all the hatred, the murderous hatred.

They stalked each other, ducking and moving warily as both tried to find an advantage. Grady landed a blow, but Frankie spun away and then there was a sharp click and the terrifying glint of a fine, very sharp blade.

Clovis was uneasy; he'd been uneasy for the past two days, uneasy over something he couldn't identify. Tonight he'd been the most bothered of all. Something was wrong and he felt it, felt it with all the cunning and radar and instinct of street-wise children. It had to do with the Clinic, with the Cowboy, he knew that much, and it ate at him, nagging him, making him pace the dark streets for hours, bringing him now to this place—to the broad, decaying stoop across the street from The Gorlin Clinic. He'd been there five minutes, listening, staring, puffing continuously on the cigarettes he'd stolen from his mother's purse. His child's face was closed in concentration as he tried to figure out what was wrong. His eyes were narrowed, thoughtful, about to turn away, when he saw it—a waving, careening light that flickered around in the lowered lights of the fifth floor. Cowboy's floor, he thought to himself, and he knew this was Cowboy's late night. He hesitated, but only briefly, for now he was certain something was wrong. "Docker Gorlin," he said out loud, "I haves to find Docker Gorlin." But he didn't know how, or where, and he ran across the street. Four steps from the Clinic door he remembered, and hastily he scrambled down to the basement window and lit a match so he could read the tiny print that appeared on a small red seal. There was a telephone number on the seal, an emergency number. The number was identified as the superintendent's, but Clovis knew better—he knew the Clinic superintendent had lasted only one week and hadn't been replaced, that the number had to belong to Nick Gorlin. Clovis fumbled through his pockets and came up with a piece of green chalk, quickly copying the number onto the matchbook cover. He ran then, ran the block and a half to the nearest phone booth and rushed inside. He jumped and dropped his dime in. He couldn't reach to dial but he managed the O, getting an operator who got him the number. It rang once, then twice, and on the third ring it was answered.

"Hello," Tessa said.

"I needs to talk to Docker Gorlin."

"He went out to get a paper, can I . . . who's this?"

"This be Clovis. From the Clinic. Where I can find him?"

"He'll be back in a few minutes, he just went to get a paper. What's the matter?"

"Now what I'm supposed to do, lady?" Clovis said angrily and jumped up to disconnect the line. He found another dime but held it in his hand, staring at it. "I should call the policemans," he said, his face twisted in disgust. "She-et, Clovis Williams calling the policemans . . . that don't make no sense. Not Clovis Williams," he muttered, but then he looked back in the direction of the Clinic and shook his head. He jumped again and with effort dialed the 911 himself. He told the police to come, to come in a hurry, and then he left the receiver dangling as he dashed back to the Clinic. He wasted no time, but galloped the stairs three at a time until he reached the fifth floor.

Nick walked into the apartment and tossed the newspaper on the couch.

"Tessa?" he called.

Tessa rushed out of the bedroom, and Nick saw she'd changed out of her robe into slacks and a blouse. "I'm glad you're back."

"What's the matter?"

"Someone named Clovis called. He sounded very agitated. I called the Clinic to see if anything was wrong and I didn't even get a ring . . . it's as if the phone was dead."

"Dead? . . . That's strange. Did you have the operator check it?"

"Yes, she didn't get anything either."

Nick's eyes clouded; worry began to creep into his expression, "Did you call the police?"

"No, I—"

"Call them," Nick said, hurrying to the door. "I'm going down there."

Tessa started for the bedroom. "All right, but I'm going with you."

"Hurry up. I'll get a cab."

There was blood all over the floor, a little spattered on the wall. An office chair had been smashed and there were pieces of glass all around the area. Clovis took a minute to look carefully at the situation, sifting it expertly through his mind, for he knew he'd have only one chance. Grady and Frankie were rolling around on the floor, Grady kicking and flailing, holding Frankie off as Frankie lashed out with his knife. Grady was bleeding from the shoulder, his clothing torn, his face badly cut; he was breathing heavily, straining for air as Frankie loomed above him. At that moment another boy, a young black boy Clovis didn't know, rose unsteadily from the floor. He reached into his pocket and then there was a sharp click; Frankie had a hold on Grady now and the other boy, Charley, stood over him, the knife in his hand only a breath away from Grady's back.

Clovis took something from his pocket and sprang, his small body catching Charley from behind, pulling him backward into the thrust of the knife he held firmly in his small fist. Charley groaned and slipped off Grady, his eyes wide and distended, dumb with surprise. Everything stopped; Frankie, his knife very near, froze; Grady stared; Charley's body was still. Clovis bent down and pulled his knife from Charley's flesh, wiping the blood on his jeans. The child looked at Frankie, but as he did so Frankie's face colored a deep, horrible red and he lunged. Grady screamed and it was a terrible sound in the night.

Nick and Tessa arrived on a street crowded with ambulances, with blue and white police cars, red flashing lights. Every window around them was open, heads clustered over every sill. Policemen, dozens of policemen, ringed the Clinic entrance, keeping back the people who'd gathered to watch the procession of white-jacketed attendants. Nick and Tessa pushed their way through the crowd and identified themselves to the police; they ran to the Clinic.

"Stay out here," Nick said to Tessa. "Until I see what's going on."

"Nick—"

"*Please*," he said, and she nodded. He was about to enter the Clinic when a stretcher was carried out, the body covered with a sheet. Nick stopped the bearers and pulled the cover back from the face. It was a boy he didn't know, it was Charley, and he redraped the body and let the stretcher pass.

A second stretcher, its cargo uncovered, approached, and he saw it was Frankie Carlino, a long, deep gash on his face barely concealed by quick, crude bandaging. Nick stared down at the boy, and for the first time in his memory he felt hate. He waved the attendant on and went inside, oblivious to the huge cry of the sirens as two ambulances took off down the street. Nick brushed by two policemen and entered the ground floor. He saw a small, black child being led from the E.R. by a policeman.

"Clovis!" Nick kneeled to him. "Are you all right? Where are Grady and Brian?" he cried, but then, from a corner of his eye, he saw Brian. "Are you all right, Clovis?"

"I be okay," the child said. He was led outside and Nick rushed into the E.R. He saw Brian leaning over a chair in which Grady sat, slumped. Grady was white, white as winter, his chest and shoulder seeping blood through his bandages. Nick gasped and Brian turned around, his face, too, deathly pale.

"He refused a stretcher," Brian said in a low, strained voice. "We have to get him to a hospital."

Grady struggled to his feet. "Nick? . . . I . . . it . . ." Grady could stand no more and collapsed to the ground.

"Grady? . . . Grady! . . . Help me, *help me*, for God's sake," Nick cried to the attendants around him. Very gently, they lifted Grady into the ambulance.

Courtney parked the tan convertible in front of a small, white house in Georgetown. She got out and checked the house number against the slip of paper she held in her hand. She nodded once and then reached inside the car for several bulky manila envelopes. She crossed the narrow street and banged the brass door knocker. It was a moment before Peter Joshua opened the door.

"I suppose I should have called," she said.

He opened the door wider. "Come in." He smiled. "All this time I've been maneuvering to get you over here and you come of your own will. People are fascinating animals. Some wine?"

"No, thanks. Is this a bad time?"

"Courtney Ames, I'm between women, between pets, between visits from children. I'm all alone in my pretty house."

She looked around and was not surprised by what she saw. It was an elegant house, elegant as Peter was elegant. The couches were fine tweed, the chairs dark, rich leather; there were two beautiful Impressionist oils and exquisite Chippendale sidetables. There was a fine old Federalist fireplace and the wood floors gleamed around the edges of a striking Persian rug. She smiled a little sadly, for she realized more about the house than its beauty; she sensed the emptiness of the house, as if its pale walls had never heard laughter or gentleness, had never seen tenderness or quiet.

She sat in an Eames chair and looked at him. "It's beautiful."

"Just something I threw together. I don't see us living here, though. I see a big, glass beachhouse. All peace and good things. Writing our books as we watch the ocean. At night, a fire, Bach playing softly, Keats to read."

"Don't talk that way," she said gently. She took a package from one of the envelopes and handed it to him. He stared at it for a moment before opening it. "Is it a present?"

"Yes," she said, and suddenly his face became very soft and a little sad.

"What's the matter?" Courtney asked. "Don't you like it?"

"I love it. Because it's beautiful. And because you gave it to me. No one . . . ," he said and looked away. "Forty-two year-old men are very foolish, Courtney Ames."

"I didn't know when I bought it . . . but it's a going-away present."

"Going away? Away where?" he asked.

"Home."

"I don't understand. This is your home. Your home

is where we can be together and write and discover some small part of what we are. I've tried very hard to find a way to you, Courtney. I've left you alone, I haven't pushed you, because I knew you would see the truth of us. We're an answer. A promise."

She shook her head. "My home is Grady. He's my promise. I had to come all the way to Washington to figure that out. It's beautiful work we've done . . . but I can't fool myself, Peter. It's *your* work. Any craftsman would take your beautiful words, your beautiful tragedy, and make it into a book. If you don't find someone to do it, if you don't do it yourself, then you *are* a fool. . . . But I am going home."

"To New York."

"To New York."

"You still have problems in New York, old kiddo."

She smiled. "I know, old kiddo. But I'm up to them now. I understand more than I did . . . before. People don't grow all at once. They grow in stages, and they need help. Someone told me that . . . I didn't understand."

"You can leave our work?" he asked coolly.

"I tried, Peter, really I did. But I'm going where I belong. Sometimes people have to travel a long way to find their way home. I know you understand that, in a way it's what you write about. Your characters never find their way, that's their sadness. . . . Maybe my sadness will be over, most of it." She smiled gently. "I hope you finish your book. I'll buy a hundred copies and I'll cheer. I'll be proud for you. But I'm leaving. I'll miss you a little," she said softly. "I'll worry about you . . . Peter so sad, so bitter. I'll wonder about you . . . what work you've done, what work abandoned . . . what good has come to you, what harm."

"Back to your bloodless little stories, your bloodless little life."

"It's not so bad. Not really so bad at all," she said softly. "Everything's here," she said and put the envelopes on the slate coffee table. "There's a note inside. It explains better than I have." She stood up then, smiling almost wistfully at Peter. "Do your book. Let all that pain come out."

"You'll be back, Courtney Ames. If for no other reason than that the last shuttle is long gone for New York. And tomorrow—"

"I've rented a car." She walked over to him and kissed him lightly. "I won't be back," she said and went to the door. She stopped then and looked back. "Peter, I'm sorry . . . sorrier than I can say, if I've harmed your dream."

He stared at her for a long moment and then turned away. She could barely hear his words. "We could have been something fine. You're a coward, though. I will always believe that because I must. The ego rises . . . recedes in us in order that we are able to do our work, you see."

24

The earliest piece of Friday morning was gray and chill. Rain would come, stiff, raw drops. Still, it was a new day and they could make of it what they wanted it to be. Their summer was over but they had yet their other seasons . . .

IT WAS A COUPLE of minutes past five in the morning and Nick walked down the corridor of City Hospital to the office of Sam Matthews. Nick had showered and changed his clothes, he'd had some coffee and a few minutes of quiet, but still his face was shot through with fatigue. Nick had regained his calm, but it was an odd kind of calm—it was a deep quiet, the sort that came of a series of stunning incidents one on top of another.

Nick tapped lightly on the door of City Hospital's Chief of Staff and entered the office. He found Sam Matthews tired but composed behind his desk. Nick sat down on the ancient, cracked green leatherette couch and looked toward the window at the far end of the room. He saw Brian then, standing in profile, and he was surprised, for even at that angle he could see that his eyes were bloodshot and puffy and that he had not changed his clothes from the night before.

"Have you been here all night?" Nick asked. Brian nodded and Nick looked away, to Sam. "Let's have it."

Sam looked down at several charts on his desk and began reading. "Juvenile male, Charles Eugene Jefferson, D.O.A. Juvenile male, Francis John Carlino, mild concussion, contusions, facial laceration—surgery performed. Being held in the prison ward by order NYPD. Female adult, Anna Maria Carlino, under heavy sedation in psychiatric section." Sam looked at Nick. "The police said they found her in the street with a kitchen knife, apparently looking for the boys who . . ." He looked back to the charts.

"Female juvenile, Marie Anne Carlino, four hours surgery, given six pints, infusion continuing. Internal hemorrhaging and contusions, broken sternum, fractured left cheekbone, bruised liver, contusions over entire body, third-degree burn on right chest." Sam looked up again. "They . . . uh, burned the letter D into her chest . . . She's catatonic, no audio, visual response, severe muscle rigidity. We'll . . . we'll hold her here as long as we can, then she'll have to be moved to an institution. Neuro believes it's irreversible on the basis of—"

"*No!*" Brian called out suddenly.

"What is it?" Nick stared at him.

"Don't give up on her," Brian said, emotion deep in his voice. "There's a chance, there's always a chance that—"

"Neuro said—" Sam Matthews began but Nick silenced him with a look.

"Brian," he said gently, "you found Marie. You saw her condition."

"I found her. It . . . it was so awful," he said and pressed a hand to his eyes. "She's so young . . . lying there, so young, in all that pain, that blood. Nick, *please* don't let them give up on her, *make* them give her a chance. If she's institutionalized she'll be stuck away in some room for the rest of her life." Nick was again shocked by the emotion in his plea. "We can work with her if she's here. I'll work with her on my own time . . . I know a few of the neuro men and a few in the psychiatric section. I'll get them to work with her. *Please*, Nick, give me that much."

Nick was silent for a moment, then he took Brian's arm. "Sit down," he said softly. "We'll talk about it—"

"No, we'll talk about it now. We can't just throw her away, *I* can't do it."

"Everything will be done for her, you have my word. She'll have the standard sixty days here, and if there isn't any progress by then . . . I'll see to it she's given more time. I promise you."

"Nick," Sam Matthews interrupted, "you're making promises for *my* hospital."

"We will do this," Nick said quietly, "*my* way."

Sam looked at him; once again he remembered his student, intern and resident; he remembered the granite resolution, the eyes that were black fire. "I didn't say a word," Sam grumbled, though he was proud of Nick, proud of the determination even in the face of pain.

Nick paid no attention to Sam. He watched as Brian relaxed somewhat and then he turned. "And Grady?"

"No changes since you called last. We had Dr. Glass look at him and he confirmed no disability in the shoulder. The knife penetrated the left quarter but it missed the nerve. He took thirty-seven stitches, but aside from soreness, he'll be fine. He has a broken index finger, left hand, and eight small lacerations on his chest, superficial. We've reduced the swelling, left optic. All told, it looked much worse than it was. No significant loss of blood, no internal injuries, no major breaks. He was stunned, of course, but there was never a question of shock. He had a few hours of sleep and he took breakfast a little while ago. He'll be fine."

"Thank God," Nick said. "Did you get a child by the name of Clovis Williams?"

"Bellevue," Brian said. "He was released a few hours ago. He's okay."

Nick looked back to Sam. "Maybe Grady should stay here a couple of days."

"Can't do it," Sam spoke quickly. "Rock bottom, absolutely, can't do it. We're jammed. Besides, he's fine. I would have released him already if he'd been any other patient. . . . Nick, have you finished with the police. Have you got a minute?"

Nick glanced at Brian and then back to Sam. "Yes."

"Where do you go from here? What happens now?" he asked seriously, concern in his voice.

"I go to a staff meeting to see who's staying. I get the Clinic cleaned up. I hire guards to be there round the clock. The Clinic *stays*. The people who want help are going to get help . . . the bastards who want a fight will get a fight. *We stay.*"

Sam smiled a little; pride deepened in his eyes. "I thought so."

Nick looked at Sam. "I made my mistakes. Bad ones, mistakes in judgment. I trusted, and so I didn't take precautions. I thought I knew all there was to know about my neighborhood . . . *my* neighborhood. The trouble is it isn't anybody's neighborhood anymore. It belongs to hate and nobody controls hate. Frankie Carlino . . . he didn't want drugs, not really. He wanted mayhem, he wanted to go out and hurt. Because he hates. He'd cut your heart out for the *revenge* . . . revenge for whatever's cut *his* heart out. The Legal Aid people are going to go into court and try for insanity . . . I know it . . . diminished capacity at the least, but I'll tell you something, if that kid is crazy he was made crazy. Bv hate," Nick said passionately, his voice rising. "Frankie'll be back on the streets within a year, his hatred deeper than it's ever been . . . and there's nothing anybody can do for him ever. His heart was destroved long ago, his soul was poisoned. Frankie and all the Frankies will be our enemy and there's no help for it. But I'll stay . . . because for every Frankie there's a Clovis . . . a child who might have become a part of the madness but won't now because we're there . . . showing him that hatred is not the only way of the world."

Nick's eyes were blazing, and Sam and Brian found themselves mesmerized. Their hearts pounded as they listened to the flow of words; Brian understood for the first time why he had joined the Clinic, why he would stay. Sam thought: on such words are men sent into wars.

Nick waved his powerful hands in the air. "Six months ago, Clovis would have joined Frankie in the looting and killing. Last night he risked his life for Grady. I'd suffer a thousand Frankies to reach a few Clovises. Goddamn it, why else are we doctors?" he demanded, and still the men were speechless. Nick's voice became very soft. "Why else?" he asked and turned away, quickly wiping at his eyes.

Sam stood up very slowly and came around the side of his desk. He went to the two doctors and quietly put a hand on each of their shoulders.

Nick was very still and then he spoke. "Thank you," was all he said. He turned to Brian. "Are you all right now?"

"Yes."

"Let's go collect Grady."

The two men left the office. They went rapidly down the corridor to the Doctors' Room where Grady waited. Nick took a deep breath, for he didn't know what Grady's emotional state would be. He steeled himself before opening the door. He was prepared for everything but what he saw—Grady, combed, fresh-looking, his eyes alert and clear, sitting erect in his chair.

"Morning," Nick said as Brian closed the door behind them.

Grady looked up. "Did you call Courtney?"

"No," Nick said. "Tessa and I decided that was up to you."

"Good. How's Clovis?"

"He wasn't hurt, Sam says. The police told me there'll be a hearing, but it's just a formality. Clovis is a hero. Saving the Cowboy."

Brian pulled some chairs from the corner of the room and pushed them close to where Grady sat. Nick flopped down and Brian rested on the arm of his chair.

"You're taking this very well," Nick said carefully.

"I didn't, not at first."

"What changed your mind?"

Grady looked away and then back to Nick. "At first, when I got upstairs and realized what was happening . . . it hurt. It hurt more than the beating, more than Frankie's knife. I thought what a fool I'd been. And then when I thought I was going to be dead . . . in those moments of sheer . . . *terror.*" He smiled very slightly. "All my old fears and insecurities ran through my mind. All of them. And everything I've ever done or not done because of them. I saw it all . . . me, stripped down naked, alone with the devils that drove me all these years. I . . . knew somehow that if Frankie didn't kill me, that if I were able to get out of there in one piece . . . I knew I was going to survive . . . and I knew I didn't have to be a superman, only me. It all came very clear in my mind. Then,"—Grady smiled—"I dove in and gave Frankie the fight of his life. Then Clovis came. I don't remember a hell of a lot after that, but when I woke up this morning all the old ghosts were gone. I went up to the residents' quarters to shave and to"—Grady began to laugh—"there I was looking into the mirror and the next thing I knew, I was saying to my face in the mirror, 'You bastard, you're gonna make it after all.' *Much* chuckling, *many* peculiar looks from the residents," Grady finished, still laughing.

Nick and Brian smiled at each other, and Brian was certain he saw the last tension leave Nick's face.

"When do we go back to work?" Grady asked simply.

Nick smiled. "Don't you want some time to recuperate?"

"I'm in great shape. I'm in the best shape of my life," Grady said quietly. "C'mon, let's get out of here."

Nick rose, and the two men stood up with him. Together they walked to the door and down the corridor to the doctors' elevator.

"The news on Marie isn't any good, is it?" Grady asked when they were inside.

"It's bad," Nick said, glancing quickly at Brian.

"We're going to help her. All of us," Brian said, vehemence still in his voice.

Grady looked in surprise at Nick, but Nick was staring down at the floor.

"I might as well get all the bad news out of the way," he said. "John Woods died early this morning. Bellevue called me in the middle of everything. He died in his sleep."

The doctors left the elevator and went through the double doors that led to the street. Grady looked around at the quiet gray sky and then at Nick. "We'll give him a nice funeral. He said he always liked the singing."

They reached the corner and the men looked at each other. Nick spoke. "You two get some sleep. I have a meeting at the Clinic and then I'm going home for a while. I'll open up again tonight."

"I'll be there," Brian said.

"No, tomorrow's good enough. I want us all rested for the A.M.A."

Grady looked at Nick. "Do we tell them about last night?"

"Yes. Let them know the worst and the best. Let them know we're still learning."

They were silent for a moment, and then Brian took a step away from them. He stopped, looking steadily at

Nick and Grady. "See you," he said and went on his way. Nick stared after him and then turned to Grady.

"And you? What about Courtney?"

Grady smiled broadly. "We'll see."

Tessa sat on the floor of the Irving Place apartment, gardening tools and soil and three small plants spread on newspaper in front of her. She looked up curiously when she heard a key turn in the door. She smiled when Nick came in.

"It's so early, I didn't expect you for hours," she said, going to him.

He hugged her close and then kissed her gently. "Hank volunteered to work tonight."

"Good, then I have you to myself." She took his hand and led him to the couch. They sat very close to each other. "You look awfully pleased and very tired," she said, stroking his face.

"I am pleased. Do you know what happened at the Clinic this afternoon? At least half the neighborhood showed up. One woman brought a cake, some kids brought a big thing of Kool-Ade, some other people brought a big poster that said, 'The Gorlin Clinic, Si.' The neighborhood threw a party. For *us*." Nick laughed. "Clovis was there with his camera, snapping away. And then some little girl read a poem she wrote about us. It was incredible. I finally called Brian and Grady to come down and see what was going on. I still can't believe it."

"It's working. Despite everything, it's working."

"It is. I stood there watching and . . . all those years of grasping for a dream . . . I saw it was real, it had happened." Nick put his arm around Tessa. "And I knew I had you to share it with, that was the most important part of all."

"I love you," she said. She smiled at him. "Why didn't you invite me to their party?"

"I said *half* the neighborhood showed up. The other

half's still waiting with brickbats. It'll always be that way . . . it won't ever be safe, not completely."

"I know that, I knew that a long time ago," Tessa said quietly. "I won't ask you to quit, I won't ever ask you to quit."

Nick looked at her, a small smile playing at his mouth. "You knew I had to hear that. You always know."

"I always love you."

They were still for a while, Tessa nestled very close to Nick. "How's Grady?" she asked.

"Terrific," Nick laughed. "He brought Clovis a new bird to keep T.K. company. When I left, Grady and Clovis were having a serious talk about bird breeding. Clovis said he'd like to have some canaries next."

"Do you think Grady's going to call Courtney?"

Nick took Tessa's face in his hands, "Hey, we've spent so much time on everybody else. Let's spend some time on us. Just on us. For tonight, at least, there are no other people, only us. How about it?"

Tessa's blue, blue eyes were very soft. "I'd like that."

"So would I."

Grady walked slowly up the stairs to his apartment. Every part of his body was sore and he was weary, yet his spirits were high; he hummed softly as he put his key in the lock. The lights were on in the apartment and he was surprised. He whirled around and then stood very still. "Courtney," he said in a whisper.

She turned around, her eyes at once shy and anxious, but then she saw the bruises on his face and her hand flew to her mouth. "Grady, what happened?"

"There was . . . uh, some trouble at the Clinic. I'm fine, no damage done," he added quickly.

"Are you sure? You're really all right? You're sure?"

"I'm sure."

"But what—"

"Another time, I'll tell you about it another time."

"You're sure you're all right?"

"Yes." He smiled.

Courtney fell silent then, shyness overcoming her, for she didn't know what to say, how to begin. "I should have called."

"You might have done that, yes," he said, and his face was noncommittal.

Courtney looked away from him. "You're making this hard for me, you could at least . . ."

But then he was holding her, holding her very tightly, laughing softly against her pale yellow hair.

"Come, sit down," he said and led her to the couch, surprised to feel both their hands trembling slightly. He brushed the hair back from her face and smiled at her. "When did you get here?"

"About an hour ago. I drove back. I . . . had some more thinking to do, so I took my time, stopped in Delaware . . ." She looked down at her lap. "I got in about an hour ago."

"And Peter?"

"Oh no, he's back in Washington. That's . . . the book, the work is over. I pulled out. I couldn't stand being there one more minute, Grady, it was all wrong."

"What about Peter."

"I don't know how to answer that." She stared straight ahead. "He's different from you and me, there's something of tragedy about him . . . like someone who lives in a high place, in the shadow of the moon. He knows all the dark places, Grady." Courtney looked at him, her eyes grave. "I didn't belong there, I came back here because I belong here."

Grady leaned back against the couch but still he held her hand. "There's been darkness around here. A lot of it. Courtney . . . do you know the hardest thing of all? It's to make a commitment, a promise to another human being. It's scary . . . because by the time we get to the age to make a promise, we've already been bruised. We're living by our fears as much as anything else. Or some of us are. The things I didn't do because of my fears . . . the things I did." Grady looked away. "I brought about the trouble at the Clinic, indirectly anyway. Because I had to succeed with the Carlino boy. And why? Because I thought I saw myself . . . at a similar age, in him. I thought I saw the same insecurity, the same loneliness, the fear. *And* because he was the biggest challenge at the Clinic and I had to take the challenge and win . . . winning, proving myself, was my only identity. All the while pulling away from you, *hiding* . . . because I didn't dare take the chance of failing, not with you. That's how I was living . . . by my fears." He looked quietly at her. "But it's not living, it's only a . . . holding action." He smiled slightly. "I found that out last night. Involuntarily. Things came clear. What I'm trying to say is I was going to call you . . . to ask you to come home . . . to tell you we have a chance despite it all. . . ."

Courtney was conscious of a deep relief and a gentle, gossamer tranquility. "There's so much to say, so much."

"There's time," Grady said softly. "We can't say it all in a night or a week . . . but we will say it, Courtney, there's time." Grady stood up and went to the windows, staring outside. "The leaves are beginning to turn, it's a new season. Maybe for us too." Courtney joined him at the window, putting her hand in his. Grady laughed suddenly. "Will you remember that old habits . . . old attitudes die hard? Will you be patient with The Kid?"

Courtney laughed, too. "Kid, I think the worst is over."

A new season comes to the city—it is a time to start again, to try, to know. It is a chance; hold it in your hand, twirl it high, high in the air, spin it like a golden top, keep it close. It is a chance . . .